Penguin Books
Bruno's Dream

W9-BJK-548

Iris Murdoch was born in Dublin of Anglo-Irish
parents. She went to Badminton School, Bristol, and
read classics at Somerville College, Oxford. During
the war she was an Assistant Principal at the
Treasury, and then worked with U.N.R.R.A. in
London, Belgium and Austria. She held a
studentship in philosophy at Newnham College,
Cambridge, for a year, and in 1948 returned to
Oxford where she was until lately a Fellow and
Tutor in philosophy at St. Anne's College. In 1956
she married John Bayley, teacher and critic.

Her other novels are *Under the Net* (1954), *The
Flight from the Enchanter* (1955), *The Sandcastle*
(1957), *The Bell* (1958), *A Severed Head* (1961),
An Unofficial Rose (1962), *The Unicorn* (1963),
The Italian Girl (1964), *The Red and the Green* (1965),
The Time of the Angels (1966) and *The
Nice and the Good* (1968), all available in Penguins.

Iris Murdoch

Bruno's Dream

Penguin Books
in association with Chatto & Windus

Penguin Books Ltd, Harmondsworth,
Middlesex, England
Penguin Books Australia Ltd, Ringwood,
Victoria, Australia

First published by Chatto & Windus 1969
Published in Penguin Books 1970
Reprinted 1971
Copyright © Iris Murdoch, 1969

Made and printed in Great Britain by
Cox & Wyman Ltd,
London, Reading and Fakenham
Set in Intertype Times

To Scott Dunbar

Chapter One

Bruno was waking up. The room seemed to be dark. He held his breath, testing the quality of the darkness, wondering if it was night or day, morning or afternoon. If it was night that was bad and might be terrible. Afternoon could be terrible too if he woke up too early. The drama of sleeping and waking had become preoccupying and fearful now that consciousness itself could be so heavy a burden. One had to be cunning. He never let himself doze in the mornings for fear of not being able to fall asleep after lunch. The television had been banished with its false sadnesses and its images of war. Perhaps he had nodded off over his book. He had had that dream again, about Janie and Maureen and the hatpin. He felt about him and began to push himself up a little on his pillows, his stockinged feet scrabbling inside the metal cage which lifted the weight of the blankets off them. Tight bedclothes are a major cause of bad feet. Not that Bruno's feet minded much at this stage.

It was not night, thank God. The cowering mind and body fidgeted, discovering themselves in time. He remembered, or somehow knew, that it was the afternoon. The curtains were tightly pulled, but there was a cold reddish glow about the edges. The sun must be shining out there, the chilly spring sun, casting a graceless light upon sinful London and the flooding Thames and the grimy ringed towers of Lots Road power station which would be visible from the window when Adelaide came at five o'clock to pull the curtains. He reached for his glasses and held his watch up towards the dim curtain-edge and made out that it was four-fifteen. He wondered if he should call out to Adelaide but decided not to. He could manage three quarters of an hour without the horrors. And Adelaide was a rather irritable servant who disliked a premature summons. Or perhaps she had become irritable only in the last year. Did she smash the best plates on purpose? There were always crumbs on the tray. He was so old now and he had been ill so tediously long.

No letters today. There would be none by the afternoon post. But when five o'clock came it was a cosy time of day, the best time really, with tea and muffins and anchovy toast and a new kind of jam and the *Evening Standard* and then Danby coming home from the printing works. It was nicer in winter when there was a coal fire in his room and it was dark outside. That lucid spring sun was his enemy and the interminable summer evenings were a torture to the mind. He would have liked a coal fire now, only it made so much work and even Nigel who thought of most things had not thought of that. Bruno would have tea, making it last as long as possible, then read the *Evening Standard,* starting with the strip cartoons, then six o'clock news on the wireless, then talk for half an hour to Danby, not about business of course but about the funny things that happened in Danby's day. Danby always had funny things in his day. Then play telephone perhaps or look at the stamps and then it would be seven and he could start drinking champagne, then read some spider books or a detective novel, then it would be supper brought by Nigel, and then talk with Nigel and then settle down for the night by Nigel. Soft padding Nigel with the angel fingers. Danby said Nigel was unreliable and threatened to sack him once. Danby must not know that Nigel broke the Simla cup. Bruno must remember to say that he broke it himself.

But of course Danby would not send Nigel away if Bruno did not want. Nigel was not really a trained nurse, he had just been an orderly or something, but he was so good with pillows and helping out of bed, he was so gentle. Danby was a kind son-in-law to Bruno. He would never send the old man to a home, Bruno knew that. It was years now since Danby had absolutely insisted that Bruno should come to stay with him and be looked after. Danby was kind, though no doubt it was all a matter of temperament and good health and being always hungry and ready for a drink. Danby was the sort of man who, if civilization were visibly collapsing in front of him, would cheer up if someone offered him a gin and French. God knows what

Bruno's daughter had seen in Danby, Gwen such a strong serious girl and Danby a shambler through pubs. Women were unaccountable. Yet they had seemed to love each other. He could remember that much, though poor Gwen had died so long ago.

He could see now in the twilight of the room the hump of the foot-cage, the big wooden box on the table which held the stamp collection, the bottle of champagne on the marble-topped bookcase, and near it upon the wall the square framed photograph of his wife Janie. Janie had died twenty years before Gwen, but they seemed equally far away now. Gwen's photo was still downstairs on the piano. He could not bring himself to ask for it to be brought. Three weeks ago he had overheard Adelaide saying to Nigel, 'He won't be coming downstairs any more.' He had felt a sense of injustice and a thrill of fright. How could he concede that 'any more'? He had not been downstairs for more than a month. But that was not 'not any more'. He could still get to the lavatory quite easily. Yet why was Nigel always talking about bedpans now and saying how easy they were and suggesting that today he was surely too tired to go? Was Nigel preparing him for that time? Well, it was not yet. He was sure of that, although he no longer wanted to know what it was that Danby and the fool doctor were whispering about on the landing. The fool doctor had said he might live for years. 'You'll outlive us all!' he had said, laughing healthy laughter and looking at his watch. Years might mean anything. He must live three years anyway, he had to do that so as to cheat the Income Tax, to live three years was a statutory requirement.

When I ought to be thinking about death I am thinking about death duties, thought Bruno. That was not really altruism. It was more like a pathetic inability, even now, to divest himself of a sense of property. It was all very confusing. He felt quite muzzy today, it was those tablets, though they did stop the pain. Or perhaps those bromide sleeping pills were poisoning him slowly. Sometimes he got muddled, a dislocated feeling quite unlike the euphoria of the champagne, and overheard himself talking aloud without knowing what he was talking about. One million brain cells were destroyed every day after the age of twenty-five, Danby had told him once, having read it in the Sunday paper. Could there be any brain cells left at that rate when one was well over eighty, Bruno wondered. Some days were clearer. There was so much less pain now. Wonderful what science can do. He must find out about a deed of gift and make the stamp collection over to somebody and not let the Income Tax have it. The stamp collection should fetch twenty thousand pounds. Twenty thousand pounds tax free was worth anybody's having. How his father had hated giving it to him at the end. He could still see with clarity, a little coloured picture in the nutshell of his mind, the thin white hand pushing the box towards him along the mahogany table. His dying father saying to him with bitterness, 'You'll sell it, Bruno you fool, and you'll be cheated royally.' Well, he had not sold it, he had even added to it a little, he had even loved it a little, though he was never a serious philatelist like his father. He had kept it for a rainy day, and now his life was nearly over and there had been no rainy day. He might have had a world tour. Or bought great works of art and enjoyed them. Or had oysters and caviare every day. Or given it to Oxfam. He must find out about the deed of gift, how it worked, only he did not like to ask Danby. Danby was very kind but he was a thoroughly worldly man. Danby must be wondering who would get the stamps. Bruno wondered too. His son-in-law Danby or his son Miles? But it was years since he had seen Miles. Miles had rejected him long ago.

Of course they all caused him pain, all the time, they just could not help it. He could spy their assumptions, their thoughts which no longer ended in him but sped away past him into unimaginable time when he would no longer be. He had become a monster to them. 'A fine old man,' he had overheard someone calling him more years ago than he liked to think of. What was he now? In his own consciousness he was scarcely old at all. He could see that his hands had aged. He noticed that with puzzlement as he promenaded the two twisted dried up heavily spotted things upon the counterpane. He no longer looked into the mirror though he could feel sometimes like a mask the ghost of his much younger face. He glimpsed himself only in the averted eyes of Danby and Adelaide, in the fastidious reluctances which they could not conceal. It was not just the smell, it was the look.

He knew that he had become a monster, animal-headed, bull-headed, a captive minotaur. He had a face now like one of his spiders, *xysticus* perhaps, or *oxyptila,* that have faces like toads. Below the huge emergent head the narrow body stretched away, the contingent improbable human form, strengthless, emaciated, elongated, smelly. He lived in a tube now, like *atypus,* he had become a tube. *Soma sema.* His body was indeed a tomb, a grotesque tomb without beauty. How differently death appeared to him now from how it had seemed even three years ago when he still had his white hair. Real death was nothing to do with obelisks and angels. No wonder they all averted their eyes.

The printing works ought to be a kind of monument only he still thought of the works as his father's creation. Gater and Greensleave. Greensleave and Odell it ought to be now with Danby in charge, only Danby had refused to change the name although old Gater had been dead these forty years. There had been a bad patch after the war when it was so hard to get spare parts for the American presses, but things had picked up somehow. Was that due to Danby? Variety was the secret, and nothing too humble: programmes, catalogues, leaflets, posters, Bingo cards, students' magazines, writing paper. Bruno had done his best for the place. He had been born to it, for it, practically in it with the clack of monotype machines in his infant ears. But he had never felt at home with printers and their strange private language had always been for him a foreign tongue. He had been always a little afraid of the works, just as he had been afraid of the horses which his father had forced him to ride when he was a child. It was different for Danby who had no natural bent and no creative gifts and was not even an intellectual, and who had taken to printing when he married Gwen as if this were the most natural thing in the world. Bruno, who never got over thinking Danby a fool, had resented that calmness. Yet it was Danby who had turned out to be the business man.

Bruno had wanted to study zoology and not to go into the printing works. His father had made him study classics and go into the printing works. How had he made him? Bruno could not remember. Only through business, only through money, had he ever really communicated with his father. Because of certain punishments he had forgotten almost everything about his father, who remained nevertheless in his life as a source of negative energy, a spring of irritation and resentment, a hole through which things drained away. He could flush with anger even now when thinking of his father, and even now the old hatred came to him fresh and dark, without images. Yet he could see his mother so clearly and see that particular strained smile on her face as she tried to persuade her husband, and the tones of her voice came to him clearly over an interval of eighty years. 'George, you must be more gentle with the boy.'

I ought to have been a recluse, Bruno thought, lived in the country like an eighteenth century clergyman with my books of theology and my spiders. The proper happiness of his life, the thing which he had so completely mislaid, came to him always associated with his mother, and with memories of summer nights when he was sixteen, seeing in the light of his electric torch the delicate egg-laying ritual of the big handsome *dolomedes* spider. O spiders, spiders, spiders, those aristocrats of the creepy-crawly world, he had never ceased to love them, but he had somehow betrayed them from the start. He had never found an *eresus niger*, though as a boy his certainty of finding one had seemed to come direct from God. His projected book on *The Mechanics of the Orb Web* had turned into an article. His more ambitious book, *The Spiders of Battersea Park*, had shrunk to a pair of articles. His monograph on the life and work of C. A. Clerck was never published. His book on *The Great Hunting Spiders* did not get beyond the planning stage. He corresponded for several years with Vladimir Pook, the eminent Russian entomologist, and Pook's great two-volume work *Soviet Spiders*, inscribed to *B. Greensleave, an English friend and a true lover of spiders*, was among his most treasured possessions. But he had never accepted Pook's invitation to visit Russia; and it was Pook who had written the last letter.

What had happened to him and what was it all about and did it matter now that it was practically all over, he wondered. It's all a dream, he thought, one goes through life in a dream, it's all too *hard*. Death refutes induction. There is no 'it' for it to be all about. There is just the dream, its texture, its essence, and in our last things we subsist only in the dream of another, a shade within a shade, fading, fading, fading. It was odd to think that Janie and Gwen and his mother and for all he knew Maureen now existed more intensely, more really, here in his mind than they existed anywhere else in the world. They are a part of my life-dream, he thought, they are immersed in my consciousness like specimens in formalin. The women all eternally young while I age like Tithonus. Soon they will have that much less reality. This dream stuff, this so intensely his dream stuff, would terminate at some moment and be gone, and no one would ever know what it had really been like. All the effort which he had put into making himself seemed vanity now that there were no more purposes. He had worked so hard, learning German, learning Italian. It seemed to him now that it had all been vanity, a desire at some moment which never came, to impress somebody, to succeed, to be admired. Janie had spoken such beautiful Italian.

As one grows older, thought Bruno, one becomes less moral, there is less time, one bothers less, one gets careless. Does it matter now at the end, is there really nothing outside the dream? He had never bothered with religion, he had left that to the women, and his vision of goodness was connected not with God but with his mother. His grandmother had had evening prayers every night with the servants present. His mother had gone to church every Sunday. Janie had gone to church at Christmas and Easter. Gwen was a rationalist. He had gone along with them and lived in casual consciousness through the life and death of God. Was there any point in starting to think about it all now, in setting up the idea of being good now, of repenting or something? Sometimes he would have liked to pray, but what is prayer if there is nobody there? If only he could believe in death-bed repentance and instant salvation. Even the idea of purgatory was infinitely consoling: to survive and suffer in the eternal embrace of a totally just love. Even the idea of a judgement, a judgement on his cruelty to his wife, his cruelty to his son. Even if Janie's dying curses were to drag him to hell.

It must be ten years since he had seen Miles, and that had been about the deeds of the house in Kensington which had been let and which Miles wanted to sell. The house was in Janie's name, bought with Janie's money, and of course she had left everything to the children. Before that he had met Miles at Janie's funeral, at Gwen's funeral, and there had been one or two other encounters about money. Miles, so cold, so unforgiving, writing those regular patronizing letters for Christmas and birthday: *I always think of you with affection and respect*. It could not be true. He had thought his son distinguished. He had admired him for refusing to go into the works, envied him perhaps. Yet Miles had not done all that much with his life. How hard it was to believe that Miles must be over fifty. He was an able civil servant, they told Bruno, but nowhere near the top. And then there had been all that poetry nonsense, getting him nowhere.

If only certain things had not been said. One says things hastily, without meaning them, without having thought, without understanding them even. One ought to be forgiven for those hasty things. It was so unfair to have been made to carry the moral burden of his careless talk, to carry it for years until it became a monstrous unwilled part of himself. He had not wanted Miles to marry an Indian girl. But how soon he would have forgotten his theories when confronted with a real girl. If only they had all ignored his remarks, if only they had made him meet Parvati, let him meet Parvati, instead of flying off and building up his offence into a permanent barrier. If they had only been gentle with him and reasoned with him instead of getting so highminded and angry. It all happened so quickly, and then he had been given his role and condemned for it. And Miles said he had said all those things he was sure he had never said. There were so many misunderstandings. Gwen tried a little. But even Gwen did not have the sense to argue with him properly. And then Parvati was killed so soon after the marriage. It was not till much later that he even saw a picture of her, a snapshot taken of her and Gwen in Hyde Park, enlaced together, their arms around each other's waists. Gwen had taken Parvati's long black plait of hair and drawn it round over her own shoulder. They were laughing. Even that snapshot might have brought him round.

Miles had forgiven nothing. Perhaps it was her death that

14

fixed him in that endless resentment. The often quoted remark about 'coffee-coloured grandchildren'. Well, there had been a judgement. Bruno had no grandchildren. Gwen and Danby, childless, Miles and Parvati, childless, Miles and – Bruno could not recall the name of Miles's second wife, he had never met her. Oh yes, Diana. Miles and Diana, childless. Was there any point in trying even now to be reconciled, whatever that meant? It was a mere convention after all that one ought to be on good terms with one's son or father. Sons and fathers were individuals and should be paid the compliment of being treated as such. Why should they not have the privilege, possessed by other and unrelated persons, of drifting painlessly apart? Or so he had said to Danby, many years ago, when the latter had questioned him about his relations with Miles. Danby had probably been worrying about the stamps.

Of course Miles's resentment had started much earlier with the Maureen business. Had Janie told them about it or had the children just guessed? He would like to know that. The dark-eyed handsome censorious pair, whispering, looking at him unsmilingly. Gwen had come back to him much later, but Miles had never come, and that old bitterness had entered into what happened afterwards, so that the two guilts seemed to be entwined. No one had ever understood about Maureen and it was now too late to try to explain it all and who could it be explained to? Not to Danby, who would just laugh, as he laughed at everything, at life, even at death. He said he found Gwen's death comical, his own wife's death comical. It was years later of course, long after that terrible meaningless leap from the bridge. Could he explain to Miles about Maureen and would Miles listen? He was the only person left in the world who cared about it any more. Could he compel Miles to see it all as it really was? Could Miles forgive him on behalf of the others or would it all be coldness and cruelty and a final increase of horror?

Janie had called Maureen a pathetic little tart. But how remote words, particularly angry words, are from the real thing at which they aim. Of course Maureen had had a lot of money out of him. Janie had forced him to reckon up how much. But money had not entered into his real relationship with Maureen, and it had not been just bed either, but somehow joy. Maureen had been sweetness, innocence, gentleness, gaiety, and peace. He bought her sheets and new curtains and cups and saucers. Playing at domesticity with Maureen gave him a pleasure which he had never had in setting up house with Janie. That had been a matter of quarrels about antique furniture with Janie's mother. Janie had equipped the house: she had not expected him to be interested. Maureen singing in her little Liverpool Irish voice *Hold that tiger, hold that tiger*. Maureen swaggering in the new short skirts. Maureen, dressed only in a blue necklace, dancing the charleston. Her little flat, full of the paraphernalia of her millinery trade, was like an exotic bird's nest. Once when he returned home covered with feathers and Janie noticed he said he had been to the Zoo. Janie believed him. Maureen laughed for hours.

Well, not perhaps innocence. How did she live? She never seemed to sell any of those hats. She said she sometimes worked as an usherette in the cinema, and she had seemed to him like a nymph of the cinema age, a sybil of the cavern of illusory love. But she had too many clothes, too nice a flat. He found a man's handkerchief once. She said it was her brother's. Yet even jealousy became, with her, a convention, a kind of game, a personal sweet game, like the chess game he had seen her setting out in a café with big handsome red and white pieces on a large board on the first occasion when he had seen her. It later appeared that she could not play chess. The chess men were simply an instrument of seduction. This discovery charmed Bruno utterly. She said she was eighteen and that Bruno was her first man. Yet even these lies were sweet as he tasted them mingled with her lipstick in long slow clinging kisses. Oh God, thought Bruno, and it all came back to him, it could come back even now with a warm rush to the centre of that dry schematic frame. Physical desire still stalked, still pounced, sometimes vague and fantastic, sometimes with memories of Maureen, sometimes with images of coloured girls whom he had followed in the street and embraced with impotent excitement in twilit rooms in Kilburn and Notting Hill long long after Janie was dead.

How selective guilt is, thought Bruno. It is the sins that link significantly with our life which we remember and regret. People whom we just knocked down in passing are soon lost to memory. Yet their wounds may be as great. We regret only the frailty which the form of our life has made us own to. Before that moment in Harrods which had changed his world he had felt practically no guilt at all. Afterwards, after Janie's awful scene with Maureen, after Maureen crying behind that closed door, he had felt the burden and the horror of it, the ugliness and the scandal. Why ever had Janie married him anyway? Stylish Janie Devlin. He must have been momentarily transformed by love and ambition into the witty dashing youth that she wanted. Her disappointment had been ironical and dry.

His pictures of Janie all seemed to belong to before the first war, to the epoch of courtship and marriage. The war itself was scarcely there in recollection. He had not been fighting, he was already over thirty, he suffered from a stomach ulcer, he hardly seemed to have noticed it at all. His father was dead and he was running the printing works which was doing well on government orders. His mother, who had gone to Norfolk because of the Zeppelins, died in nineteen sixteen. This shook him more than the holocaust. The pictures of Janie were brighter and yet more remote. Janie playing tennis in a white dress of heavy linen whose hem became green from brushing the grass through a long summer afternoon. Janie chattering Italian at a diplomatic party while her bright bold eye quizzes the men. Janie twirling her parasol surrounded by admirers in the Broad Walk. Janie in St James's Theatre on the night when he proposed. How gay, how sweet, and how infinitely far off it all seemed now. Maureen's was the more febrile gaiety of a later and grimmer world. *At the parting of the ways, You took all my happy days, And left me lonely nights.*

Society conspires to make a newly wed couple feel virtuous. Marriage is a symbol of goodness, though it is only a symbol. Janie and he had enjoyed their virtue for quite a long time. 'Is she a good woman?' his mother, who never quite got on with Janie, had asked him at the start. It was not a conventional question. Bruno was embarrassed by it and did not know the answer. His relation to Janie had fallen into two parts. In the first part, before Harrods, they had played social roles, put on

17

smart clothes, been admired and envied, lived above Bruno's station and beyond his means, and borne two handsome and talented children. In the second part, after Harrods, they seemed to have been alone, really related to each other at last, in an awful shut-in solitude, becoming demons to each other. Janie behaved so badly to me, he thought, or he tried for the ten thousandth time to frame the judgement but could not. Agamemnon was killed on his first night home from Troy. But Agamemnon was guilty, guilty. Janie's cancer came so soon after and she blamed it on him.

His love for Janie was not accessible to memory, he knew it only on evidence. She must have destroyed it systematically during that reign of terror. And he only, as it seemed to him now, knew for certain that she loved him when she was crucifying that love before his face. He only knew that she had kept all his letters when she tore them up and scattered them around the drawing-room, only knew that she had kept his proposal note when she hurled it screaming on to the fire. For weeks, months he was saying he was sorry, weeping, kneeling, buying her flowers which she threw out of the window, begging her to forgive him. 'Don't be angry with me, Janie, I can't bear it, forgive me, Janie, oh forgive me, for Christ's sake.' He must have loved her then. Maureen had vanished as if she had never been. He did not visit her again. He sent her fifty pounds. He could not even write a note. He must have loved Janie then, but it was love in an inferno: that terrible relentless withholding of forgiveness. His mother would not have punished him so for any fault. Later he became ferocious, violent. Janie said, 'You have destroyed my world.' Bruno shouted, 'You reject me. You reject everything that I am. You always have done. You never loved me.' They began to quarrel and they went on quarrelling even when Janie was ill, even when they both knew that Janie was dying. He ought not to have let Janie make him hate her. That was worse than anything.

Bruno's heart was beating violently. He hauled himself up a little further on his pillows. These million-times thought thoughts could still blind him, make him gasp with emotion and absorb him into an utter oblivion of everything else. Was there no right way to think about those dreadful things, no way of thinking about them which would bring resignation and peace? Janie had been dead for nearly forty years. How well he knew this particular rat-run of his mind. He must not, must not become so upset or he would not sleep at night and sleepless nights were torture. He did not like to call out at night, he was affrighted by his own voice calling in the darkness. Even if he did call Nigel did not always hear, did not always come. Once in extremity he had shouted so loud that Nigel must have heard, but he did not come. Perhaps he was not there at all but lying somewhere else in the arms of a girl. He knew so little really about Nigel. After that he was afraid to call in case Danby should hear and find out that Nigel was not there.

He stared at his old red dressing gown hanging on the door, a big shrouded thing in the dim light. It was the only garment now which he put on, it represented his only travelling, his wardrobe was shrunk to this. Why had it somehow become the symbol of his death? Danby offered to buy him a new one, and Bruno had refused, saying 'It's not worth it now.' Danby accepted the remark. The old dressing gown would still be there when they returned with relief from the funeral and began to get out the bottles, and then someone would say, 'Bruno's gone, but there's his poor old dressing gown still hanging on the door.'

What would it be like, would someone be there? A girl perhaps? But there was no girl. If only he could be loved by somebody new. But it was impossible. Who would love him now when he had become a monster? Perhaps he would die alone, calling, calling. He had let Janie die alone. He could not bear it. He had heard her crying out, calling his name. He had not gone up. He feared that she would curse him at the end. But perhaps she had wanted to forgive him, to be reconciled with him, and he had taken away from her that last precious good thing? The groans and cries had continued for a while and become silent at last. Tears began to stream down Bruno's face. He murmured 'Poor Bruno, poor Bruno, poor Bruno . . .'

Chapter Two

'O Adelaide, sweet Adelaide,
 The years may come, the years may go . . .'

  'Sssh!'

  Danby Odell was in bed with Adelaide the maidservant. She
had been his mistress for nearly three years. Before that there
had been Linda. Linda was smart and neat, her shiny black
handbags were like a sort of well-kept professional kit. Relaxed
and divorcée, neatness was her form of virtue, and she had kept
the affair, which she had initiated, tidy and well-organized.
Then one day she went back to Australia. They exchanged
three letters. Six months later Danby had taken up with Adelaide. She was sweet, she was there.

  These things had nothing to do with the servitude of being in
love. They had nothing to do with what it had been like with
Gwen. With Gwen it had been the once-in-a-lifetime form of
insanity. Danby had suffered. Even when he was married to her
he had suffered, as a soul might suffer in the presence of its God
simply from an apprehension of a difference in substance.
Gwen was intense and high and spiritual. Danby loved her
moral intensity with physical love. They both suffered a pain of
separation. Even when he was making her laugh, which he did
very often, there would sometimes be a spasm of pain and they
would both look quickly away. Gwen had loved him profoundly, meditating upon his unlikeness and their mutual impossibility, enclosing his separateness in the sweep of her love
and brooding over it as a saint might brood secretly upon the
wounds of the stigmata which unknown to his fellows he ever
conceals in the folds of his robe. Danby had not recovered from
her death. But his life energy was cheerful stuff.

  Danby was attractive to women. He was tall but getting
rather stout now. A bulky paunch was developing below his
waist. The long hairs which covered his chest and stomach were
still fine and golden while the straight thick hair of his head had

become pure white. His face had the glowing, very slightly wrinkled texture of a russet apple, his eyes were a clear light blue, and he had excellent regular teeth which he often admired in the mirror. He enjoyed eating and drinking and doing business. When he was younger he had been an excellent ballroom dancer and a good tennis player. He came of an unambitious tradesman's family and though he was the only child of adoring parents, neither he nor anybody else had had any particular plans for his life. He went to a mediocre grammar school and spent a year at a provincial university. His father died, his mother died, there was no money left. He realized, now that there was no one to bully and reprove him, how deeply he had loved his mother. He went into insurance. He was rescued from this fate by the war, every moment of which he enjoyed. Then came seriousness in the person of Gwen. Danby entered the printing works with some trepidation but soon found to his surprise that he had a talent for business and was indeed much better at it than Bruno was. Bruno, who was by then over sixty, was only too glad to surrender his power to his son-in-law. Danby flourished. It was not so much the money-making that he enjoyed but something much more like house-wifery or domestic neatness: keeping things tidy, making things fit, dealing with twenty tiny crises every day. The men, with whom he was regularly to be found drinking in the public bar of the Old Swan, liked Danby. Indeed almost everybody liked Danby, though there were a few people who thought him an ass. Danby liked Danby.

He had no particular pangs of conscience about Adelaide. He thought that one should do what one wanted on the whole so long as one did not make people unhappy, and he saw no reason why he should make Adelaide unhappy. She was at the age when women need the reassurance of being wanted. He had no idea whether she liked going to bed with him but he knew that she was in love with him and had been from almost the first moment when she arrived in answer to his advertisement. Bruno was just beginning to be ill. It had been a long business with poor old Bruno. Adelaide was useful and her cousin Nigel the Nurse had become indispensable. It never occurred to him, or he imagined to Adelaide, that there was any question of marriage. It was not that sort of relationship. But he had begun to feel that he was getting old and had reached resting point. Adelaide suited him. He promised to support her in her old age. He got into bed with her every night, slightly drunk, and was perfectly happy.

Adelaide, though putting on weight and no longer very young, was really rather beautiful, as Danby came to see after he had been going to bed with her for some time. She was heavy about the hips and stomach but her shoulders and breasts were classical. She had a round face and a naturally rosy complexion and a great deal of long hair of a rich brown colour. (Her hair was dyed, only Danby had never realized this.) Her tendency to overdress – such a change from Linda – gave her for him a sort of exotic almost oriental charm. Adelaide clinked and rattled with accoutrements, rustled with frills. Her wide-apart brown eyes worshipped him as she coiled the straight abundant hair into an artful bun. Her flat South London voice was to him an infinitely sexy mating call.

Danby hiccupped. It was raining outside with a gentle friendly pissing sound. It was his evening for drinking with Gaskin at the Raven. He had had a bit too much as usual. He was lying on his back with his knees up. He liked to lie on his back like that, it gave him a relaxed happy feeling. Adelaide had just switched out the light and now she was up against him, glued to his side like Eve. He could see the hump of his knees outlined against the thin curtains which glowed faintly with the light of the street lamp which shone into the yard. He and Adelaide slept in the semi-basement annexe which a previous owner had built on to the house in Stadium Street in days when the neighbourhood was a good deal less seedy than it had since become. Danby was solaced by its seediness. The neat pretty house in Notting Hill had been Gwen's house, Gwen's territory. Danby had fled from it and after years in lodgings had bought the Stadium Street house because it was so different, so shabby. And of course it was near the printing works. He loved the little yard outside his window, below ground level, always dark and covered in slippery green moss. It was always called 'the yard', never 'the garden' although it had a yellow privet bush and a laurel bush and a rose that had reverted to briar. The soil was

22

black and no grass would grow on it, only a few dandelions and weedy marigolds which struggled up each year through the damp crust of the moss. The chimneys of Lots Road power station towered above, suitable extensions of that murky infertile earth.

The printing works were situated on the other side of the Thames in Battersea, upon the water's edge, almost directly opposite the municipal wharf beside the power station, and every day Danby crossed Battersea bridge into another territory, equally dirty and seedy, but different, smelling of cattle cakes and brewing and watery flotsam. Gwen's dowry was still a source of joy to Danby. He loved the works, the clattering noise, the papery dust, the tribal independence of the printers, he loved the basic stuff of the trade, the clean-cut virginal paper, the virile elemental lead. As a child he had preferred melting his lead soldiers to parading them, and the manufacture of letters out of lead was an occupation that never ceased to satisfy. He was fond of the machines, especially the older simpler ones, and took pride in the precarious multifarious domestic economy which constantly and only just kept the concern from foundering in its own antiquity. He occasionally went into Chelsea, at least he got as far along the embankment as the Kings Arms, and more occasionally he took Adelaide to a smart King's Road restaurant, because she liked that, but he never felt at home over that particular border. Fulham, Battersea, where he knew every public house, this was the London on whose mystery he meditated. He was relieved when Bruno stopped urging him to move. He did not like disagreeing with the old man. They had always got on so well together.

'Warm enough, Adelaide?'

'Yes.'

'Your hair's all cool. Funny stuff, human hair. If you love me never cut your hair off.'

'Shove over a bit, would you.'

'Have I got a clean shirt for tomorrow? The Bowater chaps are coming.'

'Of course you have.'

'Did you hear the six o'clock news? What's the river up to?'

'Another flood warning.'

'I hope we won't have it in the back yard like we did two years ago.'

'Did you have a nice day?'

'Yes, fine. Did you? How was the old chap?'

'Same as usual. He was on about Miles again.'

'Oh.'

'Talking about seeing him.'

'Just talk.'

'Well, I think he ought to see Miles. He is his son.'

'Nonsense, Adelaide. There'd be no point after all these years. They'd have nothing to say. They'd just upset each other. By the way, did you remember to bring down the stamps?'

'Yes.'

Danby did really think there was no point in his seeing Miles. It was not just that Danby hoped to get the stamps. Though of course he did hope to get the stamps. Anybody would.

'Do you think he's getting senile?'

'Certainly not, Adelaide. He gets confused sometimes, but his mind's very clear really.'

'He will talk so about spiders. I think he imagines them.'

'I suspect he attracts them. Have you noticed how his room is always full of spiders?'

'Horrid things! How long do you think he'll last?'

'He sinks under a complication of disorders. Could be ages though.'

'You said he wouldn't talk business any more and it was a bad sign.'

'Maybe. But he's got a terrific will to live, poor old fellow.'

'I can't see why anyone would want to go on living when they've got like that. Whatever can he look forward to?'

'The next drink.'

'Well, *you* would! I think old age is awful. I hope I'll never be old.'

'When you are old, Adelaide, you will find that life is just as desirable as it is now.'

'My Auntie's senile. She's got completely gaga. She thinks she's a Russian princess. She talks some sort of gibberish she thinks is Russian.'

'Funny how mad people go for titles. By the way, is your other cousin still out of work?'

'Will Boase! He's not even trying to get work! He just draws National Assistance. They give them too much.'

'He could do that painting job for us. He needn't tell the National Assistance people.'

'He went to grammar school. So did Nigel.'

'I daresay, Adelaide, but I'm afraid I haven't any intellectual work to offer him just at the moment!'

'He ought to be in a proper job. You paid him far too much last time.'

'Well, one likes to help. He's quite unlike Nigel, isn't he. It's odd to think they're twins.'

'They're not identical twins. I wish you hadn't got Nigel to work here. It wasn't my idea.'

'Well, that was not for charity. He's terribly good with Bruno. It's almost uncanny.'

'What are Bruno and he always *talking* about?'

'I don't know. They shut up like clams when I come in.'

'I think they're talking about sex, about girls.'

'Girls? Nigel? Mmmm.'

'Fancy Bruno being interested in sex at his age.'

'A topic of enduring fascination, my dear Adelaide.'

'But he can't *do* anything.'

'We all live in a private dream world most of the time. Sex is largely in the mind.'

'I've never noticed that *you* thought it was! I think Nigel knows all about it.'

'About sex? No one knows that, my dear. You have to specialize. I intuit an interesting and unusual specialist in our Nigel.'

'You'd need to be an odd sort of man to want to be a nurse.'

'It's a very honourable profession, Adelaide.'

'Don't be silly. Do you think Nigel takes drugs or something?'

'He is a bit mystical. But I doubt it. One has enough creepy-crawlies in one's mind without positively encouraging them. Nigel has some sense.'

'Well, I'm sure he takes something or other. His face is getting all lopsided.'

'I think Nigel's rather beautiful.'

'You're mad. He's a demon.'

'I rather like demons, actually.'

'He gives me the creeps. I wish he wasn't here. I'm terrified he'll guess about us.'

'We're quite shut off in this part of the house, dear kid. Don't be so anxious about Nigel. He's sweet and perfectly harmless.'

'He isn't. I know him. He's bad. He'd tell people.'

'Well, it wouldn't matter.'

'It *would*. You *know* I don't want people to know.'

'All right, kid, all right. Sleepy-byes, sleepy-byes.'

The image of Gwen moved upon Danby's closed eyes. She was slowly turning her head towards him. Her heavily curled dark brown hair crept on her shoulder, tangled in her cameo brooch. The great-eyed brown glance gathered him into its close attention. 'Here comes your old comic relief, Gwen my darling.'

There was another image which sometimes came with sleep and which was terrible. Gwen had been drowned in the Thames. She had jumped off Battersea bridge to save a small child which had fallen from a barge. The child swam to the shore. Gwen had a heart attack, became unconscious and drowned. Danby identified her dripping wild-haired body at the mortuary. It was just like Gwen, he told himself over the years, to jump off Battersea bridge in March to save a child who could swim anyway. It was just the sort of lunatic thing she would do. It was typical. Comic, really.

Adelaide said, 'Bruno told me yesterday that spiders existed a hundred million years before flies existed.'

'Mmmmm.'

'But what did the spiders eat?'

Danby was asleep, dreaming of Gwen.

Chapter Three

Nigel, who has been sitting cross-legged on the floor outside Danby's bedroom, listening in the darkness to Danby and Adelaide talking together, rises silently, elegantly, his legs still crossed. There is nothing more now to be heard within except a counterpoint of snores. He glides up the stairs to his own room, enters and secures the door.

It is dark in the room. The door is locked, the curtains thick as fur. Deep somewhere in the darkness a single candle is burning. Nigel in black shirt, black tights, rotates with outstretched arms. The furniture against the wall is sleek and flat. The brown walls fold away into receding arcs about the glimmering sphere where Nigel turns and turns, thin as a needle, thin as a straight line, narrow as a slitlet through which a steely blinding light attempts to issue forth into the fuzzy world.

Concentric universe. Faster and faster now sphere within sphere revolves and sings. The holy city turns within the ring of equatorial emerald, within the ring of milky way of pearl, within the lacticogalactic wheel, the galaxy of galaxies, that spins motionless upon a point extensionless. The flake of rust, the speck of dust, the invisible slit in the skin through which it all sinks down and runs away.

The candle has grown into a huge luminous cylinder made of alabaster or coconut ice. It glows palely from within and impulsates and breathes. Nigel has fallen upon his knees. Kneeling upright he sways to its noiseless rhythm song. In the beginning was Om, Omphalos, Om Phallos, black undivided round devoid of consciousness or self. Out of the dreamless womb time creeps in the moment which is no beginning at the end which is no end. Time is the crack. Darkness upon darkness moving, awareness slides from being. Vibrations clap their wings and there is sound. An eye regards an eye and there is light.

27

In the dimness he is squatting huge and blocks the sky. Little hands vibrate like hairs but he squats huge and broods on self. His idly stirring foot may crush a million million while he scratches, fidgets, brushes away a myriad buzz of littlenesses whose millenia of shrieking are to him the momentary humming of a gnat which between two fingers he idly crushes as he squats still and broods on self.

The humming light is waxing, the mountainous black is waning, the screaming is swelling into a harmony, a dazzling circlet of visible sound. Two indistinct and terrible angels encircle the earth, embracing, enlacing, tumbling through circular space, both oned and oneing in magnetic joy. Love and Death, pursuing and pursued.

The sounds diminish and in the empty pallid azure the golden quoit spins away. At last, it has become a spot of radiance, a stain of gold, a fading flash, a lazar beam, a single blinding point of light which absorbs all light into itself. The colourless soundless silence vibrates and sways. He is near. Nigel trembles pants and shudders. His wide open eyes see nothing, he, Nigel, the all-seer, the priest, the slave of the god. Time and space crumple slowly. He is near, He is near, He is near. They fold and crumple. Love is death. All is one.

Nigel clutches his heart. He gasps, he moans, he reels. He falls forward on his face on the ground, his forehead strikes the floor. His eyes are screwed together against the glaring dark. The presence is agony, punishment, stripes, the extended being tortured into a single point. Annihilation. *All is one*.

Later, far away in another world, an old man calls out, calls out, then weeps alone in the dark slow hours of the night. With magnified precision Nigel hears the calling and the weeping. He lies prostrate upon the floor of the world.

Chapter Four

'Our Lodger's such a nice young man,
 Such a nice young man is he.'

Danby, singing, aimed a friendly smack at Nigel's backside. Nigel tossed his long dark hair and lowered his eyes and left the room with a spiritual smile.

Bruno said, 'Danby, I am going to summon Miles.'

'Oh Lord!'

Bruno was sitting propped up in bed. The whitish counterpane was covered with a polychrome scattering of stamps. On top of these lay an open copy of Gerhardt's *Neue Untersuchungen zur Sexualbiologie der Spinnen*. Bruno felt clearer in the head today. His legs ached and ached; but that sickening point of malaise in the middle of his being, that possibility of awful pain, had dimmed to nothing. He just felt almost agreeably limp and weak. He had had a long relaxing conversation on the telephone with the weather report man who had been reassuring about the possibility of the Thames flooding. These conversations with polite impersonal official voices soothed Bruno's nerves. He felt he was a voice himself, a disembodied citizen. After that he had had some excellent wrong numbers.

It was necessary to talk to Miles. He would talk to his son about ordinary indifferent things, about the printing works, about Miles's job, about Danby's kindness, about Nigel's skill. They would talk and talk, and the room would grow dimmer, and then by some quiet scarcely notable transition they would be speaking the names of the women, Parvati, Janie, Maureen, in grave relaxed sadness together contemplating these conjured shades. Miles would be a little formal at first, but as he listened to Bruno's voice, naming the women, speaking of them with humility and simplicity, he would bow his head and then look upon his father with great gentleness and the room would be filled with an aura of reconciliation and healing. Earlier and alone, repeating to himself the words 'reconciliation and healing', Bruno had found tears in his eyes. He wept so easily now. Any story in the newspaper about a lost dog or cat could bring tears to his eyes. Even something about the Royal Family could do it.

It all went back to the beginning. That was something which he would like to try to explain. 'Bruno' his father had named him, but his mother, who could not get on with the name, had called him 'Bruin', 'Little Bear'. How had he become corrupted and lost the innocence which belonged to his mother's only child, and how could the child of such a mother ever have become bad? Yet had he become so bad, and how bad had he become? Most men deceive their wives all the time, statistics say. He had only had Maureen. And his later excesses amounted to little more than holding hands in Notting Hill. He had lived a chaste life really. It was his accusers and not his crimes which troubled him.

It all seemed so accidental now. Yet could anything have been different on that night, when he proposed to Janie in St James's Theatre in an atmosphere of sugar and Shakespeare and the sweet craziness of the London season? He wrote *Marry me, Janie* on a page from his programme, folded the page into a paper dart, and threw it from the stalls into her box. She caught it in the air and read it with a faint smile as the lights dimmed after the interval. The play was *Twelfth Night*. Afterwards he searched for her frenziedly in the crowded foyer. Turning away with her party she tapped his arm with her fan. 'I quite like your suggestion, Bruno. Come and discuss it tomorrow.'

It had gone on, the *froufrou* and the wit and the bright artificial lights, right on it seemed to him until that moment in crowded sale-time Harrods when Maureen had been struggling with the dress. It was the early days of zip fasteners. Bruno, who often bought her clothes, was standing just outside the curtain of the trying-on room. Maureen had got the dress half over her head, but because the zip had stuck she could get it no further. She came out to Bruno, masked by the dress, her arms helplessly waving, a foot of frilly petticoat showing. 'Quick, Bruno, get it off, I can't breathe.' Bruno laughed, pulled. Then there was suddenly a moment of panic. 'Maureen, keep *still*, you won't suffocate, you fool. You're tearing the dress.' The dress came away. Bruno looked over Maureen's bare shoulder into the eyes of Janie. Janie turned at once and disappeared among the shoppers. Bruno, for whom Maureen no longer existed, darted after her. He sought for her desperately in the slow crowds as he had sought her long ago in the foyer of the theatre. He glimpsed her ahead, hurrying, and then she was gone. He came back to the department and paid the assistant for the torn dress. Maureen had vanished too. *You taught me how to love you, Now teach me to forget*.

As he waited at home for Janie to come back he felt that the quality of time had altered, perhaps forever. She did not come until the late evening. Janie made him take her to see Maureen. How had she made him? That terrible sense of being punished. Thrusting in front of him she went into Maureen's flat first and locked the door. He could hear Janie's voice speaking on the other side of the door and then the sound of Maureen crying. He knocked on the door, calling to be let in. The other lodgers in the house came out of their rooms to watch. They mocked him. 'His wife's telling off his mistress!' 'Been found out, have you?' 'Hard luck, old man.' They laughed. Bruno went home. More waiting.

He never saw Maureen again. But Janie visited her over a period of several months. 'I want her to understand what she's done.' 'I want her to know that we were happy together before this happened.' 'I want to help her.' Strong avenging Janie, weak defenceless Maureen. Years later, after Janie was dead, he put an advertisement in *The Times*. *Maureen*. *At the parting of the ways*. *Please contact BG*. *Just to talk of long ago*. There was no answer. He had not really expected one. It was an attempt to propitiate her shade. Years later still he saw a terrible news item in the paper. A Mrs Maureen Jenkins, a widow living by herself in Cricklewood, had been found by neighbours lying dead in her home, suffocated by a dress which she had been unable to pull over her head. There was a picture of a tired stout elderly-looking woman. He could not decide if it was her or not.

Danby had come to sit on the end of the bed. He pushed the stamps into a pile. 'I do wish you'd be more careful with those stamps, Bruno. I found a Post Office Mauritius on the floor the other day.'

'Nothing can happen to them.'

'They could fall through chinks in the floor-boards.'

'There are no chinks. The room is too dusty to have chinks. The chinks are full of dust.'

'There's no point in your seeing Miles, I shouldn't think'.

'You don't understand. There are things I can only talk to Miles about.'

'You want to make a life confession?'

Bruno was silent. He looked down at the stamps, caressing their gay innocent faces. He looked up at Danby's big healthy handsome face. How odd human faces were. They differed so much in *size*, apart from anything else. Danby was no fool. 'Maybe.'

'Well, make it to me. Or better still to Nigel. He's in touch with the transcendent.'

'Why are you against it?' said Bruno. He could hear his voice quavering. He had a little touch of the fear which he sometimes had now when he realized his utter helplessness. He was a prisoner in this house for ever. If they wanted to keep him from Miles they could do so. They could fail to give messages. They could fail to post letters. There was the telephone. But they could cut the wire. Of course these thoughts were insane.

'You haven't really imagined it,' said Danby. 'You'd just embarrass each other horribly. You know how you brood as it is. Something unfortunate would be said and you'd just be utterly miserable.'

'I've got to talk to him,' said Bruno. He looked at his poor blotched hands crawling over the stamps. They looked like huge spiders.

'Why this fuss all of a sudden when you've managed without him for years? You never even answer his letters.'

'There's not much – time left.' Bruno looked involuntarily at his dressing gown.

'Miles might refuse to come,' said Danby. 'Then you'd be terribly upset. Have you thought of that?'

Bruno had not thought of it. 'I've thought of that of course. But I think he'll come. I must see him. *Please*, Danby.'

Danby looked upset. He stood up and went to the window, smoothing his thick white hair down on to his neck. 'Look, Bruno, of course you can do anything you like. You don't have to say "please" to me. And I hope you don't think – Naturally I assume – It's not – I really am just thinking about you. You could be inventing a torment for yourself.'

'I'm already in torment. I want to try – anything.'

'Well, I don't understand,' said Danby, 'but OK, go ahead, no one's stopping you.'

'Don't be cross with me, Danby, I can't bear your being cross.'

'I'm not cross, for heaven's sake!'

'Would you go and see him?'

'*Me?* Why me?'

'I think it would be wise to spy out the land,' said Bruno. The new thought that Miles might simply refuse to come was frightening him terribly. It had not occurred to him for a moment. Perhaps Danby was right that the risk was not worth taking. He lived so much in his mind now. Suppose he wrote and got no answer? Suppose the telephone were just replaced when he rang up? There were worse torments, other vistas, further galleries. All the rest and that as well.

'You mean find out if he would come? Perhaps argue him into coming?'

'Yes.'

Danby smiled. 'Am I the right ambassador, dear Bruno? Miles and I never exactly hit it off. And I haven't seen him for years. He thought I was unworthy of his sister.' Danby paused. 'I was unworthy of his sister.'

'There's no one else,' said Bruno. His voice was becoming hoarse. He cleared his throat. 'You're part of the family.'

'All right. When do you want me to go? Tomorrow?'

'Not tomorrow.' His heart was suddenly beating violently. What would it be like?

Danby was looking at him closely. 'The doctor won't approve of this.'

'It doesn't matter what the doctor thinks now. Perhaps you would write a letter.'

'To Miles? Saying what? Asking to come and see him?'

'Yes. Do everything very slowly. I mean, give Miles time to think. He might be hasty. If he has time to think he'll come.'

'Well, all right. Will you compose the letter? You know I'm hopeless at letters.'

'No, you compose it. But not today.'

Adelaide came in and threw the *Evening Standard* on to the bed. A river of stamps cascaded to the floor. 'I'll bring your tea in ten minutes. Would you like muffins or anchovy toast?'

'Muffins, please, Adelaide.'

The door closed. Danby was picking up the stamps and putting them into the black wooden box. Bruno's father had disapproved of stamp hinges, which he held were injurious to stamps, and had indeed spent a lifetime vainly trying to invent an alternative device. So although he believed strongly in the aesthetic aspect of his hobby, and had often preached to Bruno that a man who did not love looking at his stamps was a tradesman and no true philatelist, he had never kept the stamps in books. He had constructed the large wooden box with a great many narrow drawers within which the stamps were supposed to lie between fitted cellophane covers, which could be fanned out when the drawers were opened. Bruno, however, whose attachment to the stamps was even more purely aesthetic than that of his father, had long ago started to jumble the carefully docketed system by which they were arranged. Of late he had started selecting out his special favourites, regardless of origin, and these were now kept heaped together in a spare drawer at the top.

'OK, Bruno,' said Danby. 'I'll do that small thing. Don't worry. We'll see. Can I help you to the lav?'

'No, thanks. I can manage.'

'Well, I'll be off. I've got an appointment at the Balloon. Cheerio.'

He thinks I won't do it, thought Bruno, gradually moving his legs towards the side of the bed, but I will. It was frightening though, the prospect of a change, something utterly new, the danger of being hurt in a new way. He got his legs over the side of the bed and rested. Suppose Miles wouldn't come, suppose he sent back a hostile reply? Suppose he came and were unkind to Bruno? Suppose Bruno felt an irresistible impulse to tell about Janie's death and Miles cursed him? Miles could curse him. He was a violent intense boy. He could hurt him now, terribly. Perhaps Danby was right. It was better to die in peace.

Bruno edged over and got his stockinged feet on to the ground. In between each trip his feet seemed to forget about walking altogether. They curled up into balls under the bed-clothes and were reluctant to flatten out again into surfaces that could be stood upon. The process of their re-education was painful. Bruno stood, stooping a little, supporting himself with one hand on the bed. Still holding on to the bed he began to shuffle towards the door. Once he got as far as the bed post he could reach out and get his dressing gown from the door without having to stand unsupported.

Of course it wasn't absolutely necessary to put on the dressing gown now that it wasn't winter any more, but it represented a challenge. It was quite easy, really. The left hand held the bed post while the right lifted down the dressing gown and with the same movement slid itself a little into the right sleeve. The right hand lifted on high, the sleeve runs down the arm. Then the right hand rests flat against the door a little above shoulder height, while the left leaves the bed post and darts in the left arm-hole. If the left is not quick enough the dressing gown falls away towards the floor, hanging from the right shoulder. It then has to be slowly relinquished and left lying. There was no getting anything up off the floor.

Bruno manages it, twitching the gown forward over his shoulders and drawing it together in front with the left hand. He is breathing deeply with the effort. He slides his right hand down slowly as far as the puckered brass door handle and begins to open the door, sidling slowly round it as he does so. His movement brings him round to face the room and he contemplates it for a moment, seeing his little prison box as an outsider might see it. The yellowish-white counterpane of threadbare Indian cotton is patterned with faded black scrolls which look like copperplate writing on a very old letter. The bed, between its four light brown flat-headed wooden posts, looks coiled up and dirty, a disorderly lair. The sheets all seem to be knotted. It has the desolate incomplete look of an

35

invalid's bed, momentarily untenanted. The cold sunless evening light from the window shows the small square of thin brown carpet, with the ragged bit tucked under the bed, surrounded by dusty varnished boarding. The wallpaper, covered with a dim design of ivy leaves, is pallid and bleached and spotted with tea-coloured stains. The little bedroom was 'the small spare room' for years. Bruno occupies it now because of its proximity to the lavatory. On Bruno's right is a bookcase topped with cracked marble on top of which two detachments of empty champagne bottles frame Janie's picture. The upper shelves contain paperback books of great antiquity. The lower shelves house Bruno's microscope and four wooden frames containing test tubes of spiders in alcohol. On Bruno's left, behind the door as it opens, is a rickety gate-leg table upon which the great wooden stamp box now rests. At night Danby usually takes it away to his own room, hoping perhaps that Bruno will forget to ask for it again, so that it can then be conveyed to the bank. The full bottles of champagne are under the table. On doctor's orders Bruno does not drink his champagne chilled. Spider books, which are too big to go into the bookcase, fill much of the rest of the room, piled on the chest of drawers, on the two upright chairs, and on the little bedside table round about the lamp. The sash window shows a segment of wet slate roof, a coffee-coloured sky in slow unseizable tumultuous motion, and one of the trinity of towers of Lots Road power station looking black and two-dimensional in the sullen light.

Bruno levers himself round and begins the journey to the lavatory, his right hand moving along the wall. A dark continuous blur upon the wallpaper, the record of many such journeys, guides his moving hand. The lavatory door is open, thank heavens. The door handle is stiff. It was Nigel's bright idea that it should always be left open when untenanted. Nigel is full of little ideas for Bruno's comfort. Bruno's hand moves on the wall. It was surely not Parvati who had made all that anger. It was Miles. Parvati must have understood. Her own parents, who were Brahmins, had opposed the match too. They never consented to see Miles. If only he had met Parvati everything would have been all right, a real girl, not just an idea of an Indian girl. He hadn't meant it anyway, it was just something he'd said once about not wanting a coloured daughter-in-law. He could not remember any feeling about it all now, any feeling that he had had. Miles said he had 'bitterly opposed' the marriage. It was not true. All he could remember was the muddle, denying he'd said things, and Miles's cold high-minded anger. It was so unfair.

Bruno was inside the lavatory leaning against the closed door. As he began to fiddle with his pyjamas something dropped to the floor at his feet. He saw at once that it was a *pholcus phalangioides* which he had dislodged from its place on the door, or perhaps in the corner of the wall, where it had woven its irregular almost invisible scaffolding, unmolested by Adelaide. The spider did not move. He wondered if he had damaged it with his sleeve. He touched it gently with his stockinged foot. The creature lay still, its long legs curled to its body. It might be shamming dead. Slowly stepping across it Bruno lowered the lavatory seat and sat down on it. He took a piece of lavatory paper and leaning forward introduced it carefully underneath the little curled up thing. The spider slid on to the paper together with a good deal of dust and fluff. It stirred slightly. He must have damaged it somehow, but without the microscope, or at any rate a magnifying glass, he could not see how. He tried to look into the spider's face but without his spectacles all was blurred. He had not kept captive spiders for a long time now. A year ago he had had a sudden yearning to see again a beautiful *micromatta virescens* and he had sent Nigel, armed with a photograph, to hunt in Battersea Park. Nigel came back without a *micromatta* but with a jam jar full of assorted spiders, two of them already dead, a poor *ciniflo ferox* and an *oonops pulcher*, probably killed by the fierce *drassodes lampidosus* with which they had been sharing their captivity. Bruno put his magnifying glass away and told Nigel to relase them all in the yard straight away. He had never really been a scholar anyway.

The *pholcus phalangioides* was showing no further signs of life. He must have half crushed it as he leaned against the wall. He dropped it on to the floor and put two more pieces of lavatory paper on top of it and brought his heel down hard on to the little resistant bundle.

Bruno felt the wretched tears near again. The women were all young while he aged like Tithonus. Supposing Janie had wanted to forgive him at the end after all? She held out her hands to him saying, 'Bruno, I forgive you. Please forgive me. I love you, dear heart, I love you, I love you, I love you.' He would never never know. The most precious thing of all was lost to him for ever.

Chapter Five

'How is my worthy twin?' said Will Boase to his cousin Adelaide de Crecy.

'Oh all right.' Adelaide looked at him distrustfully. She was never sure how close those two were. They often seemed like enemies, but she could not guess what they really felt.

'I wouldn't have his job. I can't think how he puts up with the poor old fool.'

'He's terribly good with Bruno,' said Adelaide. 'It's almost uncanny.'

'Nigel's a bit potty if you ask me. He should have stayed in acting.'

'Look where acting's got you!'

'I could get a part if only I had some decent clothes.'

'I'm not giving you any more money, Will!'

'I'm not asking you to, am I?'

'It's just as well you've got Auntie's pension!'

'Oh stop nagging!'

'Danby said you could paint the outside of the house if you'd like.'

'Tell him to paint it himself.'

'Don't be so *silly*, Will. Danby paid you a lot for that last job. Far too much in fact.'

'Exactly. I don't want Danby's blasted charity.'

'Well, I think you ought to try and make money like other people.'

'This society thinks too much about money.'

'You're just a scrounger.'

'Oh for God's sake! I'll sell my drawings. You'll see.'

'You mean those pornographic drawings, the ones you wouldn't let me look at?'

'There's nothing wrong with pornography. It's good for you.

39

If politicians stuck to pornography the world wouldn't be in such a mess.'

'Who'd buy that horrible stuff anyway?'

'There's a market. You've just got to find it.'

'I wish you'd keep on at one thing instead of starting all these things that never get anywhere.'

'I can't help it if I'm versatile, Ad!'

'Are you still going to that pistol practice place?'

'A man has got to be able to defend himself.'

'You live in a dream world. You're as bad as Nigel.'

'You wait, Ad. And I'm going to buy a really good camera. There's money in photography.'

'First it's pornography, then it's photography. You can't afford a really good camera.'

'Nag, nag, nag, nag, nag!'

'Vot serdeety molodoy!'

'The same to you with knobs onski.'

'Shto delya zadornovo malcheeka!'

'I think she's getting worse.'

'Stop gibbering, Auntie, or we'll put you in a bin. Go and write your memoirs!'

Adelaide went to Will's place every Sunday to cook midday dinner for Will and Auntie. She knew better than to call it 'lunch' to Will. It was Auntie's place, really, Will had just moved in when he was out of a job. Auntie was gaga, but she was quite capable of looking after the house. Adelaide cooked a plain dinner since neither Will nor Auntie ever knew what they were eating and Will thought interest in food was bourgeois.

Auntie, who was not a real Auntie but a devotee acquired by the twins in their early acting days when she kept theatrical lodgings in the north of England, had been parting company with reality over a period of several years. She announced periodically that she was a Russian princess, was about to sell her jewellery for a fortune, and was engaged in writing her memoirs of the Czarist court. Of late even her ability to talk seemed to be deserting her. In shops she mumbled and pointed to what she wanted, or uttered a stream of gibberish with Russian-sounding endings. *Da* and *nyet* she had probably acquired from the newspapers. Auntie lived in a dark ground floor flat in

Camden Town. Auntie's flat was genteel. It contained too many objects, including a great many small pieces of china whose number never seemed to diminish in spite of Will's habit of breaking things in fits of rage. Not everything which ought to be against a wall had a wall to be against. The sitting-room was partitioned by a long sideboard and a tall bookcase which stood out at right angles into the room. This did not matter much as no one ever went in there. Life went on in the kitchen. Will had once gone through a short phase of wanting to 'modernize' the flat, but had got no further than buying a steel chair of outstanding ugliness which now stood in the hall mercifully covered with coats.

The kitchen was dark, and darker today because it was raining, so they had the light on. An unshaded bulb bleakly lit up the cramped scene round the kitchen table where they were just finishing their roast lamb. Auntie, more than usually preoccupied with Czarism, was smiling vaguely behind thick steel-rimmed spectacles. She had a way of looking *into* her spectacles as if there was a private scene imprinted on the glass. She had been a handsome woman once. She was tall, with somewhat blue hair, and wore long skirts and very long orange cardigans which she knitted herself. Her face had become putty-coloured and podgy, but she had bright cheerful eyes. The loss of her reason did not seem to have made her unhappy.

Adelaide had always been troubled by having such an aristocratic sounding name. Her mother, Mary Boase, had married a fairly well off carpenter called Maurice de Crecy. 'We come of a Huguenot family,' Adelaide had early learnt to repeat, although she did not know who the Huguenots were or even how to spell them. At school, where she came on the roll call between Minnie Dawkins and Doris Dobby, she had been much teased about her name, but she soon saw that the little girls were also impressed. Perhaps it was her name which had made Adelaide so puzzled about her status and her identity. The puzzlement had not subsided as her life went on. Her parents were unpretentious people who lived in Croydon and ate their meals in the kitchen. When she was growing up Adelaide vainly attempted to persuade them to eat in the dining-room. Later she took over the dining-room herself and called it her 'study' and filled it with knick-knacks from antique shops. But it never looked like a real room. Adelaide's brother, who was ten years her elder, never had any puzzles. He went into computers, got married, and went to Manchester where he lived in a detached house and gave dinner parties without a table cloth.

Adelaide was clever at school, but left at fifteen and became a clerk in an insurance office. She learnt to type and hoped to become somebody's secretary. The office moved out of London. Adelaide became a shop assistant in a very superior shop and hoped to become a buyer. No one seemed to notice her talents so she left and became a clerk in a post office. She began to feel that if there had ever been a bus she had by now certainly missed it. In a moment of desperation she answered Danby's cunningly worded advertisement for a resident housekeeper. She expected a grand house. By the time she had recovered from her surprise it was too late. She had fallen in love with Danby. In fact she did no housekeeping, since Danby, who had an old maidish streak in his nature, did all the organizing and catering. Adelaide cleaned and cooked. She was the maid. Danby called her Adelaide the Maid, and invented clerihews about her. He must have invented about fifty. He turned her into a joke as he turned almost everything into a joke, and it hurt her. He once said to her, 'You have the surname of a famous tart in a story.' Adelaide replied, 'Well, I suppose I am a tart too.' 'All the nicest girls are,' he said, instead of denying it. Adelaide did not ask about her namesake, she did not want to know. She thought bitterly, 'I am just the ghost of a famous tart in a story.'

Adelaide's father died when she was about twelve and her helpless vague mother became entirely dependent on Joseph Boase, the father of Will and Nigel. So did Adelaide. Her own brother was already in Manchester. Joseph's wife, who had once been an actress, had left him some time ago because he was so bad-tempered and returned to the stage, and the trio of men became an irresistible focus and magnet to the bereaved mother and daughter. In fact the Boase family had long fascinated Adelaide and as a young child the twins, who were only three years older than her, had been much closer to her than her

42

own brother. She was in love with both of them, in those days slightly favouring Nigel. She was a bit in love with her Uncle Joseph too, although she was afraid of his bad temper. He was an extremely handsome person with a black moustache and beard who worked in a shipping office and imagined himself a seafaring man.

Her childhood with the twins had been the happiest part of Adelaide's life and she often felt its most real part. She was a tomboyish child and joined as an equal in all their games, which consisted largely of exploring building sites, climbing scaffolding, making marks in wet cement, escaping from watchmen, and stealing bricks. 'May Will and Nigel come to tea?' 'May I go to tea with Will and Nigel?' On Saturdays they played cricket with other children in the Boases' back garden. But of course they were superior to other children. They were a little secret society. It was their times as a trio that were special. Then when the twins were nineteen they ran away from Uncle Joseph and joined their mother and went on the stage.

Adelaide was working in the insurance office at the time. Their flight was a great shock to her. Although they had passed the brick-stealing stage she still saw a great deal of them. They went to plays and films together and the boys, who had stayed on in the sixth form of their grammar school, were insensibly educating their young cousin. She listened to their talk and read the books they talked about. They seemed scarcely to notice that she was growing up though they spoke teasingly of her prettiness. She was jealous of their girl friends. She was just beginning to think that one day she would marry one of them, she could not quite decide which.

Then there was a long interval during which the twins were heard of but not seen. Great things were hoped of their careers. Then Nigel was said to have left the stage and to be working at something or other in Leeds. Will appeared once on television in a small part, but Adelaide was working at the time and could not see him. The actress mother died, allegedly of drink. Adelaide's mother died, and Adelaide moved into digs. She changed jobs. She had a number of boy friends, some quite ardent, with whom she could not decide to go to bed. After the twins, they all seemed so undistinguished and insipid and dull. Will was working in repertory in Scotland. Then he suddenly started to write her love letters.

He's lonely up there, he's thinking sentimentally of when we were children, it doesn't really mean anything, Adelaide told herself. But she was very pleased all the same. She replied affectionately, trying at first to be non-committal, but soon her letters were as romantic as his. They both enjoyed the correspondence and the letters became positive works of art. Adelaide kept carbon copies of hers. Will went on saying that he was coming south but did not come. Uncle Joseph retired from the shipping office and went to live at Portsmouth. Will hinted at a big job coming up in the West End. At last he turned up in London, out of work, moved in on Auntie, and proposed to Adelaide.

Adelaide simply did not know what she felt. She had not seen Will for a long time and he had changed. He was a good-looking chap and getting to look more like Uncle Joseph. He was stouter, he had grown a moustache. He had always been more thick-set than Nigel, and now he looked like a sort of Victorian rugger player. He was big and heavy and rather mechanical in his movements, ruddy in the face, wearing his straight almost black hair neatly cut and rather long. He also seemed to be developing Uncle Joseph's temper, as Adelaide, who was not able to conceal the fact that she was dithering, soon learnt.

The trouble was that as soon as she saw Will she decided that she wanted Nigel. If only there hadn't been *two* of them! She had not seen nor heard from Nigel for years and no one knew his whereabouts. But she was haunted now by a vision of a slim dark-haired boy about whom she could not decide whether he was Nigel or whether he was Will as he used to be. She hoped Will would not guess. Will guessed and broke all Auntie's Meissen parakeets. Nigel turned up in London, working at the Royal Free Hospital. Adelaide told fervent lies to Will and went secretly to see Nigel. It was no good. Nigel was cool, vague, abstracted, not quite unkind. Adelaide was frantic. She answered Danby's advertisement. She fell in love with Danby. Will felicitously left London to work in a film at East Grinstead. By the time he came back Adelaide was Danby's mistress.

Adelaide never talked to Danby about Will except in the most casual terms and of course concealed from Will that she had any special interest in Danby. She managed to persuade Will that he had been wrong about her and Nigel, and this was easier to do now since it was true. She no longer had any tender feelings about Nigel, though he still occasioned obscure and unnerving emotions. She could not forgive him for having been so calmly unresponsive to her undignified and unambiguous appeal. He had changed too, and she felt almost a little frightened of him. He seemed to be living in another world. She had most unwisely told Danby that Nigel was a half-trained nurse and now out of work. Danby, who took to Nigel instantly, could not be prevented from summoning him and engaging him. At first she thought that Nigel's presence in the house would make her life impossible, but she had got used to it, though it still upset and frightened her. There was no reason why Nigel should know what went on behind the closed door of the annexe at night, and even if he did speculate she was sure that he would say nothing to Will, with whom he seemed to have broken off all relations. He had never told Will that Adelaide had been to see him.

Her feelings about Danby had changed without rendering her any the less slavishly in love. She had been completely captivated by his easy charm, his good looks, and the atmosphere of cheerfulness which he carried about with him. She was also strangely moved by the legend of the dead wife, whose photograph she dusted on the drawing-room piano. Big dark brooding eyes, heavy serrated dark hair, pale intense oval face, pouting finely-shaped small mouth. Whenever Danby spoke of his wife, which he did quite often, the note of his voice changed and his eyes changed and there was something serious and almost alien about him, even if he was supposed to be laughing. Adelaide liked this. It gave an alluring touch of mystery to what might otherwise have seemed too easy-going, too open. She found Danby altogether godlike, a sort of smiling vine-leaf-crowned forest deity, full of frolics but also full of power. From the first he used to smack and pat her a good deal, but then he smacked and patted the men at the printing works and the barmaid at the Balloon and the girl in the tobacconist's and the temporary charwoman and the milkman. One day he came into her bedroom, looked at her very gravely for some time in silence, then kissed her, and said, 'What about it, Adelaide?' She nearly fainted with joy.

Danby as a lover was a little less godlike. It was not that she felt that he was unreliable. He had most seriously, at the start, informed her that he intended their liaison to be lasting and that he would provide for her in her old age. Adelaide, who was not thinking about her old age and who would have accepted Danby's suggestion on any terms whatsoever, listened with some puzzlement to those protestations. Later she was glad of them. At moments when she felt, as she later occasionally felt, that she was giving up a great deal for Danby, it was a consolation to think that at least she had gained something permanent.

She did not really mind not altogether enjoying it in bed. She was anxious about contraception. She was pleased that he was pleased, and had been very moved by his tenderness and delight on learning that he was the first. It was just, she reflected, that any man, as soon as you get to know him well, turns out to be totally selfish. Danby did exactly what he wanted and never seemed to think that this might not suit Adelaide perfectly. Adelaide found it difficult in fact to recall the specific issues upon which he had crossed her, but she retained a vague sense of not being sufficiently considered. Perhaps, working deep in the whole situation, was Danby's assumption that she was not socially his equal. Adelaide sometimes felt the assumption, nebulous, pervasive, profound. She felt, almost physically, his selfishness and her own defencelessness, on long nights, after they had made love, as she lay awake wondering what that huge paunchy sweating hairy body was doing in her bed. But the discovery of his frailty, even his ordinariness, only made her love him all the more.

Will meanwhile remained terrifyingly single-minded. He settled into a condition of amazement at Adelaide's reluctance and confident expectation of her imminent capitulation. She put a great deal of energy into persuading him that there was no one else. She began to build up a picture of herself as a natural spinster. Once she thought it might be helpful to hint that she was a Lesbian, but Will got so upset and angry that she decided not to develop that idea. He never seemed to suspect Danby, largely because Will belonged to the sector of humanity that was entirely blind to Danby's charm. Will thought Danby an ass. Time, who will take over the most improbable arrangements and make them seem steady and commonplace, took over this one. Adelaide stopped being frightened of Will finding out about Danby, though she still had occasional moments of panic. She got used to coming over on Sundays and accepting Will's touchy nervy electrical devotion. She gave him money out of a small store which she was building up out of donations which Danby gave her to spend on clothes and which she promptly banked. There was usually a bad patch after lunch, after Auntie had retired, when Will would be pressing and possibly cross. But she was getting better at managing him. She had even begun a little to enjoy having, in this rather inconclusive sense, Will as well.

Although Adelaide had received, where Will was concerned, the same revelation of masculine total selfishness as she had received about Danby, she still thought of him as somehow noble and distinguished. She admired his social confidence, his sturdy conviction that he was 'working class'. In fact he was not really 'working class'. A versatile Bohemianism had rendered him classless. She even admired his ability to be unemployed without anxiety. He really was talented. He had lately shown her a series of drawings of monsters which he had done, weird embryos and hideous bristly creatures with half human faces, which frightened and impressed her. There were some pornographic drawings too of which she had accidentally seen one and it had made her feel quite sick. There was a force of violence in Will which she feared but which also a little thrilled her. But she remained circumspect and wary in her dealings with him and fell into playing the part of a sort of nagging sister.

Auntie was pottering in the hall, about to retire to rest. Adelaide was washing up. Will was sitting at the table smoking.

'What does old Bruno *do* all day?'

'He plays with his stamps. He reads those books about spiders over and over. He rings up wrong numbers on the telephone. He reads the newspapers.'

'It must be awful to be so old, Ad. I hope I don't ever grow old.'

'He's got awfully hideous too. He looks like one of your monsters.'

'Well, I suppose it doesn't matter what he looks like now, poor old bastard. Those stamps of his must be worth a packet.'

'Twenty thousand pounds, I heard Danby say.'

'Who'll get them?'

'Danby, I suppose.'

'Do you know anything about stamps, Ad?'

'No. You used to collect them, do you remember?'

'Yes. Nigel used to pinch my best ones. Nigel's a natural thief.'

'And you used to punch him. You're a natural bully.'

'Maybe. I wonder if Bruno has any Cape Triangulars.'

'What are Cape Triangulars?'

'Cape of Good Hope triangular stamps.'

'He has some triangular ones. I saw them. Don't know what kind they were. Could I have your coffee cup?'

'Ad, do you see a lot of those stamps?'

'How do you mean? Yes. I spend half my life picking them up off the floor and putting them away and bringing them out again – '

'How are they mounted? Are they in books?'

'They live in a box, in drawers, between sheets of cellophane. A lot of them are just loose in the box. He's got them into an awful jumble.'

'Could you look and see if he has any Cape Triangulars? I'll show you a picture of one.'

'Why are you interested? You chucked stamps long ago. It's a child's game.'

'Twenty thousand pounds isn't a child's game, Ad.'

'People must be mad to pay that money.'

'A Cape Triangular sold last week for two hundred pounds, I read in the paper.'

'I expect you wish you had one.'

48

'I'm going to have one, Ad.'

'What do you mean? How are you going to get it?'

'You're going to get it for me out of Bruno's collection.'

'Will!'

'Just one.'

Adelaide stopped washing. She turned round from the sink and stared at her cousin. Will was sitting with his thick legs stretched straight out, the heels of his heavy boots making yet another pair of permanent dints in the soft brown linoleum. He was looking up at Adelaide with a dreamy sly expression which she remembered from childhood.

'You want me to steal one of Bruno's stamps! You're not serious!'

'I am, Ad. That camera I told you about. In fact I've got it. The only trouble is I haven't paid for it. I need two hundred pounds.'

'Will, you're mad. Anyway, Bruno would see it was gone.'

'No, he wouldn't. You said he was getting terribly vague and gaga. And you said they were in a jumble. And no one else looks at the stamps, do they?'

'No. But I think Bruno would see. And anyway it would be perfectly wicked to steal from an old man.'

'Much less wicked than stealing from a young one. You're being soppy, my dear. He won't miss the stamp. It probably won't make any difference to the total value of the collection anyway. And it'll solve my camera problem.'

'Well, I won't, that's all!'

'You selfish bitch! Don't you want me to make money? There's hundreds of things I could do with that camera, I've got hundreds of ideas!'

'Why don't you sell those duelling pistols?'

'Because I don't want to.'

'Or get a cheaper camera. I can give you ten pounds.'

'I'm not asking you to swipe the lot, Ad. It isn't even as if Bruno collected the stamps himself. He just inherited them. Things like that shouldn't be allowed. Property is theft, really. Isn't that so, Auntie?'

Auntie had come in to fetch her orange cardigan before retiring.

'Seezara seezaroo, boga bogoo.'

'And boo to you.'

'Will, I think you're crazy.'

'So you won't do it, just to please me?'

'No.'

'You're always saying no, Ad. Come and sit beside me now Auntie's gone. Leave the washing up, I'll do it later.'

'I've got to go soon.'

'Stop saying that or I'll hit you. Come and sit here.'

They sat awkwardly side by side in upright chairs under the electric light. Adelaide rested her arms on the red and white check table cloth, grinding the crumbs a little to and fro under her sleeve. She looked ahead out of the darkened window at the rain and the jagged creosoted fence of the side passage and the dripping grey roughcast wall of the house next door. Will, sitting sideways and staring at her with his knee pressing hard into her thigh, laid a hand on her shoulder and drew it down her arm, thrusting up her sleeve and bearing down towards the wrist. The crumbs pressed painfully into her flesh. Will's other hand was beginning to fumble at her skirt. Adelaide released her arm. She captured Will's two hands and squeezed them rhythmically, still looking vaguely out of the window.

'Oh Ad, you know I'm in a state about you. I can't stop. When'll it be yes?'

'Will, don't tease me so. I don't want to.'

'I'm not teasing, damn you. This is serious, it's real, Adelaide. Sometimes I think you just live in a dream world. You ought to be shaken out of it.'

'I'm sorry, Will. I can't want things just by wanting to want them.'

'Have a try, my darling. I do love you. I can't bear my life going on and on without you. It's such a waste. Oh Adelaide, why not?'

'Just not.'

'I can't understand it. You *must* love me.'

'We're first cousins. You're like my brother.'

'Rubbish. I know I excite you. You're trembling.'

'You just upset me. Please, Will, don't be horrid, don't quarrel. We quarrelled last week and it was so silly.'

'Adelaide, is there somebody else? Be honest, please. Is there somebody else?'

'No.'

'God, I think if there were somebody else I'd bloody well kill him.'

Chapter Six

Why does one never see dead birds? How can they all hide to die?

Miles closed his notebook and moved over to the window. Earlier he had been trying to describe a dead leaf which the rain had glued to the window pane. It was a last year's leaf, in a shade of luminous dark brown, a sort of stocking brown, which reminded Miles of girls' legs. The veins of the leaf made the pattern of a tree, of which the stalk was the trunk. Only the stalk was, from Miles's side of the window, concave, a funnel divided by a narrow opening, at the base of which a raindrop was suspended, almost transparently grey around a point of yellow light.

How hard it was to describe things. How hard it was to *see* things. He wondered if, since he had completely given up drinking, he had actually been able to see more. Not that he had ever drunk very much, but any departure from total sobriety seemed to damage his perception. Even yet he was not sober enough, not quiet enough, to take in the marvels that surrounded him. The ecstatic flight of a pigeon, the communion of two discarded shoes, the pattern on a piece of processed cheese. His *Notebook of Particulars* was in its third volume, and still he was simply learning to look. He knew that this, for the present, was all of his task. The great things would happen later when he was ready for them.

Miles pushed up the sash of the window. It was evening, just coming to twilight, a time that he loved. The air was damp and warm. He reached a hand out and twisting his arm round took hold of the stocking-brown leaf by its stalk and detached it from the glass. It came away with a faint sucking noise. He examined it for a moment and then dropped it into the invisibility of the darkening air. The rain had ceased and there was a purplish gleam in the sky up above the huge humped roof of the Earls Court Exhibition Hall. The wet roof was glistening and metallic. But the narrow garden down below him was already dark between its walls except for a faint reflection of light from the windows of the summer house. Miles had built the summer house, a square box against the wall a little away from the house, in the hope that sitting in it he might write better poetry. But it did not seem to have made any difference and it got terribly damp in winter.

The garden was obscure in the vibrating diminishing light and he could just discern the grey domes of santolin and hyssop and Jackman's rue which grew in the neat squares in the pavement. Beyond the pavement was the diminutive lawn with a shaven grass path in its centre and at the end of the yew hedge with the gap in it beyond which was Diana's tool shed. That gap, which the yews were just beginning to roof over with long feathery boughs to make into an archway, somehow made the tiny garden into a dream place, made it seem longer, as if there must be more beyond, another garden, and another and another beyond that. The yew archway was black now and the yews almost as black, thickening with darkness.

How long will it be? Miles wondered. How much longer must I be patient? Will *he* come, will he really come to me at last? For nearly a year now he had been filled with a growing certainty that he was soon going to write poetry again and that it would be very much better than anything he had yet done, that it would be finally the real thing. Meanwhile he waited. He tried to prepare himself. He stopped drinking and curtailed even further his exiguous social life. Everything important, he told himself, was concerned with staying in one's place. He spent his evenings with his notebook, and if either Diana or Lisa came near him he had to prevent himself from screaming at them to go away. He said nothing to the women. At first they thought that he was ill. Later they looked at him in silence and then looked at each other. Sometimes he wrote a few lines of verse, like a musician trying an instrument. There were some isolated beautiful things. But the time was not yet when the god would come.

The poetry of his youth seemed insipid and flimsy now. And the long poem he had written after Parvati's death seemed merely turgid stuff. He had had to write that poem, to change into art and into significance and into beauty the horror of that death. It was a survival poem, born of his own outrageous will to survive. It had sometimes seemed to him like a crime to write that poem, as if it had prevented him from seeing what he ought to have seen and what he had never allowed himself afterwards to see, the real face of death. But it had come with a force of necessity which he had not known before or since. He had called it *Parvati and Shiva*.

'Lord Shiva,' he could hear Parvati saying, in her precise accented voice, as she explained to him some aspect of the Hindu religion. 'Do you believe in Shiva, Parvati?' 'There is truth in all religions.' 'But do you believe in him, in *him*?' 'Perhaps. Who knows what is belief?' Parvati's oriental ability to see that everything was, from a certain point of view, everything else, baffled and charmed his Aristotelian western mind. They had met at Cambridge, where he was reading history and she was reading economics. They were socialists of course. She was the more ardent. Parvati, in cold Cambridge evenings beside a gas fire, with her grey Cashmere shawl, as light as a cobweb, drawn round her shoulders and over her head, talking about the final crisis of capitalism. They would go back to India and serve humanity. Parvati would teach. Miles would take a course in agricultural engineering. They would work in the villages with the people. Miles began to learn Hindi. They were married immediately after their final examinations. They were both twenty-two.

Parvati came from a rich Brahmin family in Benares. Her family opposed the match. Miles could never quite understand why. Was it social, racial, religious, even perhaps financial? He questioned Parvati in vain. 'It is many things. They cannot accept. My mother has never lived in the world.' Once she translated to him a letter from her brother. It was a rather pompous letter. The brother did not seem to conceive that Parvati was serious. 'For nature so preposterously to err. . . .' What *could* it look like from their side? Parvati was greatly upset and wanted to postpone the marriage. They were both very much in love. Miles would not postpone. He was angry with her family, whose attitude he simply could not get clear about. He was even more angry with his own father who had immediately told him in the coarsest terms that he did not want a coloured daughter-in-law and coffee-coloured grandchildren. Miles broke off relations with his father. They got married and both wrote supplicating letters to Benares. After a while Parvati's mother wrote asking her to visit them. Miles was not mentioned. Parvati was overjoyed. They would surely come round now, especially when she told them that she was expecting a child. Miles saw her off at London airport. The plane crashed in the Alps. Miles had never told anybody, not even Diana, that Parvati was pregnant.

Miles never went to see the parents. Understandably they seemed to blame him for their daughter's death. He wrote to them much later when he married Diana but got no reply. He stayed on at Cambridge and did some inconclusive research and failed to get a fellowship. The war came, bringing Miles seven years of dreary misery. He saw no action. He moved from camp to camp, unable to read, unable to write, developing mysterious troubles in his intestines. He was moved into clerical work. He rose eventually to the rank of captain. When the war ended he went into the civil service.

The writing of the long poem, which took him over a year, had somehow prolonged, even in circumstances of dreadful grief, the sense of a life filled with love. He transformed the plane crash into a dazzling tornado of erotic imagery. But the poem was a *Liebestod* and although art cannot but console for what it weeps over, the completion of the poem left him sour and sick and utterly convinced of the henceforward impossibility of love. His loneliness in the army was increased by his ill-concealed disgust at the depraved casualness of his brother officers' attitude to sex. He shunned women absolutely and when certain kinds of talk began left the room banging the door. He won himself solitude and even hostility. He did not consciously wish for death but he grieved at night for some blank thing which he could not even name.

Parvati had made all other women impossible for him. Parvati plaiting her very long black hair. Parvati with quick deft movements pleating her sari. Parvati sitting on the floor with her tongue slightly out like a cat. Her delicate aquiline face, her honey-coloured skin; his sense of acquiring with her a whole precious civilization. The jewels in her ears which he was so surprised to learn were real rubies, real emeralds. How she had laughed at his surprise. Parvati ironing her saris in a room in Newnham. Then ironing his shirts. 'You represent the god.' 'What god?' 'The god – Shiva, Eros. . . . All poets have angels. You are mine.' The very small deft brown hands, the glimpse of bare sandalled feet upon the wet autumnal pavements. The red-brown grain of her lips. Her grace, which made any western woman look gauche and stiff. How coarsely made, how dumpy and disagreeably pink her college friends looked beside her. The feel of that long thick plait of hair in his hand the first time he had dared, playfully but trembling, to take hold of it. He had kissed her hair. Then he had kissed the edge of her silken sari where it slipped over her thin arm. She laughed, pushing him away. She was a clever girl who was going to get a first in economics, but she had not been very long out of that enclosed courtyarded house in Benares where her mother wove garlands to place upon images. Parvati talking about *swaraj* and the fundamental problems of an agricultural economy.

He had written hundreds of love poems for Parvati. After the war, poetry, like so much else, seemed to have come to an end. Eros had changed into Thanatos, and now even the face of Thanatos was veiled. The only person he had any real contact with was Gwen. He had not been very close to Gwen as a child. She was several years younger and he had been away at school. He first became really fond of Gwen, indeed first really noticed Gwen, when she stood up for him so fiercely when his father opposed the marriage. Gwen loved Parvati and admired her. Gwen was very partisan and given to making long speeches. He thought much later, when he a little regretted the breach with his father, that perhaps Gwen had done more harm than good. Bruno needed coaxing, and a different kind of daughter might have coaxed him instead of lecturing him. Miles had no intention of coaxing him. He wished his father at the devil.

After Parvati's death he wanted to see nobody, not even Gwen. Gwen went up to Cambridge and read Moral Sciences and started on a Ph.D. thesis on Frege. The war came and Gwen became an Air Raid Warden in London. Later on in the war Miles arrived in London, still in uniform, working in an office, and for a while a curious almost intimate relationship existed between them. Gwen was usually tired to the point of collapse. Miles felt guiltily how easy a life he was now leading by contrast. They never shared a house, but he used to go round most evenings to her little flat off Baker Street, arriving before she did, and prepare a hot meal for her. Sometimes she was very late and he sat tensely listening to the bombs and trying not to let terrible imaginings break out. Sometimes she worked at night and he saw little of her. They talked a great deal, not about themselves, never of Parvati, but about cool healing impersonal things, poetry, philosophy, art. Eventually they talked mainly philosophy and theology: Karl Barth, Wittgenstein.

Their intimacy was ended, towards the close of the war, by Danby. Miles could never understand about Gwen and Danby. It all happened very quickly. They met on an underground train. On the Inner Circle: they both seemed to attach importance to this, and reiterated it with an imbecile ritual solemnity. They had begun to talk to each other. People did this more readily in the war time. Danby surreptitiously passed his station. Gwen surreptitiously passed her. When they had been all the way round the circle they had to admit to each other that something had happened. Thus the thing began in a kind of absurdity; and Miles felt that in some way it had never ceased to be absurd. Danby was fundamentally a very absurd person, a contingent person, and Miles resented the absorption into this loose and floppy organism of his close-knit and far from contingent sister.

He felt that Gwen had deceived him. She ought not to have let things happen so fast, she ought to have consulted him. As it was, and only a little apologetically, she just introduced Danby out of the blue as her fiancé. Miles scowled politely at this plump bland constantly smiling and obviously self-satisfied person in the uniform of an artillery officer. Danby's hair was golden in those days and his complexion was pink. He looked like a schoolboy cadet. Miles questioned him closely about his background and his education. His father was a shop-keeper in Didcot. He went to a local grammar school and then to Reading university where he studied English literature for a year and then gave up. He worked in an insurance office and then went into the war where he served without drama or distinction in the artillery and later told Miles he had thoroughly enjoyed it. He appeared to have no intellectual interests. Once married he entered the printing works with an insouciance which irritated Miles, and made a success in business which irritated Miles even more. Miles could not see that Danby had any decent *raison d'être* whatsoever. 'I just can't see it, about Danby,' he said to his sister once. 'Oh well, Danby is such *fun*,' Gwen had replied. Miles had nothing with this answer.

Bruno, with whom Gwen had by now re-established relations, was reported to be fond of Danby, and after a while Miles began to tolerate his brother-in-law. Danby was anxious to please, and after Miles had made clear what he thought of the masculine jokes with which Danby at first sought to establish connivance, they did manage to achieve a sort of understanding, based on Danby's interpretation of his role as a controlled and censored fool. Danby, who was not totally insensitive, managed to extend in the direction of Miles, as a kind of propitiatory feeler, the sense of inferiority which he genuinely felt in relation to Gwen. He accepted Miles as his superior and he accepted and shared Miles's view of his incredible and quite undeserved good luck in having obtained Miles's sister. Like that, things settled down; but Miles saw less and less of them. Then after Gwen was dead there was no reason to see Danby any more.

Diana came later, as a surprise, almost as a miracle. The terrible bitterness of Gwen's death put Miles once more into the presence of that which his long poem had served to shield him from. But as soon as he was able to he ceased to look and to feel and set himself to lead a life of complete retirement and almost ferocious dullness. Writing was inconceivable. He read a good deal, as a matter of routine, mainly history and biography, but without passion. He did his job, avoided his colleagues, was classified as an eccentric and quietly passed over at promotion times. His superiors began to regard him as slightly unbalanced, but on the whole he attracted little attention. He suffered occasional fits of severe depression, but not very frequently.

Then one day in the grocer's shop in the Earls Court Road where he went twice a week with a large basket to buy his provisions a girl said to him, 'Don't look so sad.' Miles shuddered at being addressed by a woman and left the shop immediately. She followed him. 'I'm so sorry. I've so often seen you in here. May I walk along with you?' And later, 'Do you live alone?' And later still, 'Have you been married?' Diana did all the work. She explained afterwards to Miles how she had seen him several times in the shop looking self-absorbed and melancholy and had had a fantasy that everything would happen even as it did happen: that he would turn out to live alone, that he had had a great sorrow, that he shunned society, that he had no dealings with women. For Diana it was, in some extraordinary way, the perfect working out of a dream. She had been searching for Miles. She recognized him at once. It was her sense of destiny which carried them both along.

Diana had a very positive conception of her role as a woman. It was in fact her only role and one which had absorbed her since she left school. She grew up in Leicester where her father was a bank clerk. Her parents were vague people and she and her sister did what they pleased. Diana went on a scholarship to an art school in the London suburbs but left it after two years. She became an unsuccessful commercial artist, she worked in an advertising agency. But mainly she just lived. She moved to Earls Court. She had adventures. She lived with men, some rich ones who found her puzzling and gave her expensive presents, and some poor ones who took her money and got drunk and wept. All this she recounted to Miles later on, enjoying his incomprehension and his quite involuntary twitches of disapproval. She had been looking for him, she told him, all this time. She had dreamed of a separated man, a sad austere secluded man, a man with a great sorrow, an ascetic. She was a moth that wanted to be burnt by a cold cold flame.

She loved him very much and although he told her at first that he was an empty vessel, a nothing, and that her love was to him a nothing, she succeeded at last in attracting his attention. Miles was thirty-five. Diana was twenty-eight. Miles became aware that she was beautiful. She was a fair-haired brown-eyed girl with a straight assertive nose and a big well-made mouth and large flat brow and an ivory complexion and a cool enigmatic expression. She tucked her hair well back behind her ears and thrust her pale smooth large-eyed face boldly forward at the world. A quality in her which seemed at first to Miles to be shamelessness later seemed to him more like courage. In the early days of his interest he apprehended her, not without a certain pleasure, as a courtesan; and later, when he was certain that she loved him, he felt her 'adventurousness' as intensifying, not diminishing, the love which she had to offer. When he married her he still felt that she was his mistress, and that pleased both of them.

Of course Diana understood about Parvati. She knew that for Miles this had been something supreme, a love not of this world only. She submitted, in a way which touched his heart and first made him believe absolutely in her love, to being the second not only in time. She accepted indeed the fact that there was not even any question of a contest. A place in his life, a part of himself, perhaps the best part, was simply not available to her. This Miles tried to explain to her while he was still trying to dissuade her love. Soon after, perhaps even then, he was relieved to find that he had laid every vexation upon her and told her every unhappy truth without dissuading her at all. In the end he stopped fighting and let her use the whole huge force of her woman's nature to comfort him, to lure him out of the dark box in which he had been living. His pleasure in her joy was the best experience in his life for many years.

They moved to the house in Kempsford Gardens and after a while, although she said nothing about it, Miles knew that Diana was hoping for a child. Miles was not sure what he felt about children. His child, *the* one, had died in the Alps. Could there be another? He began vaguely to want a son. But the years passed and nothing happened. They looked at each other questioningly in the spaces of the house. Their life was simple. Miles had never craved for company. Now that he had Diana he was perfectly contented. He would have been happy to see no one else. Diana met her friends at lunch time. They hardly ever entertained.

Diana supported, even invented, the formalities of their life together. She made the little house in Kempsford Gardens as ceremonious as an old-fashioned manor house. Meals were punctual and meticulously served. Miles was not allowed in the kitchen. The house was always filled with flowers with never a petal out of place. Miles was forced to adopt a standard of tidiness which he found unnatural and absurd and to which he became completely used. It was as if Diana was determined to make him feel that he was living rather grandly and after a while he did begin to feel it. She had a power of making small things seem large, just as she had uncannily made the garden seem large, made it seem to go on and on like an enchanted garden in a tale. Miles suspected that, in all this, Diana was fighting back against her childhood in Leicester. She had once said to him thoughtfully, 'You were the most *distinguished* of all my suitors.' Diana had her own strict routine, her own invented personal formalities. Entirely without other occupation, she filled her time with the household tasks and enjoyments. There was her hour for working in the garden, her hour for doing the flowers, her hour for doing embroidery, her hour for sitting in the drawing-room and reading a leather-bound book, her hour for playing on the gramophone old-fashioned popular music which Miles disliked, but to which also he had become accustomed. Diana would have anjoyed an eighteenth-century country house life of peaceful ennui and formal tedium and lengthy leisured visiting. In the midst of one of the seedier parts of London she almost succeeded in conjuring it up.

A change came into the life of Miles and Diana. Perhaps in a way they welcomed it, though at first it made both of them rather apprehensive. Diana's younger sister Lisa had made a very different start in life. She read Greats at Oxford and got a first. She went to teach in a school in Yorkshire and joined the Communist Party. Diana, who was very fond of her sister, lost touch with her for a while. Lisa came south for Diana's wedding and met Miles. Then she vanished again and when next heard of she had become a Catholic and joined the order of the Poor Clares. 'I'm sure she was just attracted by the name,' Diana told Miles. 'She was always rather a literary girl.' After a few years Lisa emerged from the Poor Clares and the Roman Catholic Church and went to live in Paris. She came back to England with tuberculosis and stayed with Miles and Diana during her convalescence. She got a teaching job in a school in the East End. The idea vaguely materialized that she might stay on living with Miles and Diana. She stayed on.

All three of them needed a lot of persuading that it was a good idea but were at last entirely persuaded and soon it all began to seem quite natural. Perhaps Lisa seemed to fill the gap left by the absent child in the life of the married pair. The sisters were deeply attached to each other and Miles came to be fond of his sister-in-law and to rely upon her presence. He enjoyed the sisterness of the two women, the fugitive resemblances. He liked it in the evenings when he found them sitting together sewing. Lisa, not by nature orderly, had surrendered, even sooner than Miles had done, to Diana's domestic tyranny. It was good, after all these years *à deux*, to have an extra person in the house, to have in the house two women both devoted to his comfort. Perhaps he had been alone with Diana for a little too long. The extension of their society was refreshing and enabled him to see his wife in a new light.

Also in some vague yet evident way Lisa did need looking after. Diana used to generalize about her sister. 'She has somehow missed the bus of life.' 'She is like someone who breaks his bones if he falls over.' 'She has lost the instinct for happiness.' 'She is a bird with a broken wing.' Lisa was graver, gaunter, darker than Diana and was usually taken to be the elder sister. She was nervy and reticent and silent and solitary though she sometimes talked philosophy with Miles and was more ardent than he to complete the argument. Sometimes they got quite cross with each other and Diana had to part them. Lisa appeared to be contented in her school work and in the holidays did voluntary work for the local probation officer. Miles enjoyed her company. She puzzled him and he pitied her. She seemed a cold dewy yet wilting flower. Sometimes indeed she seemed to him simply an apparition, a shadow beside the solid reality of her sister. He and Diana shared an anxiety about her which occupied them not unpleasantly.

The sky was almost dark now, hung with a blazing evening star with tiny pinpoints of other stars round about it. The traffic was humming evenly in the Old Brompton Road. A blackbird, who always sang at the last light, was unwinding in a nearby tree the piercing and insistent pattern of his *Kyrie*. The damp air was turning chill in the darkness. Down below something pale was moving. A woman in a pale dress was walking slowly across the paving stones and along the path of clipped grass towards the archway. Which of them was it? The obscurity defeated his eyes as he watched the moving figure in silence.

Suddenly the light in the room was switched on.

Miles turned round abruptly and then with the same movement closed the window and pulled the curtain.

'Diana, I wish you wouldn't do that!'

'I'm so sorry.'

Diana was dressed in an old-fashioned blue embroidered kimono. Her straight hair, not yet grey, had paled without losing its lustre, to a sort of pearly sandy yellow. Her ivory face was unlined, like a face in a miniature.

'I'm sorry, I wasn't sure if you were here.'

'Where else would I be at this time for heaven's sake? I wish you wouldn't come porlocking. I'm trying to work. What's that you've got there?'

'A letter someone delivered by hand. It said "urgent" so I thought I'd bring it up at once.'

'Don't go, sweet. Forgive me. Who the hell's it from, I don't know the writing.' Miles tore the letter open.

Dear Miles,

I expect you will be surprised hearing from me like this out of the blue. The thing is this, your father is ill, as you know, and although there is no immediate cause for concern he is naturally thinking in terms of arrangements and all that. He would like to see you. He wants me to emphasize that he has nothing special in view here but just feels that he wants to see his son. I very much hope that you will feel ready to see him, as he is anxious to see you. As you haven't met for such a long time I thought it might be a good idea if you and I had a preliminary talk about it first, so that I can sort of put you in the picture. I very much hope that you will agree to this. I will, if I may, telephone you at the office tomorrow morning and find out what time would be convenient for me to visit you. I very much hope that all this can be arranged amicably. Your father is an old man and very far from well.

Yours sincerely,
Danby Odell

'Oh God,' said Miles.

'What is it?'

'A letter from Danby.'

'Danby? Oh, Danby Odell. What does he want?'

'He wants me to go and see my father.'

'Isn't it odd,' said Diana, pushing her hair back behind her ears, 'that in all these years I've never met either your father or Danby Odell. Is it urgent, I mean is the old man on the point of death?'

'Apparently not.'

'You'll go of course? I've been feeling for some time that you ought to do something about it.'

Miles threw the letter down on the table. He felt exasperation and an uneasy feeling rather like fear. 'Well, hell, I've been writing polite letters to the old bastard all these years and he's never replied. And now that fool Danby writes as if it was somehow all my fault.'

Diana had picked up the letter. 'I think it's quite a nice letter. He doesn't imply it's your fault.'

'Yes he does. Oh Christ.' Miles did not want this now. He did not want emotions and memories and scenes and unmanageable unforeseeable situations. He did not want to go through the rigmarole of forgiving and being forgiven. It would all be play-acting. It would be something hopelessly impure. And it might delay, it might offend, it might preclude for ever the precious imminent visitation of the god.

Chapter Seven

Danby straightened his tie and rang the bell. Miles opened the door.

'I hope I'm not too early?'

'Come in.'

Miles turned round and walked upstairs leaving Danby to shut the door. After a moment's uncertainty Danby shut the door and followed his host up the stairs. Miles had already disappeared into one of the rooms. Danby approached an open door and saw Miles standing over by the window with his back half turned. Danby entered the room and closed the door.

Danby had chosen the time of six-thirty in the evening for their interview on the assumption that Miles would be certain to offer him a drink, which would help him through the interview. He had not however omitted to drink two large gins at the Lord Clarence before turning into Kempsford Gardens. The room was dark. The sky outside was a glittering grey.

Viewed at close quarters, the idea of actually confronting Miles had alarmed Danby considerably. It was not that he was worrying about the stamps. Bruno's seeing or not seeing Miles would probably make no difference to their destination. He had not really believed that Bruno was serious about seeing his son. Bruno had speculated about this before and nothing had come of it; he had speculated about it at earlier times when he was very much more enterprising and resolute than he was now. Danby had come to feel that Bruno had settled down peacefully into the last phase of his life, wanting simply to be left alone with his routine of stamps and telephone and evening papers, with his eyes fixed, if not upon eternity and the day of judgement, at least upon some great calm and imminent negation which would preclude surprises, démarches, and the unpredictable. He had underestimated Bruno, and when he suddenly perceived the strength of will that still remained inside that big head and shrivelled body he had experienced a shock and had had rapidly to re-examine his own conception of Miles.

Miles had been filed away for years. Without reflection, Danby had assumed that he would not see Miles again. There could be no occasion except possibly Bruno's funeral. Danby occasionally imagined Bruno's funeral, how it would be. He imagined his own feelings of tenderness and regret and relief, the solemnity of the scene, the silent bow to Miles. Now suddenly there was this curiously naked and unnerving and quite unscripted encounter with a man who was a stranger and who yet was, as Danby had realized in the short while that had intervened since Bruno's decision, somehow rather deeply involved in Danby's life. He could only be indifferent to Miles at a distance. Close to, Miles was an interesting, disturbing, even menacing object.

Although Miles and Danby were about the same age Danby had always felt as if Miles were his senior. He had taken this attitude over from Gwen, who had revered her brother and regarded him as an oracle. Danby had early accepted the notion that Miles was something remarkable, and he had now to remind himself that really Miles was a very ordinary person, even by some standards a failure. Before he had ever met Miles he was already a bit afraid of him, and more rationally afraid of his power over Gwen. Miles had not concealed his opinion of Danby, and this had caused Danby considerable pain, even after he had made certain that Gwen was not going to allow her brother to forbid the banns. Danby, as he now realized, standing in the dark room looking at Miles's back, as indeed he now knew he had simply forgotten, had genuinely admired Miles in the days gone by. And the shock of his presence brought to Danby again that old familiar humiliating sensation mixed of fear and admiration and bitter hurt resentment.

Miles turned and indicated an armchair beside the fireplace and Danby sat down.

'Look here,' said Miles. He sat down on an upright chair beside the window. 'What is all this?'

'It's fairly clear I should have thought,' said Danby. 'Bruno wants to see you.'

'Does he *really*?'

'Well, he says he does and goes on saying it. I'm not a mind reader.'

Danby had thought a lot beforehand about this interview without being able to decide upon the tone of it. The tone would have to be settled impromptu. And here he was already becoming aggressive.

'It seems a bit pointless after all these years,' said Miles. He was folding a piece of paper, not looking at Danby. The room was getting darker.

'He's dying,' said Danby. He felt a rush of emotion, an obscure feeling which connected together Bruno, Gwen, Miles's profile seen against the glowing dark grey window.

'Yes, yes,' said Miles in an irritable voice. 'But children and parents don't necessarily have anything to say to each other. I'm not conventional about this and I shouldn't have thought that Father was.'

His saying 'Father' like that brought back Gwen, even the tones of her voice. Danby said, 'He wants to see you. Any discussion is just frivolous.' Miles stiffened and threw the paper away, and Danby felt that it was rather strange and wonderful for him to be calling Miles frivolous. He noticed with satisfaction that Miles's tossed hair was falling apart to reveal a bald patch.

'I'm afraid you are not being very clear-headed,' said Miles. 'My point concerns my father's welfare. An interview with me might upset him seriously. I mean, the situation has to be *thought* about. Does Father propose that we should see each other daily, or what?'

Christ, you cold-blooded bureaucrat, thought Danby. 'I don't think Bruno has thought it out beyond the idea of just seeing you once.'

'I see no point in our meeting once.'

'I mean, after meeting once you'd both just have to see how you felt.'

'I think this could be very agonizing indeed for my father, and I'm surprised you didn't dissuade him. You must have control over him by now.'

Was that a reference to the stamps? 'Bruno controls himself, I don't run him.'

'If we meet once either to meet again or not to meet again may be equally dreadful.'

It occurred to Danby for the first time that there might indeed be a problem here. Like Bruno he had not thought beyond the first occasion. 'You're complicating the matter,' said Danby. 'You are after all his only child and he is near death and wants to see you. It seems to me a matter of plain duty, whatever the consequences.'

'One cannot divorce duty from consequences.'

'Oh all right,' said Danby, standing up abruptly and pushing his chair back. 'Shall I go back and tell him you won't come?'

'Sit down, Danby.'

Danby hesitated, shuffled his feet and sat down slowly.

'I'm sorry,' said Miles. 'I probably sound rather hardhearted, but I want to see what's involved. I think we might turn the light on.' He pulled the curtain and moved to the electric light switch. Danby gritted his teeth.

Miles was not really very like Gwen, and yet there were details of her face which memory and even photographs had retained for Danby only in a hazy generalized form which were now suddenly manifest in flesh and blood clarity: the sharply marked mouth with the deep runnel above it, the brow coming closely down over the intent eyes, the heavy quality of the dark hair.

Danby looked away and looked quickly about the room which was now revealed by two green-shaded lamps. It was a book-lined room, evidently a study. A table was half drawn up under the window, covered with neatly squared off piles of paper and notebooks and an orderly row of ballpoint pens. The clean open fireplace contained a pyramid of fir cones and was surrounded by William Morris tiles which gleamed in a swirling profusion of blues and purples. Gwen would have liked those tiles. She would have enjoyed collecting the fir cones. There was a vase of daffodils on the white painted mantelshelf, and a small square gilt mirror above it. Here and there a shelf of books had been cleared to display glittering Chinese porcelain, ultramarine ducks, dogs, dragons. Everything looked formidably neat and clean. A donnish room: and yet the flowers and the ducks and the fir cones did not seem quite like Miles. Vaguely, and the thought somehow disturbed him, Danby remembered that Miles was married.

'Quite honestly,' Miles was going on. He had sat down again and was intent on folding pieces of paper and cutting them carefully with a sharp knife. 'Quite honestly, I rather dread this operation not only because of what it might do to him, but also because of what it might do to me. I'm rather through with the emotions, that kind anyway, and I've got other things to do. Is it all about money?'

'Money?' said Danby. 'Good Lord, no!' Or was it? Perhaps after all Bruno just wanted to decide the destiny of the stamps. Damn the stamps, they complicated everything.

'You see,' said Miles, concentrating upon a neat clean severance of a folded sheet. 'You *see*, I don't know whether you know this, but I've been writing to my father regularly for years, and I've never had any reply. I rather assumed he'd written me off. This desire to see me is a bit surprising. Is he senile?'

'No!' said Danby. 'He has to take various drugs and some days he gets a big vague and rambles a little, but on the whole he's perfectly clear-headed. He's certainly still a rational being.'

'Is he much – changed?'

'Physically, yes. Not in other ways. I suppose you know what's wrong with him?'

'Oddly enough I do,' said Miles slowly, raising his brooding eyes in a significant way which was very reminiscent of Gwen. 'Oddly enough I do. I wrote to his doctor about eighteen months ago. I suppose there's no new development?'

'No. Just the progress of the – thing.'

They were silent, Danby watching Miles and Miles intently examining a piece of cut paper. 'All right. I'll come and see him. But I think it's going to be awful. *Awful.*'

Danby stood up. He felt a strange defensive tenderness for Bruno combined with an acute wish that Miles would offer him a drink. He wanted to be asked to stay, given a drink, somehow comforted by Miles. He would like to have talked about the past. 'Bruno has been very brave.'

'I don't doubt it, I don't doubt it. When shall I come?' Miles had risen too.

69

'Of course he may change his mind when he knows you're coming. He may funk it.'

'You mean he's nervous too?'

'Yes.'

'Funny,' said Miles. 'I hadn't *really* thought of *him* having any feelings about it, *now* at all,' and he smiled. Miles's teeth were sharp and jumbled, too numerous for his jaw and crowded together at the front of his mouth, giving him a wolfish sweet-savage smile which Danby had quite forgotten. Danby usually despised men with uneven teeth, but Miles's were rather impressive.

'Anyway I'll let you know,' said Danby. 'I'll ring up.' He stood awkwardly. He was taller than Miles. He had somehow forgotten that too. It was the moment for the blessed glass of gin. He thought, if Bruno decides not to see Miles, I won't see Miles again, except at the funeral. Danby pushed his chair a little further back, which might have been a preliminary to departing or to sitting down again. As he did so he saw a little ball of blue tucked into the depression between the seat and the back. It was a woman's handkerchief.

'I've never met your wife,' said Danby.

Miles gave him a preoccupied look and put his hand on the door.

Danby thought, I must stop him, I want to talk to him about Gwen. If only I could think of something quickly now to say about her. He could think of nothing. He said, 'Bruno wants to meet your wife.' Bruno had expressed no such wish.

'Emotions,' said Miles. 'Emotions. It's all fruitless, fruitless.' He led the way down the stairs.

'So you talked about me?' said Bruno suspiciously, looking up at Danby.

'Yes,' said Danby in an exasperated voice, 'of course we did!' Danby had been extremely irritable on his return from Miles's house, Bruno could not make out why.

Danby was standing at the window looking out through the undrawn curtains at the lurid darkness of the London night. Bruno was well propped up on pillows. They were both sipping champagne. The whitish scrawled counterpane was covered with stamps and with the dismembered pages of the *Evening Standard*, on top of which lay the first volume of *Soviet Spiders* open at the chapter on *Liphistiid Spiders of the Baltic Coastline*.

'What did you say about me?'

'He asked how you were and I told him and I said you were longing to meet him and – '

'You shouldn't have said that.'

'Oh my God – '

'I'm not sure that I *am* longing to meet him,' said Bruno judiciously.

'Well, make up your mind for heaven's sake.'

'I can't see why *you're* so upset.'

'I'm not upset, damn you.'

Since the notion of seeing Miles, or at any rate of sending Danby on an embassy to Miles had become a real plan, Bruno had experienced a complexity of feelings. Partly he felt a kind of animal fright at the real possibility of confronting his son. Partly he was afraid of what he might feel if Miles refused to come. There was a possible madness there. Danby had reassured him at the first moment of his return. Partly too Bruno felt a quite immediate and lively sense of annoyance at the idea of Miles and Danby discussing him, perhaps making common cause against him. He imagined, 'The old fool wants to see you. Must humour him I suppose.' 'How gaga is he?' And 'How long will he last?' Would they speak of him like that? They were young and uncaged, in the legions of the healthy. He also felt an excited touched surprise that such a complex of emotions could still exist in such an old man. 'Such an *old* man,' he thought to himself until the tears came. He was pleased at these moments when he felt that he had not been simplified by age and illness. He was the complicated spread-out thing that he had always been, in fact more so, much more so. He had drawn the web of his emotions back inside himself with not a thread lost. Well, he would see Miles. It was unpredictable though, and that was scaring.

'Of course I do want to see him,' said Bruno judiciously, 'but I feel quite detached about it. You shouldn't have implied I was frantic.'

'I didn't imply it. We had a very plain talk.'

'How do you mean plain? What's Miles like now?'

'He's going bald.'

'You never liked him, Danby.'

'He never liked me. I liked him all right. He was horribly like Gwen. He still is.'

'That's why you're upset.'

'Yes. More champagne?'

'Thanks. But what's he *like*?'

'Rather brutal and preoccupied. But he'll be nice to *you*.'

'I can't think what on earth we'll talk about,' said Bruno.

His left hand strayed vaguely over things on the counterpane while the right conveyed the trembling glass to his lips. Champagne still cheered.

'You'd better see him some morning. You're best in the mornings.'

'Yes. It'll have to be Saturday or Sunday then. Will you let him know?'

'Yes. May I leave you now, Bruno? There's a man waiting in a pub. Here's Nigel the Nurse to take over.'

Soft-footed Nigel pads in and Danby leaves. Nigel's lank dark hair sweeps round his pale lopsided face and projects in a limp arc beneath his chin. His dark eyes are dreamy and he is many-handed, gentle, as he tidies Bruno up for supper time. The stamps are put away, the *Evening Standard* neatly folded, Bruno's glass of speckled golden champagne filled again to the brim. Some of it spills upon the white turned-down sheet as the crippled spotted hand trembles and shakes. Such an old old thing that hand is.

'Want to go to the lav?'

'No thanks, Nigel, I'm all right.'

'Not got cramp again?'

'No cramp.'

Nigel flutters like a moth. A pyjama button is done up, a firm support between the shoulder blades while a pillow is plumped, the lamp and the telephone moved a little farther off, *Soviet Spiders* closed and put away. The back of Nigel's hand brushes Bruno's cheek. The tenderness is incredible. Tears are again in Bruno's eyes.

'I am going to see my son, Nigel.'

'That's good.'

'Do you think forgiveness is something, Nigel? Does something *happen*? Or is it just a word? I feel sleepy now. Can I have my supper soon?'

Too much champagne. Nigel is drinking out of Danby's glass. Nigel flutters like a moth, filling the room with a soft powdery susurrus of great wings.

Chapter Eight

Danby straightened his tie and rang the bell.

The door was opened by a large-browed woman with very faded sand-coloured hair tucked well back behind her ears.

The image of Miles vanished.

'I say – Hello – I – '

'You're Danby.'

'Yes. You're Diana.'

'Yes. Oh good. I've been longing to meet you. Come in. I'm afraid Miles is out.'

There was some faint music playing in the background.

Danby followed her through the dark hall into a room into which the last evening sun was palely shining. Outside, through French windows, there was a pavement wet with recent rain, interspersed with bushy clumps of grey and bluish herbs. A very faint steam was rising from the sun-warmed pavement. But Danby had not taken his eyes off the woman.

The music, Danby now became aware, was dance music, old-fashioned dance music, a foxtrot, something dating from Danby's youth and stirring up a shadowy physical schema of memories. A slow foxtrot. Diana turned it down to a background murmur.

'How nice of you to call.'

'Well, I could have telephoned, but I was passing by and thought I'd drop in.' Danby in fact had found himself much troubled by a craving to see Miles again.

'It's about Miles seeing Bruno? I'm so glad he's going to, aren't you?'

'Yes. I wonder would Saturday morning be all right? Miles doesn't work on Saturdays?'

'Sometimes he does, but he can always not if he wants to.'

'About eleven then.'

'You know, you're not a bit like what I expected.'

'What did you expect?'

'Oh something – well, it's hard to say – '

'Miles's description of me was unflattering?'

'No, no, no, it wasn't that. I thought you'd be older, and not so – '

'Handsome?'

They both laughed.

The room was a variegated brightly coloured room, full of plump little rounded armchairs covered in chintz. There was a tall white *art nouveau* mantelpiece scattered with glistening china. The yellow and white striped walls were covered with a miscellany of small late-Victorian oil paintings and silhouettes and miniatures. It was a self-conscious eclectic room, a made-up room, a room which might have existed in Cambridge in nineteen hundred, full of cold light from the fens and an atmosphere of rather severe hedonism.

The girl, for so he immediately thought of her, was wearing a blue woollen dress without a belt, very short. She was plump inside the sheath of the dress, rounds of breasts, stomach, buttocks, well suggested and smoothed over. Her eyes were a rich unflecked brown, and her longish straight hair, now the sun was shining on it, gleamed a metallic silvery gold. She had a straight decisive nose and an intent faintly hungry enigmatic expression. Danby apprehended at once a certain sense of drama, a sense of her initiative. A nervy magnetic girl such as he did not often meet now. A rather severe hedonist.

'And am I like how you expected?'

'I'm afraid I didn't really think much about you at all. But I shall think about you now.'

'You are polite.'

They both laughed again.

'Have a drink,' said Diana. 'Miles has given up. Isn't it awful?' She took bottles of gin and vermouth and sherry and small cut glass tumblers out of a white cupboard.

Danby took the drink gratefully. The ritual of drinking, the time of day, the incapsulated moment of the first evening drink, always produced for him a rush of pure happiness along the veins. This occasion seemed, with its element of surprise, peculiarly perfect.

'I like a drink at this time of day, but I don't like drinking alone.'

'Then I'm glad I called to provide you with a drinking companion!'

'I'm glad you called! Miles is so clammed up about his family.'

'Family, yes, I suppose I count as a family connexion.'

'I think family ties are *so* important.'

'Depends on the family rather. What do you do, Diana?'

'What do you mean what do I do? I'm a housewife. I don't know what you do.'

'I'm a business man I suppose. Or a printer. I never really think what I am.'

'I never really think what I am either But I imagine that's because I'm not anything.'

'You don't go out to work?'

'Good heavens no. I'm unemployable.'

'You dust?'

'The char dusts. I garden, I cook, I rearrange the ornaments.'

'Creative.'

'Don't be silly. Have another drink.'

'When's Miles coming?'

'Not till late. He's at some office gathering he couldn't get out of. He hates it.'

'I don't imagine Miles is very social.'

'He isn't. He *hates* people.'

'You obviously rather like them.'

'Well, I'm a good deal matier than Miles is. Can I come and see Bruno too?'

'Of course. He's longing to meet you.'

'Is he? I didn't imagine he conceived of my existence.'

'Of course he does. He's all agog.'

'You make me feel quite nervous. I'll let Miles have first go. I've always so much wanted to meet you and Bruno. Is Bruno very ill?'

'Yes and no. He's not in pain and he's quite rational. He'll like you.'

'I'll like him.'

How stupid of me, thought Danby. It never occurred to me that there might be, like this, a girl. And what luck for Bruno. She would know how to deal with the old man. Girls had so much more sense. He looked about the room again. A girl who did nothing. Who sat in plump chintzy chairs and read. He saw a book on one of the chairs. Jane Austen. A woman who was perhaps a little bored. Who waited.

'I'm so very glad we've met at last,' he said.

Then, oh God, he thought, what awfully sexy music. What *is* it? It was something familiar. 'What *is* that thing on the gramophone?'

She turned it up. It was a slow foxtrot, formal, dignified, intensely sweet, bringing with it again that precise and yet unplaceable sense of the past. Danby's feet sketched a movement, sliding, catching, upon the close-woven carpeted floor.

Then the next moment he had sidled forward, slid his arm around her waist, and they were dancing in silence, advancing, retreating, circling, their slow precise feet patterning the floor and their mingled shadow climbing over the furniture after them.

The music stopped and they moved apart. Blue eyes stared at brown eyes and brown eyes dropped their gaze.

'You dance beautifully, Diana.'

'So do you.'

'I think the slow foxtrot is the best of all dances.'

'Yes. And the most difficult.'

'I haven't danced in years.'

'Nor I. Miles hates dancing.'

'I won a dancing competition once.'

'So did I.'

'Diana, will you come and dance with me, some afternoon, at one of those dance halls, you know, one can dance there in the afternoons.'

'No, of course not.'

'Miles wouldn't mind would he?'

'Danby, don't be silly.'

'Diana, slow foxtrot?'

'No.'

'Slow foxtrot?'
'No.'
'Slow fox?'
'No.'

Chapter Nine

Barefooted Nigel squats beside a railing looking down. His feet are muddied, his hands red with rust. A man passes by him on the pavement in the darkness, turns and pauses, stares. Nigel smiles without moving, flashing his white teeth in the half dark, catching a ray of light from a distant lamp post. The man hesitates, retreats, flees. Nigel still smiling returns to gaze. He sees through a divided curtain a man going to bed in a basement flat. The man is stepping out of his trousers. He leaves his trousers in a coiled mound upon the floor and goes to urinate into the washbasin. The tail of his shirt is ragged. He pulls off his shirt and scratches under his arms for some time, each hand busy scratching inside the opposite armpit. He stops and with intentness smells his fingers. Still wearing his cosy dirty vest he puts on crumpled pyjamas and crawls heavily into bed. He lies a while vacant, scratching, staring up at the ceiling, then switches out the light. Nigel rises.

These are the glories of his night city, a place of pilgrimage, a place of sin, a place of shriving. Nigel glides barefoot, taking long paces, touching each lamp post as he passes. He has seen men prostrated, writhing, cursing, praying. He has seen a man lay down a pillow to kneel upon and close his eyes and join his two hands palm to plam. All through the holy city in the human-boxes the people utter prayers of love and hate. Unpersonned Nigel strides among them with long silent feet and the prayers rise up about him hissing faintly, like steam. Up any religion a man may climb. Along the darkened alleyways the dusky white-clad worshippers are silently carrying the white fragrant garlands to lay upon the greasy lingam of Great Shiva.

Nigel strides noiselessly, crossing the roadways at a step, his bare feet not touching ground, a looker-on at inward scenes. He has reached the sacred river. It rolls on at his feet black and full, a river of tears bearing away the corpses of men. There is weeping but he is not the weeper. The wide river flows onward, immense and black beneath the old cracked voices of the temple bells which flit like bats throughout the lurid black air. The river is thick, ribbed, curled, convex, heaped up above its banks. Nigel makes offerings. Flowers. Where was the night garden where he gathered them? He throws the flowers down upon the humped river, then throws after them all the objects which he finds in his pockets, a knife, a handkerchief, a handful of money. The river takes and sighs and the flowers and the white handkerchief slide slowly away into the tunnel of the night. Nigel, a god, a slave, stands erect, a sufferer in his body for the sins of the sick city.

He reclines upon the pavement where the rising waters have lifted up the window of a houseboat near to his telescopic eye. A man and woman are sitting on a bed, the man fully clothed, the woman naked. He speaks angrily to her and brings his fist up to her eyes. She shakes her head, moving it uneasily away, her face made ugly by evasiveness and fear. The man begins to take his clothes off, tearing them off, stripping himself bare with curses. He drags back the blankets of the bed and the woman darts inside like an animal into its burrow and hides, peering, with the blankets up to her eyes. The man pulls the blankets off her and turns out the light. Nigel lies on the damp pavement and sighs for the sins of the world.

He lifts himself a little to see over a sill through an un-curtained window. Beside a cluttered kitchen table Will and Adelaide are arguing. He takes her hand which she tries stiffly to withdraw. He hurls her hand back at her. Auntie is knitting an orange cardigan. 'So there is a Cape Triangular stamp?' 'Yes, there's several.' 'You must get the right one, I'll show you a picture.' 'I'm not going to get any one.' 'Oh yes you are, Ad.' 'Oh no I'm not.' 'Sometimes I could murder you, Adelaide.' 'Let go my arm, that hurts.' 'It's meant to hurt.' 'I think you're hateful.' 'Why do you come here to torment me.' 'Let go.' 'You enjoy tormenting me.' '*Let go*.' Auntie who has noticed, not for the first time, Nigel's face risen like the moon above the window sill, smiles mysteriously and goes on knitting.

Altogether elsewhere beside a glass door he prostrates himself among feathery grey herbs. Here there is only a chink in the curtains through which he can see a thin-faced sallow man with narrow eyes and a heavy fall of dense dark hair disputing with a thin woman with stick-like arms and a gaunt ardent face. Her brown hair is wild, formless as a dark cloud about her thrusting face.

'The world is independent of my will.'

'The sense of it must lie outside it. In the world everything is as it is and happens as it does happen. In it there is no value.'

'And if there were it would be of no value.'

'If good and bad willing changes the world it can only change the limits of the world. The world must wax and wane as a whole.'

'The world of the happy is quite other than the world of the unhappy.'

'As in death too, the world does not change but ceases.'

'Death is not an event in life. Death is not lived through.'

'If by eternity is understood not endless temporal duration but timelessness, he lives eternally who lives in the present.'

'Not how the world is but that it is is the mystical.'

'Whereof we cannot speak.'

'Thereof we must be silent.'

A beautiful woman has entered the room with a brow as broad and bland as the dawn. Her night robe of midnight blue sweeps the ground. She sets a tray before the disputants and sits between them patting them both with her hands. Looking upon her with love they sip Ovaltine dissolved in hot milk and nibble custard cream biscuits.

Nigel goes home. He kneels on damp slimy moss while Danby gazes at himself in a mirror. Danby smiles at himself, admiring his double row of even white teeth. Kneeling so close to him unseen Nigel smiles too, the tender, forgiving, infinitely sad smile of almighty God.

Chapter Ten

Slow foxtrot.

With eyes half closed Danby and Diana were rotating dreamily in each other's arms. The dancing floor was filled with quiet gliding comatose middle-aged couples, all dancing very well. The lights were reddish and low. The marble pillars of the ballroom soared into an invisibility of cigarette haze. The walls were of golden mosaic with turquoise blue mosaic flowers figured upon them. Upon the pillars gilded cornucopias, cunningly fixed, leaned outward into the hall, above scalloped fringes of purple velvet. Jungles of ferns and palms occupied all corners and masked the entrance. There was a thick, sweet, powdery smell of inexpensive perfume and cosmetic. A few people sat at tables at the side, but most of those present were dancing with their eyes half closed and their cheeks glued together. A few conversed in low whispers. Most were silent. It was the afternoon.

'Danby.'

'Yes.'

'We are the youngest people here.'

'Yes.'

'Do you think all those women are dancing with their husbands?'

'No, of course not.'

'Will they tell their husbands?'

'No, of course not. Will you tell your husband?'

'Isn't it odd to think it's afternoon outside and the sun is shining?'

'Yes.'

'The afternoon is a wicked time. I think in hell it must be always afternoon.'

Diana spoke in a scarcely audible murmur as if in her sleep.

Her attention was almost completely absorbed by the pressure of Danby's cheek upon her own and by the light, firm, sensitive guiding movements of Danby's right hand upon her back.

Diana was not sure how or why she was on the dancing floor with Danby. He had rung up. There had been a sense of fatality, a craving, extremely sharp and precise, to feel those authoritative cellist fingers once again touching her back. It was all very unusual. She had spent so many years waiting for children and only lately had consciously told herself that the wait was over. She had occupied so many years – how had she occupied them? Miles had been her occupation: Miles's loneliness, Miles's shyness, his nervous animism, his inability in some ways to take hold of life at all. She had soon ceased being ambitious for him in his work. She simply wanted to preserve and prolong her sense of protecting him, of warming him to life. Meanwhile she flirted a little with her friends of both sexes. She told herself that she was not naturally monogamous while remaining strictly so. She took notice of the fact that her vaguely erotic daydreams did not always concern her husband. Yet there was no one who could interest her as Miles constantly, consistently, passionately interested her. The umbilical cord of her early love for him had never been broken. She still counted herself fortunate. Though lately, perhaps prophetically, collected quietly in the kitchen at night, she had found herself looking a little with new eyes, had felt a vague need for change, had sensed even the possibility of boredom.

She had lived upon her inexhaustible love for Miles. She had also lived on something which was perhaps not inexhaustible, her dream picture of herself. Making the house had taken her years and within it she had occupied years in posing. She posed in a silk afternoon dress in the drawing-room, in a nylon negligeé in the bedroom. While doing the flowers she posed as a lady doing the flowers. She made up her face through solitary afternoons. Miles hated social life and they hardly ever entertained. She was like a prostitute waiting among the toys and trinkets of her trade, only the man she was waiting for was her husband.

Like a religious, she had meditated for years upon her luck in getting Miles. She had never dreamed of so distinguished, so aristocratic a catch. She would even have been contented with much less. Her father was dead, but she still visited her elderly mother in the house where she had been brought up, and she was kind to the old lady, but could not help contemplating with satisfaction the gap between her mother's life and her own. Miles, without even noticing it, had lifted her across. She set herself to make a beautiful and elegant burrow for them both and within it over the years they grew together like two animals that come to develop a single telepathic personality.

She had played the passionate exacting mistress to Miles with the more conscious abandon since she knew that she was for him a second best. The idea of Parvati did not distress her, on the contrary. She charmed herself with her role of healer. She was not the damsel heroine in the castle, she was the mysterious lady of the fountain who heals the wound of the wandering knight, the wound which has defied all other touches. The role was the more grateful since the damsel heroine was long ago dead, not forgotten, but mercifully absent. There was only the fountain lady now. And the memory of the lost one remained as a guarantee of her husband's fidelity. The dead Parvati reigned felicitously over their marriage.

Lisa, poor Lisa, had come to be an occupation too, as she had been long ago in Diana's childhood, when Lisa's idealism and lack of common sense had constantly landed her in scrapes with which Diana had had to deal. Diana was devoted to her sister and enjoyed both admiring and patronizing her, and had always been helped and supported by Lisa's return of unquestioning love. With Lisa she had enjoyed by nature that animal close-ness and identity which with Miles she had after many years achieved. Adult life parted them and at their rarer meetings they had had increasingly less to say to each other, though something of the old closeness still remained. Diana was glad that Miles liked Lisa; and after Lisa's illness it had seemed natural for the married pair to ask her, for the time at any rate, to make her home with them. How she and Miles argued! It was all a novelty and somehow a felicitous one.

Diana felt infinitely sorry for Lisa, mediating her compassion through her sense of the utter alienness of her sister, through her sense of her own temperamental luck. Diana was a cheerful unanxious person, endowed with good looks and an aura of self-satisfaction. The faintly enigmatic smile which hovered about her lips like a resident cupid was really a very simple smile of satisfaction, a radiant outward sign of a totality of plump, healthy, gratified, successfully incarnate being. Lisa was without beauty, and such handsomeness as she had once had had gone with her illness. She was clever of course, and on the evidence she was tougher than she seemed. She held down a job as a school mistress at a school in the East End, one visit to which had made Diana feel quite sick. Yet in spite of this she appeared to Diana as a doomed girl. Diana had been surprised at her sister's recovery. 'Lisa wants death,' she had said to Miles. 'She certainly wants to suffer,' Miles had replied. 'That isn't quite the same thing.' 'She's a mystic,' Diana had concluded. 'She wants to be nothinged.' 'She is certainly a masochist,' Miles had agreed.

I am middle-aged, thought Diana, looking round the ballroom at the dreamy couples who were so far from young. I belong with these people. The novelty of Lisa had worn off. Had Diana now reached an age where there had to be, at last, one novelty after another? Was this a kind of wickedness? She could not feel it. She could only feel an excited sense of rejuvenation and *funniness* in the unexpected advent of Danby. Of course she had thought about Bruno and she had thought about Danby, only imagining him quite unreflectively in terms of Miles's picture. Even after Miles's recent interview with Danby she had listened quite simple-heartedly to Miles's exclamations about that fat dolt and that grinning buffoon. She had not expected to be instantly captivated. The sheer surprise of it was life-giving. Danby's smooth brown humorous face, his drooping crest of white hair, his strong confident smile, hovered in her mind as she told Miles, in somewhat curtailed terms, of Danby's visit, and while she listened in silence to Miles's stream of sarcasm. The images accompanied her to bed.

'The contact of bodies is the contact of minds.'

'You are a philosopher, Danby.'

'Think of all the ridiculous years we haven't known each other.'

'I feel I've known you for ages.'

'I feel that too. I think we're each other's type. Yes?'

'Maybe. You're someone I can be entirely light-hearted with without feeling worried. It's not so easy for a woman of my age to take this kind of – holiday.'

'Light-hearted. You don't mean frivolous, cynical?'

'No, light-hearted. You make me laugh.'

'Well, that's all right. Let's have a love affair.'

'No, Danby, nothing like that. I love my husband. I'm permanently hooked.'

'Oh. I think it's rather bad form for a woman to say that when she's illicitly dancing with another man.'

'I'm afraid it's true, my dear.'

'Let me pay you the tribute of saying that your remark has caused me pain.'

'Let me pay you the tribute of saying that I survey your pain with pleasure.'

'We might get somewhere on that basis.'

'No, no – '

'You said no last time and then yes, so I'll go on hoping.'

'Don't. I'm glad you wanted to dance with me, that's all.'

'That isn't all, since we're here together in this awfully deliciously wicked place.'

'It is rather an image of sin, isn't it.'

'Let's give the image some substance then.'

'Have you got anybody, Danby?'

'A girl, no.'

'You're not queer, are you?'

'Good God no! Diana, you make me feel quite faint!'

'All alone?'

'All alone. There was someone, but she went to Australia. I mope.'

'Poor Danby. But really I think one's thoughts and feelings are not all that important.'

'Mine are. I am thinking and feeling that I want you. What are you going to do about it? You realize that you've led me on?'

'I'm nearly fifty. It doesn't apply.'

'I'm over fifty. It does.'

'Don't make difficulties. Just for the moment really I feel young again.'

'It's the music. This place belongs to the past. It's something to do with movement, repetition. I feel young too, timeless, rather.'

'Timeless, yes. You're very attractive.'

'Then what about it?'

'No, no.'

'You aren't going to tell Miles and then write me a note saying you won't see me again? I shall really make difficulties if you do that.'

'No, of course not. But it must all be quiet and formal and romantic.'

'Those seem to me contradictory terms. You mean chocolates, flowers – '

'I mean a sort of romantic friendship.'

'Men aren't good at romantic friendships. I want you in bed.'

'You aren't really in love with me, I'm not really in love with you. We're just captivated.'

'We can't tell yet about being in love. And anyway what's wrong with being captivated? I'm not all that often captivated, I can tell you!'

'We care for each other with the less good parts of ourselves.'

'Now you're being philosophical. May I see you home?'

'No.'

'Miles won't be there, it's too early.'

'No.'

'Diana, I've just got to be alone with you for a minute. I want to kiss you.'

'No.'

Chapter Eleven

'Nigel!'

It was three o'clock in the morning, the terrible slough of the night time. Bruno had been dreaming. He dreamt that he had murdered somebody, a woman, but he could not remember whom, and had buried the body in the front garden of a house in Twickenham where he had lived as a child. People kept coming and staring at the place where the body was buried and pointing to it until Bruno noticed with horror that the shape of the body was clearly visible through the earth, outlined with a reddish luminous glow. Then he was in a law court and the judge, who was Miles, was condemning him to death. He woke up with a racing heart. He felt sudden instinctive relief at knowing it was a dream before he realized a moment later that it was true. He was condemned to death.

The room with its curtains closely drawn was pitch dark, but he could just see the time on the luminous dial of his watch. Bruno reached out to try to put his light on but could not find the lamp. It must have been moved from his bedside table to the table beside the window. Adelaide sometimes did this when she was dusting and forgot to put it back. Nigel had put the light out for him at eleven o'clock. Bruno lay with one hand pressed to his heart. His heart was jumping and missing beats like a runner who runs too fast and constantly stumbles. There was an acute pain in his chest in the region of the heart and a sense of constriction as if a wire which had been passed round his chest were being drawn tighter and tighter. He moved his feet feebly inside their cage, thinking he might get up and find the light, but he felt too weak to move. Then an agonizing cramp seized his left foot. He tried to rub it against the other foot to ease the pain. He thought, it's come, the time of prostration, of overwhelming weakness, of bedpans. The time of the dressing gown. Only, how odd, he would not be needing the dressing gown any more. The dressing gown would be a spectator awaiting its hour. But this was absurd. He had often felt weak before and it had passed off. Life is a series of unpleasant things which pass off. Except that there is one last one which doesn't.

Bruno made an effort to restrain his tears. Odd business, trying to restrain tears, he said laboriously to himself. They live somewhere there at the back of your eyes, you can feel them moving in there like animals. Then there is the weak defeated pleasure of the warm tide rising, the water overflowing on to the cheek. The tears were a little relief. He moved his hand with difficulty and touched his cheek and took his salty finger to his lips. He thought, perhaps I won't see Miles after all. His son now seemed to him the image of death. His heart was still stumbling along. And what was that noise, an intermittent buzzing noise, like an engine. Listening, Bruno could not decide whether it was a loud sound far away or a little sound near. Then he recognized it. It was the sound of a fly struggling in a spider's web. It was probably in the web of a large *tegenaria atrica* of whose friendly presence high up in the corner of the ceiling Bruno had for some time been conscious. The desperate bursts of buzzing continued, became briefer, stopped. The horror came back to Bruno. The time of the dressing gown. Then he began to call again.

'NIGEL!'

The door opened softly. 'Ssh, ssh, you'll wake Danby.' Nigel switched the light on at the door, moved to the table beside the window, switched on the dark green shaded lamp, and then switched off the centre light.

Bruno lay weak and relaxed with relief. 'Could you put the lamp beside me, Nigel? Oh dear, I seem to have knocked over my water. Could you mop it up? I hope it hasn't got on to the books.'

'Are you feeling funny?'

'I'm all right. I just got frightened. I've got awful cramp in my left foot. Could you just hold it, hold it tight, that's fine.'

Nigel's strong warm hands gripped the suffering foot and the pain immediately went away.

'Thank you, it's gone. I'm sorry I woke you.'

'I was awake anyway.'

'Nigel, could you prop me up a bit, I want to be sure I can still get my legs out.'

Bruno slowly edged up in the bed, pushing hard with his hands while Nigel raised him with a hand under each arm. Nigel lifted the bedclothes while Bruno very slowly manoeuvred his legs towards the edge of the bed. It seemed to be all right after all.

'Do you want to go?'

'No. I just wanted to be sure I could. I felt so weak just now. I had a bad dream. All right, let me be now. Nigel, would you mind staying just a short while until I feel better? Would you sit beside me?'

'Sure.'

Nigel drew the chair up beside Bruno's bed. He collected Bruno's two hands which were straying spider-like upon the counterpane and began to caress them. This caressing movement, a firm smoothing down towards the tips of the fingers, always made Bruno feel relaxed. Perhaps it eased the rheumatism in his knuckles.

They spoke in low voices.

'Why are you so kind to me, Nigel? I know I'm horrible. No one else would touch me. Are you mortifying the flesh?'

'Don't be silly.'

'I impose on you.'

'I exist to be imposed upon.'

'You're a funny chap, Nigel. You worship don't you, you believe in Him.'

'In Him. Yes.'

'Odd how He changes. When I was very young,' said Bruno, 'I thought of God as a great blank thing, rather like the sky, in fact perhaps He *was* the sky, all friendliness and protectiveness and fondness for little children. I can remember my mother pointing upward, her finger pointing upward, and a sense of marvellous safeness and happiness that I had. I never thought much about Jesus Christ, I suppose I took *him* for granted. It was the great big blank egg of the sky that I loved and felt so safe and happy with. It went with a sense of being curled up.

Perhaps I felt I was inside the egg. Later it was different, it was when I first started to look at spiders. Do you know, Nigel, that there is a spider called *amaurobius*, which lives in a burrow and has its young in the late summer, and then it dies when the frosts begin, and the young spiders live through the cold by eating their mother's dead body. One can't believe that's an accident. I don't know that I imagined God as having thought it all out, but somehow He was connected with the pattern, He was the pattern, He *was* those spiders which I watched in the light of my electric torch on summer nights. There was a wonderfulness, a separateness, it was the divine to see those spiders living their extraordinary lives. Later on in adolescence it all became confused with emotion. I thought that God was Love, a big sloppy love that drenched the world with big wet kisses and made everything all right. I felt myself transformed, purified, glorified. I'd never thought about innocence before but then I experienced it. I was a radiant youth. I was deeply touched by myself. I loved God, I was in love with God, and the world was full of the power of love. There was a lot of God at that time. Afterwards He became less, He got drier and pettier and more like an official who made rules. I had to watch my step with Him. He was a kind of bureaucrat making checks and counter-checks. There was no innocence and no radiance then. I stopped loving Him and began to find Him depressing. Then He receded altogether, He became something that the women did, a sort of female activity, though very occasionally I met Him again, most often in country churches when I was alone and suddenly He would be there. He was different once more in those meetings. He wasn't an official any longer. He was something rather lost and pathetic, a little crazed perhaps, and small. I felt sorry for Him. If I had been able to take Him by the hand it would have been like leading a little child. Yet He had His own places, His own holes and burrows, and it could still be a sort of surprise to find Him there. Later on again He was simply gone, He was nothing but an intellectual fiction, an old hypothesis, a piece of literature.'

There was silence in the room. The green-shaded lamp gave a dim light. Nigel had stopped massaging Bruno's hands and sat staring at him, his long legs hooked round the edge of the chair. Nigel's eyes were round and vague and his thin-lipped mouth hung open where he had been chewing the lank end of a lock of dark hair. He looked like a slice of a human being. He groaned faintly to indicate understanding of what Bruno had said.

'Odd,' said Bruno. 'There are people with whom one always talks about sex. And there are people with whom one always talks about God. I always talk to you about God. The others wouldn't understand.'

Nigel groaned.

'What is God made of, Nigel?'

'Why not spiders? The spiders were a good idea.'

'The spiders *were* a good idea. But I just hadn't the nerve, the courage, to hang on to them. Perhaps that's where it all began.'

'It doesn't matter what He's made of.'

'Perhaps God is all sex. All energy is sex. What do you think, Nigel?'

'It wouldn't matter if He was all sex.'

'If He's all sex how can we be saved?'

'It doesn't matter whether we are saved.'

'I can't help it,' said Bruno. 'I want to be saved. Do you love Him, Nigel?'

'Yes, I love Him.'

'Why?'

'He makes me suffer.'

'Why should you love Him for that?'

'I dig suffering.'

After a further silence Bruno said, 'I suppose one is like what one loves. Or one loves what one is like. All gods are private gods. Do you pray, Nigel?'

'I worship. Prayer is worship. Being annihilated by God.'

'Do you think one must worship something?'

'Yes. But real worship involves waiting. If you wait He comes, He finds you.'

'I never went in much for suffering,' Bruno went on. 'But I wouldn't mind it now if I felt it had any meaning, as if one were buying back one's faults. I'd take an eternity of suffering in exchange for death any day.'

'I think death must be something beautiful, something one could be in love with.'

'You're young, Nigel. You can't see death.'

'When I think of death I think of a jet black orgasm.'

'Death isn't like that, it isn't like that at all.' Bruno wondered if he could tell Nigel about the dressing gown and decided he could not. He added, 'I'm going to see my son. We shall forgive each other.'

'That's beautiful.'

Would it be beautiful, something golden, complete and achieved? Could there still be achievement?

'You understand almost everything, Nigel.'

'I love everything.'

'But you don't understand about death. Do you know what I think?' said Bruno, staring hard at the dressing gown in the dim light. 'I think God is death. That's it. God is death.'

Chapter Twelve

Danby closed the door of the fan-lighted sitting-room behind him and leaned against it. His heart was beating like a steam hammer.

Diana was standing tense and erect near the French windows. They stared at each other without smiling.

The distance between them was a huge, airy, magnetic space. Danby moved into it slowly, pushing the little rounded chintz chairs out of the way with his feet. Diana stood rigid. When he was a yard away from her he stopped again.

Then very slowly he came nearer, opening his hands, not with a grasping gesture but with a praying gesture, or perhaps a gesture of benediction. The blessing hands descended, outlining, a foot away, her figure. With a very deep sigh he put his hands behind him. Another step forward and the stuff of his jacket was lightly touching her breast. She slowly leaned her head back and, hands still behind him, he kissed her on the lips. They remained for some time, immobile, eyes closed, lip to lip.

'The metaphysic of kisses,' said Danby. He put his arms round her now, caressing her slender neck and running his hands very slowly down the length of her back. The fragility, the flexibility, of the human neck. He could feel the pain of her heart beating strongly against his own.

'You made quite a ceremony out of that.'

'The first time I kiss you is worth a ceremony. This is the first of thousands.'

'Or the first of few. Who knows?'

'What am I saying? Millions.'

Her hands were still hanging at her side.

'I am a very determined and highly organized hedonist, Diana.'

'We aren't in love.'

'Yes we are. In a way suited to our advanced age.'

' "The heyday in the blood is tame"?'

'I don't feel at all tame, my dear. What about it?'

'I've told you. I love my husband.'

'Well, that was a jolly good kiss from a girl who loves her husband. Come on, be a sport, put your arms round me. Or if you can't manage that, at least laugh at me!'

'Dear, dear, dear Danby. God, you're sweet!' She laughed. Then she threw her arms round him and burrowed her head violently into the shoulder of his jacket.

Danby tried to lift her head. He took hold of her hair and drew it back and kissed her again. 'Number two. Let's sit down, shall we?'

There was a small plump tasselled sofa against the wall. There was just room for two. The chilly lucid afternoon sun was beginning to slant into the room. 'Number three.'

'I shouldn't have let you come here,' said Diana. She was relaxed in his arms now, thrusting back his white hair from his face.

'But you did because you wanted to see me.'

'I'm afraid I wanted very much to see you.'

'Oh goodie!'

'But it's all ridiculous, Danby. This is the sort of argument that ends in bed –'

'Goodie, goodie!'

'Only that's not where we're going.'

'We'll see. There's no hurry. I've only kissed you three times. Number four coming up.'

Danby began to unfasten the front of her dress. Her hand fluttered for a moment trying to stop him and then gave in. Burrowing through white lace his hand covered her left breast. They became still, gazing at each other with wide vacant eyes.

After a moment Diana struggled to sit up. Only she did not do up her dress but left it hanging open. 'Let's try to talk rationally. Tell me about yourself. You say there was a girl and she went to Australia. How long ago was that?'

'About four years ago.'

'And how long had you been together?'

'Three years.'

'What was her name?'

'Linda.'

'You didn't think of marrying her?'

'No.'

'Why not?'

Danby thought. He had removed his hand from its first wonderful position and was beginning to edge it up a little under her skirt. She was wearing a different dress today, much smarter, a sort of oatmeal silk affair with buttons all the way down. Convenient. 'She didn't want it. And I think I couldn't marry again.'

'After – Gwen?'

'After Gwen.'

Diana sighed. 'Did Linda mind about Gwen?'

'Linda didn't mind about anything. She was a cheerful girl.'

'I wonder if I am. And you've been alone ever since?'

'I've been alone ever since.' Danby did not feel that he was exactly telling a lie. Well, in a way perhaps he was telling a lie. When Diana had asked him the question at the dance hall he had cashiered Adelaide on the spot, provisionally of course. He could probably manage to look after Adelaide somehow. Diana was an enchanting surprise. One would see what happened and meanwhile not to worry. There was no point in putting Diana off right at the start.

Danby was playing his part of the determined seducer a little dreamily. He was not in fact at all sure exactly what he wanted from Diana. He wanted to go to bed with her. That much, in ways which were far from metaphysical, was abundantly clear. But just how the thing would work he had not thought out or even considered. He remained vague, almost impassive, taking each step when he felt an overwhelming urge to take it; as he had that morning felt an overwhelming urge to telephone Diana and ask to see her.

Danby felt no general scruple about going to bed with other men's wives, though in fact he had rarely done it. He felt that one ought not to cause pain, but a discreetly conducted affair caused no pain, and might produce a great deal of happiness, fresh, gratuitous, *extra* happiness. It was a sense of that extra, of having stolen a march on dull old life, that so much pleased him and made him feel himself, really, a benefactor. He had been a benefactor to Linda and to Adelaide. Why should he not be a benefactor to Diana, who showed every sign of being a rather bored middle-aged wife at a loose end? It was clear that she had intensely wanted to see him again. As for Adelaide, well he might find some way of accommodating them both, and anyway such thoughts were premature. He might not make Diana at all. And if he did, he might find himself very much more in love with her than he yet was. He would deal with these problems as they arose. Meanwhile, the idea of cuckolding Miles, which was not absent from his mind, was rather agreeable. He would get nowhere with Miles. Here was a pleasant way of enlisting, without Miles's knowledge, Miles's kind cooperation.

'A love affair has a beginning, a middle, and an end,' said Diana. She had captured his questing hand.

'Well, let's let this one have a beginning anyway.'

'Women want things to be forever.'

'Women have an exasperating habit of talking in general terms. When and where shall we begin?' There was a difficulty here, of course. He would have preferred not to operate in Miles's house. But his own was always full of Adelaide.

'I don't want a muddle with you, Danby. I've got very fond of you. You make me feel happy –'

'What a lovely thing to say!'

'And I want that happiness to last. Not to be spoilt by – I could hold you – in a romantic friendship – let me try.'

'What you keep calling friendship looks to me like a wicked waste and impoliteness to the gods. Confess you've surprised yourself, Diana. We get on beautifully, don't we? It doesn't often happen, you know.'

Danby was indeed impressed by the peculiarly delicious ease of their communication, like an impromptu play with an impeccable form. He was enjoying the argument intensely. He had quite forgotten how delightful it was to flirt with an intelligent woman.

'Well, I want you as a friend, as a dear thing in my life, with no dramas, just always there –'

'I can be a dear thing in your life just as well if I'm your lover. Rather better, I should have thought.'

'No. It'll set off a drama. And I shall lose you.'

'At least I notice that you've moved from the conditional tense to the future tense!'

'No, no, I don't mean –'

'Anyway I don't see that there's much difference between what we're doing now and going to bed.'

'Men always say that. You know there is.'

'You're not suggesting we meet and don't touch each other?'

'No. I want to touch you, to kiss you. But nothing more. Well, I do want more but I think it would be crazy.'

'Let's be crazy then. I know what I want. All this touching and kissing would just drive me up the wall.'

'Oh God. I think perhaps I oughtn't to see you at all –'

'Come, come. You've already gone too far, Diana. You're a hedonist, just like me. You *can't* deprive yourself of me now you've got me. Can you now?'

She stared at the cold sunny window and then slowly looked at him. 'No.' She slid her arms under his and hugged him with violence. Danby looked down at the silvery golden hair which was tumbled over his sleeve. Holding her tight and questing with his chin he tried to find her mouth. 'Number –'

Danby became aware that he was staring over Diana's abandoned head straight into the eyes of a thin dark-haired girl who was standing and looking rather distraught in the doorway.

He loosed Diana, pinching her arms slightly and coughing. Diana slowly lifted her head, looking behind her, and then began quite quietly to do up her dress, her eyes still vague and a little desperate.

'I'm terribly sorry!' said the girl in the doorway in a clipped rather prissy voice. She turned as if to go, still hesitating.

'Don't go,' said Diana. She got up and Danby rose too.

'Danby, this is my sister, Lisa Watkin. This is Danby Odell.'

'Oh, hello –' The girl hesitated, extended a hand and gave Danby a crushing grip.

'Hello. I didn't know you had a sister,' he said to Diana, in an effort to make something which sounded like conversation.

Lisa, who had now pressed her hand to her heart, seemed more shocked and upset by the encounter than Diana. She was looking anxiously at her sister. Then suddenly they both smiled and the smile revealed a fugitive resemblance. Only Diana's smile was lazy and inward, whereas Lisa's was a more outward smile, like a simple animal manifestation.

'Well, then, I'll be off, upstairs.' Lisa made a quick awkward movement, rather like someone swatting a fly, and jerked out of the door without looking at Danby. The door closed and foot-steps receded.

'Gosh!' said Danby.

'It's all right,' said Diana, smiling faintly.

They stood separated from each other, stiff and momently chilled.

'Will she tell Miles?'

'No. I'll tell Miles you called in.'

'Without details, I hope?'

'Without details.'

'Better have a pretext. Say I called to say eleven-thirty tomorrow, not eleven. Are you sure she won't tell Miles?'

'Of course I am. She's perfectly discreet. She's perfect.'

'She isn't very like you. Is she ill?'

'No. She's been ill. She's all right now.'

'A pretty sister and an ugly one.'

'Lisa's quite good-looking really but you have to know her.'

'How much older is she than you?'

'She's four years younger.'

'She doesn't look it. Is she visiting?'

'No. She lives here.'

'Oh hell, Diana, how are we going to organize things?'

'Who says any things are going to be organized?'

'Don't start that again. Look, darling, I think I'll go now. The appearance of sister Lisa has put a cold finger on me. But we'll meet very soon, won't we? And don't decide anything and don't worry. We'll see how things are. But we must meet, mustn't we?'

'Yes, Danby, I suppose we must.' She looked away from him down the narrow green garden which was just beginning to quiver a little in the evening light.

'Well, don't look so sad about it, my sweet. You'll telephone me at the works on Monday. If you don't ring, I'll ring you.'

'I'll ring.'

'Number – I've lost count already.'

She stayed beside the French window, her arms hanging, as he had seen her at first, and turned slowly towards the garden leaning her head against the glass. Danby let himself out of the front door. As he turned to walk along towards the Old Brompton Road he looked up and saw a figure at an upstairs window and a pale face staring down at him. The figure hastily withdrew. Danby felt again the sense of chill, the cold finger laid upon his heart. She reminded him of somebody.

Chapter Thirteen

'Il est COCU, le chef de gare!'

Miles paused outside the house with irritation. He could hear Danby singing inside. Miles had been feeling all the morning as if he were going to a funeral. He was dressed for a funeral. He felt more than a little sick. He savoured the solemnity of his action in coming to see his father, and wished that solemnity to be recognized and respected by all concerned. He smoothed the frown from his face and rang the bell.

'Il est COCU, le chef de gare!'

Danby opened the door still singing.

'Ah, you've come, good, come in. Adelaide, meet the young master. This is Miles Greensleave. Adelaide de Crecy.'

A preoccupied young woman with a great deal of piled-up brown hair, wearing a blue and green check overall, nodded to Miles and disappeared beyond the stairs.

'Adelaide the Maid,' Danby explained. 'I don't suppose you want to go up straightaway? I think we'd better have a talk first. Would you like some coffee? Adelaide! Coffee!'

'I don't want any coffee, thank you,' said Miles.

'Adelaide! No coffee!'

Danby had led the way down some stairs and through a connecting door and entered what appeared to be his own bedroom. 'Would you care for a drink? Dutch courage?'

'No, thank you.'

Miles, who had never visited the house in Stadium Street, wrinkled his nose against the smell and the atmosphere of damp. The stairs seemed to be encrusted with earth or moss. Perhaps it was just old linoleum. Danby's room, though quite large, was masculine and austerely untidy and rather dark: a bedstead with wooden slatted ends, a dressing-table covered with a rather dusty litter of ivory-backed brushes and shaving tackle, a bookshelf full of paperback detective novels. The cheap flowered cretonne curtains were transparent with age. The big sash window showed a small garden, partly concrete, partly dark earth, sparsely dotted with dandelions. Above a dark brick wall one of the black graceless chimneys of the power station towered against a restless cloudy sky. It was raining slightly and the pitted concrete was a dark grey. Miles felt a sudden acute depression, a desolation of a quite new quality. He feared the whole experience, he feared its power to distract, to obsess, to degrade. He feared a defilement.

'Won't you take off your mackintosh? Adelaide can dry it in the kitchen.'

'No, thank you. Look, there isn't anything to say, is there? I'd better see him and get it over.'

'I just wanted to tell you,' said Danby in a low voice, 'that you'll find him very much changed. I thought I'd better warn you. He doesn't look like what he used to look like at all.'

'Naturally I'd expect him to have aged.'

'It's not just age. Well, you'll see. You won't upset him, will you?'

'Of course I won't upset him!'

'He's a poor old man. He just wants to be at peace with everybody.'

'He is expecting me, isn't he?'

'Oh God yes. He's been all agog. Couldn't sleep last night. You see, he – '

'Could I see him now, please? I don't feel in a mood for conversation.'

'Yes, yes, come on then, sorry – '

Danby led Miles back through the connecting door and up two flights of stairs. The crumbling stuff underfoot was disintegrating linoleum. On the small dark landing Danby opened a door without knocking and marched in. 'He's here, Bruno.' Miles followed.

Miles was vaguely aware of Danby slipping away behind him and closing the door. Miles stared. Then he caught his breath and put his hand to his mouth in a sudden searing heat of shock and horror. He could feel himself blushing with shock and with shame. Bruno had indeed changed.

Miles had adjusted his picture of his father. He had imagined the silver hair thinned, the back bent a little, the face more hollow. What confronted him was not a death's head. It was a huge bulbous animal head attached to a body shrunken into a dry stick. Bruno's head seemed enlarged, the completely hairless dome swollen, bulging out over big sprouting ears. The face below, so far from being gaunt, seemed to have gained flesh. The nose was immense, a shapeless heap of fleshy protuberances. Hair unlike human hair sprouted upon it and upon his cheeks, together with fungus-like stains and excrescences. The bulgier parts of the face were unwrinkled, curiously smooth and pink, almost childlike. Under bushy brows, out of which a few much longer stiffer hairs emerged like probosces, were the slits of eyes, strangely luminous and liquid. Below the thin stalk of neck the tiny narrow body, on which pyjamas hung like garments draped upon a pole, lay extended in the bed. Blotched arms, the bones separately visible, promenaded two shrivelled sharpened hands upon the counterpane.

'Miles!' The voice quavered like the voice of an old man in a play. 'My boy!'

'Hello, father.'

'Sit beside me, here.'

Miles felt a nausea which was also an impulse to weep, as if he would spew forth tears. He hoped that he was not exhibiting his state of shock. He sat down stiffly on the chair beside the bed. Perhaps mercifully Bruno did not know what he looked like. There was a sickening den-like smell of soiled sheets and old man.

'How are you feeling, father?'

'I feel all right in the mornings, that's my best time. And evenings after six sometimes, that's comfortable. But I won't ever get better again, Miles. You know that, don't you? They've told you?'

'Oh come, father. When the warm weather comes you'll be up and about.'

'Don't say that. You know it's not true. It's so cruel – '

To Miles's horror two very large crystalline tears had come out of the wet slits of eyes and were making their way down through the ravines of the face.

Miles had expected to be irritated by his father in old familiar ways, he had expected everything to be awkwardly and distressingly familiar. He had determined to play and had pictured himself playing some politer more abstract version of his old role. Then at best it might be like a sort of negotiated peace, old foes round the conference table. There would be all the old emotions and conflicts, but checked and muted. He feared the emotions but with a familiar fear. This ordeal was something he had not dreamt of. He had no resources for dealing with the monstrous thing which was still indubitably his father and which seemed to be wanting tenderness and pity. The father he had known had never wanted pity. Miles felt panic. He had relied upon dignity and dignity seemed at the first moment to be vanishing, revealing beyond it some awful naked demand of one human being upon another which he was totally unprepared to face. Bruno had changed terribly. He can't be in his right mind, thought Miles, he can't be, looking like that.

'I'm – sorry, father. Please don't – tire yourself. I won't stay long.'

'Oh, you're not going, you're not going!' The spotted claw hands with their swollen knobbly joints crawled at him convulsively.

The hands wanted to touch him. Miles moved his chair slightly back. He shrank away and could not bring himself to look into the big tearful animal face.

'No, but I don't want to – tire you, father – '

'Miles, I want to explain everything to you. There isn't much time left and I know you'll be kind and listen to me. I've got to tell it all, all, all. Janie didn't understand, she never understood, she made it all into something bad. You see, this girl, Maureen, was playing chess in a café – '

'I'm afraid I haven't the faintest idea what you're talking about, father.'

'She was playing *chess* – '

'Yes, yes, of course. I think you're getting excited. I'd better call – '

'Did you know about it, Miles? Did Gwen know? Did Janie tell you about me and Maureen? Oh, Janie was so cruel to me – It wasn't much after all, it really wasn't – '

104

'I don't know anything about this, father.'

'Janie didn't tell you? I thought she must have done, I was so sure. You were so – stern with me – and Gwen too. Oh God. Forgive me, Miles –'

'Really, father –'

'Forgive me, forgive me. Say you forgive me.'

'Yes, naturally, of course, but –'

'I must tell you all about it. I want to tell you *everything*. I had this love affair with this girl Maureen –'

'Really, father, I don't think you should tell me this –'

'I used to go to her flat –'

'I don't want to listen –'

'I lied to Janie –'

'*I don't want to listen!*'

'I would have liked Parvati, Miles, I would have accepted her and loved her, if only someone had made me meet her, if only you'd all given me a chance, it all happened so quickly, I just said something foolish without thinking and then it somehow got fixed that way, if only you'd given me a little bit more time and not got so *angry* –'

'Please, father, all this is totally unnecessary. I don't want to talk about Parvati.'

'But I do, Miles. Don't you understand that I've been thinking about it all these years, that it's been torturing me?'

'I'm sorry to hear it, but I don't see –'

'I've got to have your forgiveness. You've got to *understand* –'

'It doesn't mean anything, father. It's all over long ago, it's gone.'

'It isn't gone, it's here, it's *here* –'

'Don't excite yourself, please.'

'I would have liked Parvati. I would have loved her, we could all have been happy, I would have loved your children. Oh Miles, your children –'

'Stop it, please.'

'You must forgive me, Miles, forgive me properly, when you've understood it all. If only Parvati –'

'*I don't want to talk about Parvati.* She's nothing to do with you. Please.'

There was a silence. Bruno drew back among his pillows. His hands crawled about his neck. The narrow luminous eyes glowed. He stared at his son.

'You haven't been to see me for years.'

'You never answered my letters.'

'They were lying letters.'

'Well, father, if you feel like that I scarcely see the point – '

Bruno's pointed knees were hunched up towards his chest. His huge head lolled and rolled on the pillows as he leaned on one hand trying to lever himself up. The big bulbous face quivered. The quavering voice issued like a jet of steam.

'Why did you come here to be so unkind to an old man? You never loved me, you always sided with your mother, you never came near me, you were never affectionate and forgiving like other children, you were cold to me, and you still hate me now and you wish me dead, dead and gone, like all those things you said didn't exist any more. All right, I'll soon be dead and you can forget me and bury me and tidy me away for ever. You can't take the trouble even now to try to see what I'm really like. You just think that I'm dying and I smell of death and I've lost my mind and I'm just a heap of stinking rotting flesh that you can't bring yourself to touch, but I've still got enough spirit left to curse you – '

'Father, please – '

'Get out, get out, *get out*!' Bruno's quivering hand fumbled with a glass of water which stood on the bedside table. He made as if to hurl it, but he had not the force to lift the glass and the water spilled darkly down the side of the counterpane and the glass crashed into pieces on the floor. 'Aah – Danby! Danby!'

Miles backed away, stumbled through the door, blundered across the dark landing and began to run down the stairs. At the bottom he cannoned into Danby. For a moment Danby seized hold of his wrist. 'You've upset him, damn you! I told you not to!'

Miles wrenched himself away, and as he got out of the front door he could hear the voice above him screaming now. 'And you shan't have the stamps! You shan't have the stamps!'

He began to run away down the street in the rain. He ought

never to have gone. It was like a doom, it was more terrible than he could have imagined. He was back in that awful world of stupidity and violence and muddle. He was utterly utterly defiled.

Chapter Fourteen

'Please may we see him? We didn't telephone in case you said no.'

Danby stared at the two women. It had stopped raining and an east wind was running through a smudged grey sky. The women were wearing mackintoshes and scarves over their heads. Their faces were anxious, large and pale and looming in the sullen light. Diana's mackintosh had a harlequin pattern of pink and white and she was carrying a bunch of narcissus. The street behind them was windswept and empty.

'Come in,' he said, 'but I don't think – Look, you'd better come through to my room.'

He led them through the dark hall and down into his bedroom, closing the communicating door. 'He hears everything in the other part of the house. I'd rather he didn't – It's very kind of you to come.'

Diana pushed the scarf back revealing her brow and a strained-back strip of gleaming hair. 'Miles is *so* upset about yesterday.'

'Damn Miles, if I may say so.'

'Yes, I know, I'm sure he was awful, tactless and so on. He says he just froze up. And Bruno was rather emotional and Miles hates emotion.'

'It was hardly an unemotional situation. Miles ought to have tried.'

'He really did intend to try, I know he did. He got the impression that Bruno was a bit – sort of unhinged.'

'Bruno isn't unhinged. Miles is criminally stupid.'

'It all took him by surprise – '

'He was in such a damn hurry. I wanted to brief him beforehand but he wouldn't listen. I should have insisted.'

'Well, may we see Bruno?'

'Bruno isn't very seeable today.'

'He's upset too?'

'He's not just upset he's thoroughly ill. A man who's as sick as Bruno can't be philosophical. He was completely knocked out by that idiotic scene with Miles. I'll take the flowers up. But I'm afraid – '

'Couldn't we just go in and see him for a moment?' Lisa spoke, her head still shrouded, leaning against the door, hands in pockets.

'Well – ' Danby gave his attention to Lisa for the first time. She was much darker than her sister and very thin in the face. Wisps of dark brown hair, like thorns, emerged from under her tightly knotted damp yellow scarf. Her rather long nose was reddened by the east wind.

'You see,' Lisa went on, 'I think it's very important to do something quickly before they both settle down to thinking that they can't communicate.'

'I'm sure Lisa's right,' said Diana. 'It was her idea to come round on this sort of embassy. I think perhaps Bruno – We'd tell him Miles is sorry – Two women –'

'Two women!' Danby laughed. 'You girls think yourselves omnipotent. You're dealing with a very sick person and a thoroughly cantankerous old man. Don't imagine Bruno will eat out of your hand!'

'We wouldn't stay more than a moment,' said Lisa, 'just to give him the flowers and say a word. He could think about it afterwards. And it might give him something nicer to think about, it would make a break between *that* and now.'

Danby hesitated. 'Well, I'll go and tell him you're here. But I very much doubt if he'll see you. He's worked himself up into a real state of angry misery, and I'm afraid he's a bit confused too, it's not one of his good days.'

'Please –'

'All right, I'll see. You can come up and wait on the landing. Oh hello, Adelaide. This is Adelaide the Maid. Mrs Greensleave. Miss Watkin.'

Danby went up the two flights of stairs and put his head round Bruno's door. The unlit room was a tiny grey box suspended from the window, where racing luminous grey clouds

109

were imparting a gliding motion to the black bar of the power station tower. Bruno was sitting bolt upright in bed in a position unusual to him: he lay usually well snuggled down into the blankets. His red and white striped flannel pyjamas were buttoned up to the neck. His arms held stiffly by his sides descended into the blankets. His face was so contorted that it was difficult to discern the features or to see this prominent mass of crumpled flesh as part of a human being. Nigel, who said it was now 'too difficult to get into the crevices', had not shaved him for two days and the lower face and neck were covered with a grey fungus. Danby averted his eyes. 'Bruno, Miles's wife and sister-in-law are here.'

Bruno's head rolled slightly and Danby felt himself looked at.

'Please, we'll just – ' Danby felt a fluttering outside the door behind him and the pink and white mackintosh creaked, touched his coat.

Bruno said nothing.

Danby, turning and opening the door a little more, said, 'Just put the flowers quickly on the bed and go.' He felt upset and confused by the arrival of the women, as if he were suddenly frightened of Bruno on their behalf. He ought to have warned them about Bruno's appearance.

Diana pushed past into the room and then stood rigid. He caught the faint gasp of her breath. Lisa had come up close behind her shoulder, pushing back her yellow scarf. He saw their two juxtaposed faces with wide eyes staring, the light brown eyes, the dark brown eyes. After a moment Diana leaned nervously forward and with an outstretched arm dropped the wrapped bundle of narcissus, like a very thin baby in swaddling clothes, on to the top of the bulging foot cage. It was like an official visit to a cenotaph. Only this tomb was not empty.

Still facing towards the bed, with unfocused eyes, Diana was beginning to back towards the door, edging past Lisa who had stepped aside.

'Who did you say these girls were?' said Bruno. His unsteady voice had the hoarse gurgling note which belonged to the more confused days, but the strength and force of the question had a startling effect.

110

'They've just brought you some flowers. They – '

'Who are they?'

'Miles's wife and sister-in-law.'

'Miles's wife and sister – '

'Sister-in-law. These two ladies are sisters.'

'Sisters.' The word as Bruno uttered it sounded heavy, uncanny, meaningless.

Diana had reached the door.

'What do they want?' said Bruno. He was still sitting bolt upright and motionless and it was difficult to see where he was looking.

'We came from Miles to say that he's very sorry he upset you,' said Lisa, speaking slowly in a low clear voice.

The big indented head moved slightly. 'What?'

'Miles says he's sorry.'

Bruno was undoubtedly staring at Lisa. His face seemed to unravel a little, the mouth and eyes becoming more evident.

'Who are you?'

'I'm – '

'I think that'll do, that's quite enough of a visit,' said Danby. 'You've had a lovely visit from two nice girls. Doesn't happen every day, does it, Bruno? Bringing you flowers and all. But we mustn't overtire you, must we? Say good-bye now. Off we go.'

Since the entry of the two women into the bedroom Danby had felt an intense physical awkwardness almost amounting to sickness. Something about the juxtaposition was suddenly dreadful. Perhaps it was just the onrush of new pity, almost of shame, this glimpse of poor Bruno through unaccustomed eyes, a glimpse of the grey shabby jumbled room, the stained wallpaper and the soiled sheets, the monster-headed moribund old man imprisoned in the smelly twilit box. Danby was so used to Bruno. He saw a person there not pinned by time. But now he wanted to get the women outside and to get outside himself. He fumbled with the door-handle and put out a shielding ushering hand towards Diana.

'Danby, for Christ's sake shut up!' They paused in the doorway. 'Don't talk to me as if I were a puling infant! Do you want them to think I'm senile? I'm still a rational being, so have the decency to address me as one. You sit down here, *you*. Please.'

Bruno was still looking at Lisa. Rather laboriously he pulled one arm out of the bed clothes and moved it across the counterpane to point at a chair beside the bed. Lisa sat down.

Danby felt himself being nudged from behind by Diana. He jumped and twitched away at the contact. Diana was murmuring something to him and sliding away through the door. Trying to take hold of his hand she caught hold of a finger and pulled it. Danby half followed her through the door, shuffled with hesitation, made a reassuring gesture as she moved towards the top of the stairs, and then came back into the room and shut the door again. The smell of the narcissus was mingling with the doggy old man odour of the room. Lisa had taken Bruno's hand.

Danby leaned against the door still feeling the curious panicky giddiness. What was he afraid of? He saw Lisa's profile now, her face close up to Bruno's. Was he frightened of the old man on her behalf? It wasn't quite that.

'You don't mind me, do you, my dear?'

'No, of course not. I'm so glad to see you.'

'And you brought me flowers.'

'We both did. And they're from Miles too.'

'Miles – you – of course – Miles was cruel, so cruel to the old man.'

'He's very sorry. He got upset and muddled. He's sorry now. He hopes you'll let him come again.'

'Danby said it was a mistake to see Miles, all a mistake. A little bit of peace one needs at the end. Miles shouting at me, horrible. You see, I tried to tell him things and he wouldn't listen, said he didn't want to know.' Bruno had lowered his voice to a confidential murmur. The intensity of the girl's attention to him seemed to have stilled the room. The two heads together, so strange.

'You mustn't be too cross with Miles. It was just a muddle really.'

'He said the past doesn't exist any more, but it does exist, doesn't it?'

'It certainly does things to us.'

'Exactly. Now *you* understand.'

'You'll have to get to know Miles again. Talk to him about more ordinary things. It'll take a bit of time.'

'There isn't much time left, my dear. And no ordinary things. Only last things. Danby.'

'Yes, Bruno.'

'Pour us some champagne.'

Danby took a champagne bottle from the dusty little queue upon the floor. There were two glasses on the table. He began to ease out the cork. It flew gaily up into the topmost corner of the room, alarming the *tegenaria atrica* who was drowsing there, and the creamy champagne cascaded into the glass. The brusqueness of the gesture gave relief. He handed the glass to Lisa who handed it to Bruno. Danby filled the other glass and gave it to Lisa, reaching it across the bed.

'You two – share the glass – drink with me.' Bruno sipped the champagne.

Lisa, who was still holding Bruno's other hand, gave the glass to Danby with a smile. He drank. It was all very odd.

'Would you turn the lamp on, Danby?'

The window and the hurrying sky were gone. The shaded light shone upon Bruno's huge nose pendant over the grey stubble which grew so painfully out of the many crevices which had defeated Nigel's razor, and upon Lisa's rather long hands, one of which she now raised to release the heavy tangle of her dark hair from the scarf which was hanging loose about her neck.

'You see, my dear, when you're my age there's not much left except you want to be loved.'

'You are loved.' Lisa looked at Danby across the bed. Her face was obscure, outside the circle of light.

'At my age you live in your mind, in a sort of dream.'

'I think we all do that.'

'At the end there's nothing left to do. It's all just thought.'

'Thinking is doing something.'

'One turns into a monster at the very end. I just frighten people now, I upset them, I appal them, I know. I can't change anything in the world any more.'

'Yes, you can. You can think kind thoughts, you can send a nice message to Miles. Do send a message to Miles.'

113

'A message – Well, you can tell him – I didn't mean – what I said at the end.'

'I'm so glad.'

'Do you think it matters if people curse you? I did a terrible thing – my wife was dying and I didn't go to her – she cursed me I think – I wanted to tell Miles that – you see there was this girl – and even the spiders – '

'Oh stop it, Bruno,' said Danby. 'I mean you're getting over-excited. I think that's enough for one visit now. And don't be cross with me.'

Bruno relaxed, crumpled back a little among the pillows, the light now showing his eyes, dark liquid terribly vital slits in the chaos of his face where the lipless mouth opened amid the grey stubble. 'All right.'

'He doesn't usually have his champagne so early in the day.'

'You will come back, my dear, you'll come back and see the old man and let him tell you things?'

'Yes, of course,' she said. 'And Miles will come too. And I'll tell him what you said.'

'What did I say? Well, it doesn't matter. Drink again, both.'

Danby took a gulp of champagne and gave the glass to Lisa. She drank looking up at him, returned the glass, and leaned back towards Bruno, stroking his knotted hand and thin stick-like spotted arm.

'Ah, you have such lovely hands – and those half moons, just like – '

Lisa leaned forward and kissed him close to his still moving mouth and then rose quickly. She made a movement as if giving a benediction and retreated towards the door.

'I'll just show her out – be back – ' Danby mumbled. He fell out of the door after Lisa. He stared at her in the grey darker light of the empty landing, then with a rather timid and deliberate movement took hold of the sleeve of her brown mackintosh and pulled her across the landing and into Nigel's room, which was empty. He stared down at her.

'Look, you were so kind, so good to him – '

'I'm used to old people.'

'Would you really come again to see him?'

'Of course, if he'd like it. But he may have forgotten tomorrow.' She spoke quickly and rather brusquely as if resuming a professional role. She pulled the yellow scarf up over her head, tucking heavy locks of dark brown hair back into the upturned collar of her coat.

'He won't have. You'd have time, some morning?'

'Mornings would be impossible except at the week-end. I'm working in a probation officer's office at Poplar. I come home by tube every day about five-thirty. I could come after that.'

'Could you come tomorrow?'

'I'd better telephone first. I'll ring up when I'm leaving work. Would someone be in then?'

'Yes, yes, I'll see to it that I am. I can't tell you how grateful – '

Danby ran down the stairs after her. The hall door was open. It was lighter outside now, a grey damp metallic light shed from gleaming clouds. He caught a glimpse of Diana talking to Will Boase who was painting the iron railings in front of the house. Diana turned towards Danby and waved, her pink and white harlequin arm raised like a signal in the empty glittering street. Danby hesitated, waved, and then closed the door behind Lisa. He came back into the sad brown obscurity of the house and sat down upon the stairs. Suddenly he began to shed tears.

Chapter Fifteen

Adelaide, who could hear through the open door that some-body was coming down the stairs, attempted to release her hand which Will had gripped. Will resisted, squeezing her fingers painfully hard and thrusting his bulky body up against her. Adelaide kicked him as violently as she could on the ankle and pulled herself away. In the doorway she ran into Mrs Green-sleave who had been regarding the last part of the struggle with amusement.

'Would you mind telling Mr Odell that I'm just outside when he comes down?'

Adelaide said nothing, but went on down the stairs into the kitchen which was below the level of the street. The kitchen was rather like a dug-out and smelt of damp earth. From here she could both see and hear Mrs Greensleave and Will who were now in conversation beside the railings, outlined in a fugitive brightness of cloudy sun. Adelaide studied Mrs Greensleave's legs.

'What a pretty colour of blue you're painting the railings,' said Mrs Greensleave.

'Yes, it is rather good. A sort of Cézanne blue.'

'Oh, you know about Cézanne! Good for you. Did you choose the colour or did Mr Odell choose it?'

'I chose it. Mr Odell doesn't know one colour from another.'

'I'm not surprised! Do you work here?'

'I am working here, but I don't work here.'

'How absolute the knave is!'

'Shakespeare. I'm the odd job boy.'

'And a very learned one! Do you work for a firm or on your own?'

'I'm what they term self-employed. And as I'm not a very

exacting employer I'm usually unemployed. I'm on National Assistance.'

'Oh, hard luck.'

'For doing nothing, it's princely.'

'I see you're a philosopher, too! What's your name?'

'Will.'

'Would you come and paint our house, Will?'

'Why?'

'I'd like to help you. And our house needs painting.'

'Maybe. I'll think about it.'

'I can see you're good at painting, being an admirer of Cézanne!'

'I'm good at better things than painting.'

'What else are you good at?'

'Drawing, photography, acting – '

'Acting? That explains your knowledge of Shakespeare.'

'My general culture explains my knowledge of Shakespeare.'

'Sorry, Will! Yes, I can see you as an actor. You've got a fine head. And if I may say so, I like the way you trim your moustache.'

'You've got a fine head too. I could do your photograph. Make you look even more stunning.'

'Maybe. I'll think about it! You're a nice boy, Will. Are you what's her name's boy-friend, the maid, what is her name?'

'Adelaide. Adelaide de Crecy.'

'Dear me, what a grand name.'

'What a grand girl.'

'Well, I wish you joy.'

'Where's your house?'

'Kempsford Gardens, by West Brompton tube station. I'll write it down.'

'Maybe I'll telephone you. Maybe I won't.'

'Oh please do! Keep still a moment, Will, you've got some blue paint in your hair. I'll just try to wipe it off with this bit of paper. You've got such nice hair, it seems a pity to dye it blue.'

Adelaide opened the kitchen window a little so that she could close it again with a resounding crash. She selected the last but one teacup of the older Wedgwood set and dropped it on the stone floor. Then she left the kitchen, slamming the door behind her, and went into her own room. She saw that there was a long streak of blue paint on the skirt of the frilled chiffon dress which she had put on for Danby's day at home. She took off the dress and kicked it into a heap in the corner. She took off her Irish enamel necklace and matching bangle. She put on her oldest overall and lay down on the bed. A few tears overflowed from her eyes.

Danby had not shared her bed last night or the night before. There was nothing very unusual in this but it always depressed her. The night before he had left a note saying he would be in very late. Last night there had been something a trifle self-conscious about the way in which he had said, 'Not tonight, I think, Adelaide – I'll go in my own place tonight. I want to read a bit.' He never read, as she knew perfectly well, since he was too tired and too tipsy when he came to bed to do anything except make love and fall asleep, and indeed he very often fell asleep in the middle of the love-making and had to be shifted by savage jabs and shoves which still failed to wake him up. Last night his light had gone out and his snores had been heard immediately after he had left her.

Adelaide lived in a perpetual state of anxiety in a world of important signs the exact bearing of which constantly eluded her. She lived like an animal, seeing nothing clearly beyond her immediate surroundings, hiding at movements, sniffing, listening, waiting. She could see the kitchen, the paint on her dress, the broken Wedgwood cup. But even Stadium Street was already a mystery to her: and the two largest portents in her life, Danby and Will, were almost entirely mysterious and terrifying. In relation to Will the feeling of terror was not entirely unpleasant, and of course she had known Will such a long time. Will scaring her, shouting at her, twisting her arm, though it was incomprehensible, was at least something familiar. But Danby's quiet lazy comportment, his preoccupied smiles and unaccountable defections, although she ought by now to have been used to them, were read in trembling as one might try to read one's death sentence in a foreign language.

She wondered if life were like that for other people and

thought it could not be so. It was patently not like that for Danby. And there were married people who *knew* that they would be together for ever and if anything was nasty or muddled it was only temporary. And there were people who did important work and had their names printed on official lists. And people with grand families and property. These people belonged to the structure of the world, to which Adelaide did not feel herself in any way attached. She felt like something very small which rattled around somewhere near the bottom and could quite easily fall out of a hole without anybody even noticing. Her greatest certainty was Danby, and what kind of certainty was that? He had talked about her old age, but what did that mean? Anybody could pension off a servant. He had absolute power over her status and her being. And how little she really knew him. She could hear Danby's voice saying, 'Let's give it all a miss from now on, Adelaide, shall we?' in just the same casual tone in which he had said 'Not tonight, I think' and, so long ago, 'What about it?'

Adelaide knew that she was becoming more irritable and nervy. She knew that she ought not to have broken the Wedgwood cup and she even regretted having broken it. She had resolved not to speak to Will when he was painting the railings in case he misbehaved and Danby saw, but half-way through the morning she had felt a sudden need for Will, although she had expressed the need simply by being unpleasant to him. Then there had been the horrible spectacle of that Mrs Greensleave both patronizing Will and flirting with him, while Will simpered and answered back like a pert servant and let her paddle her hands in his hair. At that contact Adelaide had felt an automatic jealous shock, and more consciously a disgust at the failure in Will of something upon which she especially relied, his dignity: or perhaps simply his self-confidence, his peculiar pride, that which more than anything else made him the same person as the boy she had known. Will was now both a nuisance and a menace, but he was her last connexion with a real Adelaide who had once existed, a pretty girl with two clever sixth-former cousins who lent her books and flattered her, while she wondered happily in her private heart which one of them she was destined to marry.

Adelaide sat up and put her legs over the edge of the bed. There was a hole in her stocking at the knee through which a mound of pink flesh bulged out. She leaned forward and undid her hair and let it fall down heavily on either side of her face. She had that heavy graceless fat feeling which she identified as the feeling of growing old, the feeling of no return. She had made some sort of life-mistake which meant that everything would grow worse and never better. Was there no action which she could perform which, like the magic ritual in the fairy tale, would reverse it all and suddenly reveal her hidden identity? But she had no hidden identity. She got up slowly and pushed her hair, or most of it, inside the back of her overall. She opened the door of her bedroom.

The door of Danby's room opposite stood open and she could see the jumble of the unmade bed with the sheets trailing on the floor. Let him make it himself, she thought, and then changed her mind and went into the room. She began to haul the bed together. The big black box with all the little drawers in it which housed the most important part of the stamp collection was standing on Danby's dressing table. Bruno had been too upset that morning to ask to see it. Adelaide dragged on the extremely faded Welsh counterpane. The room, the bed, smelt of Danby, an intimate sweetish smell of tobacco and sweat and male. Adelaide stared at the black box. Danby usually put the stamps into some sort of order before he put the collection away at night, and Adelaide who had sometimes looked through the sheets in search of 'pretty ones', knew roughly how the drawers were arranged. She moved over and opened a drawer half-way down and fanned out the sheaf of transparent cellophane sheets. There was the set of Cape Triangular stamps. Selecting one at random she drew it quickly out and slipped it into the pocket of her overall.

'Good-bye, Will. Mind you ring me up! And don't get any more of that paint in your hair.'

Lisa and Diana began to walk away down the street in the direction of Cremorne Road. Diana had hoped that Danby might walk along with them, but no doubt he had decided that there was no point in it since Lisa was there.

Diana had been shocked and sickened by the dreary little room and its awful occupant. What she had seen seemed more like flesh, living flesh as one rarely sees it, *in extremis*, than like a person. She had expected something quite other: a silvery haired old gentleman, with an evident and affecting resemblance to Miles, whom she would coax along and charm into paying her compliments. She had expected something a little peppery and difficult, also frail, but eminently conversible. She had felt moved by the idea of the embassy once Lisa had suggested it, and she had seen herself in the rather touching role of reconciler and flower-bearer, undoing by her graciousness the harm which her husband had done. But on arrival she had realized at once that this was a case for the expert, for the professional. Familiar words like 'old gentleman' could not come near touching that reality. Lisa was good in these extreme places, she had a knack. Diana felt here, as she had felt on her few visits to Lisa's East End haunts, upset, embarrassed, and alarmed. She was glad for the old man's sake that Lisa was there.

Diana went straight out into the street to escape from the awful impression of that pathetic length of flesh, and while she was flirting more or less mechanically with the handsome dark-haired painter lad, her thoughts had already reverted to Danby. In these days Danby quietly filled her mind in a way that she was determined not to find alarming. Her nerves were calmed by the dear man's own insouciance and ease, an ease which she did not see as frivolity but rather as a kind of sincerity. With someone like Danby one knew exactly where one was. He did not pretend to the disrupting violence of absolutes. His cheerful way of asking for an affair had exhilarated her. It was easy to refuse, while at the same time one was in no way cheated of a compliment. Nor was she at all afraid that a baffled Danby would 'turn nasty'. Of course he would try, perhaps for a long time, to persuade her. But she did not on reflection really think that the argument would end in bed. There must be nothing dreadful, nothing frightening, here. The argument would have to take place, and she rather looked forward to it. But in the very length of the argument would lie the makings of the lasting sentimental friendship which Diana felt she now so very much wanted and needed to have with Danby. After all, as he was pre-eminently a happy-making man she had only to convince him about where her happiness lay. And with this thought Diana had come, over the last few days, to realize that for all the excellence of her marriage she was not by any means entirely happy.

She had mentioned both Danby's visits to Miles but had kept silent about the dancing. That episode had indeed become so dreamlike, so strangely formally romantic, in her memory that she scarcely felt guilty of any falsehood in suppressing it. That would not happen again; she could find all that she needed in a set of arrangements which would involve no falsehood. In fact even by the truth Miles was likely to be more than a little misled at present, since he could not conceive of anybody enjoying Danby's company. He had commiserated with his wife upon his brother-in-law's visitations. 'That oaf!' Diana smiled, and her smile had tenderness for both men. She did not want to deceive Miles. She would give him, in time, enough intimations of the real state of affairs. 'I like him, really.' 'He's rather sweet.' 'Guess who I'm lunching with? Danby!' Miles would get used to it, and if he could never wholly believe in Diana's predilection, in spite of her most careful factual statements, then, so much perhaps the better. So she would stretch the situation, a little from Danby's side, a little from Miles's side, until she could achieve what now her whole nature craved for, another harmless love. She would love Danby, and no one would be any the worse. As she resolved upon this she felt her heart swell again with the imperative need to love, and she sighed deeply.

'What is it, Di?'

It had come on to rain a little and the two women, their scarves pulled well forward over their heads, were walking briskly along Edith Grove.

'That poor old man – '

'Poor Bruno, yes.'

'In that sort of state they become so – repulsive and horrifying. It must be terrible to be human and conscious and utterly repulsive. I hope he doesn't know what he looks like.'

'We all interpret and idealize our faces. I expect Bruno has some idea of his appearance which is quite unlike what we saw.'

'I hope so. I can't think how Danby can manage it. Treating like a person – what isn't a person any more.'

'Bruno's not so far gone. He talked sense after you'd left.'

'You're so good. I wish I had your knack.'

'I'm more used to it.'

'What did he say?'

'He said to tell Miles he didn't mean what he said at the end.'

'You know, I think he thought you were Miles's wife!'

'I don't know who he thought I was.'

'He seemed to think you were somebody, he certainly took to you.'

'I do wish we'd known him earlier.'

'Well, that was Miles's fault. God, I hope I'll never get like that, I'd rather be dead. Don't you think there's a lot to be said for euthanasia?'

'I'm not sure. It's so hard to know what's going on inside a very old person.'

'No wonder Miles was stumped.'

'Miles will have to try again.'

'Well, you tell Miles that. You're good at being firm with him. Wasn't he cross this morning?'

'Guilty conscience!'

'Danby was thoroughly fed up with him.'

'Yes.'

The two women turned into the Fulham Road, their heads bowed to the light rain.

'Lisa.'

'Yes.'

'There's nothing special going on between me and Danby, you know.'

'I didn't think there was.'

'He's a thoughtless impetuous chap but he's really very sweet. You mustn't be hard on him.'

'I don't know anything about him.'

'You're like Miles, you're so uncompromising. I think it makes you just a little too severe sometimes.'

'Sorry!'

'Danby's a very affectionate person and I think he's a bit

123

lonely. I suspect he hasn't really talked to a woman for ages. He imagines he's a bit keen on me, but I can manage him. It's just the first shock! I know he plays the clown a bit but he's not a fool. There's no drama.'

'I didn't think there was, Di.'

'That's all right then. You worry so, Lisa, and I know you don't suffer fools gladly. You and Miles are so alike. I can't think why you're both so fond of *me*!'

Lisa laughed and thrust her arm through her sister's and gave it a quick squeeze. A little later as they were taking the short cut through Brompton cemetery Lisa said, 'Seeing Bruno like that reminded me of Dad.'

'Oh God. Lisa, I've thought about it sometimes, but I never liked to ask you. Were you actually with him when he died?'

'Yes.'

'One hates to think of these things. I'm such a coward, I was very relieved it happened when I was away. Was it rather awful?'

'Yes.'

'Like what?'

'I think one almost absolutely forgets the *quality* of scenes like that.'

'Was he – frightened?'

'Yes.'

'That must have been terrible for you.'

'It's like no other fear. It's so *deep*. It almost becomes something impersonal. Philosophers say we own our deaths. I don't think so. Death contradicts ownership and self. If only one knew that all along.'

'I suppose one is just an animal then.'

'One is with an animal then. It isn't quite the same thing.'

'He was so good earlier on in the illness.'

'He didn't believe it earlier on, any more than we believe it now.'

'We did try to deceive him.'

'We were trying to deceive ourselves. It was terrible to see him realizing – the truth.'

'Oh God. What did you do?'

'Held his hand, said I loved him – '

'I suppose that is the only thing one would want to know.'

'What was awful was that he didn't want to know. We're so used to the idea that love consoles. But here one felt that even love was – nothing.'

'That can't be true.'

'I know what you mean. It can't be true. Perhaps one just suddenly saw the dimensions of what love would have to be – like a huge vault suddenly opening out overhead – '

'Was it – hard for him to go?'

'Yes. Like a physical struggle. Well, it was a physical struggle, trying to do something.'

'I suppose death is a kind of act. But I expect he was really unconscious at the end.'

'I don't know. Who knows what it is like at the end?'

'What a gloomy conversation. Why, Lisa, you're crying! Oh stop crying, darling, stop crying, for heaven's sake!'

Chapter Sixteen

Danby was standing in the long grass in Brompton cemetery. It was Wednesday afternoon.

He had gone through the day, indeed the last few days, at the works in a kind of dream. There had been the usual round of small crises which he normally rather enjoyed. The big Columbian press used for printing small issues of posters had broken down and one of the apprentices had tried to mend it with terrible results. The bingo people had changed their mind about the format when the cards were already printing. The safety hand of the guillotine had gone wrong so that they were breaking the law now every time they used it. The lorry delivering the lead had backed into a stack of paper and ruined it. A reproduction of a modern picture in a local magazine had been printed upside down. The expensive new type had arrived for one of the composing machines and the bill was exactly twice the estimate. One of the girls in the packing department had fallen off the ladder into the storeroom and broken her ankle. The elderly eccentric for whom they printed woodcuts had rung up five times about the Japanese paper. The art school from which Danby had been trying to buy an old Albion had sent a representative to discuss the sale. Danby had left early, handing everything over to Gaskin with a preoccupied indifference which amazed the latter, who thought that Danby would at least be cock-a-hoop at the prospect of getting the Albion, a very beautiful early model which he had long coveted.

Danby had been tempted to have an encouraging quick one at the Tournament or the Lord Ranelagh which had just opened their doors, but it was better to remain sober and for once he had no difficulty in doing so. Drunk or sober was much the same now. It had been raining and now a faint evening sunlight was making everything glitter. On the other side of the tall iron railings the rush hour traffic was travelling steadily, hypnotically, along the Old Brompton Road. Inside the railings the uncut grass made the cemetery look like a field, or more like a ruined city with its formal yet grassy streets and squares: Ostia, Pompeii, Mycenae. Big house-like tombs, the dwellings of the dead, lined the wide central walk which showed in a cold sunny glimpse the curve of distant pillars. In quieter side avenues humbler graves were straggled about with grass, with here and there a cleared place, a chained space, a clipped mound, a body's length of granite chips, a few recent flowers wilting beside a name. Above the line of mist-green budding lime trees there rose far off the three black towers of Lots Road power station. *Ye are come unto Mount Zion and the city of the living God.*

It had come as no surprise to Danby when Bruno had said to him after she had gone, 'That girl looked a bit like Gwen.' Danby had taken in the resemblance earlier, when he had seen Lisa's head so close to Bruno's. He had noticed the heavy mane of dark hair, the brooding heaviness of the long face, the rapt wide-eyed attentiveness, the shaped thinking mouth with the deep runnel over it. He had gazed and brooded upon that face in the evenings that followed when Lisa had come to Bruno, and Danby had sat silent, apparently unnoticed, in the corner, occasionally moving to pour champagne, while Lisa led Bruno through mazes of self-revelation in a kind of unfaltering converse such as Danby had never heard before and which he felt that he scarcely comprehended. He had expected to be told to go. But no one suggested it, so he stayed. After she left he and Bruno looked at each other in puzzlement, in amazement. Bruno seemed sometimes on the point of asking a question. Perhaps he wanted to ask who the woman was. Or perhaps he assumed that she was Miles's wife. Perhaps it was some quite other question. In fact they said nothing to each other.

When Danby understood the troubling resemblance, he recalled at once the curious fright which he had experienced when he had seen Lisa looking at him out of the upper window at Kempsford Gardens, and he then realized what it was that he had been afraid of. It was not just of a very serious girl with a fine mouth and a formidable power of attention. Now throughout each day at the works he tried hard to scatter his thoughts, to act mechanically, not to think, not to look forward. With an intensified self-consciousness he cherished his so long accustomed being. He chatted carefully with Adelaide but told her he was ill. When Diana rang up he made an appointment and then cancelled it. He was glad that Bruno continued to be in a rather inward state and showed no signs of wanting to discuss the phenomenon on which he had commented. Danby hoped that it would all somehow fade and blow away; and yet he also knew that it would not.

Danby's relationship with Gwen had seemed to him, even at the time, something that was not quite himself, but more like a visitation from outside. He had perfectly understood Miles's looks of incomprehension and amazement. Such a conjunction was so improbable. Gwen was not his type and he was not hers. Gwen had had a kind of authority over him which seemed more an attribute of her sheer alienness than the result of any rational effect of persuasion. Perhaps it had simply been the authority of a terrifying degree of love. And in retrospect Danby saw his marriage as a pure celebration of the god of love, something almost arbitrary and yet entirely necessary, invented and conducted at the whim of that deity without the help of any mundane basis in nature. Of course Danby, though he had never opened a textbook of psychology in his life, knew that the working of nature is very often hidden and that what had so powerfully brought him and Gwen together could well be, after all, something natural, but he did not want to know. He preferred to believe in the action of the god in his life, an action which he took to be entirely *sui generis* and unique.

After Gwen's death, as he very slowly recovered himself, he felt a sense of reversion, of a return to a very much easier and more natural and Danby-like mode of existence. This was accompanied by no relief. Gwen had been a source of joy and indeed of surprise so continual that the sort of strain upon his nature of which he became so conscious afterwards could not then be apprehended as a discomfort. But in settling down to being once again himself Danby had felt as it were the pull of gravity which, after some years, had something rather reassuring about it. This was a matter which Danby had got as far as discussing with Linda, and their conclusions about him, arrived at together, had been a positive solace. It was not that Gwen had come to seem like a dream. Danby held it for gospel that Gwen had been reality and his subsequent life had been a dream. But, and especially with Linda's help, he had decided that, like most other people, he was not made for reality. In any case he had no alternative. He could not now, without Gwen, even conceive of any possibility other than the dream life of the *homme moyen sensuel* which to the tips of his fingers he so absolutely was.

Indeed, as the years went by, when after Linda, who had done him so much good, he so sensibly and quietly took up with Adelaide and felt the smooth weighty powers of initiative of one who is entirely assembled inside his own nature, he began, without in any way thinking it to be sacrilege, to doubt whether he had ever truly been awakened even by Gwen. Gwen had been a sort of miracle in his life the nature of which he would never entirely understand. Such a thing could only happen once, and it had left him a sacred relic upon which he could meditate with profit until the end of his days. But had he ever really existed in the world of which his love for Gwen had given him intimations? As time went by he began to doubt it. Not that he doubted Gwen's value. But he began, as with middle age his exploration of his own nature became more confident, to wonder how far a person like himself had genuinely participated in that feast of love. Danby was aware that one forgot things. But on the whole he felt that the god must have found him, for all the frenzy of his enthusiasm, something of a disappointment. He had loved whole-heartedly but with too ordinary a heart.

The appearance of Diana had in no way startled Danby. Diana was a kind of mixture of Linda and Adelaide and in a way more attractive to him than either of them. She had Linda's coolness and Adelaide's peculiar kind of animal sweetness and charm. He had loved talking to her as much as touching her. Her delightfulness had reminded him how unambitious he had lately become about women and how few of them he took the trouble to meet nowadays. She had also reminded him of his power to attract. He had enjoyed dancing with her more intensely than he had enjoyed anything for years. Naturally he would have liked to go to bed with her. However she was married to Miles, and though at first it had seemed a rather jolly idea to cuckold Miles, a more extended reflection suggested snags.

Danby, though he would not have admitted to being afraid of Miles, regarded the mystery of Miles as something rather formidable and deserving of a certain respect. After all, Miles was Gwen's brother, and that was not the place in which to risk having some kind of mess. Danby did not doubt that he could easily overcome Diana's professed scruples. But, as he thought about it longer he began to feel that perhaps it would be nicer after all to explore the sentimental friendship which she had said she wanted. She was indeed, like himself, a devotee of 'cool self-love', and it would go hard but their confederate hedonisms would not find out some way of enjoying each other without risk. What the meeting with Diana did however also lead Danby to resolve was that it was time to go hunting again. He would find another, less problematic, equally marvellous girl and take her to bed. And he would look after Adelaide too. Everything would be all right and everybody would be happy. These reflections however belonged to the period prior to last Sunday. They had nothing whatever to do with what had actually now happened.

Danby, who had stationed himself beside the defunct Chelsea pensioners' enclosure, moved up closer to the railings, stumbling upon hidden stones in the arching grass. His eyes were tired and dazzled by following in the rather pale bright light the endless stream of people who were emerging from West Brompton tube station. She had said that she would not see Bruno today because he must not be made too dependent on her visits. It was during the afternoon, when Danby had realized just how appalling it was that she was not coming, that he had had to cease deceiving himself about what had happened. She had said she usually came home about half past five. Danby had been in position since five and it was now after six. It was possible that he had missed her, it was possible that she was spending the evening elsewhere, it was possible that she had come home by another route and entered Kempsford Gardens from Warwick

Road. Danby was feeling dazed and a little light-headed as if he were not getting enough air. Outside the cars were moving and the people were filing endlessly past in the weak bright heartless sunshine. Inside the cemetery there was emptiness and distance and expanses of shady green. Danby had no clear intentions and had shunned formulating any. It was simply necessary to be here and to see her.

Danby darted to the cemetery gate and shot through it. Lisa, who had just passed close by the railings, was waiting to cross the road. She turned, frowning, a little dazzled by the sun, as Danby blundered up to her.

'Oh, excuse me – '

'Oh, hello.'

As she turned back from the roadway and looked full at him Danby felt a crushing constriction about the heart and a sort of black explosion.

'I er I saw you and I wanted to, just a word, if you can spare a moment – '

'Certainly. Are things all right? Bruno no worse I hope?'

'Bruno – no – just the same. Well, he's missing you awfully –'

'He knows I'll come tomorrow?'

'Yes, yes.'

'You see, I couldn't always come, sometimes there are meetings and things – and it's better not to have too rigid a pattern.'

'I quite understand –'

'What was it you wanted?'

'It's, well, about Bruno, about seeing him, could you – Look, could you just come into the cemetery for a moment, there's such a crowd here.'

Danby touched the sleeve of her coat. It was the same brown mackintosh but he could not now have closed his fingers to grip it. He turned into the gate of the cemetery and felt her moving just behind him. Once inside he walked a little way towards one of the side alleys and stopped under a lime tree beside a tall square lichen-freckled tomb with an urn on top of it.

Lisa joined him and reached out a hand to the tomb. Her fingers moved upon its crumbling surface. He saw the long hand with the clear half moons as Bruno had said, so like.

'I hope I don't overtire Bruno?'

'No, you're doing him so much good.'

'When people talk from the heart they sometimes regret it later.'

'You're just what Bruno needs. He's been longing to get all that stuff off his chest.'

'We'll soon get on to talking about ordinary things. It's just a matter of transition.'

'You're so wonderful at controlling him! You can make him talk about anything.'

'Well, if he says all these things to me perhaps he won't feel he's got to say them to Miles!' She was pushing back the yellow scarf and hauling her hair out again. She looked tired.

'You look tired.'

'I'm all right. Look, about Miles seeing Bruno – '

'Had a hard day?'

'Much as usual. Miles says he'll go again on Sunday if you think Bruno's really ready for him.'

'You'll come too, won't you?'

'Maybe – '

'If you bring Miles into the room it might help.'

'It might. I'll think about that. Would the same time on Sunday morning do for Miles?'

'Yes, that's fine.'

'Good. Well, if that's all I'll be getting along.'

'Oh er wait just a minute, Lisa, would you – '

She had moved away and now turned again attentive. Behind her were graves of children, tiny pathetic stones half lost in the meadowy vegetation. The silent sleepers made a dome of quietness. The traffic and the people were elsewhere.

Danby stumbled into the long wet grass, getting in between her and the gateway. He almost held out his hands to prevent her from going away.

'What is it?'

'You will come tomorrow, won't you?'

'Yes, of course. I said so.'

'You don't mind my calling you "Lisa"?'

'No, of course not.'

She was staring at him in that terribly attentive way, her

mouth pouting a little, her eyes narrowed against the sun.

'Lisa, when you come to see Bruno tomorrow could you stay on with me afterwards, I mean have a drink or something?'

'Was there something special you wanted to discuss?'

'No, yes, that is – '

'About Miles and Bruno?'

'No, not really. I'm sorry, it's hard to explain – '

'*Is* Bruno suddenly much worse?'

'No, no, Bruno's fine.'

'Then what did you want to talk about?'

'Oh nothing special you see, I just wondered – I mean perhaps we could have a drink, perhaps we could have lunch – Would you have lunch with me tomorrow?'

She smiled. 'You don't have to be so grateful. I like coming to see Bruno. You don't have to invite me to lunch.'

Danby groaned. His feet seemed to be getting tangled together in the grass. 'You don't understand – it's nothing to do with Bruno – it's about me – '

'How do you mean?'

'I'm in a difficulty – '

'Oh. I'm sorry to hear that.'

'You'll think me a bit mad – '

Lisa was frowning and looking down, fumbling at the buttons of her mackintosh. She took a step away and a step to the side, glancing towards the gateway. 'I really would rather not discuss with you anything about my sister.'

'Oh God – '

'I really don't regard – anything like that – as my business. So if you'll excuse me – '

'*It's not about your sister.* Oh Christ!'

'Well, then I don't understand you. And anyway I must be going.'

'Lisa, will you lunch with me tomorrow?'

'I'm always busy at lunch time.'

'Lisa, don't you understand, I just want to see *you*.'

'I doubt if I can help you with any of your problems.'

'It's not *that*. You'll stay, after Bruno, tomorrow, talk to me – ?'

'I don't quite see the point.' She was staring at him now in a hostile way, pulling up the collar of her mackintosh like a brown crest.

'There may not be any point for you. But for me – '

'I must be going.'

'Please see me, please – ' He spread out his hands in appeal and to bar her in from the gate.

'I don't know what's going on between you and my sister and I assure you I don't want to know. Now get out of the way, please.'

'You mustn't think I'm – It's not like that – With Diana it was just – nothing much – nothing – '

'Well, I don't want to discuss your nothings. I must be going home.'

'Please, Lisa, just consider seeing me, I'll write to you, don't be so cruel – '

'I'm not being cruel. I see no point in this sort of discussion. You seem to me to take a very peculiar view – '

'I haven't explained properly. Let me explain. Let's meet more and talk, please – '

'I'm a very busy person and I have a life of my own as I'm sure you have too. Now will you get out of the way?'

'I can't let you go like this, I'll write, you will come tomorrow, won't you – ?' Danby contorted himself in front of her and then stretched out a hand which brushed the sleeve of her coat as she stepped quickly into the long grass to get past him. 'Lisa!'

She was hurrying towards the gate. In another moment she was outside and had disappeared into the steadily moving crowd. Danby looked after her for a moment. Then he turned back and began to walk slowly away down the long avenue of tombstones.

Chapter Seventeen

Miles Greensleave, returning from the office, stopped abruptly in the Old Brompton Road as he saw in a shaft of sunlight Lisa and Danby Odell deep in conversation inside the railings of the cemetery.

Behind the railings in the green shaded meadowy expanse with its distant vista of pillars in the rainy sunlight the two figures looked large, clear, significant. There was something too about their attitudes, their intentness, which suggested a great seriousness, something at issue. Miles felt a sense of disagreeable shock, as if of fear. He stopped and watched. As he watched, Danby suddenly threw out his hands in a theatrical gesture as if he were trying to prevent Lisa from passing him. Miles looked on with amazement. Still keeping them in view, he began to walk quickly along in the direction of the gate. But before he reached it he saw Lisa dart past Danby, who appeared to be making a sort of lunge at her, and emerge on to the pavement. She dodged between the passers-by and had crossed the road before Miles could catch up with her.

He ran across the road after her and came up beside her as she reached the corner of Eardley Crescent.

'Lisa!'

'Oh, Miles, good, hello.'

'Lisa, what on earth was going on? I saw that fool Danby – what was he doing?'

'Oh he just – We were talking about Bruno.'

'Was he trying to make a pass at you or something?'

'No, no. He had some problem or other. He – he wanted me to have lunch with him.'

'To have *lunch* with him?'

'He said he wanted to see me –'

'To *see* you? I hope you told him to go to hell. He seemed to be behaving in a damned impertinent manner, standing in front of you like that and making a grab at you – '

'It's all right, Miles, don't take on.'

'I will take on! You didn't say you'd have lunch with him, did you?'

'No, I didn't.'

'I should think not, that pathetic ass, making a scene like that in public.'

'I don't think he was very serious.'

'Probably blind drunk. Fancy his wanting to have lunch with you!'

'Is it so very odd that a man should want to have lunch with me?'

'No, no, Lisa, of course not. I mean you're – Danby's such poor stuff. You wouldn't think he'd have the nerve to approach someone like you. He drinks like a fish. He's probably making passes at girls all the time.'

'Maybe. I expect that explains it.'

'Let me know if he annoys you again.'

'Really, Miles, I'm not a Victorian maiden. I can look after myself.'

'I hope you won't go round to that house again, to Stadium Street.'

'I did say I'd go and see Bruno.'

'Well, go sometime when Danby's out at work. I suppose he does work. Or let Diana go. The old man probably can't distinguish you anyway.'

'Diana, well – '

They turned to mount the steps of the house in Kempsford Gardens. Diana, who had been watching out for them from the front window, as she so often did, threw open the front door. 'Come in, come in, your poor tired things, let me take your coats. Lisa, your mac is quite wet, you can't have hung it up properly this morning, you are bad. Oh Miles, you've got me the *Evening Standard*, good, I meant to remind you, come on in, I've lit a fire in the drawing-room and now the sun's doing its best to put it out. I bought a new sherry decanter, eighteenth century one, in that shop in the Fulham Road, you must both have a sip of sherry before you do another thing. Look, cut glass, isn't it lovely? It was quite cheap too. Do sit down, you both look exhausted, did you meet on the train?'

'No, just outside the station,' said Miles. He sat down. The sun was shining into the little neat coloured drawing-room which Diana kept so fanatically tidy. A small fire was burning gaily in the grate. On a bright Scandinavian tile-topped table the new sherry decanter stood with three glasses. This was his home.

Diana poured out the sherry and gave a glass to Lisa who was still standing in the doorway unknotting her scarf.

'Any dramas?' Diana often asked them this question when they came home in the evening.

'No, no dramas,' said Lisa. She took the glass.

Miles lifted his head towards her, but she had already drifted away through the door taking the sherry with her.

In fact he had already known, even without the hint from Lisa, that it would be better not to tell Diana about the scene with Danby. Why?

'The fragile pearly shaft sinks into the table and located where there is a dim red blotch, a shadowed unred red, reflection of a flower. Above yet how above is stretched the surface skin of grainy wood, a rich striped brown. Red reddest of words. Brown luscious caramel word. Yet also loneliest of colours, an exile from the spectrum, word colour, wood colour, colour of earth, tree, bread, hair.'

Miles closed up his *Notebook of Particulars* and stared at the red and purple anemones which his wife had placed upon his work table. A page which he had torn out and crumpled up was uncrumpling quietly with a little mouse-like sound in the waste paper basket. It was late in the evening and the curtains were drawn. The women knew better than to come porlocking at this hour. The expanse of dark time was his.

However he could not work. He had intended to describe the anemones, to continue what he had begun to write about them yesterday evening in daylight. He had wanted to catch in words the peculiar watery pallor of reflections in polished wood. But now it suddenly seemed pointless. The anemones, the *strength* of whose rather thick thrusting stems had struck him yesterday, now seemed to him just a bunch of rather vulgar flowers, pert faces with frilly collars. Diana had put them in a little cheap Chinese vase which increased if anything the vulgarity of their appearance. He could not see them properly any more. They were not worth looking at anyway. He felt distressed, hurt.

That idiotic scene in the cemetery between Lisa and Danby had unsettled him, given him a sense of pointlessness, that old pointlessness which he remembered so well from the war time. He knew the vulnerability of his strength. Seeing Bruno, that had made everything go wrong, it had made him feel guilt, and with the guilt had come that fatal weakness. Miles hated muddle and thinking ill of himself. If only he had kept his head with Bruno and not got excited and upset. How easy it was afterwards to see this and to see how simple it would have been to have acted otherwise. But he had been so shocked and moved by simply seeing Bruno again and had not had time to collect himself. He knew now that he had quite deliberately tried not to foresee what it would be like, tried not to use his imagination. The father to whom he wrote respectful letters twice a year, and whose fault it patently was that they never met, had been long settled in the background of his life, a venerable image housed in a niche, looking rather like a sage represented by Blake. The terrible sick old man in the shabby little room in Stadium Street was something quite else, something requiring thought, something demanding, something frightening.

I shall have to see him again, Miles had thought, even before Lisa brought him the reconciling message. Things could not be left like that, all mangled and awful. It would wreck his work, it would haunt his dreams. The pitifulness of it all had sickened Miles. He did not want to hear Bruno's confessions. As far as he was concerned now, Bruno had no past. He had long ago forgiven Bruno, that is he had amputated from his mind and his heart all further consideration of Bruno's offences. He did not want to think about the past in the company of his father. The past was terrible, sacred, *his*. He would have been prepared to enact the dutiful son if this could have been done in a dignified rather impersonal sort of way. Or he would even have been prepared to chat with Bruno, if that would have helped, only what can one chat about with a stranger who is dying? What he could not do was enter into a live relationship with his father which involved the reopening of the past. He could not bear the presence now to both of them of *those* things, that they should see them together. The idea was hideous, sickening. Of course no one could be expected to understand this. It was inexplicable but absolute. He could share no intensity with Bruno. And he would certainly accept no briefing from Danby. Yet he had to go there again and get through it somehow and act some sort of part. And when he did now try to think about how to do it he said to himself; my gods do not know about things of this kind.

His mind reverted to the scene in the cemetery. This was somehow part of the same business, he felt it was somehow caused by some emanation from that awful room in Stadium Street. Of course Danby was just a clown, but the scene had been in some way horrible. The whole thing was partly Danby's fault anyhow. Not that Miles imagined Danby had put Bruno up to summoning him. Danby was probably rather unnerved by Miles's late appearance on the scene. Miles recalled the wording of the message which Bruno had sent him through Lisa: 'Tell him I didn't mean what I said at the end.' What did that signify? Was it just a general revocation of an old man's curse, or did it mean that Miles would get the stamps after all? Miles had not thought about the stamp collection in years. He had settled down to assuming that Danby would have it. However, supposing Miles did get it it would certainly not be unwelcome. It would mean that he could give up the office and spend all his time writing poetry.

Miles banished the vulgar idea of the stamps from his mind. He got up restlessly and began to walk about his room. Three paces took him across it and three paces took him back, past the lighted grainy polished table which he kept so neat with his *Notebook of Particulars* and his row of vari-coloured biros and his fountain pen and his silver ink pot, which Diana had given him, and his neatly aligned sheets of blue blotting paper and the little Chinese vase of red and purple anemones. He paused to look at his face in the small square mirror. He used to think that he resembled the young Yeats. What he saw now in the gilded square, a little blurred as in a small painting by Cézanne, was a long thin crooked face with a lopsided tremulous mouth and a long pointed nose and frowning eyes and an anxious insecure expression, surrounded by jagged wavering stripes of limp dull dark hair well streaked with grey. He showed his wolf's teeth unsmilingly. It did not matter any more what he looked like. He began pacing again. He thought about Lisa in the cemetery.

His reaction had indeed been, to use Lisa's expression, rather Victorian! Of course Lisa could look after herself. She was a hundred times tougher than a drunken trifler like Danby. It was odd that although he had got so used to seeing Lisa through Diana's eyes as a 'bird with a broken wing' he had also, and as it now seemed to him from the start, apprehended her as a person with strength. Lisa was somebody. It must be no joke being a teacher in that school. Miles had visited it once and been appalled by the atmosphere of dirt and poverty and muddle, the smell, the haggard mamas, the children brawling in the street. Lisa lived in a real world which seemed very unlike the reality which in his poetry he was attempting to join. That was her vocation and he respected and admired it.

Why then, since Lisa was so patently able to deal with Danby's foolery, had he been so upset? And why had it seemed so clear that Diana must not be told? Lisa was a part of the household, a part of his life. He and Diana had long ago decided that Lisa would never marry, that she would be with them for ever. Diana had asked did he mind. No, he did not mind, he was glad that Lisa should be there, very glad. She had become a part of his contentment. She gave him a kind of companionship which Diana could not give, she could talk to him about things which Diana did not understand. Miles had come to think of her as a person secluded, segregated, enclosed. She did her work and she lived with Miles and Diana. She was not as other women, she was a kind of religious. After all, she had actually been a nun for several years and the experience had marked her with a coldness and a separateness. Was that why he had been shocked then, as if one had seen a gross man insulting a nun, dragging her by her habit?

'Is it so very odd that a man should want to have lunch with me?' No, it was not really odd. Lisa was not pretty as Diana was. Indeed one had to know her well before one could see her

140

attractiveness at all. Miles could see it. He could even, he felt now, see her beauty, her secret beauty, that dark intensity of eyes and mouth. This must be invisible to an outsider. He could imagine how Lisa must look to the outsider, like a gaunt untidy middle-aged schoolmistress. Yet even such people occasionally got invitations to lunch he supposed. Only not Lisa. Danby's gyrations were meaningless of course, probably the outcome of drink, but they had posed a question, and Miles had begun to be aware of the question like an infixed dart. How would he feel if Lisa had a suitor?

In a way he knew very little about Lisa. In a way the concept of the broken-winged bird had served to conceal her. He had never discussed her past with her. He had imagined, it did not now seem very clear why, that she preferred not to speak of it. He knew nothing about her sex life, if it had ever existed. Diana had mooted a theory that Lisa was not interested in men, and Miles had rather vaguely taken the theory over. When he asked his routine questions about Lisa's 'day' it had never occurred to him to wonder if the day had included a man. In fact he did not imagine that Lisa had any secret life. But what he had now received from that glimpse of the by-play in Brompton Cemetery, and what he now knew that he could never rid himself of, was the idea that it was *possible* for Lisa to be courted. She was loseable. She was free.

As Miles continued to pace his room, brushing the mantelpiece at one end and the doorhandle at the other, he began slowly to take in the significance of the prophetic terror which he had experienced beside the cemetery railings. He had discovered something new and dreadful and growing with which he would now have to live, a deep and unpredictable menace to his peace of mind. Something at the very heart of his world which had been sleeping was now terribly awake. Lisa belonged at Kempsford Gardens. He loved Lisa. Lisa was his.

Chapter Eighteen

'DANBY!'

Danby, who had just completed a letter to Lisa and put it in an envelope, cursed and laid his electric razor down on top of the envelope. As there was no table in his room he had written the letter standing up beside the chest of drawers.

'DANBY!'

'Coming, Bruno, coming!'

Danby went up the stairs two at a time.

'Don't shout so, Bruno.'

'Danby, one of the stamps has gone.'

'I daresay it has the way you scatter them around.'

'But it's *gone*, it was there in its case, last time I looked and I'm certain I didn't take it out.'

'You probably did, you know. Don't get out of bed, Bruno. I'll look for the damn thing.'

'It's one of the Cape triangulars, it's worth two hundred pounds.'

'Don't get out of bed! And don't fuss so. I'll search, Adelaide will search, it's probably somewhere in this room on the floor.'

'It *can't* be –'

'Adelaide! ADELAIDE!'

It was late evening, nearly Bruno's bed time. Rain was beating against the windows. The lamp shone on the pale scrawled counterpane, Bruno's supper tray with half-eaten beans on toast, the usual litter of stamps, *The Spider Population of East Anglia*, and the *Evening Standard*. Danby had spent the evening in a frenzy. Lisa had visited Bruno in the afternoon and he had missed her.

A champagne glass rolled off the bed on to the floor and broke. Adelaide came in looking tired and irritable and began to pick up the pieces of the glass.

'Adelaide, Bruno has lost a stamp, a triangular stamp. It must be somewhere here on the floor. You do that side of the room and I'll do this side.'

'It can't be in this room, I'm sure it was in its case –'

'Oh shut up, Bruno. Lift the carpet up at the corners, Adelaide. I'll help you shift the books. Mind you don't put your knee on a bit of glass. Oh Nigel, hello, Bruno's lost a stamp, a triangular one. Could you help us look? It must be on the floor.'

Danby and Adelaide crawled slowly along the floor towards each other while Nigel stood dreamily at the door and watched them.

'I'll do under the bed, Adelaide. There's that hole in the carpet, it might have got underneath there.'

'It's no good your looking, Danby, I *know* it's not in this room.'

'Well, where is it if it's not in this room?'

'I don't know, but I know –'

'Oh stop blithering. You're being jolly helpful aren't you, Nigel. Bruno, get back into *bed*. Well, it looks as if it's not on the floor, I'll look in the drawers and on the shelves. You can knock off, Adelaide, just take that damn glass away, will you, don't leave it in the waste paper basket. And the tray. And don't bang the bloody door like that!'

Adelaide was heard noisily descending the stairs. Nigel continued to watch while Danby searched the chest of drawers, moved it away from the wall and looked behind it, looked behind the bookcase, looked behind the books in the bookcase.

'It may have got *inside* a book. And if it has, God knows when it'll turn up. It doesn't matter anyway. Bruno, can't you be philosophical about a bloody stamp!'

'It's the best one of the set. It's worth two hundred pounds.'

'Well, that doesn't matter to *you*, does it? Oh Christ, Bruno, don't take on so, I've had a ghastly day. I can't stand all this damn fuss about a stamp. Nigel, will you either help me or fuck off? Bruno, I'm sorry, don't look so awful.'

'I know you're only waiting for me to be gone, you're only waiting –'

143

'BRUNO, stop it! Look, I'll search the landing and the stairs, all the way down to my room. It may have got dropped somewhere on the way. Do try to compose yourself. You haven't even opened your *Evening Standard*.'

'I want *that* stamp – '

'Don't be so childish. I'll go on looking. You just read the paper for Christ's sake. Read about the Thames flood menace. That'll take your mind off stamps.'

Danby came out, followed by Nigel, and shut the door. As he began examining the linoleum on the landing he felt a soft touch on his shoulder.

'Oh clear off, Nigel. This is one of your dream days.'

'Could I talk to you a moment?'

'No.'

'It's about the stamp.'

Danby straightened up. Nigel had moved on into his own room and Danby followed him.

Nigel's room presented a stripped and drear appearance. All the furniture had been pushed back against the walls and the dressing table had been banished on to the landing. The centre light showed a square of shabby brown carpet in the middle of the room, a surrounding section of unstained boards, and a further section of much worn cheaply stained wood floor. Some Indian painted wooden animals stood on the chest of drawers together with two jam jars containing anemones and narcissus. The narcissus had faded to the colour and texture of old thin paper. Nigel stood on one leg in the centre of the carpet stroking down his long lank sidelocks of dark hair so that they met under his chin. He motioned Danby to shut the door.

'What do you do in here?' said Danby. 'Dance?'

'I know where that stamp is.'

'Oh. Where is it?'

'What will you do for me if I tell you?'

'Nothing.'

'You'll owe me something.'

'Stop babbling, Nigel. Where's the stamp?'

'Adelaide took it.'

'*Adelaide?*'

'Yes.'

144

'That can't be true,' said Danby. 'You're romancing, you've had too much of whatever bloody stuff it is you take.'

'Truly. She didn't take it for herself. She took it for Will Boase. It was his idea.'

'For Will Boase? Why on earth – ?'

'He wanted a camera.'

'Christ! But why should Adelaide do that for Will Boase?'

'Better ask her.'

'Nigel, is this true?'

'Yes, yes, yes. Cross my heart.'

Danby left the room and bounded down the stairs. 'Adelaide!'

Adelaide was in her room sitting on her bed staring in front of her. She looked as if she had been crying.

'Adelaide, Nigel says you took that stamp, but this is ridiculous – '

'It's true.'

Danby sat down on the bed beside her. 'He says you took it for Will Boase.'

'Yes.'

'But why?'

Adelaide shook her head slowly from side to side and tears began to course down her cheeks. She still stared, not looking at Danby. She said nothing.

'Well,' said Danby after a moment, 'whatever the reason you can bloody well get it back again, and if your worthless thieving cousin has sold it he can bloody well give us the money or see the police. I'll write him a letter and you can take it over straightaway. Bruno wants that stamp. I'll tell him we found it somewhere. How could you be so unkind to the old man?'

Adelaide began to sob.

'Oh stop it, Adelaide. I've had enough today. Sorry I was rough, but it's all a bit much.'

Adelaide began to scream. Sitting stiffly and still staring at the door she uttered a series of low piercing bubbling screams which crowded in her throat as they fought for utterance. Saliva foamed down on to her chin.

Danby turned her round towards him and slapped her face.

The screams stopped, but the next moment Danby felt himself gripped by the shoulders and almost hurled off the bed. Punching, kicking, biting, Adelaide had attached herself to the whole length of his body. Caught off his balance he could not get his hands between them. He felt her teeth at his neck. The next moment they had both fallen heavily on to the floor.

Danby pulled himself up. Adelaide lay where she had fallen, leaning on one elbow, her hair rolling about her, looking up at him with a contorted face.

'Adelaide – please – what is it – you've gone mad – '

'You despise me,' she said. 'You regard me as a servant. You treat me as a slave. You wouldn't dream of marrying me, oh no. I'm cheap trash. I'm just good to go to bed with for a while. I'm convenient, easy. You don't really care about me at all. *I hate you, I hate you, I hate you.*'

Danby was trembling. 'Adelaide, please don't speak like that. Don't worry about the stamp. We'll deal with it tomorrow. Better get yourself to bed. Shall I bring you a hot drink, some aspirins or something?'

'*I hate you.*'

He hesitated at the door. Then he went out closing it behind him. He went straight up into the hall and out of the house into a dark continuum of light driving rain.

Adelaide got up from her bed. She felt bruised and stiff and her face ached with crying. She thought, I'll kill myself. She looked in the mirror and the sight of her terrible face brought on more tears. She leaned against the wall gasping with sobs.

It was nearly three o'clock in the morning and Danby had not come back. Or perhaps he had come back and gone out again. During the first two or three hours after his departure Adelaide had been crying too frenziedly into her pillow to be at all conscious of her surroundings. Later she thought that she heard Bruno calling. Now there was only the rain.

She could not yet understand what had happened or why it had happened. She had been mad to take the stamp. She had known that even before she gave it to Will. She had gone over to Camden Town with the stamp in her handbag, still undecided about whether to give it to him or to return it. After

Auntie had gone to bed they had started quarrelling as usual. Adelaide had made some sarcastic remarks about Will's flirtation with Mrs Greensleave. The memory of this scene had begun to torment Adelaide. She particularly resented the ease with which Mrs Greensleave had got into conversation with Will. For Adelaide to converse with Will was difficult, even flirting with Will was awkward, inarticulate, perilous. Mrs Greensleave had seemed to find it all very easy. Adelaide told Will he had behaved like a flattered servant and simpered like a petted boy. Will had been extremely angry. Adelaide declared that if Will telephoned Mrs Greensleave she would not see him again. Will professed himself quite unmoved by this threat and announced his intention of telephoning Mrs Greensleave forthwith. Reduced at last to tears of rage and helpless misery Adelaide had thrown the stamp on to the table. The scene had ended with Will delighted, attentive, loving, promising never to communicate with Mrs Greensleave again.

It was all unworthy, horrible, muddled, nasty to look back upon. Oh she had cried so much in these last days. And it had ended in this insanity, which must have broken Danby's love for her for ever. Even if he was kind to her now he must regard her as a mad person. He would always be nervous of her, watching for a recurrence of that awful fury. Indeed she had frightened herself. Yet Adelaide knew that she was not mad, she was just driven somehow beyond the bounds of her endurance.

She opened the door of her room. Danby's door opposite was still open and the room was dark. She walked across and turned the light on. The bed was still made up, not slept in, the curtains were not drawn across the black shiny rainy window, the room was desolate. More tears came to Adelaide. She went across and pulled the curtains. Then she took the Welsh counterpane off the bed and turned back the blankets neatly, dropping her tears on to the sheets. She stood looking about the room.

Then she saw that there was a letter lying on top of the chest of drawers. Her first thought was that Danby had come back while she was still weeping hysterically and had left a message for her. She moved over and pushed Danby's electric razor aside. The envelope was addressed to Miss Lisa Watkin. It was unsealed.

Adelaide listened for a moment. Only rain. Then after another moment's hesitation she pulled the letter out of the envelope.

My dear Lisa,

I am sorry to have behaved so badly in Brompton cemetery and perhaps startled you. I am not much good at writing letters but I must write this one. I want you to know it's serious. Not that I have any hope anyway, why should I have? But it's not a light thing. You may find this incomprehensible. I've only seen you a few times. But oh God Lisa, please believe it's serious, it's terrible. I do love you and I do want to see you and get to know you and I ask you *please* to consider this as a serious possibility. I will behave very well and do anything you want. Don't just blankly say there's no point. How do you know there's no point until you try? I know I'm nothing compared with you, but I love you terribly and *one is not mistaken about something like this*. I have only loved like this once before. It is quite different from ordinary trifling affections and just wanting to get into bed with people. I feel a sense of destiny here. You *must* listen to me, Lisa. That you may think badly of me (for instance because of what you saw that first time) and think I am a frivolous person somehow doesn't matter. I am a frivolous person, but not about you, and if you attended to me at all you might be able to forgive me and you have already changed me. Don't regard all this as drunken babbling or something. It is the heart speaking and one knows when that is happening. Please recognize and I dare to say *respect* the fact that I love you, and *see me again*, Lisa. You have got to. There is no way round this. I will write again and suggest a meeting. Please think of me seriously. I love you, Lisa, and everything else is utterly blotted out.

Your slave
Danby

Adelaide put the letter back into the envelope and put the envelope back under the electric razor. She switched out the light and returned to her own room and locked the door. She lay rigid and tearless until the window began to lighten with the dawn.

Chapter Nineteen

Very quietly Miles opened the door of Lisa's room in the darkness.

It was about two o'clock on Saturday morning. During the two previous days Miles had taken his meals, gone to the office, done his work, talked in an ordinary way to the two women. He had made his usual pithy comments on the morning newspapers and departed punctually to catch his train returning equally punctually in the evening. But amid the old machinery of his life his inner heart was in a boiling seething ferment. He had watched Lisa closely. The physical space between them had taken on a new and terrifying significance. The near approach of hands at the breakfast table, the exchange of a book, the movement of a cup, an encounter on the stairs, these things were passages of anguish. The familiar house which he had called his home had disappeared. In its stead there was a structure of movements and views and distances which racked his body like an instrument of torture.

It was also impossible not to look and look. He stared at her compulsively and it seemed to him that she stared back. A magnetism which it would have been blinding agony to resist drew his eyes towards hers, compelled her eyes by his. He could not forgo these looks which were now so appallingly weighted with meaning. With a slightly giddy deliberation he refrained from varying the ordinary routine of his day. He made no attempt to be alone with her, and since they usually left home and returned at different times, and as Diana was always about in the house where doors were left open to be called through and looked through, he had not been alone with her.

However there are communications which can be made and certainly made without speech. By the time Friday evening had been reached Miles knew that Lisa knew and he knew that she knew that he knew. He had still absolutely no idea of what she thought about it, and indeed, absorbed in observing the painful evolution of his own feelings, he had not yet very much considered this. He was moreover not yet prepared to admit that he had entered a disastrous situation. The experience of falling in love, or as it seemed here to Miles, of realizing that one is in love, is itself however painful also a preoccupying joy. It increases vitality and sense of self. And this rather black joy was still preventing Miles from looking ahead or indeed from making any plan whatsoever. He did reflect: she did not want to tell Diana about Danby. But that might be and doubtless was, just an effect of her general discretion and tactful reserve, since she could hardly have foreseen what the witnessing of that little drama was going to do to the sanity of her brother-in-law.

Late on Friday evening, just as the women, who went to bed earlier than Miles, were in course of retiring something did happen. Diana was talking to Lisa at the foot of the stairs. Miles was still in the drawing-room, standing near the window which he had just been fastening. Lisa came back into the drawing-room to fetch a book, and for a moment they were both out of sight from the hall. Miles stared at her. Lisa picked up the book and arrested her movement for just a second to look back at him. Miles made a gesture with his hands, a gesture of entreaty and surrender, whose meaning was quite unmistakable. Lisa looked at him blankly and turned back into the hall, answering a question of Diana's.

Miles went up to his study, as he always did. Time passed. The agony became greater. At last, treading very softly, he went to Lisa's door.

The room where Miles and Diana slept was on the same landing as Miles's study. The room where Lisa slept was on a separate landing down some stairs. Miles was not afraid of waking Diana who was a prompt and sound sleeper.

He did not knock on the door but turned the handle very quietly and stepped noiselessly through into the darkness of the room.

The intensely enclosed darkness and silence seemed for a moment to stifle him and he put his hand to his throat. The violent pounding of his heart was making him feel sick and faint. He stood still, releasing the door handle, trying to breathe normally. He could see nothing, but after a while he began to hear the soft sound of Lisa's sleeping breath. He moved very quietly forward with hands outstretched, his feet questing carefully for obstacles. He could see the whiteness of the bed now and very dimly discern the shape of her head and the dark hair fanned out upon the pillow. She was lying on her back, one arm outstretched upon the counterpane. Miles put a hand out towards the bed. He was trembling so violently that his fingernails scratched the sheet with a tearing sound. Uttering a sighing groan he fell on his knees beside the bed. He could see her profile outlined against the window. He touched her hair.

'Oh! Miles!' She moved quickly, half sitting up.

Miles put his arms out gropingly. In a second she had put her arms round his neck and drawn his head violently against her breast.

Miles did not afterwards know how long they remained thus, quite motionless. Perhaps a long time. It was a moment of black blissful death. It was also a moment of absolute certainty.

'Oh God,' said Lisa.

'I love you, Lisa.

'I know. I love you too.'

'Oh my darling – '

'I'm sorry, Miles.'

'Don't be sorry. It's wonderful.'

'I never thought you – Why suddenly now, Miles, what happened?'

'I don't know. I feel I've loved you for years only I was blind to it. You were so necessary.'

'Yes, perhaps. But it wasn't like this.'

'I know. This is sudden. And oh my God it's violent, Lisa. I feel I shall die of it.'

'Was it something to do with Danby?'

'I'm a fool, a fool, Lisa. You've been so close to me for years. I took you for granted. I didn't see my own needs – '

'But was it?'

'Yes, I suppose so. Not that I imagined that that imbecile – But it suddenly made me see how free you were.'

'But I'm not free, Miles. I've never been free. Not since I met you.'

'Lisa, you don't mean – '

'Yes. I fell in love with you on your wedding day, the day when we first met.'

'Oh my heart – '

'I'm sorry. It's a relief to tell you. But it's also – a sort of death warrant. It's all my fault, Miles. I should never have come to live here. I didn't imagine you could ever have any interest in me except wanting to talk philosophy. I only came because I thought it inconceivable that I should ever reveal – what I have now revealed.'

'Oh Lisa do forgive me.'

'Don't be silly.'

'All these wasted years. Oh my darling – '

'You mustn't think of it in that way – '

'May I turn the light on?'

'No, no light for heaven's sake. Diana isn't awake, is she?'

'No.'

'Miles, it's wonderful even though it's death. I never in my wildest dreams imagined that I would ever be able to touch you like this.'

'Oh Lisa, I can't express to you – To think that you suffered – And I might never have known – '

'Well, you know now and I shall have to go away.'

'Don't say that. You are *not* going away. I won't let you. Do you want to kill me?'

'Miles, it's hopeless, don't you see? Oh God, to have found you like this, to hold you like this, and to know it's death at the same time – '

'Lisa, don't, don't cry, my heart. We must hold this situation because we've *got* to. There is a way. This is only the first moment – '

'It's practically the last moment, Miles. Do try to face this, my dear. We simply must not delude ourselves. And really for you – This has been something very sudden and odd like a quick storm. The real thing is Diana, all those years of sharing her bed – '

'Lisa, Lisa – '

'You must hang on to reality, Miles. Don't worry about me. I'm infinitely grateful to you for this, it will be a sort of jewel for my whole life and I shall be a far far richer person. I'm so grateful and glad that you came to me now like this in the night. If you hadn't come just like this I might never have told you. And I'm so *happy* that you know, even though it's absolute pure pain too. But there is nothing more, nothing to do or plan, just this.'

'I don't understand you, Lisa, I'm not going to listen to you. We've both been taken by surprise. We've got to *think* about it.'

'Thinking would be fatal. There must be no thinking. You know where thinking about it would get us.'

'Oh Christ.'

'You do see, Miles.'

'Lisa, I know so little about you.'

'Better so.'

'You say it's a sudden storm. It's not really so sudden. Sudden things are prepared for. Do you know what I noticed long ago, that we resemble each other, physically I mean?'

'Yes. I noticed too that we resemble each other. It's because I've thought about you so much.'

'No, it's because you were made for me. You are *the one*.'

'No, no, Miles. You are emotional and it is the black night time. You don't know what you're saying. What you are saying is blasphemy.'

'Parvati.'

'And Diana.'

'Diana was different. You know Diana was never like this. Nothing has been like this.'

'So you believe now, but – '

'I'd like to talk to you about Parvati. I think I could. I was never able to talk to – anyone else.'

'I've thought so much about Parvati. I wanted to see a picture of her only I never liked to ask you.'

'She was pregnant when she was killed.'

'Oh Miles – '

'I never told anyone, even Diana.'

'It still seems very close?'

'Yes. Sometimes as if I'd never really woken up to it yet. I'd have to go back and make it seem like yesterday but I can't. It's a permanent nightmare, not something real. I wrote a long poem about her afterwards.'

'That helped?'

'Yes. It was necessary to – celebrate her death. I don't know if you understand.'

'Yes, I think so.'

'I sometimes feel, Lisa, as if I never really *experienced* her death at all. I poeticized it, I made it into something unreal, something beautiful. I had to.

'We'd all do that to death if we could.'

'Perhaps. But it remains like a kind of barrier, a falseness. I think it prevents me from writing. It's like a curse. And yet I think it might be too terrible to experience – even now.'

'Perhaps you will experience it – when the times comes.'

'You could help me. I could relive it all with you.'

'No, no, I'm the last person – I mustn't touch this – That's another reason – '

'Lisa, you're the only one I could connect with Parvati – It would give meaning to everything.'

'No. You must do that alone.'

'Lisa, you can't leave me now that you've found me, it isn't conceivable. We're intelligent people. We can *manage* this. Will you promise you won't go away?'

'No, I can't promise that Miles.'

'Well, promise you won't go away tomorrow?'

'I promise I won't go away tomorrow.'

'Thank God. We'll talk it over properly tomorrow. We'll hold the whole situation, Lisa. *We've got to.*'

'Go now, Miles, please. Diana will wake.'

'All right. Let me kiss you. God, I've never kissed you before!'

For a moment they struggled awkwardly, finding each other's lips in the black dark.

'Go, go.'

'Sweetheart, don't betray this, don't abandon it.'

'Go, please.'

'Promise you'll try. We'll both try. We'll succeed.'

'Go, Miles.'

'Tomorrow, Lisa. Say "tomorrow".'

'Tomorrow.'

Miles stumbled out of the room. Joy overwhelmed all other feelings. He knelt down on the stairs between the two landings and closed his eyes, giddy and choking with joy.

After a few minutes he tiptoed up and opened the door of his own bedroom.

The curtain had been pulled back and the light from the street lamp faintly illuminated the room. Diana was lying on her back, her arms outside the counterpane extended by her sides. As Miles entered he caught a reflected glint from her open eyes. He approached the bed and looked down at her. Then he put a hand to her cheek. It was wet with tears.

'Hello.'

'Hello.'

'Miles, things will never be the same again. Never, never, never.'

Miles undressed and got into bed. He lay beside his wife, rigid like her, on his back with his arms extended. Never, never, never. The black joy returned to him and stretched out his extended body upon a rack of ecstasy.

Chapter Twenty

Bruno was holding Lisa's hand. The curtains were pulled against the dazzle of the afternoon sun and it was shadowy in the room.

'You see, I'd like to know what I'm *like*.'

'Perhaps there isn't any such thing, Bruno.'

'I want to get it into focus, what I really feel about it all.'

'One doesn't necessarily feel anything clear at all about the past. One is such a jumbled thing oneself.'

'I'm a jumbled thing, my dear, an old jumbled bedraggled dislocated thing.'

'We all are. When one tries to get a really clear memory one's usually doing it for some definite purpose, for revenge or consolation or something.'

'It does all go away – '

'Let it go.'

'But what really happened? What did Janie do to Maureen?'

'You can't know. You may have been a very small interlude in Maureen's life.'

'Oh. I suppose so.'

'You seem disappointed! But for so many people one is just a blind force.'

'But I wasn't a small interlude in Janie's life. I wrecked Janie's life.'

'In the world things happen as they do happen. Think how much of it was accidental.'

'You mean – to let myself off?'

'The question doesn't arise. There were the things that happened. But thinking about wickedness usually just comforts.'

'I was a demon to her.'

'Human beings are not demons. They are much too muddy.'

'I ought to have gone to her when she was dying.'

'There are things one can do nothing with. Try to draw a sort of quiet line round it.'

'I can't draw a line round it. It's myself. It's here. It's me.'

'You live too much in yourself.'

'Where else can I live, child?'

'Outside. Leave yourself. It's just an agitating puppet. Think about other things, think about anything that's good.'

'An agitating puppet. Yes, I feel so tired out with waving my arms about.'

'Brooding about the past is so often fantasy of how one might have won and resentment that one didn't. It is that resentment which one so often mistakes for repentance.'

'Do you know, there's something that hurts me even more than not having gone to Janie.'

'What?'

'Being mocked on that landing by the lodgers.'

'You mean – ?'

'When Janie went into Maureen's flat and locked the door, you remember I told you – Well, no, I didn't tell you, I left that bit out, it was too awful. When Janie made me take her to see Maureen, Janie went into the flat and locked the door against me and I could hear Maureen crying inside and I was knocking on the door, and the other lodgers in the house came down and mocked me.'

'Poor Bruno.'

'Something which ought to be quite unimportant turns out to be the most important thing of all.'

'A demon wouldn't feel this. Don't you see that you can't get it all clear?'

'If there were God one could leave it to God.'

'If there were God one could leave it to God.'

'Do you believe in God?'

'No. Listen. Miles will be coming to see you. Be very quiet with him and don't expect him to do anything for you.'

'I think I wanted him to go through some kind of ceremony, like a rite of exorcism. Funny thing, I'd forgotten, I'd just forgotten, how awfully much he irritated me!' They both laughed.

'Well, be kind to him, anyway.'

'You do love Miles, don't you?'

'Yes.'

'He's lucky. That girl who came before, your sister is it?'

'Yes.'

'Does she live with you?'

'Yes.'

'Miles doesn't mind?'

'No.'

Lisa drew a cool ringless hand back over the soft damp fleshy folds of Bruno's furrowed brow and down over the shiny bony dome of the skull to the ring of thin silky hair.

'I don't horrify you, my dear?'

'Of course not.'

'I daren't look in the mirror. You know that? And it must smell horrible.'

'No.'

'Very old people still feel sex, you know.'

'I know.'

'It gives me such joy to hold your hand.'

'I'm glad. I'll tell you something you may not believe.'

'What?'

'You're still attractive.'

Tears surged over the bulges of Bruno's cheek and soaked into the huge spade-shaped expanse of grey hair which was just beginning to look less like prickles and more like fur. The growth of hair was painful as it forced its way out through the fleshy folds and crevices of the tumbled face. But Bruno had not even tried to make Nigel change his mind about shaving him. It had soon begun not to matter.

'I must go now, Bruno.'

'You'll miss Danby. He'll be home in half an hour.'

'Never mind. You didn't mind my coming unannounced?'

'No, it was a lovely surprise. A sort of – apparition.'

'Yes, a ghost.'

'A heavenly ghost.'

After the girl had gone Bruno lay back on his pillows and stroked his bearded face. He had had a moustache very long ago when he had been courting Janie. He had never worn a beard. How it pricked and tickled. Yet perhaps it was a good idea after all. It concealed the bulbous fleshy contours into which his face had collapsed. It might make him look more human. Of course the girl didn't mean it, but how wonderful of her to say it. It had been a happy surprise, her visit, and now there were suddenly a lot of quite new and agreeable things to think about. It was good to find that there could still be pleasant surprises and absolutely new thoughts. Bruno said to himself, perhaps the doctor was serious, perhaps I might last out those years after all. He reached out his hand for *Soviet Spiders*.

'I'll kill Nigel.'

'Well, he's not here.'

'And you can tell that swine Danby what he can do with himself. I'll get even with that swine after I've fixed Nigel.'

'Don't shout so, Will.'

'Writing me a damned condescending letter saying would I be so kind as to return the stamp and if a trifling loan would assist he'd be very glad to oblige!'

'You still haven't given me the stamp.'

'Here's the bloody stamp. I wish you'd never snitched the damn thing.'

'Well, it was your idea!'

'Don't keep saying that!'

'Mind the camera, you're banging it against the kitchen table.'

'Fuck the camera. It's all the blasted camera's fault.'

'Never your fault, I suppose.'

'Shut up, Ad, unless you want your head punched.'

'Will, stop shouting, and *go away* for heaven's sake. You know I don't like having you in the house.'

'The way you're going on you soon won't have me in any house.'

'Well, that would suit me down to the ground!'

'Oh, it would, would it – well, *good-bye*.'

Will pulled the strap of the camera case over his head and hurled the camera down violently on to the stone floor of the kitchen. He bounded out of the door and up the stairs and slammed the front door after him. Adelaide dissolved into tears.

After a while she dried a glass which had been standing on the draining-board and went to the kitchen cupboard. She had been down to the Balloon Tavern that morning and bought herself a half bottle of gin. It helped a little bit.

She had not seen Danby. She had kept her bedroom door and the kitchen door resolutely shut and locked. She had heard him coming and going. Twice he had tapped on the door and called her name and she had not replied. She was beginning to need desperately to talk to him, but she could not bear to see that frightened pitying look upon his face again. She felt that before she saw him she should have something to confront him with, she should have made a plan and developed an attitude, but she had no plan and no attitude, only tears and total misery. She had been glad to see Will, but then of course they had quarrelled.

After sipping a mixture of gin and tears for a while she leaned forward and picked the camera up from the kitchen floor. Her body felt heavy and stiff and old. She wondered if the camera was broken. It must be. Yet when she shook it it didn't seem to rattle so perhaps it was all right. She hung it round her neck and shed a few more tears.

A little later she heard someone coming down the stairs. She had heard someone mount the stairs earlier in the afternoon and enter Bruno's room, and she had assumed that it was Nigel, though she had prudently told Will that Nigel was not there. She moved out to the foot of the stairs. Ought she to warn Nigel about Will?

Lisa Watkin passed through the hall and out of the front door. Without a moment's hesitation Adelaide dashed up after her.

She caught up with Lisa just as she was turning into Ashburnham Road.

'Miss Watkin – '

'Oh, hello.'

'Could I have a word with you?'

'Yes, surely. I do hope you don't mind my going straight up to Bruno? I didn't like to ring the bell in case he was asleep.'

'That's all right. Look, there's something I want to tell you.'

'Oh yes. About Bruno?'

'No. About Danby.'

'About – Danby?'

'Yes. You see I know all about you and Danby.'

Lisa slightly quickened her pace and her face put on a cold stiff slightly amused expression which enraged Adelaide. 'I am unaware that there is anything to know about me and Danby.'

'Don't give me that. You know he's been making advances. He wrote you a letter.'

'Really.'

'Or are you denying it?'

'I object to your rude and aggressive tone of voice.'

'Well, you'll just have to put up with it, won't you.'

'I have no intention of putting up with it. You seem to be under some sort of misapprehension. But I am certainly not going to discuss it with you.'

'You can put on airs, but I bet you're dying to know what I've got to tell you.'

'If you have something to say, say it.'

'There you are you see! Well, before you get going with Danby there's something about him you ought to know.'

'There is no question of my, as you put it, getting going with Danby. I scarcely know Danby.'

'I bet that's a bloody lie. Anyway, you keep away from Danby. Danby is my lover. We live together. We've been lovers for years.'

'I cannot think why you trouble to press this information on me. It's of no conceivable interest to me and it doesn't concern me. I can see you're upset and I'm sorry if I was rude to you just now. Now will you please go back. Bruno may be needing you.'

'I'm not your servant, madam. Do you believe me? If you don't believe me ask Danby, just *ask* him.'

'I have no plans for seeing Danby. You are upsetting yourself about nothing. I haven't the slightest intention of interfering with your arrangements. Now be kind enough not to trouble me any more with this nonsense. Good afternoon.'

They had reached the King's Road. Lisa darted quickly into

the traffic and crossed the road leaving Adelaide standing on the kerb. Adelaide stood for a moment, then slowly turned back. Then she paused and pulled off the camera, which had been bobbing round her neck, and hurled it down violently on to the pavement. This time all its inward parts came out and scattered themselves in the gutter. She left them lying there.

Chapter Twenty-one

It was Sunday. Miles was walking along the crowded pavement of the Fulham Road in the rain. With vague unfocused eyes he sidestepped his way through the oncoming crowds. His hair was plastered darkly to his uncovered head and the raindrops moved down his face like tears. He came to the discreet doorway of the Servite church and went mechanically through it. He needed somewhere to sit and think.

Miles had been to see Bruno. It had been all right. He had said that he was sorry and almost felt it. Bruno had told some rambling story about a stamp being lost and Danby finding it stuck underneath the stair carpet. None of the women had been mentioned. They had talked at random, darting from subject to subject in a way which Bruno seemed to find quite natural. They had talked about the house where they used to live in Fawcett Street and Miles had said it was all let out in flats now. They had talked about the printing works and about Miles's job and about the state of the economy. They had recalled a dog called Sambo who had been part of the family when Miles was a child. Miles had discussed whether Bruno would like to have a cat since he knew someone whose tabby had just had most attractive kittens, and Bruno had said no, he would get too damned attached to the cat and then it would be certain to run away or get run over. They had discussed the difference between cats and dogs. They had talked about spiders. It had all been quite easy. Bruno was quite rational and much more relaxed, and looked a good deal less appalling. No terrible memories had been stirred, only innocent and sad ones. Miles had not thought about Sambo in years. He came away, moved by the old man, and with a fresh and strangely pathetic sense of himself.

Now however he had already ceased to think about Bruno.

He went through the corridor into the cold inward light of the church. There was a plaintive urgent melancholy sound of chanting, but after he had stood for a moment just inside the door he made out that there was no service in progress. The singers must be the choir who were practising invisible to him in a side chapel at the far end. The body of the church was almost empty, though here and there between bunchy brown granite pillars he could see one or two people kneeling before the shrines which arched along the side walls in a series of rich shadowy caverns. The plain-song chant ceased, leaving an intense quietness behind it. Miles knew the place. He had come here in the past to meditate. He took off his dripping mackintosh and hung it over the back of the pew in front. He sat down and began to dry his face and hair with his handkerchief.

What on earth was he going to do about Lisa? She had avoided him on Saturday, leaving for work early and coming back late. He had managed to see her for a moment early this morning in the garden, when all she had said to him was, 'I've got to go away. Don't let it start, don't let it *start*.' But this was impossible, it had already started. On Saturday evening, after Lisa had resolutely planted herself in the drawing-room with Diana, he had withdrawn to his study. What had the women said to each other after his departure? Perhaps nothing. Before going to bed he had tried Lisa's door. It was locked.

He had not spoken of the matter to Diana either, after a very brief exchange which they had had after Miles came to bed in the early hours of Saturday morning. Diana had of course *seen* what had happened between him and Lisa. It must have been fairly obvious: those looks, those sighs, those shudderings, those significant almost-touches. She said, 'I knew it would happen one day.' Miles did not believe her. He did not believe the possibility had occurred to Diana for a single second. She said, 'She's much better for you than I am. You ought to go away together.' Miles said, 'Nonsense, Diana. I'm married to you. Now shut up.' They had lain rigid and sleepless side by side until the daylight came.

Miles had thought at first in these terms: as it is utterly impossible and inconceivable that I should part from either of them there is really no problem. The only question is how exactly to manage it, how to juggle it. There is no question about whether it should or can be managed. And fortunately the question of concealment does not even arise. This extremely simple and as it seemed to him radical way of seeing the problem persisted with him, together with sensations of mad joy, throughout most of Saturday. It had been almost a relief to be at the office, to perform neutral compulsory activities, and to think about Lisa dreamily and abstractly without considering any plan of action whatsoever. Saturday evening had been rather a trial, particularly the experience of leaving the two women behind together in the drawing-room, reading their books. No eyes had been raised to meet his as he lingered at the door. The light head and the dark head both remained resolutely bowed. After he had walked for about half a mile up and down the three pace extent of his study he had considered the possibility of creeping downstairs to see if they were talking about him, but the idea seemed too sickeningly nightmarish.

The nightmarish aspect of the whole situation had then begun to be a little more obvious. He had, he realized, thought about the problem so far simply in relation to himself, as if it were all somehow neatly enclosed within him. He had to decide how to deal with the two women and manage them both somehow: this part remained vague, but as there was evidently no alternative some arrangement would doubtless prove to be possible. He would *hold* the situation: this form of words which he had used to Lisa recurred to him together with an atmosphere of comfort; he would hold the situation together and not let it fall to pieces, and this holding would be an embrace which strongly enfolded both Lisa and Diana. Love would triumph.

But now he had just begun to see, and the glimpse of it made him grit his teeth together with pain and terror, the absolute awfulness of the situation for the other two. Diana loved him, deeply, completely, she was his wife, she had shared his bed for years. He had had so many conversations with her about Lisa, as if they had been Lisa's parents. They had talked with benevolent superior connivance about the failed nun, the broken-winged bird. They had worried about her together and speculated about her sex life and wondered if she were a

Lesbian and made all sorts of plans to protect and cherish her. How could Diana tolerate this sudden monstrous change in her sister's status? The sisters loved each other. What would happen now? And how could Lisa, with her rigid views of duty and her uncompromising life bear to become the instrument which should destroy her sister's marriage? Miles's vague vision of holding the situation had simply ignored both Diana's claims and Lisa's conscience. Oh how happy he had been before, he suddenly thought, living simply in the house with the two of them in a state of unconsciousness. Yet all that time Lisa must have been suffering.

There were certain impossibilities. He could not abandon Diana. Nor had he the faintest grain of inclination to abandon Diana. He loved and needed Diana, she had rescued him from desolation, she had been faithful to him and served him, he was bound to her by every tie of duty and indeed of deep marital love. The women were so different. He loved them both, but in different ways. Why was there not some dispensation for a situation which must be as common as this? However he had meant, and he still meant, what he had expressed to Lisa by saying, 'You are *the one*.' This was no blasphemy against Parvati. Parvati was twenty-three years old. Miles was fifty-five. Parvati would understand. It was simply true that Lisa fitted him, fitted into his soul, in a way that Diana did not. It was true, he realized with a terrible new pain, that if he had met Lisa first he would have married her.

Suppose he were to take lodgings for Lisa in another part of London? He could divide his week between them. It would seem odd at first, but they would all soon settle down to it and it would begin to seem natural. But as Miles started to imagine the details he saw that it was a perfectly abominable idea. He could not ask Diana, whose entire life consisted of caring for him, of waiting for him, to endure days of absence about which she would want to know nothing. And, even more strongly, he felt that it would be monstrous, if he were going to offer Lisa anything, to offer her less then everything. But this was exactly what he had decided at the start that he could not do. Terrible and unendurable possibilities began to structure themselves in the background of his mind. Unable to envisage them, Miles said frantically to himself, Suppose I just run off with Lisa after all?

Kyrie eleison, Kyrie eleison, Kyrie eleison. The choir were singing again. It was like a bird's cry, piercing, repetitive, insistent, wearying God with petition. Or perhaps more like a kind of work, a close attentive intricate laborious toiling. How happy are those who believe that they can pray and be helped, or even, without being helped, be listened to. If there really existed an all-wise intelligence before which he could lay the present tangle, even if that intelligence held its peace, the knowledge that the right solution somewhere existed would soothe the nerves. As it was, it was indeed the opposite conjecture, that in fact there was no solution, that it did not matter very much what one did, which produced the impulse to struggle and plunge about like a terrified horse whose cart has been overturned. A vision of chaos came suddenly to Miles: the blotting out of the ordinary world of ordinary obligations. Perhaps all ordinary obligations were fakes, and all meticulous lives based upon illusion?

Miles leaned forward, crossing his hands across his eyes. There came back to him not exactly as a memory but as a hallucination, the moment when he had received the news of Parvati's death. An acquaintance who had seen the newspaper account, with the names of the dead, had come round to his house. Miles had made the man go away at once. He had stood there alone in the hall holding the newspaper. He had believed it instantly. Hope would have been too great an agony. And as it seemed to Miles now, he had begun, even in those first seconds, to *plot* how to cheat himself of any full recognition of what had occurred. His excuse was indeed a convincing one: a full recognition might have destroyed his reason. He acted as other human beings act, only with a different and in some ways more refined apparatus. He began to write the poem within three days. He continued it for over a year. His pain went into it almost raw.

It certainly seemed strange, when Miles reflected about it, that throughout his life, so much of which now seemed to have slipped dully away, he had retained his deep conviction that he was a poet. He had published a volume of young man's poems just before Parvati died. He had continued to publish occasional poems in periodicals. There had been another small collected volume. His work was to be found in one or two anthologies. But he had always felt these to be weak preliminaries. His Duino visitation, his great angels were still to come. He had never lost this faith. Yet on the evidence it seemed so unlikely. He had become duller with the years, more pleasure-loving, less conscious. All those years with Diana, coming home on the tube to sherry and dinner and Diana's latest flower-arrangements. Even Lisa's coming had left him still blind. It was only lately, when he had started the *Notebook of Particulars,* that his vague faith had turned into a sharper hope, and had he perhaps even here misinterpreted what had happened? Was that sharper sense of life, that thrilled apprehension of being, not perhaps due rather to Lisa's presence in the house and his still sleeping awareness of being in love with her? Perhaps it was Lisa, not poetry, which would complete his destiny.

Kyrie eleison, Kyrie eleison, Kyrie eleison. Christe eleison, Christe eleison, Christe eleison. Can I not unriddle myself, thought Miles. Being in love, *l'amour fou,* is very like a spiritual condition. Plato thought any love was capable of leading us into the life of the spirit: perhaps because falling in love convinces so intensely of the reality and power of love itself, which dulled life knows nothing of. But falling in love involves also an enlivening and magnifying of the greedy passionate self. Such love will envisage suffering, absence, separation, pain, it will even exult in these: but what it cannot envisage is death, utter loss. This is the vision which it will on no account tolerate, which at all costs it will thrust away, transform and veil. Miles struggled in thought: he said to himself, the key is somewhere here, but where? Do these fragments really fit together? I scarcely make sense to myself at all, I babble, I rave.

As if yielding to a pressure upon his shoulders he slid forward on to his knees. He had knelt down occasionally in churches in recent years, always a little self-consciously, well aware of satisfying an emotional need which had more to do with sex than with virtue. But now he scarcely noticed what he had done. Eros and Thanatos: a false pair and a true pair. In transforming

Parvati's death into something which he could bear to contemplate, and in using for this purpose the one talent which he held as sacred, he had acted humanly, forgivably; yet it somehow seemed to him now that this almost inevitable crime had set his whole life moving in the wrong direction. Of course he had really loved Parvati, he had loved her with the total and as yet unspecialized passion of a young man. But such a love could not be expected to fight it out with death, and the defeat had mattered. Why did it all suddenly seem so alive and so close and so important now? Was he being given a second chance? I am raving, thought Miles, I am raving.

He knew, and knew it in fear and trembling, that good art comes out of courage, humility, virtue: and in the more discouraged moments of his long vigil he had felt his continued failure to be simply the relentlessly necessary result of his general mediocrity, his quiet well-bred worldliness and love of ease. There was a barrier to be surmounted which he could not surmount, and the barrier was a moral barrier. Was it still possible somehow to cleave his heart in twain and throw away the worser part of it? Miles knew that such a thing could never be simple, could scarcely be conceivable. A human being is a morass, a swamp, a jungle. It could only come from somewhere far beyond, as a dream, as a haunting vision, that image of the true love, the love that accepts death, the love that lives with death.

Lisa, he thought, Lisa. I cannot and I will not give you up. But how, oh how, was it all to be lived, and could that vision ever come to his aid, could it reach out into the final twisted extremity of his need? *Kyrie eleison, Kyrie eleison, Kyrie eleison.* Help me, help me, Miles prayed, pressing his hands desperately against his eyes. He did not feel at that moment that his cry was unheard. But he knew, with a deeper spasm of despair, that the deity to which he prayed was his own poetic angel, and that that angel was without power to help him now.

Chapter Twenty-two

Danby was walking down Kempsford Gardens. It was about ten o'clock on Sunday evening. The rain was pouring down, appearing suddenly in the lamplight, dense, sizzling, glittering like gramophone needles.

Danby walked in a state of abandon, his mackintosh unbuttoned, water soaking his hair and pouring down his neck. He had spent the day in a mounting frenzy, unable to eat, wanting to be sick and unable to be sick. He had been driven wild by missing Lisa's last visit and he could scarcely hear the old man speaking so placidly about her without groaning. He had posted her two more letters. He had not seen Adelaide, the thought of whom now inspired both guilt and fear. He had felt relief at tapping on her door in vain. He had written her a note saying that he hoped she felt better, and later found it torn into small pieces on the stairs. In fact on both Saturday and Sunday, since Lisa had told Bruno she would not come, he had been absent almost all day, leaving early and returning late, wandering aimlessly about and spending every possible moment in the pubs. He was by now thoroughly drunk.

Sitting in the Six Bells in the King's Road he had attempted to write a letter to Diana. He had written,

Dear Diana,
   You will think me crazy but I am in love with your sister. I can't explain this. It's something absolute. Please forgive me for having played about. It wasn't serious and it should not have happened. This other thing is serious. Forgive me and forget me.

                                                                    Danby

He stared at the letter for some time, making rings upon it with his glass. Then he tore it up. He could not write thus to Diana. It sounded too shabby. He could not ask her to forget

him, that was simply silly. Then something even more important occurred to him. Supposing Miles saw the letter? Miles
already thought ill enough of him without this further intimation of Danby's tendency to play about, and what is more to
do so with Miles's own wife. With any luck Miles might never
know about that episode. Miles doubtless regarded Lisa as his
sister, and would be just as opposed to Danby's suit in this
context as he had been in the earlier one, and for the same
reasons. And he's quite right too, thought Danby, he's quite
right; but I do love her and somehow that makes all the
difference.

Yet what was the difference? His love could hardly make
Danby more eligible, more presentable, more sober. How
could he ever make it plain that it had cured him of frivolity? If
only Lisa had not seen him kissing Diana! But in truth the letter
to Diana sounded shabby because the facts were shabby. In an
agony of humility Danby surveyed himself as he walked
through the windy rainy streets waiting for the evening pubs to
open. His impertinence in loving this girl was fantastic. He had
no attributes which could possibly interest her. He had remained absurdly vaguely confident of his ability to charm long
after even his more vulgar attractions had begun to fade. Because poor Adelaide had loved him he imagined that he could
obtain all women by crooking his finger. He was an obese elderly man with white hair and a face coarsened by drink. He was
ridiculous, he was pathetic, he stood no chance, his suit was
meaningless, and by not admitting instant defeat he would
merely prolong a useless agony.

Yet love has never for a second lent an ear to arguments of
this kind, and Danby's humility coexisted strangely with a lusty
confidence. Danby could not but feel himself, especially after
the evening pubs had been open for an hour or two, at the
beginning of a wonderful and hopeful adventure. This sense of
adventure, heightened by yet more drinks, had now led his feet
in the direction of Kempsford Gardens.

Danby stood in the rain swaying slightly while he checked
and rechecked the number of the house. There were no lights
on in the front. They could hardly have gone to bed. He was a
little vague about the time, but the pubs were still open so it

could not be very late. He went up the steps to the door and laid his hand upon it. Now that he was actually here fear and emotion sobered him a little. What in the world did he think he was doing? He stooped down and peered cautiously through the letter box. There was a line of light somewhere ahead from a closed-in lighted room. Danby straightened up and began to stroke the smooth painted surface of the door. He lifted his hand but could not bring himself to touch the knocker.

He thought, I think I won't try to talk to her after all. I'm too drunk. I would just disgust her, appearing like this. Besides, there's Miles and Diana. More deeply he thought: let her have a little more time to reflect about me. I'll wait until she has answered my letters. More deeply still he thought: as things are now I can still hope and imagine. If I see her she may kill hope. He turned away from the door. But the sense of her proximity arrested him magnetically like a jerked-upon rope. He would not talk to her. But he could not go away. He stood a moment in puzzlement. If only he could see her without being seen.

The houses in Kempsford Gardens formed a terrace with no gaps between. Danby began to retrace his steps towards the Old Brompton Road. There must be some way round the back. He walked down beside some garages and surveyed the back of the terrace, scattered with lighted windows, curving away into the flickering rainy dark. The walled gardens ran down to meet their opposite numbers in Eardley Crescent. There was no pathway, were no back gates. Danby gauged the height of the nearest wall. At the next moment he was on the top of it. As he felt just then he could have swarmed up the side of St Paul's. He slid rather muddily down, tramped across a dark garden and got himself up on to the next wall. He sat astride it for a moment. What was he supposed to be doing? Oh yes. But he ought to be counting the houses. He had lost count already. Somebody behind him opened a window and he fell down into some extremely thick and prickly foliage in the next garden. He pulled himself out, hearing his trousers ripping quietly. A long thorn seemed to be imbedded in the soft flesh of his thigh. He blundered clear and stood for a moment retrieving his sense of direction. Straight on, where an uncurtained window lighted a tract of green rain-beaten grass, another wall, or was it two walls, three walls.

An increasing amount of bricks and rubble seemed to be coming off the tops of the walls and weighing him down, lodged in his shoes and in his pockets. Stumbling forward his leg came into contact with something which as it keeled over and subsequently broke he recognized to be a leering red-capped gnome. That couldn't possibly be in Miles's garden. Where was he? Panting now a little he negotiated the next wall, taking off from a stout branch of wistaria which cracked loudly under him. He was suddenly feeling very weak and tired and the St Paul's sensation had quite gone. There was a throbbing pain in his left knee which he must have knocked rather badly without noticing it. He stood in the middle of the lawn, breathing deeply and trying by sundry jerks and wriggles to dislodge the thorn which still seemed to be piercing the inside of his thigh. Then in the dim light from the next door house he recognized the yew archway, the humpy mounds of small shrubs, and the gleaming expanse of wet pavement. The thorn came away.

The French window, outlined in light from within, was well curtained. Danby, who felt that up to a moment ago he must have been making a great deal of noise, moved forward as quietly as he could, stepping from the grass on to the pavement. The soles of his shoes seemed to stick to the wet pavement from which they detached themselves with a soft sucking sound. But the steady hissing of the rain absorbed the little noise. The two sides of the window showed no chink, but there seemed to be a tiny gap left in the middle where the curtains just failed to meet. Danby's questing hand touched the glass and he shuddered at its brittle feel and steadied himself on wide-apart legs. Leaning forward from the waist, his eyes trying to grow out of his head on stalks, he attempted to look through the gap. He took another cautious shuffle forward and now he could see into the room. It was a peaceful scene. Miles, Lisa and Diana were all curled up with books. Miles and Diana sat in armchairs on either side of the fireplace where a very small wood fire was burning. Lisa sat a little way back on the sofa, facing the window. Danby controlled his breathing and with a strong hand contained the acceleration of his already violently beating heart.

Miles, who had his back half turned to Danby, was raising his head from his book. He looked first at the bowed head of Diana and then at the bowed head of Lisa. As Diana began to raise her head Miles returned his attention to his book. Diana looked first at the bowed head of Miles and then at the bowed head of Lisa. As Lisa began to raise her head Diana returned her attention to her book. Lisa looked first at the bowed head of Diana and then at the bowed head of Miles. As Miles began to raise his head again Lisa returned her attention to her book. Profound silence reigned. Danby stared at Lisa. Her legs were half tucked under her and her heavy dark sweep of hair drooped down to brush the pages. She was wearing a sort of navy blue shift dress with a shirt collar and a green scarf tucked in at the neck. It occurred to Danby that it was the first time he had seen her without her brown mackintosh on. It was the first time he had seen one of her dresses. It was the first time he had seen the tension of her body inside her clothes, observed the silky sweep of her stockinged knees, contemplated her legs. She was wearing soft blue and green check bedroom slippers. Danby apprehended the curled weight of her body, the thrust of her breasts against the navy blue dress, the sleek stretched curve of the hip, the bony slimness of the ankle, and what it would be like to kneel down and very quietly take one of those soft-shod feet into his hand. He closed his eyes for a moment, When he opened them he realized that Diana was looking with a startled expression straight at the gap in the curtain.

Danby swung round and sidled quickly away from the window, trampling upon soft earth and springy wet vegetation. He stumbled back off the pavement on to grass, and with long quiet strides retreated down the garden. The yew hedge loomed up and he passed through the black space in the middle of it into the little enclosure between the hedge and the wall. He blundered through a heap of wet clinging stuff which might have been the remnants of a bonfire. Lighted windows of houses seemed to be all around him now, vague blank accusing eyes. A little diffused light showed him the wall, the outline of roofs and chimney pots and trees, the faint lines of the rain against the reddish-black London sky. He began to fumble at the wall. It seemed to have grown higher. He tried to pull himself up but his arms were as weak as putty and he fell violently back into the heap of sticky ash.

A figure materialized suddenly very close to him.

'Danby, is it you?'

'Diana!'

'Sssh. The others didn't see you.'

'Diana, I'm terribly sorry – '

'Whisper, don't shout! However did you get in here?'

'I came over the walls.'

'Well, you'd better go back over the walls!'

'Yes, of course, Diana. I was just trying to climb up when you arrived.'

'You are an absolute fool. You shouldn't come here at night like this.'

'Diana, I've been meaning to write to you – '

'Thank God Miles didn't see you. Now for God's sake go quietly. Can't you get up?'

'No, it's a bit difficult. The thing is this, Diana, I meant to write – '

'Don't *write*, you idiot. You can easily see me during the day. All you've got to do is telephone.'

'Diana, I want to *explain* – '

'I couldn't think what had happened to you. I thought you'd got cold feet, or something. And now this!'

'Diana, I *must* – '

'Are you drunk?'

'Yes.'

'Well, get out. Darling Danby, I'm not really cross with you. All right. You suddenly felt desperate. You felt you had to see me. I quite understand. Only now for heaven's sake go!'

'Diana, I – '

'I don't want any fuss, Danby. Just *go*.'

'All right. I just feel all weak. I can't get up the damn wall.'

'You'd better have something to stand on. There's a wooden box here somewhere. Wait a minute.'

'But how will I get out of the next door garden?'

'I don't care a damn how you get out of the next door garden. I want you out of this garden.'

'Would you mind if I took the box with me?'

'Oh *Danby*! Here –'

'Sssh. Diana, I thought I heard someone moving just over there.'

'There's no one. They didn't see me coming out. Could you help me with the box?'

Danby leaned forward. He could see the harlequin arm of the wet mackintosh close to his. The box seemed to be half embedded in the earth. It came away with a squelching sound and a rattle of stones.

'Sssh!'

Danby fumbled the box and placed it on end against the wall. He began to mount.

'Oh Danby, this is all so mad.'

'I'm afraid it's madder than you know, my dear.'

'Do be careful. Don't break your ankle, will you?'

'You're getting soaking wet, Diana. Better go in. I'm all right now.'

'Where's your hand?'

Danby stretched out his hand in the darkness and felt it gripped violently by Diana's two hands. He returned the pressure and drew quickly away.

A bright light suddenly flashed in the archway of the hedge and focused upon Danby, who was in the act of lifting his leg to the top of the wall. 'What on earth is going on here?' said Miles's voice.

Diana stepped quickly back. Danby withdrew his leg, but remained standing on the box. He covered his eyes which were dazzled by the beam.

'What is this farce?' said Miles. 'What the hell are you doing in my garden?'

Danby got down slowly off the box. 'Would you mind not shining that torch in my face?'

The torch was lowered, revealing lines of rain drops, a circle of ragged grass, and a scattering of earth and bonfire ash. Danby could now make out the figure of Miles, very upright underneath a large black umbrella.

'I'm sorry,' said Danby.

'You haven't answered my question,' said Miles. 'What are you doing here?'

'I just wanted to see – '

'You mean you were spying?'

'No. You see, I hadn't the nerve to knock on the door, so I got over the wall and – '

'Blasted bloody cheek, climbing on our wall, breaking down our roses!'

'And then Diana saw me and – '

'Where did Diana see you? What are you talking about?'

'He was looking in through the drawing-room window, through a chink in the curtain,' said Diana in a clear cool voice. She had retreated and was standing in darkness near to the other wall.

Miles swung the torch in her direction, revealing dark splashed stockings and muddy bedroom slippers.

'Why the hell didn't you tell me?'

'I wasn't sure who it was.'

'You mean you went out by yourself to tackle an intruder?'

'Well, I mean I really knew it was Danby, but – '

'Everyone around here seems to have gone stark staring mad.'

'If you'll excuse me,' said Danby, 'I think I really must be going.' He climbed up again on to the box.

'Oh no you don't. You'll stay here until I've told you a thing or two.'

'I don't feel in the mood for conversation,' said Danby. He began to lift his leg.

'You're drunk, aren't you?'

'Yes. Now I really must be getting along.'

'I know why you came here tonight.'

'Miles – ' said Diana.

Danby lowered his leg.

'Miles,' she said, 'I think it would be better if we talked – '

Danby stepped heavily down off the box. He said, 'Diana, don't say *anything*. Everything will be clear later.'

'Yes, Diana, go away would you?' said Miles. 'Go inside, please. And don't say anything to Lisa. I'll deal with this drunken lunatic.'

With a faint resigned gesture of farewell the harlequin mackintosh faded into the darkness.

The torchlight made a bright circle on the ground between them.

'I want to tell you something,' said Miles, 'and I hope that you'll have the decency to act upon it.'

'What?'

'You wanted to see her, didn't you?'

Danby tried to assemble his mind. Who was Miles talking about? 'Yes. No.'

'You're fuddled. I'm not surprised you were ashamed to knock on the door.'

'I didn't want to cause any trouble,' said Danby. 'Not any – trouble.'

'Don't worry, you can't. Though I admit your nuisance value is high.'

'What do you mean I can't?'

'Because you're going to get out and stay out.'

'I wonder if we quite understand each other?' said Danby. 'I wanted to see Lisa.'

'I know. But you're not going to. And you can stop pestering her with impertinent letters.'

'Christ! She didn't show you my letters, did she?'

'No. But she said you'd written to her more than once.'

'Well, why the hell not? It's not a crime to love somebody. And why are you taking a high line about it? It isn't quite your business is it? You aren't her father. You aren't even her brother. She's a grown-up woman. She's free.'

'She isn't free. That's the point.'

'What do you mean?'

'Her affections are engaged. She's a committed person. She loves somebody else.'

Danby leaned back against the wall. The rain beat on his face and trickled quietly down his spine, cold at first, becoming warmer as it reached the middle of his back.

'Are you sure?'

'Yes, I'm sure. I'm sorry to sound bloody minded, but you ought to know this. So perhaps from now on you'll keep away.'

Danby breathed deeply. He stared down at the lighted circle of soggy mauvish wood ash. 'Look, Miles, I hear what you say. But I'm in love. I mean I can't just take this from you – '

'In love!'

'Yes. Is Lisa actually engaged – ?'

'Lisa is no concern of yours. Even if she were not already attached – she could have no conceivable interest in you. Your attentions merely cause her embarrassment. I trust they will now cease.'

'I don't think you can order me about in this way, you know –'

'I know her mind on this subject. I am merely informing you of it. I presume this sort of drunken romping after girls is a pretty regular pastime for you. Well, you've made a mistake with Lisa. I suggest you move on to the next one.'

'I'm serious, damn you.'

'You're tedious. And now you can go. Get off my land. Go the way you came.'

The circle of light on the ground wavered, then darted upward and Danby covered his eyes against it. It sank again and was switched off, the outline of the umbrella was steady.

'Listen *please* – '

'There's nothing more to say. I'm going in, once I've seen you over the wall.'

'Damn it, I'm not going to have you telling me what Lisa thinks. I'll go on behaving as I think fit.'

'If you communicate with her any more you'll be behaving like a cad.'

'She doesn't need your protection! What's it got to do with you, for Christ's sake?'

'Miles, what is it?' A dark figure was silhouetted in the archway and then faded as it moved closer to Miles against the gloom of the hedge. The rain had begun to sizzle with increased force. Danby spread out his hands and pressed the palms back violently against the hard uneven surface of the wall.

'Lisa!'

'Who is there, who are you talking to?'

'Danby.'

'Oh. I thought I heard a noise.'

'I've told him to go. Go back inside, would you, Lisa.'

179

'Wait a minute.'

A flurry of rain filled the silence with a sort of long sigh.

'Miles, I'd like to speak to Danby for a moment. Could you leave us?'

'Lisa, don't be silly! He's drunk.'

'Please, Miles.'

'The fool might do anything.'

'No, no – '

'Well, come inside then. There's no point in getting soaked and talking in the dark.'

'No, here. You go, Miles. I won't be more than a moment. Please.'

'You'll get all wet. And I don't at all like leaving you.'

'Just one minute, Miles.'

'Oh, all right. I'll go back to the terrace. Call if you want me. Here, take the umbrella and the torch.'

'I don't want the umbrella and the torch. Just go, just for one minute.'

Miles walked heavily away through the archway, dipping the umbrella, and his feet could be heard stamping across the grass.

Danby let go of the wall and lurched forward. Then he half fell half threw himself on his knees in the wet sticky hillock of earth and ash. 'Oh Lisa, Lisa – '

'Get up please. Why did you come here?'

'I wanted to see you. I looked through the window. Oh Christ – '

'Are you very drunk?'

'No.'

'Get up then.'

'Lisa, I want to tell you it's serious, it's terrible, it's absolute.'

'I'm sorry – '

'Lisa, Miles said you loved somebody. He said you were engaged.'

'Oh God – '

'It's true then?'

'Yes, it's true,' she said, after a moment's silence.

Danby rose slowly to his feet. It was difficult to get up. His knee was extremely painful. He said in a dull voice, 'I shall hope all the same.'

'Don't. I just wanted to thank you for your letters. I am grateful to you. And God knows I don't want to hurt you. But please try not to think of me in that way. I have nothing for you and it's just no good. Please believe this. I don't want you to waste your time on something quite fruitless. It's absolutely no good.'

'Don't say any more,' he said, raising his voice, 'don't say any more. Forgive me.'

'Come through the house. There's no need to – '

Danby was already on top of the wall. How he got through the intervening gardens he could not afterwards remember. Perhaps he flew. Someone shouted after him. It was not Lisa. He fell off the last wall into the lane beside the garages, stumbling and falling. He blundered into a garage door and came down heavily on to the ground. He crawled, got up, emerged on to the wet lamp-lighted pavement.

He stood for a while in the rainy murk between two lamp posts, vague and dazed, swaying a little on his feet and looking back down Kempsford Gardens. Then he set off slowly in the direction of the Old Brompton Road. He paused once more and looked back. Then he began to look more intently. A dark figure had emerged after him from the side laneway and was now gliding away quietly in the opposite direction towards Warwick Road. Danby stared hard through the lines of rain. There was something familiar about the slim form and the gliding gait.

Danby started to walk quickly back. The figure quickened its pace. Danby began to run. The figure ran. Danby ran harder. He caught it up just short of Warwick Road underneath a lamp post and grabbed it firmly by the collar.

'Nigel!'

Nigel twisted and struggled and squirmed but Danby held him fast. 'Nigel, you swine, you spy! You were there in that garden!'

'You're choking me, let go!'

'Were you there in that garden?'

'Yes, yes, stop it, stop it – '

'You heard it all!'

'You're killing me.'

'You bloody spy!'

'Please, please, please –'

Danby shook the limp and now unresisting figure violently to and fro and then hurled it away from him. Nigel staggered, slithered on the wet slippery pavement, and fell, the side of his head meeting the lamp post with an audible crack. He lay still. Danby, who had started to walk away, paused a moment until he had seen Nigel stir and begin to get up. Danby turned again and faced the force of the rain and the wind, walking unsteadily in the middle of the road.

Chapter Twenty-three

Nigel was kneeling beside his twin brother's bed. Will was sleeping heavily. Soft rain was running quietly, ceaselessly down the glass of the skylight. A very faint illumination from the lamp-lighted street showed the old brass-railed bedstead and Will's large round face, flushed and swollen with sleep, a weight upon the pillow, the moustached upper lip twitching slightly.

The tossed bedclothes also revealed an outflung right arm clad in purple and white spotted pyjama, a hand drooping over the edge of the bed, and a large plump left foot peeping out of another expanse of purple and white pyjama. Nigel, armed with a length of rope, two thick bands of perforated rubber, and a smooth stick about twenty inches long, carefully contemplated the position of the hand and the foot.

He decided to start with the foot. He laid the stick and one end of the rope silently down upon the floor and approached the other extremity of the rope to the well-padded and rather fragrant sole of his brother's foot which seemed to be regarding him with an insolent expression. The rope ended in a slip-knot with the perforated band of rubber threaded on to the rope within the area of the knot. Nigel began very gingerly to draw the slip-knot over the insolent protruding foot without bringing it into contact with the sole. As the band of rubber descended on to the sheet it very lightly touched the roughened edge of the heel and Nigel quickly looked round. A faint smile appeared on Will's face, but he continued to sleep, now uttering very light snores like little sipping noises. He shifted slightly, moving his legs, and as he did so Nigel, holding the upper side of the noose clear with his left hand, thrust his right hand deep into the mattress and drew the slip knot loosely up over Will's ankle. He laid the upper part of the noose very lightly down across the pyjamaed leg, observing Will's face again, which continued to smile a little and twitch in between the snores.

Rising very quietly from his kneeling position Nigel now lifted the other end of the rope from the floor, and after contemplating the brass rails at the foot of the bed for a moment or two, led the free end of the rope between the rails close to the slumbering foot, out again two rails further back, and round the brass bed post on the far side of the bed. Holding the end of the rope bunched and high, he sidestepped noiselessly to the head of the bed and slid the second slip knot with its perforated rubber bracelet through the head rails of the bed, past two rails, and out again round the brass bed post on the near side of the bed. The wrist, which was dangling free, presented fewer difficulties. Holding the centre portion of the rope well up with his left hand, Nigel caught the wrist in the swinging slip knot and ventured to pull the knot tighter until it was touching the pyjama cuff very lightly all round.

The machine was now almost complete. Nigel slung the loose centre of the rope over his shoulder and attended once more to the foot, tightening the knot very carefully just above the bone of the ankle. He adjusted the rope at the head and foot of the bed, pulling it down the rails towards the mattress, and then stood back, drawing the middle of the rope steadily towards him. He picked up the stick and laid it against the rope and began quietly and deliberately to shorten the rope by twisting it about the stick.

Will woke up with a flurry and an exclamation. Nigel retreated, pulling hard on the rope and twisting faster. The slip knots tightened, the rubber bracelets clung, and Will's wrist and ankle were drawn up taut against the rails at the head and foot of the bed. Will yelled.

'Sssh, Will, you'll wake Auntie.'

'Damn you, you've done it again!'

'It's more ingenious this time,' said Nigel. 'I doubt if you will be able to get out.'

'You bastard!'

'The rubber is the essential thing. I ought to have thought of it earlier.'

'Loosen the rope, for Christ's sake, you're breaking my wrist.'

'I doubt that. Excuse me while I just manoeuvre this chair.'
Keeping the rope taut with one hand, Nigel reached the other
for a wooden upright chair which stood against the wall. Leaning over he threaded the stick through, twisting it so that it was
held braced against the two wooden rails under the seat of the
chair. He sat down on the chair.

'Nigel, loosen it a bit, fuck you, the bloody rail is cutting into
my wrist, it'll open a vein.'

'I remember hearing a story like this once before. I shouldn't
struggle if I were you, it'll only make things worse.'

Will, stretched out between the head and the foot of the bed,
had contorted his body, his left hand struggling to curl round
the brass rails to reach his captive right wrist. The fingers
clawed without force at the tightened surface of the rubber
bracelet.

'This damn thing will stop my circulation. Do you want to
kill me?'

'Not quite. Stop struggling, Will, you'll feel better.'

'Loosen the rope, you're pulling me apart.'

'Say please.'

'Please, bugger you.'

Nigel moved the chair a fraction forward.

'That's not enough.'

'Lie still and relax your muscles and listen to me.'

'How can I listen when I'm in the most frightful pain?'

'You're not in the most frightful pain. The pain is negligible.
Listen to me.'

'Go to hell.'

'If you get treated like this it's your own fault for being so
violent. That's something which you would have understood
long ago if you had been capable of thinking. Of course violent
men get put into cages and stretched on racks by men who are
less violent but more clever. It's the only way to make them
listen.'

'I'll never listen to you, not if I have to scream for an hour.
Loosen the rope, my ankle's breaking.'

'No, it isn't. You *have* listened, Will. The violent men do
listen in the end, because it's to their advantage. You remember
that time when we were ten and I hung you up by your wrists

185

from the scaffolding on the building site because you wouldn't do what I wanted?'

'Yes, and I remember what I did to you after you let me down!'

'All right, but you also did what I wanted.'

'And damn stupid it was too. You always were a crazy pervert.'

'You see, you've quite forgotten that you're supposed to be in pain.'

'I haven't. You'll kill me one day with one of your damn contraptions. I can feel my wrist bleeding. Could you look?'

'You can't catch me that way, Will. If you don't mind I think I'll turn the light on. You're an interesting sight.'

Nigel tilted his chair slightly and turned the electric light switch. An unshaded electric bulb above the bed revealed Will outstretched and twisted between his pinioned wrist and his pinioned ankle. The unbuttoned pyjamas showed his braced polished chest with a runnel of jet black curls running down the centre of it. Will jerked again, clawing at his caught wrist with his free hand. Then he lay still panting, eyes bulging, his flushed face turned full to Nigel, his gritted teeth flashing under his moustache. 'You've tightened the rope again, damn you.'

'A little, possibly. There.'

'If you play this trick once more I'll kill you.'

'No, no. Last time I admit was a little inefficient, but the damage you did to yourself getting out was entirely your own fault. If you'd just stayed still and heard what I wanted to say you'd have been quite unhurt.'

'You ought to be in a bin.'

'Don't be silly. Ever since I was a child you've been using your fists upon me. My cleverness and ingenuity just make us quits. I wanted to tell you something important, entirely for your own advantage I may say, and as I knew you'd rush at me like a mad bull if I turned up without taking precautions I decided I must tie you up just once again.'

'You enjoy this sort of thing.'

'Perhaps I do, Will. You must just try to see it as a form of brotherly affection.'

'Christ!'

'Blood's thicker than water, Will, especially twin blood. You are the other half of myself, a weird brutish alien half, doubtless a lesser half, but connected to me by an ectoplasmic necessity for which love would be too weak a name.'

'You've always detested me, Nigel.'

'I am afraid you are very stupid and understand very little.'

'You peached on me about that bloody stamp.'

'A routine castigation, my dear Will. I have to set some limits to your misdoings.'

'You've always persecuted me.'

'In self defence. And also a little because you need me. You need me as the brute needs the angel, as the tender back needs the whip and the suppliant neck the axe. Any juxtaposition of brutish material and spirit involves suffering.'

Nigel shunted the chair an inch backward and Will screamed.

'Stop it, Nigel, stop it, I'll faint with pain!'

'Nonsense. There, is that better. Now will you stop twisting yourself about and attend to what I have to say.'

'Who's been punching you? I'm glad to see somebody has.'

One side of Nigel's face was severely bruised, the bluish shadow turning to purple as it ringed the eye.

'Danby.'

'Danby? Why ever Danby? Not that I care. I'll black the other eye for you when I get out of this.'

'Never mind. Listen, Will. Are you listening or do you want to be strung up any tighter?'

'I'm listening, bugger you, get on with it. Loosen the bloody rope a bit more, will you.'

'Please.'

'Please.'

'All right. Now listen. It's about Adelaide.'

'About Adelaide? What about Adelaide?'

'You love Adelaide, don't you?'

'If I do it's no bloody business of yours. I know you've been after her. You tried to get hold of her when you came back to London.'

'No, I didn't.'

'You keep away from Adelaide, or I'll really do you. That

187

girl belongs to me and I'll have her. I'll get her if I have to kill her in the process. What's more she loves me.'

'So you imagine. But suppose there was somebody else?'

'How do you mean, somebody else? No one could possibly be after Ad, she doesn't see anybody, she doesn't go anywhere.'

'She doesn't need to. It all happens at home.'

'What on earth do you mean? Christ, do you mean you –'

'No. Danby.'

'What do you mean, Danby? Don't torture me!'

'Danby is Adelaide's lover. Adelaide is Danby's mistress. It's been going on for years. I thought you ought to know.'

Will lay still, breathing deeply. Then he said quite quietly, 'Nigel, let go of the rope. I promise and swear that I won't hurt you.'

Nigel got up and drew the stick out between the rungs of the chair. He unwound the rope and the tension was loosened. Will turned stiffly and began to sit up on the bed. He groaned and began to pull at the tightened rubber manacle at his wrist. Nigel helped him to pull it off, and then loosened the anklet. Will, groaning softly, chafed the bruised flesh at wrist and ankle. He said, 'I don't believe you, Nigel.'

'It's true.'

'Prove it.'

'Ask Adelaide. Meanwhile take a look at this. You know Danby's writing.'

Nigel handed Will a small piece of paper which had been torn across several ways and put together again with adhesive tape. The paper said, *Sweet Adelaide, I think I'll spend tonight in my bed and not in yours, as I'll be in rather late. Sleep tight, little one. Your D.*

Will studied the paper carefully. Then he uttered a long piercing shriek and turned and fell with his face into the pillow.

'Sssh, don't make such a noise –'

Will sat up again, his face contorted, his jaw shuddering, grinning with pain and rage. 'I'll kill that man. I'll kill her too.'

'Don't be crazy, Will –'

'I'll kill them. Years, you say. Years. And her stringing me along all that time and swearing there was nobody else and letting me give her presents and kiss her hands.'

'Yes, I know, but listen to me still –'

'And saying she wasn't the marrying sort! Well, she's not, she's a bloody harlot! And I laid my life at her feet. I'll cut her into ribbons. And I'll kill him. I'll go now and find them in their bed. *Sweet Adelaide!* Oh Christ, I'll die of this. Where are my clothes?'

'Stop, Will, stop and *listen*. I've hidden your clothes anyway, you won't find them. Just listen to me –'

'Then I'll go naked. Get out of my way, Nigel. You've driven me mad.'

'The door's locked. Sit down, *sit down*.'

Will let go of the door handle which he had been rattling. He stood rigid for a moment, his eyes rolling, and then collapsed back full length on to the bed with a moan, burying his face in his hands. 'Oh Adelaide, Adelaide, I loved you, I loved you so.'

Nigel drew the chair up close. He caressed the mop of shaggy dark hair and the shoulders which were shuddering with dry sobs.

'Stop it, Will. You can't do anything tonight. You've got to think it over. You know the truth now, and that gives you power over both of them. Think it out. And don't try to hurt Adelaide. Leave her to heaven and to those thorns that in her bosom lodge to prick and sting her. As for Danby, we'll think of some way of punishing him. I'll help you. We'll do it together.'

Will had stopped sobbing and was sitting up, once more twisting and chafing his right wrist. His eyes were dull and vacant with misery, his mouth half open, dripping saliva. 'To think that she –'

'Even she. I didn't really cut your wrist, did I?'

'After our being children together and all. I thought – It's like being betrayed by one's mother.'

'Every man is betrayed by his mother.'

'I trusted her absolutely. I thought she had no other life. For years, you say. With that fat swine. I'll carve him. And she

189

loved me so much when she was a girl. And so pretty. And so innocent. We were happy then.'

'The three of us.'

'The three of us. We used to go about arm in arm, remember.'

'With her in the middle.'

'And have tugs of war going round lamp posts.'

'You always won.'

'Do you remember the day when we told her about sex?'

'And she wouldn't believe us!'

'God! It's all so clear, so near.'

'And the building site and the waste land where we used to pick dandelions.'

'And climbing on the scaffolding.'

'And stealing the bricks.'

'And playing French and English.'

'And Grandmother's Steps.'

'She belonged to the beginning of our life when everything was good.'

'Before we ran away.'

'Before the theatre.'

'Before all those awful things – you know.'

'I know. She was separate from all that. I felt she'd kept the early part somehow, kept our childhood, kept it for me.'

'Kept it all fresh, all pure.'

'Are you laughing at me, Nigel?'

'No, no. Come, you promised – '

'Did Adelaide go to see you, go to your place, after you came back to London?'

'No.'

'She was very funny about you then. I thought you were after her.'

'No, indeed.'

'Well, what's your motive for telling me all this? What's in it for you? You love her and you're trying to come between us!'

'No!'

'You can't have her and you don't want me to.'

'No, I swear.'

190

'Well, why then? Is it just craziness? Or wanting to hurt me? Or wanting to hurt Danby?'

'Just craziness.'

'You hate Danby. You've got some sort of grudge against him. Is that it? What made him hit you, anyway?'

'No, Will, that isn't it, that isn't it at all.'

The increasing rain tapped on the dark skylight and ran down it in a steady stream. The brothers stared into each other's eyes, sitting close together in the brightly lighted attic room with their knees touching.

Chapter Twenty-four

The whiskey bottle was nearly empty.

Danby was sitting on his bed with his face in his hands. Adelaide was sitting on the floor with her back against the chest of drawers. Her face was swollen up and her eyes practically closed with crying. Her mouth, through which she was breathing heavily, hung open. Every now and then she shuddered and another two large tears came out of the slits of her eyes. She was wearing a blouse over her petticoat but no skirt.

The window curtains were half drawn. It was nine o'clock on the following evening and already dark outside. It was raining violently, abandonedly. A strong gusty wind was driving the rain almost horizontally, bringing it in sharp pattering flurries up against the window, like the crack of handfuls of small pebbles hurled against the glass.

A distant voice was calling. 'Danby!'

Danby groaned and rubbed his face deeper into his hands.

'*Danby!*'

Danby got up and without looking at Adelaide stepped over her outstretched legs and began to go up the stairs. He felt stiff and aching and bruised all over.

'DANBY!'

Danby pushed open the door of Bruno's room and looked in, frowning against the light and peering at Bruno from underneath his hand. The lamp illuminated the comfortless untidy bed which had been twisted and turned in all day.

'Danby, what's the matter?'

'Nothing's the matter. What do you want?'

'Why are you looking at me like that?'

'Like what?'

'As if you can't see me properly.'

'I'm drunk. What do you want?'

'Where's Nigel?'

'I don't know.'

'He hasn't been here all day. And he wasn't here last night.'

'It doesn't matter. Go to sleep, Bruno.'

'It's too early to go to sleep. And I haven't had any tea. I called and called and nobody came.'

'I'll make you some tea.'

'Danby, don't go away, please, shut the door. You will forgive Nigel, won't you, you won't be cross with him?'

'I expect Nigel's cleared off.'

'Nigel? He *can't* have done. He *can't* have, have left me – ' Bruno's voice quavered upward. He was lying low down in his rumpled bed, only the big head and one claw-like hand visible above the bedclothes. Danby frowned at him over the hump of the foot cage. He seemed to be a long way off.

'I'll get the tea now. Want anything with it?'

'Don't go Danby. The rain is so awful and the wind. I thought I heard somebody screaming downstairs a little while ago.'

'I expect you did.'

'What was it?'

'Adelaide screaming with laughter. Want any toast or anything? I'll bring up the *Evening Standard*.'

'What's that girl's name?'

'What's what girl's name?'

'That girl who comes. I mean Miles's – '

'Lisa.'

'She didn't come today.'

'Oh forget that girl, Bruno.'

'What do you mean, forget her?'

'It doesn't matter any more.'

'What do you mean it doesn't matter any more? What has the doctor been telling you, has he rung you up?'

'No, of course not.'

'He's told you I'm done for and you've sacked Nigel and told the girl not to come – '

'Oh stop it, Bruno, the doctor hasn't said anything.'

'Of course it doesn't matter any more if I'm going to be dead – '

'Bruno, shut up. You're raving. I'll get you some tea.'

'I don't want any tea.'

'Well, go to sleep then. I'll turn the light out.'

'I can't sleep with that noise, with the wind rattling the window. Is it rain or hail?'

'Rain. It just sounds like hail.'

'Danby, don't go away. Sit with the old man for a little bit. I've been alone all day. You just threw that tray at me at lunch time.'

'Sorry.'

'Sit beside me, please, Danby, please.'

'I can't. I'm drunk.'

'Please – '

'Do you want the light on or off?'

With difficulty Danby focused his eyes upon the head lolling on the pillow, the bearded chin dug deep into the sheets, the shrunken form which scarcely lifted the blankets to reveal its presence, the brown gaunt hand pawing a little in supplication.

'Will you make my bed, Danby? Do my pillows anyway.'

Danby strode across the room, punched the pillows perfunctorily and went back to the door. 'Do you want the light on or off?'

'Danby, I'm frightened, don't go.'

Danby saw that tears were beginning to run down Bruno's face, finding their way across the reddened creases and bulges underneath his eyes.

'Oh go to sleep Bruno, will you.' Danby switched the light off and closed the door. He stopped at the top of the stairs to listen but there was no more sound from the old man's room. He went down the further flight of stairs and reached his own room. Adelaide had not moved.

Danby reached for the bottle and poured the rest of the whiskey into his glass. He sat down heavily. 'Better go to bed, Adelaide.' The rain hurtled across the windows in a series of cracks like bursts of machine gun fire. The wind howled, rose to a scream, then howled again.

'I love you, I love you, I love you.'

'Oh stop it, Adelaide, there's a good girl.'

'Did you ever think of marrying me, did you ever *think* of it for a single second?'

'I don't know. Do stop it, will you, I've had enough.'

'You knew it couldn't last. You just amused yourself with me. You just took me on till something better turned up, something serious, something in your own class.'

'Class has nothing to do with it.'

'Hasn't it? Then why do you feel you can treat me like dirt, walk out just the way you walked in?'

'You were glad enough when I walked in.'

'That's a bloody rotten thing to say.'

'OK. Agreed. Now let's stop talking.'

'You never thought our thing was real.'

'Yes I did, Adelaide. I just didn't know this would happen, I didn't think.'

'You didn't think! Of course you didn't think! You just took what you wanted.'

'If it's any satisfaction to you I know I'm an absolute bastard.'

'Well, I hope you'll be happy with her, after destroying me and taking all my life away from me.'

'I've already told you she isn't interested in me, she's got somebody else, she doesn't want me, she's told me to clear out.'

'I don't believe a word of it. You're saying this to put me off. And tomorrow you'll give me the sack.'

'Don't be silly, Adelaide. Don't start all that again.'

'I'm not being silly. I'm a servant. I'm your servant. Have you forgotten? I'm your paid employee.'

'You've said all this before.'

'And I was glad to be your servant, *glad*.'

'Oh go to bed, for Christ's sake.'

'To think how I worshipped you! You'll never know how I worshipped you.'

'Well, more fool you.'

'You took my love, you were glad enough to have it, and now you just call me a fool!'

'I'm sorry, I didn't mean – '

'Anyway, I told her, I *told* her.'

'What on earth are you talking about?'

'I told that stuck-up bitch about you and me. You didn't know that, did you? I told her we were lovers. I told her we'd been lovers for years. I told her to bloody well keep off.'

'Oh Christ.' Danby got up. He stood hunched, staring at the empty whiskey bottle. 'When was that?'

'Last week.'

'What did she say?'

'She pretended not to care.'

'Adelaide, I'm sorry you did that.'

'I'm glad you're sorry.'

'Not that she could think any worse of me – Well, she could – Anyway it doesn't matter.'

'You just kept mum about little me, didn't you? Thought you could tidy me away, sweep me under the carpet – '

'Oh never mind, never mind. It doesn't matter. Nothing matters.'

'I loved you so much – '

'Don't start crying again, I can't stand it.'

'I loved you so much and I was so happy – so happy – ' Adelaide choked in sobs.

'Go to bed – or else I'm going out – '

'I'll kill myself. I can't go on existing now. I'll kill myself – ' Danby made for the door.

Suddenly there was a different sound at the window. The rattling spatter of the rain had been resolved into a steadier and more insistent tapping. Danby stood rigid. Adelaide stopped crying. The tapping came again, louder, purposive, menacing against the wailing background of the wind. Adelaide and Danby stared at each other and then at the window. Between the half drawn curtains the space was blank, quartered with reflections. Danby strode across and dragged back the curtain, leaning forward and peering. A hand was clearly visible, pressed against the glass from without. Adelaide screamed. Danby could now see a bulky figure standing directly opposite to him in the darkness outside. The next moment there was a sound of shattering glass and Danby leapt back as the fragments of the glass pane came showering after him into the room.

Danby spun round, jumped over Adelaide's legs, and ran up the stairs two at a time. He threw open the front door. Through the swaying curtain of the driven rain he saw a hurrying figure just reaching the corner of the road and disappearing. Danby stood for a moment on the verge of the rain, with the wet wind blowing into his face and his heart beating hard. Then as he began to close the door he saw that he was standing upon an envelope. He picked it up and went slowly back down the stairs.

Adelaide had risen. She stood clutching her blouse against her throat. The cold air was blowing in through the big jagged hole in the window pane. 'Who was it?'

'I don't know. Whoever it was he probably left this note. It's addressed to me.' Danby ripped it open. It read as follows.

I know about your life with Adelaide. She was mine but I discard her as trash. You may keep her. Just tell the hell-bitch to stay out of my way if she wants to keep her looks. You I shall punish in my own fashion. I challenge you to a duel. The weapons will be pistols. You may select the place. If you refuse this challenge I will brand you as a coward, I will publish your degrading liaison with your servant, I will persecute you at your home and at your place of work in every way that I can devise, until I have made your life a misery. If you accept the challenge I will do my best either to kill you or to maim you.

Will Boase

Danby read this curious missive with raised eyebrows. Then he handed it to Adelaide.

Adelaide looked at it. It fell from her hands to the floor. She crushed her fingers into her mouth to stifle the issuing cry. Then her voice came bubbling forth. 'I've lost him, I've lost him, I've lost him, the only man who ever really loved me!'

Chapter Twenty-five

Lisa stood in the door of the drawing-room dressed in her brown mackintosh with the collar turned up. A large tartan suitcase stood on the floor beside her. A sunny rainy light filled the room with a peculiar brightness. Miles was standing by the window.

'Close the door, Lisa.'

Lisa made an interrogative gesture, pointing behind her into the hall.

'She's upstairs,' said Miles. 'Anyway she doesn't suppose you'll leave the house without seeing me!'

'I don't want to add anything – anything – '

'To her pain? It makes no difference. What about our pain?'

'It's better not to talk,' said Lisa. She closed the door.

'But we have talked. It was essential.'

'Maybe. But one of the good things is that we haven't talked more than was essential.'

'You treat this thing – surgically.'

'It's the only way.'

'It may be the right way. I'm not even sure about that. It's certainly not the only way. It's unnatural.'

'What is right is often unnatural.'

'God, you chill my blood, Lisa.'

'I know. I love you, Miles.' She uttered the words coldly.

'I love you. I love you terribly. I'll love you always to the very end of my life. I shall think about you all the time.'

'Not all the time, Miles.'

'And if you imagine this is the end of the story you're bloody mistaken. You can't dispose of a thing of this size in this cool way.'

'I don't feel cool, Miles. Now I am going to call Diana.'

'No, no, no, not yet.'

Miles crossed the room to the door. As he reached the door Lisa moved back into the room. They faced each other.

'Lisa, take off your coat.'

'No.'

'It's not too late to decide something else. It will never be too late and it certainly isn't too late now.'

'No talk,' she said, 'no talk. The more we talk the more agony it will be later. And we know that we have no other course of action at all.'

'We've discussed it so little.'

'You know what discussion is like in a case like this.'

'Oh Lisa – we're acting like mad things.'

'*See* it's hopeless, Miles, *see* it. Before you loved me, all right before you knew you loved me, it was possible for me to live here. It was painful, but it was good too. It was a manageable life. But now it would be torture to me, and torture to Diana. And you know you can't leave Diana. Anyway you love her. And you can't run us in two houses. I wouldn't tolerate it even if you and Diana would. Just *see* it, see the pattern, see the machine. You can't struggle against necessity.'

'Is there nothing else, nothing we haven't thought of?'

'Nothing.'

'I could leave Diana. We haven't really considered – '

'You couldn't. Miles, this is just the sort of talk we mustn't have. We've got to go on functioning as people and we *can*. No ones dies of love. It's all crazy and inflated now. But we'll feel better in six months' time, though people in love hate to admit this.'

'I won't feel better in six months' time, Lisa. I don't think you realize how important this is for both of us. It's something I've waited for all my life.'

'I have realized it, Miles. You know how much I love you. And I've waited too. I've lived for years with this love. I didn't know it would end like this. Though even if I had known I would still have loved and waited. But we can't run a course straight into ruin, ruin of Diana, ruin of you, ruin of me. How could we live together, abandoning her? Could you write poetry, could I go on doing any of the things that I do for people, if we were living with an action like that?'

'You say we exaggerate things. Perhaps we exaggerate this thing about Diana. Perhaps she'd be all right, better off – '

'You're married to Diana, she's given you her life. It's not just a calculation.'

'Oh God, I know it's not just a calculation – '

'You see the case for me now. If we went away together you'd see the case for Diana.'

'It's that I can't face it, Lisa, now it's come. I didn't believe it before, that was why I allowed you to argue in that way, saying it was all inevitable. Now that there's something quite unendurable to endure I just know that the argument must be wrong. There *must* be an alternative. I feel you just can't be going away, all that terrible long way away – '

'Believe it, Miles, believe it. Look, here is my aeroplane ticket. London – Calcutta.'

Lisa opened her bag and took out the red aeroplane ticket. She displayed it, holding it up with her two hands.

'When?'

'It's better you don't know. Miles, I love you desperately, I love you more in this moment than ever before. I could faint with it. I love you so much now when I can see that you are beginning to believe that I am going. We must keep this love uncontaminated even if we *kill* it. Don't you see?'

'Love and death. It doesn't seem very romantic to me, Lisa.'

'It's not romantic, Miles. This is real death. *We shall forget each other.*'

'No, no, no. You are sacrificing – for Diana and me – too much – '

'I am not sacrificing anything for Diana and you. I make the sacrifice to my own love. I can't, with so much love, do anything else.'

'You mean accept any compromise?'

'Accept *any* compromise. The only thing is the impossible thing – if I had only met you before – '

'Oh God, oh God, before, first – Why is it impossible, it can't be impossible – '

'I won't be here any more.'

'We shall meet again.'

'We shall not meet again.'

'You're going to Parvati's country.'

'I've always wanted to.'

'And there really is this job?'

'Yes. I fixed it all up with the Save the Children Fund people. I'll be at their office in Calcutta and then somewhere out in the country. I shall have to learn Hindi. I shall be terribly busy.'

'I shall not be busy. I shall be here with grief. I shall be yearning for you.'

'You will be writing poetry. Oh believe it, Miles, see it, accept it.'

'I can't. It wouldn't change me, Lisa. I just feel completely crippled by this.'

'You have gods, Miles. They may reward you.'

'They don't give rewards for this kind of thing.'

'You can't know that.'

'Will you write to me?'

'No.'

Miles stretched out his hand towards her, drew his fingers along the mackintosh sleeve to the warmth of her wrist. Then quite slowly he took her in his arms. She stood limp in his embrace, only inclining her head on to his shoulder. She said into his coat, 'It was my fault, Miles, for coming here at all. I ought never to have come. There are secrets that can't be kept.'

'I love you. It wasn't just your secret.'

'I infected you with love.'

'It's not leprosy. Oh Lisa, this won't get less. Have some mercy – ' He began to kiss her brow and her cheeks.

She pulled gently away. 'We shouldn't have had this conversation, Miles. You will try to help Diana, won't you. This will be your task so you won't be idle. You'll have to help her positively. She has her pain which is different from ours. Only I mustn't speak of that.'

'Lisa, don't talk in that awful tone as if you were condemning us to death.'

'Now I really must go. I'll call Di.'

'No, no, no, not yet, please – Oh Lisa, there must be more to say – we haven't arranged anything – I don't know where you'll be – we'll meet again in a few days, when we've had time to think things over. I *can't* just let you *go*.'

Lisa opened the door and called 'Diana.'

Diana came slowly down the stairs. She was carefully, even smartly, dressed in blue tweed. She was wearing earrings. She had been crying.

'I'm just going, Di. Don't be cross with me. And don't forget to go and see Bruno.'

'Bruno, also, wants you, not me,' said Diana in a strained voice, staring at her sister.

'He'll soon want you. Just hold his hand and stroke him, I mean really stroke him – '

'All right, all right.'

'Di, will you just walk with me as far as the station? No, Miles, don't you come. Di will just see me to the station. Get your mac, darling, it's still raining a bit.'

Lisa went across the hall and Diana followed her slowly without looking at Miles. He stood in the doorway and watched them. The hall door was opened revealing the street full of blue rainy light.

'Good-bye, Miles.'

The door closed. They were gone. Miles returned to the drawing-room and sat down.

He thought, it's not final. Now I've simply got to *think*. Hope stirred in him, lessening the pain. He looked out through the window into the soaking garden where a little rain was falling through the bright air. She would not say where she was staying, but he could find out. Perhaps Diana knew. Anyway he could always fly to Calcutta. She was not really dying, she was not really going away for ever. No, no, no, he thought to himself, I will not accept Lisa's sentence of death.

Chapter Twenty-six

Bruno was asleep. His huge head, made even larger by the ragged unclipped beard, lolled uncomfortably sideways, his mouth open, a moist lower lip showing amid the dull grey growth. He drew his breath in and out with a long shuddering sigh. His dark spotted hands with their swollen knuckles trembled and clutched a little on the yellowish white surface of the thin counterpane. Diana wondered if he was dreaming.

He had asked for Lisa. Diana had told him Lisa was away. He had asked when she would be back and whether Miles was away too. He seemed to imagine that Lisa was married to Miles. Diana had answered vaguely. He had been peevish and abstracted and twice said aloud, as if unconscious of her presence, 'Poor Bruno, poor Bruno.' At last she had managed to induce something like a conversation, and they had talked, about the various houses he had lived in and about the merits of different parts of London. They talked about how London was changing, and whether it was as handsome as Rome or Paris. Bruno showed a little animation. Diana could not bring herself to stroke him as Lisa had enjoined, but, a little self-consciously, she had taken his hand which he let her hold, squeezing her fingers rather absently from time to time. She felt rather less physical horror of him, but the smell was hard to bear and she had a terrible intuition of his inward parts and of his pitiable mortality. There was something so strange and pathetic about the thin wispy emaciated body, so scarcely perceptible under the bedclothes, as if it were doing its best to shrivel right away leaving nothing but the head. An hour of the afternoon had passed in something like talk. She did not want to risk meeting Danby, whom she did not yet feel quite ready to encounter, and had just begun to say that it was time to go when Bruno had suddenly, still holding her hand, fallen asleep.

Diana had been disconcerted and had immediately wondered if he was dying. She released her hand cautiously from his and stood up. His breathing seemed to be regular and steady. Even as she was moving the chair and rising to her feet she was able to measure the intensity of her attention to Bruno by the sudden violence of her misery at remembering about Miles and Lisa. She stood for a while looking down at Bruno until he became ghostly and almost invisible. Then as she began to make her way to the door she saw, clear and separated like a detail in a Flemish picture, a big bottle of sleeping tablets which was standing upon the top of the marble-topped bookcase. She knew what they were, because Bruno had mentioned them in reply to a question of hers about how he slept. Diana stood still again, staring at the bottle of tablets.

Diana had so far found herself quite unable to discuss the situation with Miles. He had made one or two half-hearted attempts to refer to it, but had seemed relieved when she had, with a kind of submissive animal gesture, simply turned her head away and refused to reply. In the two days since Lisa's departure they had lived in the house together like two maniacs, each totally absorbed in a tempestuous inferno of private thoughts. Yet with all this they managed to behave with a certain degree of normality. Diana went shopping, Miles went to the office. They slept in the same bed, or rather lay awake for hours side by side, motionless and silent. Diana cried quietly, not wiping her tears, soaking the pillow. By day they were immensely polite and considerate and solicitous and rather formal. The only evident change in their routine was in the matter of meals. By tacit mutual consent they had abandoned any pretence of serious eating. Diana laid out, at intervals, a sort of buffet in the dining-room at which, usually not together, they occasionally picked, a little shame-faced at being able to eat at all.

Diana had not at any point talked to Lisa either. She had made no comment to her sister, nor had Lisa attempted to speak to her, although twice she had taken Diana's hand and squeezed it and laid it against her cheek, while Diana looked back at her blankly without responding. Diana conjectured that Lisa had determined on her flight immediately after Miles's nocturnal visit. Then she had kept her silence during the time in which she was arranging for the job in India. She announced her departure on the morning of the day on which she left, and Diana could see that Miles was just as stunned as she was. On the final walk to the station Lisa had been cool and business-like, talking fast, and Diana had been silent. Lisa had been trying to impress upon her that she must prevent Miles from trying to find Lisa before her departure to India, and that he would certainly fail if he tried. She did not tell Diana where she was going. When they got to the station she spoke again about Bruno. They embraced with closed eyes, clasping each other hard. Then Lisa was gone.

Diana had walked about the streets on that day and on the next day. She had sat on benches in parks and in churchyards. She rehearsed the situation endlessly in her mind, trying to find some way of thinking about it which was less than torture, but she could not. She had begun by believing that Miles and Lisa would run away together. Now she believed that they had finally and definitively crucified their love for her sake. It was not at first clear to her which was worse. In thinking them capable of running away she had made a judgement which seemed to bear not so much upon the honesty of either as upon the intense and terrible thing which was their love. Diana had fully taken in the scale of it, as with her first violent shock of horror she realized that the unthinkable had happened and that her life was utterly changed. She had apprehended with cer-tainty this thing, huge, full-fledged and monstrous in the house, when at a certain moment she had seen Miles and Lisa looking at each other across the dining-table. She had not foreseen it. The pity for Lisa which she had so long shared with Miles had made her incapable of seeing her sister as pre-eminently able to charm her husband.

Her appalled and frightened imagination could not now in-habit the alternative. Once the dreadful fear of Miles's flight had become less it began to seem to her a far worse and a far more difficult thing to accept their sacrifice. It would have been better to be their victim. That at least would have justified and made endurable the extreme jealousy and resentment which she could not stop feeling, and which she felt undiminished and intensified as she now saw Miles frantic-eyed at Kempsford Gardens, pacing and shuddering inside the walls of the house like a creature in a cage. For her too the house, the garden, had become utterly changed, a prison, a desolation. He could not expect her to be grateful, even though he had in a sense behaved impeccably. That impeccable behaviour tormented her almost more than anything. The situation somehow demanded her gratitude in a way which humiliated her utterly. How had they spoken of her? She had tried not to watch them. They could have spent the days together outside the house while she, at home, sat waiting for their judgement upon her – 'You can't leave poor Diana.' 'Poor Diana would break her heart.' 'After all, she is your wife, Miles. She has nothing but you.' 'She is not strong, Lisa, and independent as you are.' How strangely she and Lisa had now changed places. Now it was Diana who was the bird with the broken wing who would ever after be trailing her feathers in the dust.

If only they had gone away, thought Diana, I could have survived. Of course it would have been terrible. She tried to imagine the house suddenly empty, deprived of that dear familiar animal presence. They had lived together for so long like animals in a hutch. But all she could feel was the hollow misery of her irrevocably transformed marriage. 'Things will never be the same again, never.' But if they had gone, she thought, then all the energy, all the pride, all the sense of self would have been on the side of survival. I would have wanted to show them and to show the world how well I could survive. I would have felt less bitter. I could have sought for help and found it in other places. As the wife, retained, triumphant, I can appeal to nobody, least of all to myself. Every way I lose. She has taken him from me, she has destroyed our married love, and I have no new life, only the dead form of the old life. They have acted rightly, and just by this I am utterly brought low. My pain and my bitterness are sealed up inside me forever. I have no source of energy, no growth of being, to enable me to live this hateful role of the wife to whom they have together planned to sacrifice their great love. I am humbled by this to the point of annihilation. Sooner or later Miles will begin to speak about it. He will speak kindly, gently, trying to make me feel that his love for me is something real. But I *saw* that thing, their love. Miles and I never loved so.

They had decided not to run away together. But supposing Diana were to run away, and leave them to each other? Was there somehow somewhere here an issue from the circle of her pain? Almost blindly she considered it. She might go abroad somewhere leaving no address. But they would scarcely believe that she had gone for good. They would search for her lovingly *together*. In any case Diana had no money and no skill to earn it with. With a conscious sense of madness she even considered going to Danby. If she went to Danby would Miles and Lisa *then* feel convinced, released? Diana had kept, during all her awful preoccupations, the idea of Danby in reserve. She had retained a feeling for him, gratitude, affection, a sense of him as a holiday from Miles. Here at least there was a new place of love. It had struck her as odd that Miles had said nothing to her about Danby's drunken visit. Doubtless his own agony had rendered Danby's activities invisible. Yet did it really make any sense to run to Danby? He might simply not know what to do with her. It would end in a muddle which would merely reveal her as, after all, irrevocably and slavishly attached to Miles. Was there no other way?

Diana looked at the bottle of sleeping tablets and then looked back at Bruno. He was a little propped up, as he had been when he was talking to her, the head fallen sideways. It was not easy to tell, even when regarding him full face, when his eyes were open and when they were not. Perhaps he was quietly watching her now? Diana turned back to him and moved to the side of the bed. Holding her breath she leaned over him. His eyes, amid the pudgy folds of flesh, were tightly closed, the little sighing breath issued from the mouth, the moist red lower lip extended and retracted rhythmically with the breath.

Diana stood in the middle of the room half-way to the door and looked out of the window at the plump grey folds of cloud which were passing in a rapid seething surge behind the chimney of the power station. A sick fear rose up in her throat. She had the power to blot out all the suffering years. She had loved Miles, she still utterly and agonizingly loved him. But was not the future now simply the long grey time of the extinction of

207

love? He would never forgive her because of that sacrifice. And she would never forgive him. They would watch each other grow cold. But if she quitted the scene, if she went, utterly went, she would be the preserver of love: his love, hers, Lisa's. Was not this, so plainly and for all of them, the answer and the only answer?

Diana caught her breath and almost staggered. She moved to the door and picked up the bottle of sleeping tablets. She opened the door.

A lanky dark haired man was standing on the landing just outside the door.

'Oh!' said Diana. The immobility and sudden closeness of the figure seemed menacing and uncanny.

'I beg your pardon,' he said softly. 'I didn't mean to startle you. I was listening to see if anyone was with Bruno.'

Diana closed the door and slipped the bottle of tablets into her handbag. 'I was talking to him but he fell asleep.'

'My name is Nigel. I'm the nurse. Nigel the Nurse. I suppose I should say the male nurse, the way people say women writers, though I don't see why they should, do you, as more women are writers than men are nurses. Wouldn't you agree?'

'I'm afraid I must be going,' said Diana. She began to go down the stairs.

However before she could reach the front door Nigel had darted past her into the hall. He now stood with his back to the door. 'Don't go just yet.'

'I'm in a hurry,' said Diana.

'Not just yet.'

She stood uncertainly, facing him. His face was very bland, almost sleepy, as he leaned floppily against the door with arms outspread against it. She felt confused and alarmed. 'Get out of the way, please.'

'No, Mrs Greensleave.'

'You know who I am –'

'I know you well. Come in here a minute, I want to speak to you. Please.'

He took hold of the strap of her handbag and tugged her gently in the direction of the front room. The room smelt of dust and damp and disuse and the curtains were half drawn.

'This is the drawing-room. But no one ever comes in here, as you can see. Please sit down.' He gave Diana a little push and she fell over on to the brown plush sofa, raising a puff of dust which made her sneeze. Nigel pulled the curtains back and let in the cold cloudy afternoon light.

'What do you want?'

'There's something you ought to know.'

'What?'

'Danby loves your sister.'

Diana stared at him as he swayed to and fro against the window. 'I think you are confused,' she said. 'Danby scarcely knows my sister.'

'He knows her enough to be madly in love with her.'

'I think you must be mixing my sister up with me. Not that Danby – Anyway it's nothing to do with you.'

'I'm not mixing you up. He liked you. Then he met Lisa and fell in love.'

'You are mistaken,' said Diana. She began to rise.

'Well, look at this.' Nigel thrust into her hand a much torn piece of paper which had been reconstituted with the help of adhesive tape. It was a first draft of Danby's second letter to Lisa.

Diana read through it. Then it fell from her fingers on to the floor. She leaned back into the sofa and stared ahead of her. This was surely a sign. She knew now, and knew it quite clearly, that Danby's love would have kept her from suicide. But now – Lisa had taken Danby too. Diana clutched her handbag, feeling the bottle of tablets inside it. She thought I will go home, no I will go to a hotel, and do it at once. This is the end. Danby too. Lisa had annexed the world. A tear rolled down her cheek. She had forgotten Nigel's presence.

He had sat down beside her. 'I thought you ought to know in case it made any difference.'

'It makes no difference,' she said, wiping away the tear. She began to get up.

'Wait. I've got something else to say.'

'What about?'

'About Miles and Lisa. You mustn't be desperate.'

'How do you know all these things?'

'Because I am God. Maybe this is how God appears now in the world, a little unregarded crazy person whom everyone pushes aside and knocks down and steps upon. Or it can be that I am the false god, or one of the million million false gods there are. It matters very little. The false god is the true God. Up any religion a man may climb.'

'Let me go,' said Diana. Nigel had taken her by the shoulders.

'You must not be resentful. You must not be angry with them. There must be not a speck of resentment, not a speck of anger. That is a task, that is *the* task. To make a new heaven and a new earth. Only you can do it. And it is possible, it is possible.'

'Let me go. It's no business of yours.'

'It is my business. I love you.'

'Don't be silly, we've never met before.'

'We have met. I was painting the railings. I had paint in my hair.'

'But surely that was – someone else – ' Diana put her hand to her face. She felt she must be going slightly mad.

'Besides I love everybody.'

'Then it can't be love. Take your hands away, please.'

'Why not? Didn't I tell you I was God?'

'I think you must be mad – or drugged.'

'Maybe. May I call you Diana, Diana? Do you know that you're rather beautiful?' Nigel began to slide his arms round the back of her shoulders. Diana struggled, but he was amazingly strong.

'Do you want me to start screaming?'

'You won't scream. Besides, who would rescue you? Bruno? I just want to hold you ever so lovingly while I talk to you.'

Diana, her arms pinioned, tried to get some purchase with her knee. More clouds of dust arose out of the old sofa. Diana began to sneeze again and Nigel's grip tightened. Tears of helplessness and misery coursed down her face. She stopped struggling.

'There, there, don't fight poor Nigel, he loves you. You must forgive Miles and Lisa.'

Diana let the tears flow for a while. She was unable to wipe them away because of the closeness of Nigel's embrace. She said at last, 'How?'

'Let them trample over you in their own way. Perhaps they have done the right thing, though they have done it proudly, riding on horses. Their pride has its little necessities. See and pardon.'

'There is also my pride,' said Diana.

'Abandon it. Let it fall away like a heavy stone.'

'It hardly concerns me,' she said, 'that they have done the right thing. They have made a great sacrifice. I've got to be grateful. But I can't be. They love each other terribly.'

'Each loves himself more. Their love for themselves and for their own lives left them no other way. They have sacrificed nothing. They have just decided to do what will make them flourish.'

'I can't discuss this with you,' said Diana. But she did not now try to draw herself away.

'You are discussing it with me, my dear. The terrible thing is that nobody will die of this! Miles will flourish, and you will watch him kindly, as if you were watching a child.'

'They should have gone away together. He'll resent it for ever. He'll despise me. There can be no love between us any more. I cannot bear his thoughts, his thoughts about her, his thoughts about me.'

'A human being hardly ever thinks about other people. He contemplates fantasms which resemble them and which he has decked out for his own purposes. Miles's thoughts cannot touch you. His thoughts are about Miles. This too you must see and forgive. He will be pleased with himself and you will see him smiling.'

'But what about me?'

'That is what they all cry. Relax. Let them walk on you. Send anger and hate away. Love them and let them walk on you. Love Miles, love Danby, love Lisa, love Bruno, love Nigel.'

Diana had laid her head against Nigel's shoulder. Her tears were drying upon her cheek and upon his coat. 'I don't think I know how to do it.'

'You know how to try to do it. Everybody knows that.'

'It's all been so mad. Danby and Lisa too. It all seems like a dream now, a nightmare, with nothing clear.'

'It is mostly a dream, Diana. Only little pieces are clear and they don't necessarily fit together. When we suffer we think everything is a big machine. But the machine is just a fantasm of our pain.'

'It did seem like a machine,' she said. She began to sit up and push back her hair. Nigel had relaxed his hold.

'You see, it is already passing.'

She sat back and looked at him. A bluish purple bruise covered one side of his face, darkly ringing the half-closed eye. 'Whatever have you done to yourself?'

'I ran into a piece of the real world. It can hurt.'

'Poor Nigel – '

'And let me take these away. You won't be needing them.' Nigel's hand, burrowing in her handbag, had got hold of the bottle of sleeping tablets. He lifted them out and transferred them to his pocket.

Diana rubbed her face, smoothing the dried tears into the skin. 'No, I suppose I won't. But I don't know why. You've just talked nonsense to me.'

'Of course, of course. I am the nonsense priest of the non-sense god! A false doctor is not a kind of doctor, but a false god is a kind of god, Diana. Let me see you home.'

Chapter Twenty-seven

Danby switched on the light. The big lower room of the printing works, musty with mingled smells of ink and paper and years-old papery debris, looked desolate, untidy, cluttered, cold, caught off its guard, and yet peculiarly immobile and suddenly attentive against the line of black uncurtained windows. It always looked very odd without the bustle of people and the clattering noise. It was nearly five o'clock in the morning.

Danby began to cross the room. On the way he paused beside the old Albion press which had arrived the day before from the art school. The cast iron was dulled and a little rusty. It needed paint, oil, love. Even in its humbled disused condition it was a thing of strength and beauty. *Cope, London*. 1827. He caressed the big iron flower which served as a counter-weight, and when he swung the bar the press moved easily, silently, with quiet power. He left it and went on across the room.

At the far side a door led out on to a flight of stone steps. The steps led down on to a diminutive wharf, now disused, from which an iron ladder led on down into the river, or at low tide to the muddy banks of the Thames. Danby unlocked the door and opened it and looked out. He could now see a very faint suggestion of light in the sky, a grey dimness contrasting with the thicker black below. He tried to make out the outline of the power station chimneys opposite but could not find them. Two or three lighted windows on the other side of the water distracted his eye, and he thought for a moment about Bruno, although he knew that Stadium Street could not be seen from the printing works. The surface of the river seemed now to be becoming visible. Or perhaps it was an illusion. Perhaps too there was a faint rivery sound, or perhaps just a steady murmuring in his ears. There was a smooth cool smell of mud and water. It was still a little time to low tide.

Danby stepped back inside and looked at his watch. He took off his mackintosh, shivered, and put it back on again. The cold air was making his bruised shoulder ache. He went over to the little rickety wooden office which jutted out like a hut into the main room, and switched on the light inside it. The office, which was used by Danby and Gaskin, was untidy, the desk piled with letters, some still unopened. Danby had been unable to work himself and unable to delegate his duties. The walls were papered with old handbills, announcing sales and theatrical performances of sixty years ago. Danby opened the cupboard and poured himself out a glass of neat whiskey. He was feeling ridiculously nervous.

He had accepted Will Boase's absurd challenge to a duel for reasons which had seemed compelling at the time, but which were now by no means quite so clear. Of course he knew that the 'duel' would be a farce, something staged by the twins with theatre pistols loaded with blanks, and designed to confuse and humiliate him. Nevertheless it now seemed like a frightening trial, something unforeseeable and violent, a happening in which he would have to play a rapid and impromptu role, and in which he might find it difficult to act resolutely and impossible to act with dignity. He felt that he had delivered himself entirely into the hands of hostile men.

Yet such a handing of himself over had been what at first he had thought that he wanted. He had wanted to become the victim of a violent event. He had been arrested by the word 'punish' which Will had used in his letter, and it had seemed to Danby that the twins, whom he now connected together into one agency, were the instruments of a fate, directed against him, and yet indubitably his. The idea of the duel was the idea of an ending, a fake ending of course, as Danby vaguely knew, but at any rate such a sort of forced small catastrophe as might symbolize the closing of an era.

He knew that Lisa had gone away. He had gone round to Kempsford Gardens and Diana had showed him the empty room. Diana said that she had gone abroad, for good. Danby did not ask for details. He did not suppose that she had gone abroad alone. He had stood silently with Diana in the empty room. Only after he had departed did he realize that Diana now seemed to know about him and Lisa. Miles must have told her. He went to the office the next day and the next day. He tended Bruno as usual, coming back to feed him at lunch-time. Nigel, after an absence of three days, returned and resumed his ministry. Only now Nigel was a hostile presence, a thin sardonic judging angel. Danby spoke to him awkwardly, apologetically, and shrank away from his smile. Adelaide had packed her belongings in several suitcases, which she had to unpack every day to find things she needed. She had announced her intention of going but had not yet gone. She spent most of every day away from the house. The kitchen was filled with dirty crockery and decaying food. Danby held a used plate under the hot tap every time he had to feed Bruno. He took his own meals in pubs.

Danby felt very sorry about Adelaide. What had seemed so natural and simple and pleasant while it was going on nicely now seemed much more like a crime. He could not work out quite why it was a crime. It was not what Adelaide said, about his not wanting to marry her because he thought her inferior. He did not, he believed, think her inferior. He simply would not have married anybody whom he loved in that rather simple mediocre sort of way. He would not have married Linda either. Perhaps the crime was that of letting himself be loved so much more than he loved. Perhaps it was that of allowing someone to be committed, to be utterly bound, for the sake of a second rate kind of loving. It was not that it was a casual loving exactly. It had its own kind of reality, it was domestic, it belonged, like some humble house spirit, to the house at Stadium Street, to the kitchen and bedrooms there. Yet it was after all a poor weak thing, instantly broken at the touch of what now seemed to Danby to be the re-entry into his life of a reality which he had shamefully forgotten.

Yet which was the reality? He told himself sometimes that Lisa was, must be, a dream figure, an apparition, and that as time went on he would more and more realize this, until it would seem to him in the end that he had never really met her and that she had never really existed at all. He had become momentarily insane because of a girl who resembled Gwen, a serious intense girl with a dark wig of hair and a thinking mouth whom he had seen about half a dozen times in his life.

He had become insane because she had suddenly reminded him of what it had been like, of what he had been like, of how he had been made to be, so long ago during his marriage. Lisa was just an angel of memory, a reminder of loss.

Yet he knew really that she was not simply an apparition. She was not Gwen come back from the dead. She was very different from Gwen. And he was very different from Gwen's husband. He was an older fatter more drunken man than the one whom Gwen had so unaccountably loved. But he was also perhaps, and this intimation somehow entered into the deepest part of Danby's pain, a wiser man. The years had brought him something which, potentially at least, was good. That obscure small good seemed to suffer and ache inside him as he thought vaguely but intensely about all the might-have-beens of a quite other life with Lisa. It seemed to him that in spite of his casual mode of being and his bad behaviour to Adelaide and his general willingness to play the fool, he had found something in the world, some little grain of understanding which that glimpse of Lisa had made suddenly luminous and alive. He felt obscurely the dividedness of his being, the extent of what was gross, the littleness and value of what was not. But these thoughts, when they came, were never entirely clear to him, and he spent most of his days in a coma of misery, thinking about Lisa and the other man, inducing physical pains of yearning and jealousy which made him gasp, and putting off the attempt to pull himself together.

The prospect of the crazy 'duel' had been, to his desperate mood, almost a relief. It had seemed the image of something destructive and mad, and also of something appropriate and necessary. The aching and deprived heart yearns for necessity. Danby would have been glad to be arrested, imprisoned, scourged, judged. Now in his dreams, in some huge echoing courtroom, a woman's voice rehearsed misdoings which dated back to his earliest childhood. Anything which could show his present situation as inevitable would have been an alleviation of his pain. It was not enough that his rational mind could display to him the utter improbability of his success. It was its impossibility that he needed to have the proof of. As it was, the torment of accidents continued. If only he had met her earlier, if only there were not this other man, if only she had not seen him kissing Diana, if only he were the different and better person which it seemed to him he might easily be. He had accepted and even welcomed the idea of the duel because it seemed somehow to belong to the other order of things, the legal, the necessary.

But now, shivering in the cold cramped little office underneath the electric light, with all the familiar things looking alienated and eerie, the craziness of the plan took on a different and more sinister air. From the moment of the tapping on the window and the receipt of Will's pompous letter, Danby had thought of nothing but himself. He had thought of the encounter in relation to himself, as something that he was going to bring about or do. He had not thought of Will except as of a blind agency destined somehow to act upon him. Now, as he poured himself out another glass of whiskey, he thought about Will more carefully. He really knew very little about him. The one thing which he certainly knew about Will was the degree of his hatred. But how exactly would that hatred make him behave? Will had loved Adelaide since they were children. He had thought of her as ever the pure sweet maid who was somehow reserved for him. This much Danby had gathered from Adelaide's tearful outpourings after the delivery of the letter. How would Will feel towards a man who had casually, unseriously, seduced this dream woman, and what fate would he deem appropriate for such a man? That Will intended in some way to humiliate him became clearer to Danby now. Had he proposed the dawn hour, the deserted place, for some quite other purpose of his own? Perhaps he and Nigel would arrive with other men, tie Danby up and thrash him? He had heard of such things.

He put the glass down and came out into the main workshop. The windows were paler. He switched off the lights and could now see the nearer shore and the surface of the water gleaming and shifting in flakes of very pale yellowish grey. The opposite shore was veiled by a mist which seemed to quiver and vibrate, casting out a diffused yellow radiance which revealed the debris-strewn river bank below the printing works in a faint but horribly clear morning light. Danby shuddered.

He heard a sound behind him and jerked round. He had left

the outer door open, as they had agreed. There were two figures on the other side of the room, one tall and thin, the other shorter, stouter.

'Oh,' said Danby, 'good morning.' He did not like to turn the electric light on again. There was just enough illumination to recognize his visitors. His heart beat violently.

Will, who was carrying a large case under his arm, stayed by the doorway. Nigel came forward, tiptoeing or gliding across the floor. When he came up to the window Danby could see his face quite clearly.

'You've no one with you?'

'No. I thought I'd dispense with a second!'

'That's a bit irregular, you know,' said Nigel. He stood for a moment staring at Danby. His face seemed stretched, beaming with a blissful excitement, the purple bruise still visible along the cheek and under the eye.

'Isn't this all rather absurd?' said Danby in a loud voice. 'I think we should forget it and go home. I can't think why I came at all.'

Will moved forward from the door. He stopped about five paces away, put the case down on the level tray of one of the colour-printing machines, and looked at Danby with a gaze of cool intense hatred.

'All right,' said Danby. 'Do what you like. Play out your little game. But let's do it quickly. I want to get home.' He thought, this man is in the theatre, and yet he's horribly in earnest too. I can't get away now. If I tried to go he'd spring on me. At any rate there seemed to be only the two of them.

'Let's go down then,' said Nigel. 'The tide's out, isn't it? It was a good idea of yours to have it here.'

Danby opened the door. The cold water-scented air filled the doorway. He could smell the sea. He took a deep breath and went a little unsteadily down the steps, trailing his hand on the wall. He crossed the wharf and began to climb slowly down the iron ladder to the river shore. As he stepped off on to the yielding gravelly mud, he could see the large rubber-soled boots of Will on the upper rungs of the ladder.

The expanse of shore, some twenty feet from the base of the

wall to the water, was quite clearly lit now by a light still faint but rather lurid which seemed to emanate from the curtain of mist which hung now at the centre of the river and arched over the shore, enclosing it in a capsule of bright haze. A quietness, which seemed also to be coming out of the mist, held the scene poised, and Danby was startled by the sound of his own footsteps moving over the rather sticky gravel. He stood staring at the water's edge. The tide had not yet turned and the river was still running steadily downstream. A sleek line of mud was reflecting the yellowish light. Above it, the surface was more irregular, lumpy, stony, strewn with plastic bags and old motor tyres and bottles of green and clear glass and very pale smooth clean pieces of driftwood which the Thames had long had for her own. The clear glowing light made the littered scene seem over-precise, purposive, as if one had wandered suddenly into the very middle of a work of art.

Will was still standing beside the ladder, leaning the edge of the case against one of the rungs and fumbling with the clasp. Nigel, with the same lilting gliding motion, came over to Danby. The light fell on his face which was strained into a semblance of an archaic smile.

'How would you like to proceed? Have you any special wishes?'

'Anything you like,' said Danby.

'There are various possibilities – '

'You decide. Only get on with it.'

'What Will wants is the system where you measure out twenty paces in the middle and draw a line on each side. Then you each stand another twenty paces behind the lines. After I give the word you can walk forward as far as the line and fire at any point before you reach it, or when you reach it. No order of firing, just fire when you want to.'

'Look, Nigel, can't we call off this farce?' said Danby in a low voice. 'Couldn't Will and I just have a talk? I know how he feels – '

'Do you want to apologize to him?'

'No! I just mean a sort of civilized talk – '

'It's impossible. You don't understand. Will couldn't talk to you, he *couldn't*.' Nigel had laid his hand on Danby's arm.

Nigel's teeth were chattering.

'It's all perfectly insane – '

'Wait here. I'll just report to Will.'

Nigel's footsteps, crunching, sucking, moved away over the gravel and Danby could hear the murmur of voices. He felt light-headed, a sensation as at the onset of extreme drunkenness. The lurid detailed scene seemed to be tilting a little sideways. Nigel was back beside him and was thrusting something into his hand.

'Here. You know how to fire a pistol, don't you?'

Danby lifted his hand, which was holding a rather beautiful duelling pistol with a long slim barrel. The handle, very smooth and already warm in his hand, was made of a rich rosybrown wood with a curly grain. The barrel and the butt end of the handle were ornamented with a flowery silver inlay. Danby stared with fascination at the strange weighty object.

'You sight along the barrel. Better keep a straight arm. It doesn't kick much.'

'I trust you and your brother are enjoying yourselves,' said Danby.

'It's loaded. If you don't want to hurt him fire well wide. Remember you don't have to walk as far as the line.'

'You ought to be in films!'

Danby, who was well acquainted with revolvers and had sometimes played with pistols, examined his weapon. It was indeed loaded. A blank of course, but loaded. It appeared that the twins were going to carry their theatre scene through to the end.

'I'll drop a handkerchief, and after that you can fire when you like.'

'All we need now is a surgeon!'

Nigel gave him the ecstatic beaming stare, giggled and glided away.

The light was growing. Will had moved away on the other side of the iron ladder. Danby watched Nigel pacing the shore, making marks with pieces of driftwood. A chilly breeze had begun to blow and the mist had receded a little without yet revealing the other side of the river. Danby turned up the collar of his mackintosh. He thought, supposing this were all real and

I was perhaps going to die. He thought, Lisa, where are you now.

'Back here please,' said Nigel. He motioned Danby back behind a line which he had scored in the stony mud. A long way ahead of him he could see the figure of Will, rigid, upright, compact, small, a focused pellet of menacing significance. He could see a blotch of purple which must be Will's scarf, perhaps his shirt.

'Sixty paces between you,' said Nigel. 'The next line is there, marked with driftwood, which you mustn't cross, but you can fire before you reach it.' His hand touched the sleeve of Danby's raincoat, gathered up some of the stuff and fingered it.

'I'm sorry I pushed you into that lamp post,' said Danby. 'I didn't mean to.' A very fine misty rain had begun to fall. Nigel's black hair was filmed over with glittering pinheads of rain.

'That's all right. Good luck. If you fire first, stand sideways, there's less risk. The light's still a bit uncertain, he'll probably miss you.'

Nigel moved away. This performance is designed to frighten me, thought Danby. They want me to break down, lose my nerve, beg them to stop, run away. It's all ridiculous. But all the same he found that he was trembling.

Nigel had returned to the middle point, half-way between Will and Danby. He was flourishing a white handkerchief above his head. The two lines marking the twenty paces in the centre were plainly marked with wood. A boat on the river hooted distantly. The handkerchief fluttered to the ground.

Will had begun to walk very slowly forward, carefully lifting his pistol with outstretched arm and gazing along the barrel. Danby stared. Then as if compelled by a magnetic line of force stretched between himself and his opponent he began to move too. His heart seemed to be pounding and rattling at an incoherent speed. He put his left hand to his breast. It's theatre, he said to himself, just theatre. But the power of the scene had already made him its actor and he found himself raising the pistol, feeling for the trigger. It was all idiotic, but it was also awful, a grotesquerie, a piece of obscene unworthy mumming. Get it over with, he thought. Instinctively he turned the gun away from the slowly advancing but still distant figure of Will, and lowering the barrel in the direction of the river he pulled the trigger.

The leap of the gun, the deafening noise of the report, overlaid another event. A green glass bottle which had been lying upon the mud at the very edge of the water disappeared into fragments with a high splintering clang.

Danby stood quite still, the echoes of the report still roaring in his ears, and stared at the bottle. So the pistol had been really loaded after all.

He dropped the pistol, which was wreathed in white smoke, and it fell with a dull thump into the glistening greyish mud. He stooped to pick it up again and saw straight ahead of him in the enclosed dome of golden luminosity the still advancing figure of Will. Danby tried to think. He said to himself, I must do something quickly, I must stop him, it's all a mistake. He tried to move, but his limbs seemed too heavy to stir. He stood paralysed, watching with fascination as the figure with the pointing pistol grew larger. Yes, he was wearing a mauve shirt. A mauve shirt.

Danby thought, supposing this man kills me. He wants to kill me, he wills my death. I should have known it wasn't play acting. But he must know that I'm harmless, I didn't mean to hurt him, I must explain it's a mistake, I mustn't die by mistake. Who would understand? He raised his hand. He tried to move his foot but it seemed to be rooted in the mud. He stood there with a raised hand, like a signal, a totem. The rain was increasing.

Will had reached the line of driftwood and stopped, pointing the pistol with care. There was about thirty yards between them.

He must be stopped, thought Danby, I must call out to him. But his body had become rigid with fear and expectation of the impact of the bullet. His mind seemed to float above him in some other sphere. He saw himself lying dead on the bank of the Thames with Will's bullet in his heart. He thought I am dying for a girl I didn't love, I am dying because I failed to love, I am dying just upon the brink of love. I was not worthy. He tried to will to move, to sidestep, even to stand sideways as

222

Nigel had advised. But he could not stop staring at Will, who was still taking aim, clear and detailed in an ellipse of bright vision.

'No, no, no!' Something black had shot across the centre of the scene, something capering, agitated, Nigel waving, shouting, spreading out his arms. He capered in front of Danby, dancing in the gravelly mud, his feet spraying pebbles.

'Get out of the way, damn you!'

As Will shouted Danby rushed forward and seized Nigel around the waist. They swayed together. Over Nigel's shoulder Danby could see the steady pointing pistol. Danby crooked his foot round Nigel's ankle and threw him stumbling to the ground. Will shouted again and fired.

As Danby heard the bullet whistle past his head the explosion loosened his limbs and he sat down heavily on the stones. Nigel was lying full length. He gazed on Danby. Then his eyes closed and there was an expression of bliss upon his face. The echo of the shot died away and there was a curiously intense silence.

Danby reached out to Nigel's shoulder with the intention of shaking him, but he had no force in his arm and remained leaning there, staring down into the swooning beatific face. There was a sound of crunching footsteps.

Will, the still smoking pistol hanging limp at his side, said 'Which of you have I hit?' His face was white, his mouth open and shuddering.

'Neither of us, fortunately for you,' said Danby. He began to get up.

'Nigel, Nigel – ' Will fell on his knees beside his brother.

Nigel's eyes opened. 'Hello, Will. I think I've been in heaven.'

'Are you all right, you bloody fool?'

'Yes. But look. I spy police.'

A uniformed figure had appeared on the next wharf, which belonged to the cattle cake mills. Somebody was distantly shouting. Danby turned about and began to walk in the opposite direction along the slippery shore. Then he decided it was silly to walk and began to run. The mist was lifting and he could see through the light now rather luminous curtain of rain a line of barges, the outline of the bridge, and the surface of the river smoothed and pitted with rain.

The water was lapping the base of the brick wall below the churchyard. The strand was coming to an end. Danby's feet splashed in the water. He heard shouts behind him. He plunged in deeper, wildly splashing, and then with a sudden sense of blissful release gave himself to the Thames, losing his footing and falling forward into the deeper water. He began to swim towards the line of barges. He passed under the stern of the last barge and the shore behind him was blotted out.

Now there was a sudden peace and silence. Danby swam slowly, breast stroke, scarcely stirring the surface of the quiet water. It did not seem cold. The still flowing tide took him gently with it. He felt a strange beatific lightness as if all his sins, including the ones which he had long ago forgotten, had been suddenly forgiven. The mist had lifted and the rain was abating. A little pale sunlight began to glow from behind him, and he saw that a perfect rainbow had come into being, hanging over London, bridging the Thames from north to south. Danby swam towards it. He swam under Battersea bridge.

Chapter Twenty-eight

It was raining, raining, raining. Adelaide stood in her bedroom with the light switched on. She felt frightened. It had been dark outside for so long now that it was hard to know if it was evening or night. The rain had darkened the whole afternoon. Her watch had stopped. It must be night by now.

There had been another flood warning. But there had been so many and nothing had happened. The darkness was just so hard to bear and that continual violent rain battering the windows. The house had become terrible to her. It was as if it had been taken over by an evil spirit. She could not bear even to look into the kitchen. She feared Nigel, she feared Danby, she feared Bruno. She was afraid that Bruno would suddenly start to die when there was no one there but herself. The others came and went mysteriously. Perhaps one day they would go and not come back. She wanted to go herself, she had packed her bags days ago, but she had no will to move herself and nowhere to go to.

I can't stay here, Adelaide kept thinking, I must go to a hotel. But she did not want to spend her money on a hotel. She had never stayed in a hotel in her life, and did not know how to choose one to go to. She thought, I must find another job. But the idea was nightmarish. She felt utterly incapable of working, of seeing new people. She felt incapable of living any more. She had at last understood that the person she had always loved was Will. That jerky violence which had so plucked at her nerves now merged magnetically with the sovereign forces of her own nature. She responded, she submitted, but too late. The years with Danby seemed an insubstantial dream. She should have recognized this lord out of her childhood, she should never have questioned his authority over her. Beside that brute reality the charm of Danby faded to a wisp. Adelaide had forgotten her love for Danby. It seemed to her that she had been kind to him for some other reason which she could not now understand. She had ceased to feel animosity against Danby, though she was still very anxious not to meet him. She did not feel that he had used her unjustly. Her sense of being, through her new indifference to him, Danby's equal, had removed all sense of grievance. Her anger was against herself, for her frivolity and her blindness. She had had him at her feet, the only one, for years and years, and now had lost him utterly.

Adelaide sat on the edge of her bed crying. She had rehearsed in her mind a hundred scenes of reconciliation, of throwing herself before him and accepting his anger and receiving his forgiveness. But she knew really that it would be profitless to try to see him, she knew him well enough. He was capable of assaulting her, hurting her, and this would have none of the splendour of imagined violence. It would be ugly, humiliating, final. She had thought of asking Nigel to intercede for her, even of asking Auntie. But for all she knew Will detested Nigel, and she dared not go near Auntie for fear of an encounter with Will. She had written him a letter. *Please forgive me. I know now I love you.* But it looked unreal, flimsy, utterly unlike the terrible force which she now felt rising up underneath her heart. She had posted the letter just for something to do, as an unbeliever might light a candle in a church. He would never forgive her now. He would hate her for ever.

'Adelaide!'

He had called before and she had taken no notice. Dully she got up and began to mount the stairs.

'Adelaide!'

'I'm coming, I'm coming, don't shout.'

It was cold in Bruno's room. The centre light and the lamp were both on. The uncurtained window was a shiny black void full of beating drumming rain. Bruno's bed was disordered and one pillow had fallen to the floor. He lay sideways in the bed, his head drooping awkwardly towards one side as if the neck were broken. A spider book fell heavily off the side of the bed.

'What's the matter?'

'Where's everybody?'

'I don't know.'

'Where's Danby, where's Nigel?'

'I don't know.'

'This rain is so awful.'

'Do you want tea or something?'

'No. I feel rotten. Could you arrange my pillows, Adelaide? No one looks after me. I could be dead and no one would even notice.'

Holding her breath and gripping the thin fleshless bone of his shoulder Adelaide threw the vagrant pillow in behind him. She straightened the blankets and the counterpane. Bruno with some difficulty arranged his two thin arms upon the counterpane, pulling down the sleeves of his red and white striped pyjamas.

'Could I have that book? Could you pull the curtains?'

Adelaide dragged the curtains across the window and threw the book on to the bed. 'Anything else you want?'

'Could you turn on the electric fire? It's like winter in here.'

'If you didn't disarrange your bed so you wouldn't feel so cold.'

'All my limbs are aching so, I can't stay still. Adelaide, the wireless says the Thames is flooding.'

'They're always saying that.'

'There's a north westerly gale blowing and the flow over the weir at Teddington – '

'Oh don't worry your head.'

'Could you bring up the *Evening Standard*?'

'It hasn't come.'

'Adelaide, could I have a hot water bottle? I'm so cold. I'm sorry to trouble you.'

Adelaide went to the bathroom and filled a bottle at the hot tap. She dried it hastily on a towel and brought it back and held her breath again as she pushed it in at the bottom of the bed underneath the foot cage. 'Can you reach it?'

'Yes. It's terribly hot.'

'I'll wrap it up in something.'

'No, don't bother.'

'Do you want another blanket?'

'No, no, I couldn't stand the weight. Adelaide, could you go out and see if it's really flooding?'

'Don't be silly! They'd warn us if it was. It's just a high tide. They're always making something out of nothing.'

'Adelaide, please go out and see. Oh God, I wish Danby would come back.'

'I don't know what you mean go out and see! There's nothing to see but the rain. And if I go out in that I'll be soaked to the skin.'

'Well, ring up someone, would you, ring up the police – *Please,* Adelaide –'

'I can't think what you're so fussed about. All right. I'll ring up.'

Adelaide closed Bruno's door and went down the stairs. The stairs seemed darker than usual. In the hall she fumbled for the telephone book and had to take it into the drawing-room to look up the number. The drawing-room looked empty and crazy, the big front bow windows black and roaring. Adelaide saw that a stream of water was finding its way in from the window and making a long dark stain upon the carpet. She went back to the telephone and lifted the receiver. She began to dial. Then she realized that there was no dialling tone. The telephone was dead. She put the receiver down and lifted it again. Still dead.

Adelaide left the telephone. She stood in the dimness of the hall, cramming a hand into her mouth. She went to open the street door, but closed it quickly again as a blast of violent rain screamed against her out of the darkness. The rain was so thick that the street lamps were obscured by it and all seemed dark outside. If only someone could help, she thought, if only someone would come. The neighbours were all elderly people and anyway she scarcely knew them. If only Danby would come. The loneliness, the noise, the terrified Bruno were suddenly intolerable. Adelaide thought, I'll just go out as far as the Kings Arms on Cheyne Walk. There would be bright lights there and joking people who would laugh at her alarm. She called up the stairs to Bruno, 'It's all right. The police say it's all right. I'm just going out for a moment to look. I won't be long.'

She put on her mackintosh and drew a scarf over her head

and, holding the latch key in her hand, opened the door. Once she was outside it was quite difficult to close the door again. The sheer weight of the rain and the wind, driving obliquely, pressed the door away from her hand. She pulled it to, went down the few steps and began to go along the street. The gutters were overflowing and the pavements were running with water. The road was like a stream and the water was squelching inside her shoes. After a few steps she paused, already soaked to the skin. The air was a blackness of thick water. It was insane to go through this deluge. But then she thought again of the lights and laughter of the Kings Arms and she began to hurry on.

By the time Adelaide got to the turning into Cremorne Road she was panting with exhaustion and with terror. Her clothes were clinging to her and impeding her movements. The water appeared to be round her ankles. With the rain hissing and splashing so it was hard to tell. Some way off, beyond the curtain of the downpour, she could now hear a strange awful roaring noise. She stood at the corner, looking towards Cheyne Walk, but the rain was too thick for her to see anything. Someone called to her from a doorstep, then banged the door against the rain. Adelaide could feel the water now, tugging at her ankles, moving with greater force. A man appeared out of the darkness, running or trying to run. He shouted to her, 'Don't go down there!'

'What's happening?' shouted Adelaide. The noise almost drowned her voice.

'The water's coming over the embankment wall. Don't go there, get back! The police – ' The figure disappeared, plunging and splashing and hopping in the stream of rising water.

'Oh, oh, oh!' Adelaide cried to herself with fear as she began to run back along the road. Already it was not any more like running. It was more like wading. Each foot as it came down was gripped by the moving water. One of Adelaide's shoes came off and she kicked off the other one. She grabbed at railings, gasping. Then she began to lift her feet higher and splash along, wailing in panic. Someone at an upstairs window was calling out hysterically. Just as Adelaide reached her own front door and had mounted the steps out of the stream and thrust the key frantically into the lock something happened. She had been seeing the glint of the rain, a diffused glitter of swirling water, little chips of light moving about in the dark. Now there was only blackness as if a velvet band had been wrapped around her head. She thrust the door open and stumbled in. It took her a moment to realize what had happened. The lights in the house had gone out. The power station must be flooded.

Adelaide had to lean against the door to close it, still crying to herself with fear. She could hear Bruno's voice calling shrilly upstairs. The interior darkness was thick and stifling. She groped her way to the stairs.

'Adelaide, Adelaide, come quickly, the lights – '

She blundered, hands outstretched, to Bruno's door.

'Adelaide, what's happening? Is there a flood?'

She crossed the room and felt in the dark for his hand. It was like holding a few dry twigs. 'It's all right. It's just rain water. The power station must have got swamped.' Not to frighten the old man. If he gets panic-stricken I shall break down.

'You didn't ring the police at all, I heard – '

'Yes, I did. Everything's all right.'

'No, it isn't. That noise isn't just rain. The Thames must be coming over the walls. It'll be coming in downstairs. Go and see. And bring some candles, it's so awful in the dark – '

Adelaide groped her way to the door and descended the stairs holding on to the banisters on each side. It's only water, she told herself, it doesn't matter if it does come in, we should be safe upstairs. If only the noise was not so terrible. If only Danby would come. But through that downpour nobody could come. She thought, there's a torch in the drawer of the hall table. Her sense of direction and distance seemed to have been destroyed. She blundered about, found the table and got her fingers on to the torch. She switched it on and directed the beam down the stairs which led to her bedroom and the kitchen. There was a strange new sound coming from down there, a gurgling and a hissing. The little light pointed down into the darkness and was quenched. Adelaide took several steps down the stairs. The circle of light revealed the surface of moving water. Adelaide stared, appalled, fascinated. Then she thought, my clothes, my things!

She splashed down into the water which was now almost ankle deep at the foot of the stairs, and on into her bedroom. There were two suitcases on the floor and one on the bed. She seized her handbag, picked the cases out of the water and began to struggle with them back up the stairs, holding the lighted torch against her thigh. She bumped them up stair by stair as far as the ground floor landing. Bruno was shouting. She paid no attention but darted back down the stairs for the third suitcase. What else should she take? Her overcoat. She took it off the peg and began fumbling with it trying to put it on over her soaking clinging mackintosh. It was impossible. Her arms felt like putty and she was shuddering and crying with cold. She dragged the suitcase and a bundle of overcoat and dressing-gown up to the landing and ran down again. There were candles somewhere in the kitchen, but where? She stood on the stairs flashing her torch on to the race of water just below her. She could not make out if it was rising. The gurgling hissing sound was now very close to her and she made out that it was caused by the water from the street running down the steps at the side of the house and into the yard at the back which was below street level. The waters must be coming in under the side door.

Must find things, rescue things, thought Adelaide. She stepped down into the water, forcing her legs against it, and went into Danby's room. She flashed the torch at the window trying to see into the yard but could see nothing beyond the glass. She moved over and pushed up the sash of the window. The hissing and the roar filled the room with a chaotic hubbub. There was no light outside. Adelaide shone the torch, bringing it low down outside the window. There was a strange biting sensation in her hand. She realized she was touching water. The flood was mounting up in the yard and had reached a higher level than the water inside the house. The yard was like a lake. Adelaide began frenziedly to try to shut the window again but it seemed to have stuck and her hands were without power. Before long the water outside would have reached the level of the window sill. Crying, almost screaming, she pulled at the sash, then turned back to the room flashing her torch. A large hairbrush of Danby's was lying on the dressing table, looking curiously peaceful and ordinary and separated from the din of its surroundings. She picked it up and with the light of the torch flickering wildly from her left hand, began to bang the frame of the open window. There was a crash of glass and she could feel the fragments of the pane falling all about her.

Adelaide staggered back from the window. She felt a sharp pain in one foot and sat down abruptly upon Danby's bed. As she did so the wavering torch light showed her something which was floating upon the water quite near to one of the legs of the bed. It was the big black wooden box which contained the stamp collection.

'Adelaide! Adelaide!' Bruno's voice had somehow pierced the uproar which seemed to possess the house.

Adelaide tried to pick up the box with one hand, then used two hands and put it on to Danby's bed. She sat back and lifted her stockinged foot. It felt as if a piece of glass was sticking into the sole. Holding the torch carefully she examined her foot, running her hand over it cautiously. A rapid stain of red was tingeing the soaking stocking. Adelaide stared and moaned. Her questing hand was stiff with cold.

'Adelaide, get the stamps!' Bruno's scream reached her again.

Adelaide turned the torch on to the wooden box. It was tilting over sideways and several of the drawers had fallen open. The familiar coloured faces of the stamps could be seen inside their cellophane wrappings. Something fell down over Adelaide's eyes. It was the dripping scarf which she had not thought to remove from her head. She thrust it back. She could hear herself still moaning amid the roaring darkness of surging water and driving rain. Her body was shuddering with cold and her feet had contracted into balls of pain. She stared at the stamps. The thought occurred to her, suppose I took some of these stamps to Will. Would he forgive me then? I could pretend they had been lost in the flood. They might have been. If I hadn't been here they would all have been lost. It's the deluge, it's the end of the world anyway, so what does it matter what one does. She steadied the torch and reached out a wet hand clumsy with cold. Where were the Cape triangulars? If only she knew which ones were valuable. Get it up the stairs, she thought. Upstairs, dry clothes, get warm again, think what to do. She stood up and felt the sharp pain in her foot again. Crying, standing on one foot, she tried to lift the box, but it was too heavy.

'*Adelaide, the stamps, the stamps!*' The screaming voice seemed suddenly nearer.

Adelaide, with one knee on the bed, began trying to pull the drawers out of the box, but the drawers seemed to be attached at the back. They only came out so far and then stopped. With hands clumsy with cold, she pulled helplessly at the cellophane envelopes. They were attached too.

Suddenly there was a new echoing splashing spilling sound and something gripped Adelaide about the leg. She let go of the box and clasped the end of the bed. The piled-up water must be coming in through the open window. Adelaide cried out and plunged towards the door. It was now impossible to lift her feet out of the racing water. She pulled herself round the door and fell towards the stairs, grabbing at the banisters. She managed to get her foot on to the lowest stair. The lighted torch was clasped in the palm of her hand and she saw the illumined flesh like alabaster as her hand reached out before her.

'ADELAIDE, THE STAMPS, GET THE STAMPS!' Bruno's terrible cry was just above her.

As she reached the next step she managed to shift the torch and cast its ray up ahead of her. She shrieked. Bruno was standing at the top of the kitchen stairs, leaning against the newell post. He was wearing only the jacket of his pyjamas and his thin legs, like the legs of an insect, were bending at the knees. The great swollen head swayed above, checkered by the light into huge cubes, like a wooden head in a carnival. Bruno swayed, leaned forward, his thin twigs of hands grasping for the banister, his knees crumpling. The next moment he had fallen headlong, his head hurtling down into her shoulder. Adelaide dropped the torch and fell straight backwards, with Bruno on top of her, into the black surge of water below.

Chapter Twenty-nine

'You know,' said Miles, 'one can actually hear the crack of the swallows' beaks as they catch the flies. Listen.'

'They're early this year,' said Diana. 'I wish they'd stay here with us and not go on somewhere else.'

'I don't blame them. They're making for some peaceful country farmhouse.'

It was a quiet sunny evening, one of those spring evenings which have the intensity of autumn, when growing things vibrate with colour and seem to breathe out silence. Miles and Diana were walking very slowly through Brompton Cemetery. They were near the centre now, where sounds from the Fulham Road and the Old Brompton Road had faded to a distant hum like the murmur of insects. Miles and Diana sat down on a seat. Miles put his arm round her shoulder.

'How quiet it is here, it's like the country. I don't see why the swallows shouldn't stay.'

'Are you warm enough, dear?'

'Yes, Miles. The sun is warm, isn't it? How green everything is, it's like a great water meadow.'

'I think one forgets about *green* in the winter.'

'One forgets so many things. Every spring is a surprise.'

'Every spring is a surprise.'

'Just the grass growing again is so wonderful. Look at the light on it over there.'

'How was Bruno when you saw him today?'

'Much the same. He doesn't know who I am. I think he doesn't know who Danby is any more. He talks occasionally and it sounds like sense only it doesn't connect with anything. He just seems to live in the present.'

'A good place to live, Diana. It's a miracle he survived that fall.'

'The doctor says it won't be long now. He's awfully sort of cut off. Well, you saw.'

'He's pathetic.'

'No, not pathetic. Just cut off.'

'He still hasn't asked about the stamps?'

'No, thank heavens.'

'I'm rather glad they've gone.'

The stamp collection had perished in the flood. The box had evidently floated out of the window. When the water subsided it was found in the yard, tilted over with some of its drawers missing. The few stamps that remained in the box were completely ruined.

Miles gently squeezed his wife's shoulder. Everything that had happened to him lately had been completely unexpected. What a terribly complex thing his life must be to be able so utterly to surprise its owner! Miles felt as if everything had been somehow turned inside out. The shape was much the same, but the colour was different, the feel was different. It was the old world made new or else perhaps really seen for the first time.

For several days after Lisa's departure he had lived in a state of stretched tense physical pain. He had let Lisa go, he had let her walk away down the street, and he had thought then that he was suffering. He did not experience her departure until nearly a day later, as if the news needed time to penetrate his body. When it had at last done so the real pain began. He could not eat or sleep. He did not attempt to go to the office, though he left the house every morning as if he were going to. He walked the streets all day. One day in Warwick Road he passed Diana on the pavement and could see from her strained inward face that she was similarly employed. She did not see him. In the evenings he sat in the drawing-room and pretended to read. Diana went off to bed about eight. Miles, who could not now bring himself to share her bed, stretched himself out on the hearth rug and lay there stiff and open-eyed through the night hours. He began to think that he would soon die simply from lack of sleep.

He had thought at first that he would find Lisa, that he *must* find Lisa. He could not conceive how he had ever let her go out of his sight. Two houses. It would have worked. He could have forced it on her. He had asked Diana where she was, but Diana obviously did not know. The Save the Children Fund people did not know either. They said her forwarding address was their Calcutta office. He imagined finding her, meeting her in the street perhaps, or stopping her at the airport. He imagined the light sound, one evening, of her key in the door at Kempsford Gardens. 'Miles, I've come back, I had to. I'll never leave you again.' He imagined a meeting in India, the circle of wondering dark faces as Lisa laughed and cried in his arms. Yet he did not visit travel agents or haunt London airport. He did not even write to her. Something very small inside him believed that she was gone, that he had really lost her, and he bent over in physical agony to contain that small searing lump of belief.

All this while he and Diana had scarcely spoken to each other. Diana spent an increasing amount of time in the bedroom, indeed in bed, and seemed to be crying a good deal. Once or twice she had made pitiful attempts to smile at him when they met on the stairs, but Miles's face could not smile, and once when she touched his arm beseechingly he jerked away as if he had received an electric shock. Diana had passed by and gone on into the kitchen with a wailing sob. Miles knew that he was becoming crazed by lack of sleep but had no will to do anything about it. He waited patiently, resignedly, for his exhausted body to commit some merciful violence upon his tormented mind. On about the fifth day towards evening he found himself not so much falling asleep as entering a state of trance. He could see his surroundings with an increase of vividness but seemed to have withdrawn from them into a condition of remote dream-like helplessness.

Later he woke from an unconsciousness which had not seemed like sleep. It was night and the moon was shining into the drawing-room where he was lying on the floor. It seemed to Miles that he must be dead. He seemed to see himself lying there, as if his soul had left his body and was standing like a tall sentinel beside it. He lay in the moonlight trying to remember who he was and what had happened to him. Then he remembered. Parvati had been killed yesterday in an air crash. He recalled how he had parted with her so lately at the airport. She had a shy way of waving, with one thin little hand fluttering beside her hair, then darting to toss the heavy pigtail back over her shoulder. She was wearing the red and gold sari which he so particularly liked. She was still so slim, the child not yet showing within her. She waved, and he could see the flash of her smile, and then she was gone through the doorway. It was the first time they had been really parted for years. 'Soon back, darling, soon back,' he had repeated to himself, as she had said it to him, as he looked at the empty doorway. And now she was dead, broken and scattered upon a mountainside, utterly gone out of the world, existing no more anywhere, Parvati and his child. Miles turned away from the moonlight and rested his forehead upon the carpet. He lay there open-eyed and gazed and gazed upon the fact of her death. She was utterly gone out of the world for ever. She did not exist any more at all.

Diana had found him in the morning still lying there, apparently paralysed and unable to move. She had sent for a doctor and Miles was persuaded to hobble up to bed. After a while he seemed more rational, complained like an ordinary invalid, accepted hot water bottles and soup. He become pathetically dependent upon Diana, and could scarcely bear her to leave him for a moment, although he spoke to her very little. Then at last he began to talk. He talked to her for a whole day, for two whole days, about Parvati, he told her everything, about the child, everything, everything that he could remember right from the very beginning. He described to her in detail how he had first met Parvati when she was bicycling along King's Parade, and he had thought, if only that marvellous girl's sari would catch in the wheel of her bicycle I could go up to her and speak to her. Then the sari had caught in the wheel of the bicycle and Miles had run up to help her to free it and had asked her to have tea with him. She refused. Two days later he met her again at a political meeting, and she accepted. He told Diana everything that he could remember, down to the way she had waved and tossed her pigtail at the doorway at the airport. And he told her about standing alone in the hall with the newspaper. And Diana listened with tears streaming down her face.

After that they talked about Lisa. Diana told him about their childhood and what Lisa had been like then. She found some old photographs and showed them to Miles. They talked about their marriage and why it had happened and what it was like. 'I coaxed you into love, Miles. It was not like Parvati, not like Lisa.' 'You coaxed me back to life. Perhaps only you could have done it.' They talked of Miles's loves and whether he had really loved Lisa from long ago and whether he would have married her if he had met her first. They talked in quiet voices like two very old people talking about things that had happened long ago in the distant past. It was then that Miles began to notice that some change had come about, that the world looked quite different, that it had been turned inside out.

The pain was not less. Or perhaps it must have become less since he could behave normally, eat meals and go back to the office. It was as if the pain remained there but he had grown larger all round it and could contain it more easily. It no longer bent and racked his body. He carried it inside himself gently, almost gingerly, as if it were a precious egg. He sat very upright in the tube train, sat quietly at his desk in the office, nursing his pain, letting his body hold it carefully, lightly. He thought a great deal about Parvati and a great deal about Lisa. Their shades travelled with him wherever he went. And he experienced his loss as if it were one loss, blankly and without consolation, and his eyes seemed to open upon it, wider and wider, as he stared at what had happened and nursed the great egg of pain inside him.

During this time he often heard Diana telling him to leave her and to go to Lisa. He heard her words, to which he gave no reply except to smile and shake his head. The words had no connexion now with practice or with the everyday pattern of his life. He knew now that Lisa was an impossibility and had to be an impossibility. That was indeed her role, her task, her service to him. He would never cease to love her. But he felt that he would probably never meet her again. She was dedicated, separated, withdrawn for ever beyond a grille, behind a curtain. And he would worship her cold virtue until he could see her no longer. He recalled the superb negativity of her last appearance. 'No talk.' 'Will you write to me?' 'No.' Indeed in his thought she was already changing. The girl whom he had known for so many years, the sick girl, the deprived one, the silent one, was already being obscured by something else. A tall cold angel, chilly and strong as a steel shaft, seemed to be materializing, never more to leave his side. The angel of death, perhaps of Parvati's death.

Of course Miles knew what was going to happen next. He smiled his secret smile, he smiled alone, and he smiled at Diana, smiled through Diana, as she urged him that it was not too late to go to Lisa. He was in no hurry now, for he was in the hands of another power. On warm sunny spring evenings he sat in the little summer house, disregarding Diana's anxiety about it being damp. When the weather was cold or rainy he sat at his study window watching the fast grey clouds falling down over the top of the Earls Court exhibition hall. When it grew dark he sat there in the darkness and looked out into the red glowing London sky. His thoughts became vague, floating, warm. They began to distintegrate as the darkness below them stirred and shifted. They began to fall apart into images.

Miles started writing poetry. He wrote easily. Huge chunks, great complicated pieces, arrived complete. Images fluttered about him, practically blinding him with their multiplicity. There is a grace of certainty about being in love. There is a grace of certainty in art, but it is very rare. Miles felt it now as he heard in poetry for the first time his own voice speaking and not that of another. And he knew that the moment had come at last when he could with humility call himself a poet. He had waited long enough and he had tried to wait faithfully. Yet it seemed to him now that he had simply not known how to wait, and that his attempts to prepare himself for the great service into which he was now entered had all been mistaken ones. He had strained and pulled and scratched fretfully at the surfaces of life, while the great other watched and smiled. What had availed him now, what had bundled him through the barrier into the real world, this Miles knew too, but now that his life's work had begun he averted his gaze. And more deeply and calmly he knew that when the frenzy left him – for it could not last for ever – he would be left with all the tools of his trade.

Diana and Miles had begun to walk back through the cemetery, with their arms round each other's waists. They walked very slowly, like an old couple. The evening sun shone upon the shining arches of the new grass and a rich smell of wet earth floated in the warm air. The avenue of lime trees was misted with young leaves.

Diana said, 'I think you ought to have an electric fire in the summer house. It wouldn't be too difficult to arrange.'

'Warm days are coming now.'

'Yes, but it *is* damp in there. And if we made it really warm you could work there in the winter too.'

'I should like that. Especially if it snowed!'

'Especially if it snowed. I'd have to make the whole place completely draught-proof of course. What's the name of that stuff that you put round the doors and windows to seal them?'

'I can't remember.'

'I'll ask the ironmonger tomorrow.'

Chapter Thirty

Adelaide's tears dropped into the open drawer, making damp spots on the pink and blue jumble of her underwear. They fell, as she straightened up, on to the sleeve of her new black suit which was made of a corduroy so fine that it carried a grey surface haze like shot silk. She smudged the tears away with her hand, hoping that they would not make a mark upon the corduroy. She peered at herself in the dressing-table mirror. The hotel room did not provide a long glass. The frilly white blouse, also new, seemed to be the wrong size after all. She had bought it in a hurry. The frills refused to emerge elegantly at the neck of the jacket but remained crushed and jumbled inside, and if she tried to pull them out the blouse came adrift at the waist. But it was too late to do anything about that now, or about the blue necklace of Venetian beads which just did not look right on top of the blouse. She should have realized it was the wrong length. She took off the necklace and dropped it into her suitcase. Then she adjusted the mirror, stood back, and began cautiously to mount on a chair. By this method she could see the reflection of her lower half, see the black cord skirt, the invisible nylon stockings, the black patent leather shoes with the steel buckle. Well, she thought, I certainly look right for a funeral.

She got down again very carefully. Adelaide was always afraid of falling and felt giddy standing on a chair. She picked up her little black velvet hat and began to dust it, holding it well away from herself, and leaning forward a little so that the tears should fall on to the floor and not on to her suit or hat. How is it possible, thought Adelaide, to go on crying for such a long time, one would think that the supply would run out. Where do they come from, these tears? She pictured a great lacrymose reservoir, the tears of a lifetime: and at the thought of how many she would still without doubt have to shed, the flowing stream redoubled. I've cried so much lately, it'll damage my eyes, she thought, it'll alter my appearance permanently. I really must stop, but how? She studied her face in the mirror. Her eyes were puckered and oozing and surrounded by great red circles of swollen skin. Her whole face was red and swollen and hot, its surface shiny with dried and half-dried tears. God, I look terrible, thought Adelaide. How can I put make-up on to that?

She began to comb her hair, dropping the little balls of loose hair at intervals into the hotel waste paper basket. Her hair seemed to be coming out more than usual. It was not the right colour either. She had had to go to a strange hairdressers and the girl had tinted it to a much lighter brown. She wondered how noticeable this was. She had not yet got used to having short hair and got a shock from her looking glass every morning. The great length of cut hair travelled with her. The hairdresser had offered to buy it, but Adelaide could not consent to this, although the weird severed object caused her horror. She patted her new head. She had hoped that short hair would make her look younger. Now she thought it just made her look blowsy and untidy. She could not decide whether to push the short light brown locks back behind her ear or to let them hang. They looked wrong either way. Perhaps it had been an awful mistake to have her hair cut off. But she knew perfectly well why she had done it.

Adelaide looked at her watch. She had still not finished packing. She could leave the big suitcase downstairs with the porter. She began to stuff her underclothes into the smaller bag. She went through the drawers and checked the wardrobe. She searched the unmade bed and found two damp handkerchiefs. She must remember to buy some paper ones. She had not been long in the hotel, but the sheets looked grimy and grey. Everything was ready now except her face. She had put off making it up in the hope that she would be able to stop crying. Now she would just have to put the make-up on and trust that it would somehow check the tears. Leaning well over the washbasin she mopped her face for some time with cold water. Then she dried it and began to smooth on a foundation cream. The touch of her fingers soothed her burning cheeks. She closed her eyes for a moment. Now for the powder. Just as she was preparing to apply the pearly pink lipstick to her swollen lips two great tears rolled down making two deep long furrows over the smoothly powdered curve of her cheeks. 'Damn!' said Adelaide. Her hand slipped and the lipstick went on to her chin. She thought, I shall have to wash my face and start again. Well, no I won't. It doesn't really matter any more what I look like. Then she repeated to herself, it doesn't really matter any more what I look like. She felt that it was true and that it was an index of great changes in her life. The solemnity of the thought elicited two more big tears. She tried to rub the errant lipstick off with her handkerchief. It would not quite come off, but the pink blur blended well enough with her flushed face. She mopped her cheeks over lightly and put on her hat. The telephone rang to say that the taxi had come.

Adelaide carried the two bags down the narrow stairs, past the dusty potted plants in the brass bowls, and left the larger bag with the porter. She got into the taxi. She thought, Oh God now I shall really start to cry again. And she did. Curiously watched by people in neighbouring cars, she abandoned herself to sobbing as the taxi crawled slowly through the north London traffic. At last they had arrived. Adelaide dabbed her face with a soaking wet handkerchief and tried to powder it again, only now the powder puff seemed to have got wet too. She paid the taxi driver out of her new black patent leather handbag. She crossed the busy pavement between a newspaper stand and a stack of crates of fruit which were just being delivered to the greengrocer. A tomato rolled across the pavement and broke, revealing its damp blushing interior at her feet. Adelaide skirted it and went into the little dark doorway and up the stairs to the office on the first floor. She knocked and went in.

Auntie and the twins were already there. Auntie was wearing a very long black coat with a fur trimmed collar and a hat which appeared to be made entirely of peacock's feathers. She was also wearing a big red and green brooch and a number of flashy rings. The twins were in dark suits, Will sporting a red rose and Nigel a white rose. The registrar came forward to welcome Adelaide.

'Hello,' said Adelaide, looking past him at the twins.

Nigel advanced and kissed her a little awkwardly on the cheek. He was smiling. Will's face was thunderous. He had trimmed his moustache into a Hitlerian toothbrush. He came and kissed Adelaide, also on the cheek. He said, 'Christ, your face is hot.' Auntie said, *'Moya meelaya devooshka.'* Will said, 'Shut up, Auntie.' Adelaide felt that she was going to faint and had to sit down.

'Now then,' said the registrar a little coyly, 'must remember why we're here, mustn't we. Now let me see, which of you gentlemen is going to be married? Mustn't marry the lady to the wrong one, must I?'

'I'm the groom,' said Will. 'Oh Ad, do stop crying, turn off the waterworks, will you? Have you got no dignity? Anyone'd think you were going to be executed.'

'I think we all feel like that on our wedding day, ha ha,' said the registrar.

Nigel smiled.

Auntie said, *'Svadba, soodba, slooshba.'*

Will said, 'Ba ba black sheep to you, Auntie. Now Ad, do pull yourself together. You don't want to call the whole thing off, do you?'

'Nooo,' Adelaide wailed.

Auntie said, *'Ya tosha,'* and began to sniff.

'Tosh off, Auntie. Ad, try to behave like a rational being or I shall really get angry with you. Come and sit here beside me, come on. Now stop it, or I'll give you something to cry for!'

Adelaide came forward. She had knocked her hat sideways by her exertions with her handkerchief and she had smeared her lipstick again. Her breath hissed through shuddering lips. Tears had begun to course down Auntie's face. Nigel was smiling.

'Now I think you both know the procedure,' said the registrar. 'This is a very simple little ceremony, but it has the force and solemnity of law and society behind it, and is just as binding as if you were being married in a cathedral.'

Adelaide moaned and put her damp handkerchief to her mouth. Nigel, still smiling, wiped away a tear from his eye.

'First I must check your names please, your full names, and also your fathers' names. You, Adelaide Anne de Crecy . . .'

Nigel's face was streaming with tears. He was still smiling.

'And you, Wilfred Reginald Boase . . .'

'Oh Christ!' said Will. His face became red, and his eyes filled and overbrimmed with tears. 'Christ! Sorry, Ad.'

'And your father's name – Oh dear – Oh dear me – ' The registrar's pen faltered and he began to reach for his handkerchief.

Adelaide had anticipated pains and difficulties in her married life, and her anticipations were fulfilled. Will's temper did not improve as the years went by, and a chronic dyspepsia, caused by the irregular life of the theatre, did nothing to soothe his frequent tantrums. Adelaide submitted meekly at first. Later she learnt how to shout back. But she always felt ashamed and tired after their rows. Will never seemed even to remember that there had been a quarrel. Yet if Adelaide had certainly foreseen the bad things it was also true that she had not managed to foresee the good ones. She had married Will in a mood of cornered desperation because she felt that Will was her fate. She had not even framed the idea of happiness in connexion with her marriage. Yet there was happiness too. Adelaide had not realized beforehand how very much she would enjoy being in bed with Will and how greatly this enjoyment would lighten the way for both of them. Nor did she, as she wept and signed her new name, Adelaide Boase, for the first time, dream of much later and sunnier days, in spite of Will's cantankerous temper, when her tall twins would be up at Oxford (non-identical, Benedick and Mercutio), when Will would be one of the most famous and popular actors in England, and a greatly transformed Adelaide would be Lady Boase.

Nearer in time, and a financial godsend to the young household, was the surprise they got when Auntie died and her jewels turned out to be worth ten thousand pounds. Auntie's memoirs too, when translated into English, proved a best-seller, as well as being a mine of information for historians about the last days of the Czarist régime. Adelaide and Will kept saying that they would learn Russian one day so as to read Auntie's memoirs in the original, but they never did. However Benedick became a Russian expert. Mercutio was a mathematician.

Chapter Thirty-one

Danby was sitting on the edge of his bed. It was ten o'clock in the evening. The walls of the room were still a bit damp, but he had managed to dry the bed out with hot water bottles. On warm days he put the mattress in the sun. The electricity had been off for weeks, as the whole house had had to be rewired. Fortunately the government were going, if he filled in enough forms, to pay for that. Fortunately too the weather had been exceptionally warm for the time of year.

The room had not suffered too much. Getting the mud off the floor had been the difficult thing. It was fantastic how much mud that water had brought in with it. The carpet had been mud-coloured anyway, but the walls were darkly stained up to about four feet from the ground. It was no good having the place redecorated until the walls had dried. With luck, the government would pay for that as well. Danby had been sleeping upstairs, but he was wondering if tonight he wouldn't move back into his own room. He didn't like it upstairs, though of course it was nearer if Bruno called in the night. But Bruno very rarely called in the night now. He seemed to be sleeping better, and indeed spent quite a lot of his time asleep.

Danby had stopped going to the printing works and spent his days at home now. Someone had to stay with Bruno. Nigel had simply vanished from the scene, leaving most of his belongings behind, and Danby felt there was no point in engaging another nurse at this stage. The doctor was surprised that Bruno had lasted so long. Diana came nearly every day in the late afternoon and Danby went out for a breather and a visit to the pub while she sat with Bruno. He could hear her talking to Bruno sometimes, as he went out of the hall door, but he never asked her what they talked about. He talked a little with Bruno himself, usually about immediate things, food, the weather, Bruno's room. Bruno could talk quite sensibly about these things, but the background of his mind seemed to have come adrift, and Danby often caught Bruno looking at him with a puzzled expression, as if he did not know who Danby was and did not quite like to ask. Diana too was a source of puzzlement, though Danby lost no opportunity of repeating, 'Diana, you know, Miles's wife.' But Danby did not explain his own identity. He did not want to remind Bruno about Gwen.

With Diana Danby had achieved a sad but strangely sweet relationship such as one might have with a wife one had divorced long ago. They kissed each other on the cheek and squeezed hands. The tending of Bruno made a solemn and melancholy bond between them. 'How is he today?' 'Not too bad. He took some soup.' Danby knew that Diana was afraid that Bruno might die when she was alone with him and Danby was not there. She never said this, but Danby understood what it meant when she asked anxiously, 'You won't be too long away, will you?' It was strange and terrible, this waiting for death. Every morning Danby wondered if Bruno had not died quietly during the night, and then saw, with a shock of pain and relief, the bedclothes still rising and falling a little. He had come, during this last time, to love Bruno with a blank almost impersonal sort of love, and he was able at last to measure that vast difference, that distance between presence and absence. Bruno's presence in the house was something real, so positive, so profoundly touching. And yet it was also impossible not to feel it as a defilement. Danby looked forward with dread and yet with longing to the time when he would come home and take off his coat and get out the whiskey bottle in a house utterly empty of Bruno. Yet between that moment and now there was that terrible unforeseeable *thing* to be endured.

Bruno had changed physically too since his fall. He had stopped wearing his false teeth and the lower part of his face had collapsed. His head seemed to be shrinking generally as the chunky flesh which had made his face look so lumpy and strange began to subside and fall in towards the bone. The ring of thin silky white hair which had fringed the base of the skull had mostly come off, rubbed away upon the pillow, and the skull was almost completely bare. Only Bruno's eyes remained the same, narrow, moist and terrifyingly full of puzzlement, speculation, and a weird kind of intelligence. With these puzzled hostile rather frightened eyes he surveyed the people who served him. Only sometimes for Diana would his shrunken face strain into a smile and his eyes wrinkle up with something like pleasure.

Miles had called two or three times and conducted rather one-sided conversations with Bruno. Once Danby, passing the door, had heard Miles talking about cricket, though he had not heard Bruno reply. Miles carried with him an atmosphere of complete unconcern. He was almost debonair. He approached Bruno with a kind of cheerfulness which irritated Danby extremely. He made brisk inquiries about what the doctor had said. He behaved like a man performing a duty and pleased with himself for doing so. He seemed completely uninvolved in the pain and the mystery of what was about to take place. He left the house smiling secretively and humming to himself. Danby decided that he detested Miles. The strange emotion, which had once seemed like love, which Miles had inspired in him, had faded away. He no longer even thought that Miles resembled Gwen. He saw him as a large smiling rat. He also sensed Miles's increased dislike of himself, and wondered if Diana had talked. Probably not.

Danby had heard the news of Adelaide's marriage with distress and relief. Now that he was no longer deafened by her cries he was able to remember her charm. She had been a sweet girl-friend to him during those years and he felt a shamed gratitude which he would have liked to express to her in some way. He thought of giving her fifty pounds as a wedding present and got as far as writing the cheque but then could not decide whether it would be proper to send it or not. When things have gone hopelessly wrong one simply does not know how to behave. In the end he did not send the cheque. Will would only tear it up and send back the pieces.

Danby drew the curtains. It was very dark outside, a moonless night and a little rain falling. He went to check that the door of the annexe was propped open so that he could hear Bruno if he called. The old man had been fast asleep when Danby went up to see him earlier. Oh let him die in his sleep,

Danby prayed with a sad pained heart. Let him die peacefully in his sleep and not know. Only not tonight, not tonight. Poor Bruno. Danby pulled back the sheets and blankets and felt the mattress, wondering if it was dry enough to sleep on. It seemed to be all right. The Stadium Street house had never felt entirely like a home to Danby, but he liked his little room with the dreary outlook on to the yard. The yard was just an expanse of grey mud now, caked and cracking in dry weather, in wet weather like thick glue. Danby vaguely intended to clear it up, but could not see how this could be done.

He sat down again on the bed and looked at himself in the dressing-table mirror. A fat man with a lot of white hair and rather good teeth. He sighed. If only he had not seen Lisa, if only he had not been given that glimpse of something else, of really being alive or whatever it was. He had been quite happy sleeping with Adelaide, quite happy flirting with Diana. These beings belonged to his ordinary dull world and his ordinary dim consciousness. Meeting Lisa was the sudden exchange of twilight for daylight, greyness for colour, shadow for substance and shape. He had forgotten what these things were like. Perhaps he would forget again. Perhaps he would come through it all and out on to some great placid lake where the sun shone hazily and with a difference. Perhaps he would achieve some sort of peace, the peace of an elderly man, a peace of cosy retirement without angels. Without women, too, he thought. Could he find another girl now? After seeing Lisa he simply didn't want to.

He wondered where she was now, in some unimaginable abode of bliss with her other man. He could not think of her as belonging to this world and inhabiting the same space as himself. He pictured her enclosed in some kind of radiant extra-galactic egg, some strange fold of the space-time continuum which wrapped her absolutely away. This vague image was necessary to him to soothe what would otherwise have been a crippling degree of jealousy and desire. If there was no place for possibility there was no place for yearning. Lisa had been a vision, an apparition, not a possibility. Yet however much he tried to refuse the knowledge, he knew that what he had seen and, oh God, *touched* was a real woman who might have loved him.

Danby thought that he might soon start to cry. For years he had been incapable of tears. Now quite lately, he had found himself weeping in the late evening and the early morning. The tears were strange, sweetly soothing and a little unnerving, as if his body were suffering some weird physical change. He must be careful not to let Bruno see him crying. He got up and went to the door for a moment to listen. There was no sound from upstairs. Then he thought that he had better go up and check that he had locked the front door, and he went up the stairs on tiptoe. Thank God poor Bruno slept at night.

A letter, which must have come by the second post, was lying on the mat. Danby saw at once that the writing was unfamiliar and it instantly seemed to him that the letter must be from Lisa. In trembling haste he tore it open. It was rather long and appeared to be from Nigel. Danby locked the door and fixed the chain and went slowly down the stairs again. He sat for a while staring sadly at nothing and holding Nigel's letter crumpled in his hand. If only there were not these vain ghostly hopes, these sudden inane shadows of possibilities, these unfulfilled conditionals of hopeless desire. He closed his eyes and a tear trickled down his cheek. Then he began to read Nigel's letter.

My dearest Danby,

I hope you will try to forgive me for my dereliction of duty, my unannounced departure, my taking of leave without consultation or permission. I am sorry to leave Bruno and had not intended to do so before the end. I hope he is calm and I would send my love if I thought he still remembered Nigel, only I trust that mercifully he does not. Since in a sense Nigel never really existed, he probably casts no memory image as he casts no shadow. I write to speak to you, just once, since it is a delicious joy to do so (see below) and because I feel I should try to explain why I went away. That, and other things.

Love is a strange thing. There is no doubt at all that it and only it makes the world go round. It is our only significant activity. Everything else is dust and tinkling cymbals and vexation of spirit. Yet on the other hand what a trouble-maker it is to be sure. What a dreamer-upper of the impossible, what an embracer of the feet of the unattainable. It is a weird thought that anyone is *permitted* to love anyone and in any way he pleases. Nothing in nature forbids it. A cat may look at a king, the worthless can love the good, the good the worthless, the worthless the worthless and the good the good. Hey presto: and the great light flashes on revealing perhaps reality or perhaps illusion. And alas how very often, dearest Danby, does one love alone, in solipsism, in vain incapsulation, while concealment feeds upon the substance of the heart. It is not a matter of conventions. Love knows no conventions. Anything *can* happen, so that in a way, a terrible terrible way, there are no impossibilities. Ah, I have thought of this too, my dear, and it has not been the least part of my suffering. You might have loved me. It was, alas, logically possible. But what made me go away was not simply my sense of the improbability of the conceivable, but my knowledge that my very great love was a very great destroyer. If I had been the saint that I could be I would have loved you and let you know it and stayed near you and done you no harm at all, surrounding you like the harmless air and making you almost not notice how much I loved you. As it is, the unpredictable force of that immense angelic thing, once let loose from its dark concealment, would have dragged us – where? I know not, but down. You would have had to act a hateful part. And I –

The other great love of my life is, well you can guess who. To have you both before me pointing loaded pistols at each other was the acting out of a fantasy. And how absolutely, when it came to it, you were both of you clay in my hands. How easy it proved to make you do exactly what I wanted! But I must not think about my godlike power – that way lies the possible-impossible torment which I have determined to end. It was a great happening, was it not, our duel? Not knowing the outcome was heavenly pain, was Russian roulette of the soul. Forgive me.

I have decided that the only way to deal with myself as I now am is to leave England. A friend has told me how I can get a job in India, with the Save the Children Fund, and I am going to Calcutta. I leave no address and I sign no name. I am a spirit that wished you well and will wish you well for however long or short a time it preserves your memory. I kiss your feet.

Danby stared at the letter. It caused him an extraordinary and novel kind of pain. He wished he had known that Nigel loved him. Yet what on earth would he have done about it? Would he have acted that 'hateful part'? Yes, what a troublemaker it was. Every man jack craving for love, and how rarely it all worked out. Nigel loved Danby who loved Lisa who loved – How sad and crazy it all was. Oh God, I feel so bloody lonely, he thought. The voice of love, even though it was not the right one, came to him with such an unmistakable accent out of that inaccessible real world. His eyes seemed to be filling with tears again. 'Oh hell,' said Danby aloud. He shook the tears away and took off his jacket and his tie. Better go to bed and drown all this self-pity in decent oblivion. Misery and drink made him a sound sleeper. He stood for a moment listening to the rain which had grown fiercer and listening to the wind which was rattling the windowpane. He undid the front of his shirt.

Suddenly there was a strange sharp regular noise very close to him. Danby stood paralysed, clutching his shirt. In a moment the sound came again, loud and several times repeated. Someone was tapping urgently upon the window. Will! Danby thought, it's Will for sure, come to do me properly. He stood perfectly still. The tapping came again, insistent, demanding, violent. He'll break the glass in a minute, thought Danby. Whatever shall I do? Call the police? Pretend not to be here? Can he see me through the chink in the curtain? Oh God, why did this have to happen. Danby felt tired and old. He wanted to go to bed. He did not want to be forced to fight with a half crazy young man. It was all ridiculous. He called out, 'Who's there?' There was no answer, only the tapping on the window, once more repeated, fierce and sharp. Danby hesitated. Then he moved silently out of the room and into the kitchen. He picked up a long carving knife and then laid it down again. He returned and went up to the window. *'Who is it?' Tap, tap, tap, tap.* Danby pulled back the curtains. He could not see out into the darkness and the rain. Then he violently pulled up the sash of the window and retreated across the room.

At once a long leg with an extremely muddy shoe appeared over the window ledge. But it was a woman's leg. 'Help me, would you?' said Lisa.

Danby closed the window and pulled the curtain again. Lisa was sitting on the bed. She had taken off her mackintosh and was removing her shoes. Her hair, which had been uncovered, was plastered to her head and curled in wet arabesques down her neck.

She said, 'I'm sorry to come in this way and I wouldn't have done so if I'd known how much mud I would bring in with me. I didn't like to ring the bell because of Bruno. Would you mind getting me a towel?'

Danby went to the kitchen and returned with a towel. She began to dry her face and hair. Danby stood by the window, leaning on the chest of drawers, staring with his mouth open. An extreme pain, passing up the centre of his body like a white hot rod, kept him clenched and rigid.

'I'm sorry to arrive unannounced,' said Lisa. She had rubbed her hair into a mass of rather frizzy small ringlets which she was now trying to smooth down. 'Could I borrow your comb?'

Danby, moving gingerly because of the pain, handed her the comb, leaning stiffly. His teeth had begun to chatter and he closed his mouth grinding his teeth together.

Lisa was combing her hair. It was difficult. 'What a stormy night,' she said.

'Oh God!' said Danby. 'Oh Christ!'

'Do sit down, Danby. Sit on that chair by the window, would you? How is Bruno?'

Danby sat down, still stiffly. That pain made him groan. He put his hands to his face and groaned again. He said in a low stumbling voice, 'Why are you here?'

'I said how is Bruno?'

'All right. No, dying. But quiet, O.K. Why are you here?'

'I will explain,' said Lisa. 'And I must begin with an apology. It might have been better to write to you. But I have been a long time in a great deal of doubt and when things at last became clear I found that I wanted to see you at once and to, as I say, explain.' She spoke rather coldly, staring at him and still combing her hair.

'You don't know what you've done,' said Danby.

'Not yet. But a little time will show.'

'I mean, coming to see me like this. It makes it all a thousand times worse. There's nothing to explain. I wasn't complaining. I wasn't even looking for you. And there's absolutely nothing you can do. I've just got to suffer it. Oh God, I wish you hadn't come!'

'I'm afraid you'll have to undergo the explanation,' she said. 'It is necessary – for me.'

'There isn't any explanation!' said Danby. 'I just love you like a crazy fool. Anybody can love anybody. The worthless can love the good. A cat can look at a king, queen, princess, angel. I've just got to grit my teeth and sit it out. I don't want your sympathy or your bloody explanations!'

Lisa was looking at him with a frowning faintly curious look, her mouth pouting as if with a slight disgust. Her face was a glowing pink after her exertions with the towel. Her hair, which she had finished combing and smoothing back, curled damply down her neck, blackened by the rain. She pulled up one wet stockinged foot and tucked it under her, arranging the pillows behind her back against the wall. When she had made herself comfortable she said, 'Now I want you to listen.'

'I'm inclined to tell you to go,' said Danby. He felt something curiously like anger.

'No. You would find yourself incapable of that, I think.'

She's right, he thought. Oh God, Oh God, why do I have to endure this?

'I am going to talk, and I may ask you some questions,' said Lisa. 'I want to start with a question. When you came that night to Kempsford Gardens Miles told you I was in love with somebody. Do you know who that person is?'

'The person you're in love with? No.'

'It's Miles.'

Danby looked at the floor. He leaned slowly forward with his elbows on his knees and his face in his hands. He thought, I simply mustn't start crying. If I started I wouldn't be able to stop. Miles. *Miles.* He was silent.

'I'm sorry,' said Lisa. 'I know this hurts you but it's necessary. I have been and am in love with Miles. I fell in love with him when I first met him, on the day of his marriage with Diana. I loved him all through those years and I imagined that I would never let him know it.'

Danby was silent, pressing his hands into his eyes.

'Quite recently however he found out, or rather I told him. I ought not to have done so, but it was very difficult not to, psychologically difficult I mean, because by then he had fallen in love with me.'

Danby was silent.

'I don't know how long he has loved me,' Lisa went on in the same cool precise even voice, 'he imagines that it has been a long time. But my own guess is that he only really fell in love quite lately.'

Danby lifted his head. There were tears and he did not try to conceal them. 'God blast you, why are you torturing me with this damned love story?'

'It is necessary to make this quite clear. I love Miles and he loves me.'

'Oh get out, will you,' said Danby.

'However,' said Lisa, paying no attention to the interruption, 'the fact remained that Miles was married to Diana.'

'This is a nightmare,' said Danby. 'What's the point of all this? Oh Lisa, Lisa, you are thoughtless and cruel, or else you don't realize what kind of state I'm in. If only I hadn't seen you again, talked to you again. It would have stopped hurting so much sooner. And now you come here and talk about Miles, about *Miles* of all people. You must be insane to hurt somebody like this.'

'I am sorry,' she said. 'But you will see that it has been necessary.'

'What's necessary about it? If you want to see how much power you've got well you're seeing it. If you want to see a man reduced to – '

'Stop it, please, and listen – '

'I'd managed to find some sort of peace with Bruno here. Well, not peace, but it's been real. I was starting to realize that you were – just something impossible. And now you've spoilt it all. You just can't know what you've done, coming here, coming into my room – '

'Naturally, you were beginning to recover – '

'I wasn't beginning to recover! I'll never recover! Oh damn you, damn you, damn you!'

'Don't shout so. Will you listen to what I've got to tell you? I need your help.'

'I'm to help you get hold of Miles I suppose! Oh Christ, Lisa, you don't mean that – You can't mean – ' Danby sat upright, glaring at her, his face puckered up with pain.

'What are you supposing?'

255

'When I first saw you, Lisa, I was, oh God, I was holding Diana in my arms. What hope have I ever had of convincing you that I love you, that it's serious, different, terrible? You think I'm just a man who chases women. You think I'm really just as interested in Diana. You want me to occupy Diana, to take her away, so that you and Miles – You absolute fiend!' Danby stood up. He raised his hands, half desperate, half threatening.

'Sit down and stop shouting at me.'

'That's devil's work. You're driving me straight into madness. Do you want me to kill you?'

'You're being very stupid. Don't dare to touch me!'

'Touch you – I'd like to strangle you!' Danby moaned and turned about and leaned against the chest of drawers, covering his face. 'Oh Lisa, Lisa, Lisa – '

'I want you to listen and I want you to *think*. If you'd been using your mind you wouldn't have said what you said just now. I don't want you to take Diana away from Miles. You couldn't do it anyway.'

Danby moaned again.

'Miles and I knew at once that there was no future for us together. What sort of people do you think we are?'

'People in love,' he said.

'Romantic love is not an absolute.'

'People who are in love think so.'

'It's an overprized condition. Besides one recovers. Even you began to recover!'

'I didn't. Nor did you. You say you've loved Miles for years.'

'Absence cures.'

'Anyhow, you and Miles will find a way. You're both so damn clever.'

'Listen. There was and is nothing that we could do with our love. Miles could not leave Diana. He is married to Diana, Diana has given her whole life to Miles. And after I had told my love and tasted his I could not remain in the house – '

'There are other houses in London.'

'Not for Miles and me. We couldn't live like that.'

'You could try. Did you go to bed together?' Danby was standing with his back to her, staring down at his hairbrush.

'No, of course not.'

'I don't see why of course. You're not saints.'

'No. We are cool self-interested people. We did not want to set a course into ruin and madness.'

'Well, I'm still waiting to see what aspect of your cool self-interest has brought you to me with this practically unbearable story!'

'As I told you, we decided that we must part and I decided that it would be easier for both of us if I went right away and I fixed up a job for myself in India, in Calcutta, with the Save the Children Fund.'

'Then why aren't you in Calcutta,' said Danby, 'why are you in Stadium Street, in my bedroom, sitting on my bed with your shoes off?'

There was silence. He looked up at last. She was looking at him with a peculiar hard intensity. After a pause she went on. 'I decided not to go to India. It was a difficult decision and a very crucial one.'

'So you're going back to Miles after all, and you thought you'd drop in on me on the way and tell me all about it!'

'No, I'm not going back to Miles.'

'Then what are you going to do?'

'That,' said Lisa, 'depends partly on you.'

Danby sat down very slowly in the chair by the window. He stared at her fiercely, sternly. 'Lisa, just what are you talking about?'

She looked at him now almost with hostility. 'I want to make it all crystal clear,' she said, 'and it's not easy to make clear.'

'I'll say it isn't!'

'I don't want you to be in any way cheated.'

'I look like being killed not cheated.'

'I had to make it plain about Miles –'

'You've made it plain! What do you want, Lisa, do you want to use me to make Miles jealous?'

'It's odd,' she said, 'I think it was seeing you talking to me that day in the cemetery that made Miles suddenly realize he loved me – when he saw that someone else might.'

'You can spare me the touching reminiscences. So that *is* what you want?'

'No. I have no plans which concern Miles.'

'It's impossible,' said Danby. 'You love him. He loves you. As you've explained ten times. It's impossible. You must intend to go back to him.'

'*No.*'

'Well, then what *do* you want me to do?'

For the first time since her arrival Lisa showed some confusion. She sighed, dropped her gaze, and began to push her hair back, fingering the damp rings on her neck into dry dark brown tendrils. 'I decided not to go to India –'

'Go on.'

'I spent all those years – in that house – loving Miles and knowing where he slept – every night –'

'Cut that bit.'

'I could have gone on, you see, indefinitely, and I thought I would go on indefinitely. Only then that suddenly happened, his loving me like that and my telling him –'

'Lisa, don't take me round again, I can't stand it.'

'When I thought I'd go away I imagined I was the same person, the person of before. It was the person of before who decided to go to India –'

'Go on, go on.'

'Well, I found I wasn't that person any more.'

'What on earth are you talking about?'

'I'd also like you to know,' she said, looking directly at him again, 'that I do absolutely believe that you love me, and that it is, as you put it, serious, different, terrible.'

Danby stared at her. He felt as if he was going to faint and slide forward off the chair. He said hoarsely, 'Christ. You want me to console you.'

Lisa was looking at him with great intentness. 'There is something, yes, which might be put like that. As I said, it is extremely difficult to be precise. That – experience – with Miles altered me. Maybe for the worse, time will show. I found I couldn't just go away – and be alone. I didn't want to go away – any more.'

'Oh Lisa,' said Danby. He put his hand to his eyes. 'It's no good,' he said. 'I should die of it.'

'Possibly. Possibly not.'

Danby leaned forward, glaring at her. 'You listen to me now. You are simply deluding yourself. You said you couldn't go away and be alone. All right, but what's the point of coming to me when you don't love me and you do love somebody else? Don't you realize there's only one cure for your loneliness and this isn't it? You don't love me. You certainly don't know me. Perhaps just at this moment you are grateful to me for being in love with you. I might cheer you up, amuse you, for a short while, days, weeks maybe. Then you'd go back to Miles. And I should kill myself. Or Miles. Or you.'

'No,' said Lisa carefully, leaning forward with an equal intentness, 'I've thought all this out. You have to believe me that I won't go back to Miles. You must see. Miles is the one man who is entirely impossible.'

'I don't see. Nothing is impossible when people are in love. You're mad, you're absolutely mad. And you obviously haven't understood what you're trifling with here. It's a great fire, Lisa, it's a killer.'

'I want to get over Miles and I will get over Miles,' said Lisa. 'I know how to do it. I shall suffer pain and I shall inflict pain, I know that. Miles feels I'm in a nunnery or dead. His peace depends on seeing me as unattainable, as an angel. It will hurt terribly when it turns out that I am only a woman after all.'

'Then he'll come round and get you.'

'No. Then he will stop loving me.'

'So it's all in aid of a cure for Miles!'

'Don't be a fool. Danby, listen, can't you conceive that I might care for you and find you attractive, that something did happen that day in the cemetery and that night in the garden? I'm grateful that you love me, but it isn't just that. It means a lot to be wanted, but it isn't just that. I loved Miles but I could see you too. I wouldn't come to just anybody like this and ask to be consoled and helped. I've been thinking about you for days and weeks. Thinking about you made me decide not to go to India. Does it seem so strange after all that I should want to make somebody happy and be happy myself? I've thought about the way you fell on your knees in the ashes in the garden and how very much at that moment I wanted to touch you. In all those years at Kempsford Gardens I lost my instinct of self-preservation. I've been living in a dark cage. Now I'm out of it. It has been painful, this coming out, and it will go on being painful for some time, but that's a simple clean pain such as one might live with. I am not mad, Danby. I have never been more sane, coldly sane, *self-interestedly* sane. I am a woman. I want warmth and love, affection, laughter, happiness, all the things I've done without. I don't want to live upon the rack.'

'You don't know me at all – '

'I have seen your heart. You don't know me. You imagine I'm good, But those self-denying years prove nothing. And you think I am – like someone else.'

'No,' he said, 'no. I can see you. I can see *you*.'

'Then let us trust each other.'

'Wait a minute,' said Danby, 'before I start screaming. Just what are you suggesting?'

'Something very simple. That we try to get to know each other better. For instance, you might invite me out to dinner.'

'*Invite you – out – to dinner!* I am going mad, I must be,' said Danby. He began to sob with laughter. 'It's no use, Lisa. It's all fantasy. You'd leave me and it would kill me.'

'Well, if you prefer not to take the risk – ' Lisa stretched out a long leg and massaged her ankle. Then she thrust her feet into her shoes and reached for her coat.

Danby fell on his knees and put his head on to her lap. With a tired sad triumphant smile she caressed the dry white hair.

Chapter Thirty-two

Bruno was waking up. Thank God it was not the night time. Waking up was different now. It was a kind of entry into pain which was like a very slow quiet entry into warm water. The pain was not physical pain though there was physical pain. Sometimes there were sudden wrenches with a sense of something inward griping and collapsing. But these were brief and rare. There was the general restless itching aching unease of the body which could find no rest now and to which even sleep came like an anxious cloud trailing its twilight over tensed knotted limbs. This other pain was of the mind, or somehow of the whole being as if in the doomed animal mind and body were fusing into almost diaphanous ectoplasm, only vaguely located in space, which vibrated blindly with the agony of consciousness. The return from sleep into this ectoplasmic consciousness was always misery. I am still here, he thought.

Days had lost their pattern. There was soup, bedpan, soup, bedpan. There was darkness and light, rain upon the window, sunlight which was worse than anything, which showed the limp crumpled greyness of the sheets and the stains on the wallpaper and the puckered brass door handle which had not been cleaned for years. Bruno knew that he was unable to think properly. Perhaps it was those latest tablets which the doctor had given him for the pain. They were new tablets, a different colour. He felt as if the centre of his mind was occupied by a huge black box which took up nearly all the space and round which he had to edge his way. Names not only of people but of things eluded him, hovering near him on the left, on the right, like birds which sped away when he turned his head. He did in fact turn his head, heavily, in puzzlement, searching for an area of clarity which he knew must be near to him because he could somehow see its light but not it.

People came and went. Danby and Gwen often sat with him together and talked sometimes to each other, sometimes to him. He liked that. There had been a young man with dark hair, only that was a long time ago. Bruno wanted to ask for the young man but could not recall his name. He heard himself say, 'The young man, the young man – ' No one seemed to understand. Miles had come. Bruno knew Miles and knew his name and said his name. But he had not talked to him. Miles's visits were like being in the cinema. Miles moved, spoke, performed and Bruno watched. When Miles leaned forward and spoke with an unusual intensity Bruno would nod to him and try to smile. It was difficult to smile now because of the pain ectoplasm, but with a lot of effort he could smile, though sometimes he wondered if this strange thing was really smiling. And there was a woman with pale hair and a very sweet radiant face who was with him a lot of the time now. Bruno did not know who she was.

Time passed and Bruno watched it pass, his face contracted with a kind of cunning. Time had never been *visible* to him before. People came to him and brought him things, soup, bedpans, the *Evening Standard*, his own book in two volumes, *The Great Hunting Spiders*. He looked at the pictures in the evening paper and in the spider book, but even with his glasses on the print had become vague and furry. If he woke at night he moaned and made the time move on by moaning, dropping a moan into a little cup or sack of time which was then taken from him. Sometimes he moaned for what seemed like hours on end. Sometimes Danby or Gwen would come, talk to him, tuck in his bedclothes, arrange his pillows. When they had gone he moaned again.

That was what the present was like. Somewhere quite else there was the past, perfectly clear, brightly coloured, stretching out quite near to him in some sort of different kind of extension. He saw moving pictures. It was not quite like remembering. One day he saw Sambo's grave in the garden of the house at Twickenham. Miles was walking slowly towards it. They had got a little plain stone to mark the dog's grave. They had meant to have his name engraved upon it, but this had never been done. Often he saw his mother, sometimes by lamp light combing out her long hair, sometimes by sunlight, calling through screens of golden leaves, 'Bruin, Bruin, where are you, my darling.' Once he saw Maureen in a very short skirt lying fast asleep in a nest of feathers. That could not be a memory. *Ten cents a dance, that's what they pay me, Lord how they weigh me down.* He saw Gwen in a gym slip with pigtails holding *Kennedy's Latin Primer*. He used to help her with her homework. He saw the page with her big childish writing side by side with his precise small writing. *Amo, amas, amat.* Latin begins where everything begins. But where does everything end, thought Bruno, *where* does it end?

I am dying, he thought, but what is it *like*? Is it just this pain, this fear? For there was fear, fear of something. Would death, when it came, be some unimaginably more dreadful physical agony, would one experience death, would it be long? Yet it was not really this future thing that Bruno feared. He feared something that was present with him, the whimpering frailty of his being which so dreaded extinction. What moaned in the night was different and less terrible. There was something in him which was capable of a far more awful suffering and which he must somehow cheat out of a full awareness. He must, with a part of his mind, look always away from *that,* and not let the structure of his personality be destroyed by what it could not bear. Some old habit of uprightness must serve here, some habit bred to deal with quite different matters, and which must somehow be coaxed into helping him now. There were tears. Bruno did not mind the tears, they were a kind of contemplation. He wept as he looked at the slow movement of time and at the coloured pictures. This was not the terror. The terror must be kept in its corner. He must play the game of survival until the very end. That was one important thing.

There is another important thing, thought Bruno, or is it the same thing? What is the other thing? It's something I've got to do. If God existed He would do it for me. Bruno had had a dream about God. God had hung up above him in the form of a beautiful *eresus niger*, swinging very very slightly upon a fine almost invisible golden thread. God had let down another thread towards Bruno and the thread swung to and fro just above Bruno's head and Bruno kept seizing it and it kept breaking. The light fragile touch of the thread was accompanied by an agonizing and yet delightful physical sensation. Then suddenly the *eresus niger* seemed to be growing larger and larger and turning into the face of Bruno's father. The face filled up the whole sky.

God would do it for me, but God doesn't exist, thought Bruno laboriously. He began to think about the women. He saw Maureen sitting in the café with the chess board on the table in front of her, staring at the red and white pieces and moving one of them every now and then. *She's got eyes of blue, I never cared for eyes of blue, But she's got eyes of blue, So that's my weakness now.* Maureen was wearing a little round red and white checked cloche hat pulled well down over her ears. Why had it never occurred to him before that the hat matched the chess men? Had she done it on purpose? He must ask her sometime.

'Must ask her,' he said aloud.

'What's that, Bruno?'

'Must ask her.'

The pale-haired woman came and sat on his bed and took his hand in both of hers as she often did. Her big oval ivory-complexioned face looked tired and sad. Twice he had seen her crying quietly when she thought he was asleep. Who was she? He wondered how old she was. Her face was quite unlined but it was not the face of a young woman.

'What is it, Bruno, dear heart?'

'Fly in the web,' said Bruno.

A big *araneus diadematus* had made a very handsome orb web across a corner of the window outside. It was usually to be seen hanging head downwards at the hub of the web or else sitting in a crack at the side of the window, in a little bower made of threads, attached to the centre of the web by a strong signal thread. Bruno had been watching it for days. It had had no prey. Now a large house fly was struggling in the web and the spider was rushing towards it.

'Shall I rescue the fly?'

Bruno did not know whether he wanted the fly rescued or not. The spider had already reached the fly and cast a thread around it. Now the woman had opened the window and put her hand into the web, destroying its beautiful symmetry. The

264

spider retreated. The captive fly dangled from a thread.

'Too late. Bring them here both. In the mug, the cup.'

The woman detached the fly into the mug and with more difficulty captured the spider in the cup. She brought them both to Bruno.

The fly was struggling feebly, moving its legs and its head. Its wings had already been crushed up against its body by the circling thread. The spider was agitated, trying to rush up the slippery side of the cup. The woman kept moving the cup with a light circular motion against the direction of the spider, so that it kept falling back again to the bottom. After a while it was still.

'Such a fat spider.'

'You're not afraid,' said Bruno. 'Most women are afraid.'

'I'm not afraid of spiders. I rather like them. I like flies too.'

'It's a sad thing. Look at the cross, big white cross on her back. In the middle ages they said she was holy because of the cross.'

'Do you think we'd better kill the fly?'

Bruno considered. They had interfered with nature and were now at a loss. 'Yes. And put the spider back.'

The woman dropped the fly on to the floor and stepped on it. She carefully reintroduced the spider to the web. The spider ran straight into its bower, cowering back so as to be almost invisible.

'Leave the window open, please.'

The warm early summer air filled the room. The smell of dusty streets, the special smell of the Thames, a sort of fermented rotting yet cool fresh smell, was mingled with a vague scent of flowers.

What do they feel, thought Bruno. Had the fly suffered pain when its wings were forced back and crushed by the strong thread? Had the spider felt fear when it was in the teacup? How mysterious life was at these its extremities. And yet was the mystery less when one returned from the extremities to the centre? Perhaps if God existed He would look down upon His creation with the same puzzlement and ask, what do they feel?

But there was no God. I am at the centre of the great orb of my life, thought Bruno, until some blind hand snaps the thread. I have lived for nearly ninety years and I know nothing. I have watched the terrible rituals of nature and I have lived inside the simple instincts of my own being and now at the end I am empty of wisdom. Where is the difference between me and these little humble creatures? The spider spins its web, it can no other. I spin out my consciousness, this compulsive chatterer, this idle rambling voice that will so soon be mute. But it's all a dream. Reality is too hard. I have lived my life in a dream and now it is too late to wake up.

'What *was* the other thing?' said Bruno.

'What other thing, my dear?'

'The *other* thing.'

If only one could believe that death was waking up. Some people believed this. Bruno stared at his dressing gown hanging on the door. He never used it now since he did not leave his bed, and it had hardened into folds which were every day the same. How well he knew those folds. It seemed to be getting taller, larger, darker. Even the sunshine did not dispel that darkness now. The pity of it all, thought Bruno. I've been through this vale of tears and never seen anything real. The reality. That's the other thing. But now it's too late and I don't even know what it is. He looked round him. The sunshine revealed the terrible little room, the faded stained wallpaper with the green ivy design, the dull puckered door knob, the thin Indian counterpane with its almost invisible spidery arabesques, the row of champagne bottles getting dusty in the corner. He could not drink champagne any more now. And the dressing gown.

Tears came out of Bruno's eyes and ran down over the bones of his face and into his beard.

'What is it, dear heart? Don't cry.'

'I can't remember, I can't *remember*.'

It's something simple really, he thought. Something to do with Maureen and Janie and the whole thing. One sees now how pointless it all was, all the things one chased after, all the things one wanted. And if there is something that matters now at the end it must be the only thing that matters. I wish I'd known it then. It looks as if it would have been easy to be kind and good since it's so obvious now that nothing else matters at all. But of course then one was inside the dream.

'Does it work backwards?' said Bruno. 'It can't, can it?'

'What do you mean, my dear?'

The woman was holding his hand again, sitting close up against him on the bed. He felt no sexual desire any more. The fear had killed it.

'If only it could work backwards, but it can't.'

Some people believed that too. That life could be redeemed. But it couldn't be, and that was what was so terrible. He had loved only a few people and loved them so badly, so selfishly. He had made a muddle of everything. Was it only in the presence of death that one could see so clearly what love ought to be like? If only the knowledge which he had now, this absolute nothing-else-matters, could somehow go backwards and purify the little selfish loves and straighten out the muddles. But it could not.

Had Janie known this at the end? For the first time Bruno saw it with absolute certainty. Janie must have known. It would be impossible in this presence not to know. She had not wanted to curse him, she had wanted to forgive him. And he had not given her the chance.

'Janie, I am so sorry,' murmured Bruno. His tears flowed. But he was glad that he knew, at last.

The dressing gown had moved forward towards him and was standing at the foot of the bed.

I believe he's going, thought Diana. Oh why have I got to suffer this?

Bruno had been talking a kind of nonsense for days and intermittently crying. He could scarcely eat and all power of movement seemed to be leaving his body. The limp shrunken form lay inertly under the counterpane. Only in the head, only perhaps in the eyes, there burned with a fierce almost violent strength the flame which was so soon to be put out.

Diana held on to his hand which just perceptibly returned her pressure. He was blinking the tears away from his eyes. Diana put up her other hand to brush his cheek. He had not the strength now to raise his hand to his face. How strange it was that when almost all the other functions of the body had dwindled and fallen away into the hand of nature the eyes had not surrendered their mysterious power to manufacture tears.

Diana felt the tears rising into her own eyes, and she drew her free hand back to mop them. Her tears and Bruno's were mingled on her cheek. She had come to love Bruno so much in this terrible time.

If Bruno went now, Danby would feel very bad about it. He and Lisa had gone away for the night. Diana had persuaded them to go. Then Bruno had suddenly begun to sink.

It seemed to Diana that Danby and her sister were scarcely sane. They both seemed to be drunk with ecstasy. The physical change in Lisa was so great that Diana could scarcely recognize her as the same person. She looked not ten but twenty years younger and more beautiful than she had ever looked in her life. She laughed almost all the time, with a new laugh which Diana had never heard before. Or perhaps it was that throughout the years she had just forgotten the sound of Lisa's laughter. Had she and Danby been to bed together? Lisa's appearance left the matter in little doubt. Their attempts, in that house of death, to conceal their felicity were touching and unsuccessful. They could not help presenting a picture of life at its most explosively robust and hopeful. They could not help presenting a spectacle of triumph.

Miles's indignation had been extreme and comic. Her perception of the comicality of Miles in this situation had been one of the things which had helped Diana herself to bear it. It had been some time before Miles would even believe what Diana was telling him. He regarded it as *impossible*, as *strictly contradictory*. He stared at Diana with wild amazed eyes. It was all a *mistake*, she would find that she had been mistaken, she had certainly got it wrong. For nature so preposterously to err. ... When at last Diana did succeed in persuading Miles of the truth of what she said, that Lisa was not leading a dedicated life in India but was to be seen riding about London in Danby's new sports car and dining with Danby at riverside restaurants, dressed in extremely smart new clothes, Miles gave himself up to a day of rage and execration. He cursed Danby, he cursed

Lisa. He said it could not possibly last. She would be sorry, my God, she would be sorry! He announced himself irreparably damaged. The next day he was silent, frowning, concentrating, refusing to answer Diana's questions. On the third day he said to Diana enigmatically, 'It's all over now,' and returned to work in the summer house. It was another week before Diana, walking down the garden, saw once more the strange angelic smile upon his face as he wrote.

Lisa had sent no communication to Miles and offered no explanation to Diana. Diana had simply discovered her with Danby one morning at Stadium Street. They had assumed that she would immediately understand. They looked upon her golden-eyed, a little apologetically, coaxingly like children. And, as it seemed to Diana, almost at once started treating her as if she were their mother. It had taken Diana herself some time to see and to believe what was there in front of her face. It had been a very bitter revelation. Diana, when she had first taken it on herself to visit Bruno regularly, had come to find a certain sweetness in her renewed relationship with Danby. She felt she had not really got over him and saw no reason why she should try to. She experienced his attractiveness now in a more diffused and peaceful way as a comforting warmth and a consoling presence. There was healing for her in their coexistence with Bruno. She could see that Danby was unhappy. She respected his grief and looked forward to a time when she might be able in turn to console him. She felt vague about this. There would be no extremes. But something would have survived the wreck. When poor Bruno is dead, she thought, I'll consider about Danby and I'll see what to do. In fact, she thought a lot about him, especially in the evenings when she was alone in the drawing-room at Kempsford Gardens, and his image brought her a kind of happiness.

But now, Lisa had taken Miles away from her and now she has taken Danby too. While she listened to Miles's outraged cries she struggled with her own pain. How could her resentment ever have an end? She realized now just how much she had been relying on Danby. Indeed it was not until Miles told her that at least she ought to be pleased by this definitive removal of her rival that this aspect of the matter occurred to her at all. Danby was far more final than India. A Lisa in India would have become a divinity. A Lisa sitting in Danby's car with an arm outstretched along the back of the seat, as Diana had last seen her, was fallen indeed. Miles said venomously, 'Well, she has chosen the world and the flesh. Let's hope for her sake she doesn't find she's got the devil as well!' Naturally it did not occur to Miles that Diana would be other than pleased. In fact, he was not concerned with Diana's feelings, being so absorbingly interested in his own. He will manage, she thought, he will manage. We've all paired off really, in the end. Miles has got his muse, Lisa has got Danby. And I've got Bruno. Who would have thought it would work out like that?

Diana felt that she had emerged at last into a vast place of loneliness. Danby and Lisa, with their solicitous concern about her and their submissive politeness, were as lost to her as if they were dead. And she was beginning to realize how little Miles really reflected about her, how little he tried in his imagination to body forth the real being of his wife. His imagination was engaged in other and more exotic battles. He had seemed very close to her when he had talked to her about Parvati, but it seemed to her now that she had simply been made use of. Miles had needed a crisis in his relations with the past, he had needed a certain ordeal, and she had helped him to achieve it. Now he had returned into himself more self-sufficiently than ever before. She thought of startling him into noticing her by telling him that she too was in love with Danby. But that would be merely to add absurdity to pain.

And now, she thought, I have done the most foolish thing of all, in becoming so attached to someone who is dying. Is this not the most pointless of all loves? Like loving death itself. The tending of Bruno had had at first simply a kind of consoling inevitability. It was something compulsory, a task, a duty, and it took her away from Kempsford Gardens where Miles sat smiling his entranced and private smile. It also brought her into a natural relationship with Danby. Later Danby's proximity was a torment. But by then she had come to love Bruno, to love him with a blank unanxious hopeless love. He could give her nothing in return except pain. And it seemed to her as the days went by and Bruno became weaker and less rational, that she had come to participate in his death, that she was experiencing it too.

Diana felt herself growing older and one day when she looked in the glass she saw that she resembled somebody. She resembled Lisa as Lisa used to be. Then she began to notice that everything was looking different. The smarting bitterness was gone. Instead there was a more august and terrible pain than she had never known before. As she sat day after day holding Bruno's gaunt blotched hand in her own she puzzled over the pain and what it was and where it was, whether in her or in Bruno. And she saw the ivy leaves and the puckered door knob, and the tear in the pocket of Bruno's old dressing gown with a clarity and a closeness which she had never experienced before. The familiar roads between Kempsford Gardens and Stadium Street seemed like those of an unknown city, so many were the new things which she now began to notice in them: potted plants in windows, irregular stains upon walls, moist green moss between paving stones. Even little piles of dust and screwed up paper drifted into corners seemed to claim and deserve her attention. And the faces of passers-by glowed with an uncanny clarity, as if her specious present had been lengthened out to allow of contemplation within the space of a second. Diana wondered what it meant. She wondered if Bruno was experiencing it too. She would have liked to ask him, only he seemed so far away now, wrapped in a puzzlement and a contemplation of his own. So they sat together hand in hand and thought their own thoughts.

The pain increased until Diana did not even know whether it was pain any more, and she wondered if she would be utterly changed by it or whether she would return into her ordinary being and forget what it had been like in those last days with Bruno. She felt that if she could only remember it she would be changed. But in what way? And what was there to remember? What was there that seemed so important, something that she could understand now and which she so much feared to lose? She could not wish to suffer like this throughout the rest of her life.

She tried to think about herself but there seemed to be nothing there. Things can't matter very much, she thought, because one isn't anything. Yet one loves people, this matters. Perhaps this great pain was just her profitless love for Bruno. One isn't anything, and yet one loves people. How could that be? Her resentment against Miles, against Lisa, against Danby had utterly gone away. They will flourish and you will watch them kindly as if you were watching children. Who had said that to her? Perhaps no one had said it except some spirit in her own thoughts. Relax. Let them walk on you. Love them. Let love like a huge vault open out overhead. The helplessness of human stuff in the grip of death was something which Diana felt now in her own body. She lived the reality of death and felt herself made nothing by it and denuded of desire. Yet love still existed and it was the only thing that existed.

The old spotted hand that was holding on to hers relaxed gently at last.